Monday and the Counterfeit Corpse

Andrew Kirschbaum

Acknowledgements

It has been said that writing a novel is a solitary pastime. Fortunately, that has never been the case for me. My editors, good friends, and family, have been with me every step of the way, and I thank them here, once more, for that gift. They are: Curtis Barton, Katherine Bunting, Anandi Gandolfi, Nicole Geada, Lila Kirschbaum, Richard Kirschbaum, Rebecca Kletnieks, Lisa Lassner, and Marcus Roth. The errors that managed to creep in despite their efforts are entirely my doing.

Dedication

This book is for Anandi Gandolfi:
Friend, partner, and inspiration.
Thanks for showing me the magic.

Monday and the Counterfeit Corpse

Chapter One

My name's Zachariah Monday. I'm a detective for hire, personal investigator, occasional body guard, professional pain-in-the-ass, busybody, snoop, and accidental do-gooder. Actually I'm a world-class do-gooder, it's just that I don't get paid for it, and not getting paid is something I rarely do on purpose. Fortunately, I do mostly get paid for all the rest, so I'm getting by just fine, thanks for asking.

Detective work comes in two basic flavors, boring and deadly. Luckily for me, it changes back and forth pretty frequently so I usually don't get too bored. Or dead. The real payoff doesn't have much to do with money, though. Most cases pay, but a few precious ones are actually fun. I was about to wrap up one of the best cases I had ever had the pleasure of solving. In fact, I was actually going so far as to kill time before I ended this one.

Okay, making the bad guys a little nervous and hopefully throwing them off their game was the official reason I was stalling. That, and the fact that I was counting on one more player to show up for my little production, but if I'm to be completely honest, it was only a little bit of the former and a whole lot of the latter. I had my whole game plan worked out, all my lines carefully rehearsed, and every possible contingency covered. My partner says I love showing off. I tell him he's crazy, but man, is he going to be able to say 'I told you so' after this one.

I leaned against the mantelpiece at the head of the room. I had chosen my position and facial expression carefully. The key was to look relaxed and calm, but ready for anything. It wasn't an easy thing to do, but I think

I pulled it off. I looked around the room at the collection of witnesses, suspects, victims, and innocent bystanders. I smiled, carefully showing a little bit of tooth.

In the center of the room, in an impressive high-backed chair sat Mrs. Belinda Stanhope-Crane, also known as the Widow Crane, also known as my client. Here's a hint for anyone who wants to go into the detective-for-hire business: always have a rich client if you can possibly swing it; it just makes everything easier. Mrs. Stanhope-Crane was richer than King Midas wished he had been and she was a great client. She had hired me to find out who killed her husband Malcolm Howard – her latest husband that is. Mrs. Stanhope-Crane had outlived half a dozen husbands in her time. The deceased spouse in question had been half his wife's age, at the time of death two weeks ago.

I had read about the murder in the papers before she came to me with the case. It was front-page stuff, 'Scandalous Marriage Ends in Bloody Murder.' All sorts of tawdry allegations were flying. Popular gossip had it that hubby Howard had been killed by criminals plotting to steal all of his wife's money. And of course, everyone suspected that Howard had been in on it, what with his history as a convicted felon. It had all the makings of a first-rate soap opera and I was smack dab in the middle of it all. It didn't get much better than this in the detective-for-hire business.

I asked Belinda (she insisted that I call her Belinda) if she wanted me to prove her husband innocent or if she wanted me to solve the crime. Her answer had surprised me. She said neither; she only wanted justice to be done. I may have fallen just a tiny bit in love with Belinda right then and there. Plus she offered to pay me nearly double my usual rate.

Two people sat on the couch to her left. One was Nate Crane, the oldest son from her first marriage and heir to the bulk of the Stanhope-Crane fortune – now that Howard was dead, anyway. To Nate's left was Margaret Stanhope-O'Shaughnessy, my client's sister. For a while Maggie O'Shaughnessy had been my primary suspect, but I knew better now. I hadn't revealed this publicly yet; it was better if the real bad guy didn't suspect what I didn't suspect until it was too late. I reached into my back pocket and pulled out my trusty notebook. It's times like this that I'm glad I take copious notes. Also, it's easier to ignore people nonchalantly when you have an excuse not to look at them. I checked my notes and ignored up a storm.

Sitting across from those three and staring daggers at everyone was Brigid Howard, a woman who had emerged after the murder and alternately claimed to be Malcolm Howard's sister, secret wife, and criminal partner at various points in my investigation. She had also tried to seduce me, or possibly kill me. I'm still not sure which. I had her pegged now. She was just a gold-digger with a talent for lies. Her real name was Mildred Drood and she wasn't directly related to the case at all, but she sure had confused me for a while.

The entire serving staff was standing against the back wall: the chauffeur, three maids, a stable master, a cook, and a butler. Everyone in the room was human except for the butler. He was a goblinblood, which is to say that he was of mixed human and goblin ancestry. Accordingly, he was nearly an inch shorter than the next shortest person in the room, who was a 5 foot, 2-inch maid named Ginny. I didn't remember Ginny's last name, but I couldn't be expected to remember everything, could I? I flipped several pages back in my notes. Ginny's last name was Prescott.

The goblinblood butler made up in width what he lacked in height; he easily weighed three hundred pounds and it looked to be entirely muscle. His traditional butler's uniform did little to hide his powerful physique. Not for the first time, I thought about being on the business end of those sledgehammer fists and, like every other time, I decided that I didn't want to have that particular experience. He smiled at me, revealing huge slabs of teeth like pearly white tombstones.

Full-blooded goblins are like snowflakes – or they would be if snowflakes could bench-press motorcycles before a light lunch and shrug off injuries that would kill me three times over. What I meant by the snowflake thing was that no two goblins look very much alike. They were often some shade of green and they were usually about 4 or 5 feet tall. After that things got more complicated. Some goblins are hairless and scaly. Some goblins have great big pointy ears. A lot of them have long and lanky heavily-muscled limbs. But some of them had none of those qualities.

Scientists have theories on why goblins vary so widely from one to another. Wizards have theories as well. Maybe the most ancient and learned members of the goblin race know the answers. Then again, maybe they don't. Most of the goblins that I know really didn't care about the reasons behind why they were the way they were. Goblins are like that.

Mixed-race goblins, like the butler against the wall, were an even bigger bag of complicated. Some of them could pass for human if they wore baggy clothing; others – like the butler – could nearly pass for goblin. His head was wide and hairless and covered with tiny green scales, his ears were big and pointy and rose inches above either side of his head. And did I mention the teeth? Because the teeth looked like they could easily grind me into paste, and I like to mention things like that.

I turned to a blank page in my notebook and started sketching teeth. Again, this wasn't relevant to the case in any way, but I was, after all, stalling for time. I snuck another quick glance around the room again. If my last invitee didn't show up soon, someone's temper was going to blow and then things would get harder.

"Blast it, Monday!" exclaimed Nate Crane as he burst up from the couch. "How long are you going to make us sit around here? You promised us answers!"

I sighed. Why am I always right when I least want to be?

"Mr. Crane," I said in a soothing voice. "If you'll just be patient for a few more minutes, I'll be able to explain everything."

Just then the door banged open and an enormous man stormed into the room. He was well over six feet tall and hugely overweight. His great bald dome of a head gleamed brightly in the large room's witchlamps and a great shaggy sprawl of red beard covered the lower half of his face and spilled down his chest. He wore a New Jerusalem Police Department badge on his shirt and a tie that defied all taste and decorum.

"Lieutenant Mandrake!" I greeted him warmly, as an old friend deserves. "I'm so glad you could make it. I was just telling Mr. Crane here that you were on your way."

"Fuck you, Monday," Mandrake growled. "You asked me to be here and I'm here. Show me what you want me to see, but remember that you owe me big time for this. I don't make house calls."

I cleared my throat ostentatiously and straightened my tie. Jasper Mandrake was a real charmer, but he was also the closest thing New Jerusalem had to an honest cop. Mandrake cared and that was worth a whole lot in my book. Also with the piles of cash that Belinda was paying me, I could afford Mandrake's bribes, which was worth even more. Justice indeed, Mrs. Stanhope-Crane; justice indeed.

"Now that we're all assembled," I said in my best public-speaking voice. "Let's begin. As you all know, Mrs. Stanhope-Crane hired me to determine who was behind the murder of her husband, Malcolm Howard, and why he was murdered. I have asked you all to be here today because I have the answers to those questions and more."

I paused and let my gaze travel slowly across the large room, resting my eyes briefly on each of the assembled. Some of them looked me in the eyes, but others glanced away. Nervously, shyly, guiltily? I let the moment linger. The butler shifted slightly, moving into a stance that would allow him to move quickly, or possibly start a fight. I noted that and moved on.

"Mrs. St – I'm sorry – Belinda," I began in what I hoped was a comforting tone of voice. "Your husband was not involved in a scheme to steal all your money. All of the evidence that I've found shows nothing but honest motivations. I believe that your husband truly loved you and wanted to spend the rest of his life with you. I am truly sorry."

I paced back and forth a little bit before going on, partly because it makes me look thoughtful, but also because it provided a nice dramatic pause.

"Malcolm wasn't killed by your sister or your son," I continued. "In fact, no member of your family was involved in the crime at all. The true killer planted all of that evidence to throw investigators off the track. And it worked, at least for a little while."

"The handgun in Nathan's room?" asked Margaret Stanhope-O'Shaughnessy.

"The plans to the family safe in Margaret's room?" asked Nathan Crane simultaneously.

"All put there by the true killer," I assured them both. "To set you against each other and to stall for time. Sort of like I've been doing for some time now. Jasper, have your men found it yet?"

"Of course they have," Lt. Mandrake replied testily. "What do you think took me so long?"

"All right then," I smiled. "Bring it in, please."

"Bring it in!" bawled Mandrake in a huge ear-splitting voice.

The door opened once again and a uniformed police officer came in carrying a two-foot tall statuette of a crying woman. It was nicely sculpted and looked pretty valuable. It was also the motive for Malcolm Howard's murder.

"The Weeping Lady?" asked Belinda Stanhope-Crane in disbelief. "What about it?"

"Not the Weeping Lady," I replied. "This is a counterfeit. In fact, it's one of nearly a dozen counterfeits which have been moving through New Jerusalem for the last month."

Out of the corner of my eye, I noticed the butler edging slowly backwards. Unless I missed my guess – and I didn't – he was about to make his move. So it was time for me to make mine.

"Belinda," I said. "A trusted member of your staff has betrayed you, stolen from you, and most tragically of all, when your husband discovered their crimes, committed cold-blooded murder."

"But who?" cried Belinda. "Who did it?"

"Perdition take you all! I'm not going back to jail!" snarled a voice.

Twelve sets of eyes swept the room, looking for the source of the snarl. It was the cook, and he had produced a handgun from somewhere and he was pointing it right at Belinda Stanhope-Crane. Both Lt. Mandrake and the uniformed officer were too far away to do anything, I was even further away and if I moved at all the crooked cook would surely shoot. Fortunately, I had planned ahead and had a shill in the crowd.

From behind the cook and well out of his field of view, a massive sledgehammer of a fist crashed into his head. The gun dropped from his suddenly slackened fist and clunked to the floor loudly, followed by the cook's unconscious body a moment later. I definitely never wanted to be on the business end of those enormous mitts.

"I got him, Boss," said the butler who wasn't a butler. His voice was so deep I could feel it in my chest; no fully human throat would ever produce a voice like that.

"Good job, Baxter," I replied with a grin.

Baxter Kline was my partner. Technically he was my employee, but that only went so far as me paying him. He was a great partner and he added a lot of value to the firm. When it came to actually following orders, he wasn't so great. But that's okay as he frequently tells me that I'm not so great as a boss either. We had infiltrated Baxter into the household a few weeks ago and today it had paid off.

"Wait," began Nathan Crane. "The butler is working for you?"

"Yep," I replied with a grin. "He's my partner, Baxter Kline."

"Thank goodness!" exclaimed Belinda. "He was an awful butler. When all of this was over, I was going to have to let him go."

Baxter actually looked contrite. "Sorry, Ma'am. I was so busy running Zack's errands, I barely had any time for you at all."

"Lt. Mandrake," I called. "If you and your associate would be so kind as to drag the cook away in manacles I can get back to explaining what exactly has been going on here for the last three weeks."

"I ain't your errand boy, Monday," Mandrake growled, a dangerous edge to his voice. "But seein' as this jerkhole pulled a deadly weapon on an upstanding citizen, I guess it's my civic duty to haul him in."

Mandrake turned towards the uniform and jerked a thumb towards the groaning cook, "Kovacks? Haul the jerkhole in."

"Yes, sir!" Kovacks replied smartly before busying himself with the aforementioned task.

Right about then the room exploded into a dozen different voices asking a hundred different questions. I flipped my notebook open nonchalantly and smiled.

"Let me start at the beginning," I said.

About an hour later everyone was finally satisfied with my answers, or at the very least they were as satisfied as they were ever likely to get. Mrs. Stanhope-Crane and I shook hands, she gave me a fat bonus check – which I had totally earned, thank you very much – and we said our good-byes. Lt. Mandrake and Officer Kovacks had long since left with their collar, and everyone else had something important or at least distracting that needed doing.

Baxter and I left together in a shared cab. Sure we had made a good profit on this case, but there was no sense in throwing away perfectly good money. We rode in silence for a time while I deconstructed recent events. I had expected things to go worse, frankly. The cook was a career criminal; he had been part of an underground fighting ring years ago before graduating to more sophisticated things like counterfeiting rings. I had expected him to give Bax a run for his money in the thug department. Which is not to say that Baxter Kline wasn't a damn fine thug, because he was. He was also a true gentleman, and quite possibly the heir to the Goblin Throne.

I realized Baxter was staring at me.

"What?" I asked.

"Why'd you lie to her?" he rumbled.

"I didn't!" I protested.

"Howard the hubby was in it up to his neck and you know it!" Baxter rumbled.

"At the beginning, sure!" I replied easily. "But he really did fall in love with Belinda and his partner killed him for it. Can you tell me what purpose would be served by hurting her with a meaningless truth?"

"You could argue that it would be doing the job she paid us to do," Baxter suggested.

"She paid us for justice," I said. "Justice is exactly what she got. It's bad enough she lost her husband. I'm not going to be the one to take away his memory as well."

"Boss, you are even more of a romantic sap than you are unabashed hambone." Baxter grumbled, but his smile softened the words and made a lie of the grumble.

"I thought I did quite well in there," I observed, changing the subject to an area in which I was more comfortable.

"Yeah, yeah," Baxter admitted. "You did just fine."

"Ahem," I said, holding out my hand.

Baxter glowered at me, but he shoved one of his massive paws into a jacket pocket and pulled out a money clip. He peeled off a twenty and laid it in my hand. I made a show of examining it, holding it up to the light to look at the paper and such.

"I didn't actually think you'd blow it, Boss," Baxter rumbled. "I just think you've gotten too reliant on your pocket watch lately, and with it in the shop for repairs…."

"I'm more than my tools," I sniffed in a fair approximation of Nathan Crane's voice.

As much as I refused to admit it, Baxter had a point. My charmed pocket watch was a powerful tool, and it helped me out quite a lot. A few seconds warning right before any physical danger threatened my person was a pretty handy thing to have around. I patted the jacket pocket I usually kept the thing in to remind myself that it wasn't there. I was operating without a net until the danger charm got out of the shop. And that was okay. Sometimes it was good to leave the safety nets behind.

"This was a damn good case," I said. "And the perfect end to a perfect day."

"Not quite," Baxter said. "We still don't have any idea what's going on with the counterfeit statuette. Why are they smuggling art into the city? And where is it coming from? We don't know any of that stuff."

"True," I agreed. "But none of that stuff is our problem. It's Jasper's job not ours, not until someone pays us to do it."

Baxter revealed a flask from within the folds of his trench coat.

"I'll drink to that," Baxter said.

And that is exactly what we did.

Chapter Two

I work and live in the city of New Jerusalem. If you ask me there isn't a better burg in all the worlds. My city has everything: art, culture, great food, and where else can you find so much magic? There's wonder around every corner if you know where and how to look. And if there's one thing that I know it's knowing where and how to look for things. There are more witches and warlocks per square mile in New Jeru than anywhere else I know.

And where else could you brush shoulders with this many faeries? Outside of Faerie proper, or the Mists, there's maybe one full-blooded fae royal for every twenty-thousand humans, and most of those who choose to live in the solid world live right here in New Jerusalem. The city boasts thousands of commoner fae and faerieblooded humans, and at least a hundred thousand goblins and their kin. Sadly, most of those goblins live in overcrowded ghettos. All cities have problems and my city is no exception.

I can't work magic myself; I don't have the right kind of smarts for that business. Don't get me wrong, I've got plenty of street smarts, and I know my times tables, but magic relies on following very specific instructions very specifically. There are a thousand different schools of magic, but they all boil down to two very basic sorts. There's witchcraft which uses spells, rituals, and tools passed down from one witch to another for millennia.

Some witches take on a single apprentice, while others run entire schools for hundreds of students. The specifics are all different, but the point is the same: get the recipe wrong and boom! And no one is writing new recipes, what the previous generation of witches passes on is all there is, so every scrap is precious.

The other sort of magic is warlockery. Warlocks are the bad boys and girls of magic and definitely aren't the studious types. They dig up, piece together, or out and out steal their spells from wherever they can find them. Warlocks frequently get together at trade conventions where they trade, sell – and yes, steal – spells with, to, and from each other. And according to what my buddy Tim the Warlock tells me, it isn't always in that order either. My point is, both approaches require doing something in exactly the same precise way again and again and again. The very idea of that makes me literally nauseous.

Even though I can't do magic myself, I can still use other people's magic, and I absolutely do. I like to keep a collection of useful items around at all times. Sadly, my pockets are only so deep – both metaphorically and physically – so I could neither afford nor carry as much of a toolbox or arsenal as I might prefer. I intended to take the bonus money Belinda had paid me to go shopping for a few new toys. I love going shopping, but I love it even more when I can actually afford to buy things. There was a new shop I had heard about over in Houdiniville and I was itching to check it out. Sadly, the Houdiniville neighborhood was very much out of my way and I hadn't had an excuse to get out there yet.

Houdiniville is the part of New Jerusalem that the wireless networks use when they want to set a motion picture in New Jerusalem. It's the part of town that still looks like the old post cards. It's a fun neighborhood, what with all the tower observatories, transplanted castle sections, and at least one genuine decaying Edwardian manse; it also garners a lot of tourist trade and therefore some very cool shops have sprung up.

But shopping is pleasure and even on the day after I closed a big case, business still came first. There were more than a few bills that I had let slide over the last couple of weeks and what with actually having some money and all, I thought now would be a good time to catch up. So I had enjoyed a quiet morning of solitude and paperwork. Baxter somehow manages to be real busy anytime there's a lot of filing or bill paying to do. In what passes for his defense, Baxter really is terrible at most office work. I've thought about hiring another employee to help me with the fiddly bits, but I'm actually pretty good at the boring stuff and it probably isn't worth the money it would cost to get somebody better than me.

The suite of offices I rent included a waiting area and three offices. The offices were mine, Baxter's, and the big one we used for impressing clients and having meals in, respectively. Those offices were located on the 23rd floor of the Flood Building and while they weren't exactly palatial, they served my purposes well enough.

So there I was putting papers into alphabetical order, then wrapping them into bundles, putting the bundles into folders, and then putting the folders inside filing cabinets. The reasons for doing all of this escapes me, but it's the way things are done, so I do it. I closed the drawer on the last folder of the day, the drawer made a satisfying sound as it clicked shut, and I allowed myself the happy smile of a man who doesn't have any more filing to do.

My thoughts began to fill with visions of quaint little shops (possibly even shoppes) where I would be offered an espresso while I browsed happily. And that's when there was a knock on the front door to my offices. I wasn't startled. I am a man of action, a man who's always aware of his surroundings and such a man can never be taken by surprise, let alone startled. Therefore, the high-pitched squeak I made and the little jump in the air were not the signs of startlement; they were merely side effects of a man who is preparing for action.

No one was supposed to be able to knock on my door without passing through my security system. I have a very good security system; it cost me a lot of money and it very rarely fails. The fact that my visitor had gotten past it with nary a squawk (other than the one I made) told me quite a bit. It told me that my mystery visitor had enough magical mojo to fool, shut down, or overpower my defenses. It told me that he, she, or it, didn't want me to have any warning. The fact that they had then knocked politely instead of simply barging in told me that they had enough confidence to throw that advantage away. The odds are good that they wanted me to know all of these things and that is why they were patiently waiting outside my door while I worked it out in my head. All of this led to one inescapable conclusion: I was not going to get any espresso today.

I went out to the waiting area. I could see the general shape of a woman through the translucent glass that made up the top third of my door. I could also see the reversed letters that spelled out Monday Investigations.

Below that in a smaller font, there was the jumble of letters and numbers that made up my private investigator's license number.

"Come in," I said in as calmly as possible. It was possible that my squeak had gone unheard and if there was any chance at salvaging my precious ego, I was going to take it.

The door opened and my visitor glided in. She was a tall woman with an elegant sweep of raven-black hair lightly accented with silver. Her dark eyes sparkled with intelligence over a strikingly aquiline nose graced with a slight bend at the bridge. All her clothing was black from the tip of her pointy black hat to the equally pointy tips of her low-heeled black shoes. Her name was Adriana Gray, and she was probably the most powerful wizard I had ever met.

Remember all that stuff I said about witches and warlocks? Forget it. Throw it all out the window. Witches and warlocks are craft workers, laborers, people who work a trade. Wizards are artists, geniuses, explorers of the unknown. The average wizard was as far beyond the average warlock as a Dutch Master was beyond a marginally-talented house painter. I had met Ms. Gray last year on an inadvertant expedition to a place called the Old City. The Old City was – quite literally – a whole other world so I was quite naturally surprised to see her here.

"Good afternoon, Mr. Monday," said the wizard in her clear contralto voice. "I have a case for you."

"You want to hire me?" I asked, sounding a bit stupid even to my own ears.

"Isn't that what most visitors to your offices desire?" Gray replied archly.

"Well, yes," I admitted. "But most visitors to my offices aren't Adriana Gray."

She laughed at that. She had a rich and wholly-unselfconscious laugh. I liked it and I liked her as well. My affection for her was due in part to her having helped me out of a serious jam last year. She had charged me a small fortune for the help, but I still felt like I owed her one.

I offered her a cup of coffee and she declined, explaining that she had picked up a cup on the way. That was fortunate for me, actually, since making coffee for clients was one of Baxter's jobs. No one liked coffee the way I made it, so in a small and quiet retaliation upon an uncaring world, I only ever made enough for myself. We went into the big meeting room and we each sat in one of the nice high-backed leather chairs that surrounded the big impressive table. I had spent a pile of money on both the chairs and the table, but it made me feel like I was running a real business whenever I got to use them, which on slow days amounted to having lunch. We got settled; I opened up a case file, wrote 'Adriana Gray' on the tab and looked at my prospective client in a sensitive and open-minded way. I practiced that look in the mirror, and believe me when I tell you it's a good one.

"Tell me more about this case," I said. "I'll help if I can."

"An associate of mine has been murdered," she said, matter-of-factly. "I'd like you to find out who did it and why, and if possible, help me bring them to justice."

I nodded; this was familiar ground to me. With very few notable exceptions, the law wasn't much interested in solving murder cases. They were certainly interested in making it look like they were interested, but violence is a part of life in New Jerusalem. The government was mostly about making money and keeping the peace and that involved working hand in hand with organized crime whenever and wherever necessary. In the cloudy space between peace and justice, I manage to make my living.

"Have you informed the authorities?" I asked.

"This case is," she paused as if deciding on the proper turn of phrase, "… outside of the jurisdiction of the authorities."

"How far outside?" I asked.

"From our past encounter, I know you've done some traveling," she began by way of reply. "How much do you know about the Soft Realms?"

"Not as much as I'd like," I admitted.

Already I wasn't liking this case so much. Creation was an awfully big place, but only a relatively small part of it was solid and defined. The world was a tiny little blue ball floating in a great big ocean of cold, dark mystery. There were places out there, goblinside, faerieside and other even scarier places.

"I am one of the custodians of a small holdfast deep in the Mists," Adriana Gray continued. "It is a small realm and a fragile one. The man who has been murdered was another of the custodians. I need to know whether this is a plot to destabilize and destroy the realm, or if it was a different matter entirely. I need someone to dig deep into the entrenched secrets and politics. And I need an outsider to do it."

I breathed in deeply. How big a favor did I owe her? I wasn't looking for work right now and this case sounded like an awful lot of trouble. I'd be outside my area of knowledge and expertise, and the thing about murderers is that they're generally willing to kill people who bother them.

The last time I had been out there, I ran into all sorts of strange and powerful things. In addition to the wizardly Ms. Gray, I'd met and dealt with a genuine fire-breathing dragon, an angel of salvation, and an enterprising devil called the Duke of Sorrows. Everything had worked out relatively well in the end, but I was in no rush to repeat the experience.

"I'll pay you $1,000 a day no matter how long it takes, minimum of $5,000, half of which I am willing to pay up front. Right now, if you accept the case, which I very much hope you will."

My train of thought spontaneously derailed. That was about twice as much as I usually got in exchange for risking life and limb. And $2,500 would pay for some very nice toys. Actually, come to think of it, I could do better than the quaint little magic shop in Houdiniville and make the deal a little bit easier for Ms. Gray in the process.

"How about $2,500 worth of goods from your shop in the Old City as a down payment instead?" I asked.

A dark eyebrow arched elegantly over an equally-dark eye. "Did you have something particular in mind?" she asked, a smile playing about her thin lips.

"In fact I do," I replied. "But we can discuss that later. If you agree, the terms are acceptable to me as well."

"The terms are acceptable," she said. "How shall you proceed?"

"I'll have plenty of questions for you before we're done. You've hired yourself a private detective. I'll give you a full report once a week. We'll pick a time that's convenient for you. When the job's done, you'll get an itemized list of everything I've done and everywhere I've gone and exactly how I've spent your money. Results are guaranteed. I never back off, and I'm good at my job. When you hire Zachariah Monday, you get the truth, whether you like it or not."

"Oh my," Ms. Gray chuckled indulgently. "Do you practice that speech very often?"

In fact, I did, but it seemed to lessen the effect when I admitted it, so I just grunted and made a few notes. My notebook is an invaluable conversational tool.

"Let's begin," I said after a moment. "What can you tell me about the victim?"

"His name was Peter Starbourne and he was an artist and a Pillar of Patchwork."

"Patchwork?" I asked.

"That is what we call our holdfast," she replied.

"Okay," I said, making a few notes. "Please go on."

"Mr. Starbourne was one of our leading citizens," she continued. "His sculptures and paintings are famous throughout Creation."

The name Peter Starbourne sounded familiar to me now that I thought about it, "Has his art made it to the solid world?" I asked.

"Very much so," she replied. "His work is bought and sold extensively in your world."

"He had enemies, I assume?"

"Not enemies as such, no," she answered. "All famous and important men have those who disagree with them. But he didn't have as many as some, or even most. He was an artist, not a politician."

"He had at least one enemy," I said grimly.

That eyebrow expressed itself again as she said, "Aren't you leaping to conclusions, Investigator? Mightn't it have been a crime of passion or opportunity?"

I gave her my very best charming grin.

"I went to detective school, Ms. Gray," I said. "So, yeah, it could have been any of those or a dozen more. It could even be an accident that just looks murdery. It happens. But there are two rules I follow. The first one is called the Zebra Rule. If you hear hoof beats in the distance, think horses, not zebras, unless you're in Africa."

Gray smiled, "And the second rule?"

"That one's called the Spenser Rule," I said. "And it goes like this: We can assume a thing or not, but if not assuming it gets us nowhere and the other way gets us somewhere, we're better off if we assume the way that gets us somewhere."

"And all of that means?" Gray asked, a hint of laughter in her voice.

"Until we know better," I said, the smile falling away from my face. "Peter Starbourne had enemies and they murdered him."

I would have loved to end the interview there; a dramatic note is a nice way to wrap up an interview, but I had more questions and not even my love of drama took precedence over my curiosity. Working together with Ms. Gray, I assembled a list of people to interview. Some of them were on hand or nearby when the body had been discovered; others were local experts that might provide me information and context about recent events. I would be taking a look at Starbourne's home, his studio, and his business office, and almost certainly other locations would pop up that needed snooping into. Before we were done, I had scheduled significantly more than a week's worth of investigating.

"Well," I said, glancing up from my notes. "I think that's enough to start with. Maybe we'll get lucky and one or more of these leads will pan out. I need to make some arrangements, pack my things and make a few surprise preparations."

I tore a page out of my trusty notebook and handed her the list I had compiled.

"Can you get me these things from your shop?" I asked. "And do they amount to less than $2,500 worth of supplies?"

She glanced at the page very briefly before nodding, "All of this looks acceptable."

"How long do I have before you can make the crossing back to the Mists?" I asked. "And where do we need to be? I know where a few ley lines cross near here."

She gave me that thin smile of hers again as she rose from the chair.

"There are certain spots where it is easier to cross over," she said. "But to a wizard of my experience such things are not necessary. When and where would it be convenient for you to embark? We shall meet there and then."

"Are you saying you could leave right here and now?"

"Certainly, if that was what you wished," she replied.

"Huh," I said intelligently.

My buddy Tim is a damn good warlock. He told me once that moving from world to world was the very hardest thing any magic practitioner ever attempted. The fact that the ley lines crisscrossing New Jerusalem made it a whole lot easier to perform this herculean feat was a big part of the reason the city even existed. New Jerusalem had been founded because of the ley lines and the power they represented. And here was Adriana Gray, wizard of the Old City, telling me that she didn't need the lines, that even being in the same city with the biggest concentration of lines anywhere on the continent, she didn't even need to go a few blocks out of her way to use one. Was she showing off to impress me? Maybe. Was I impressed anyway? You'd better believe I was.

Adriana Gray and I wished each other a good day and she went off to do whatever it is wizards do when they're not being cryptic and scary.

Why did a wizard as powerful as Adriana Gray need me to poke my nose into a whodunit? Didn't she have other resources? What else was going on here? And how badly was I going to regret taking this case? The answers to those questions lay on the other side of the answer to another question: Who murdered Peter Starbourne? Any way you looked at it, it was going to be a busy week.

Chapter Three

The rest of the morning and a piece of the afternoon were spent preparing. If I was going to be out of town for Salvation knows how long, there was some stuff I had to do first. I called my neighbors and asked them to field any packages or post that arrived while I was gone and I put the cleaning service on hold. That was pretty much it for personal stuff; I live a simple life. Or at least I try to. I left a written message on Baxter's desk to call me when he got in, that handled the business stuff. Now all I had to worry about was the romantic stuff.

For the previous couple of months my social life had been … complicated. My number one girl was Audrey Talbot, a fiery redhead with a very full dance card. Audrey was a high-powered executive and she had always insisted that we both date other people, to keep it from getting too serious, she had said. That was fine, really; I had the hang of it and was doing fine, thank you very much … until my ex-wife Carin came back into the picture. A case had brought me to her door and somehow all the problems just didn't seem to matter anymore. Carin and I were dating again, pretty seriously.

Neither woman was putting any pressure on me to choose between them, although in some ways that actually made things worse. There were rules, perhaps unspoken ones, but rules nonetheless. I saw Audrey at least once a week, I saw Carin as often as our schedules allowed, which was considerably less often than once a week. As fate would have it, the stars and our schedules both aligned three days ago and Carin and I had enjoyed dinner and a show, followed by a few drinks at an upscale bar.

The show was great, and Carin's theater connections had scored us great seats, even at the last minute. The drinks were better, and spending the night at Carin's place turned out to be the best part of all.

Which would be great, except for the fact that my little jaunt out of town (way, way out of town) would mess with the laws of reciprocity; I was going to miss my date with Audrey, and I was not looking forward to that conversation. I thought about trying to reach Baxter directly, but suspected my motives were more about stalling the inevitable than being a good employer. With a huge and melodramatic sigh, I picked up the telephone handset and dialed Audrey's office.

"Samaritech. We pave the way," chanted the pleasant baritone voice of Audrey's latest assistant.

"Toph, this is Zack. Is she in?" I asked the phone.

"Hi, Zack," answered Toph's disembodied voice. "Nope, she's in a meeting with McGregor. Again."

"Sooooo …" I drawled. "She'll be in a really, really bad mood when she gets out?"

Toph allowed himself a dry chuckle. "If we're lucky."

"Well," I said after a moment's pause to run a thousand terrible possibilities through my fevered brain. "I certainly don't want to bother her at a time like this. Tell her I called. No message."

"Sure thing, Zack," Toph reassured me. "Have a good one."

I assured him that I would, wished him much the same in return, and hung up the phone. I ran an exasperated hand through my hair and sighed again, perhaps with even more melodrama this time. I knew that putting things off wouldn't make them any better, in fact it was likely to have the opposite effect, but I figured that future me would just have to worry about that one. Future me got that kind of treatment a lot. You might think I'd have learned better by now, but no such luck.

I reached for the phone to call Baxter after all; right as my fingers brushed it, the phone rang, startling me rather badly. I looked around embarrassed at my own behavior even though I knew no one was watching. Then I waited a moment to get my heartbeat back under control and snagged the handset.

"Audrey! Thanks for calling back," I began.

"No such luck, Boss," rumbled my goblinblooded employee, interrupting me before I said something unmanly. "It's me."

"So it is," I replied. "What's the situation?"

"Mrs. Stanhope-Crane's check has cleared, the wolf is officially away from the door," Baxter rumbled. "You want me to start looking into that counterfeit art business?"

"Nah," I said, casually. "There's no percentage in it right now. Besides, I'm going to need you to mind the office for a while. I've got out of town business."

"New case?" Baxter asked. "So soon? I thought you were going to go antiquing or something?"

"Shopping is not the same thing as antiquing," I replied, with a little bit of my exasperation seeping into my tone. "You are a green-skinned barbarian with no appreciation for the finer things."

"You got it, Boss," Baxter agreed happily. "You called Audrey yet?"

The problem with working with detectives is keeping secrets from them. We detectives are real nosy-parkers. I really had no ground for complaint; I have been mounting a steady campaign of wheedling, haranguing, and spying to figure out some of Baxter's own secrets for years. The fact that Baxter knew much more about my life than I did about his was merely because I am less devious and has nothing to do with his allegedly superior detecting skills. That's my story and I'm sticking to it.

"So tell me about this case," Baxter rumbled, waking me up from my momentary musing. "Where are you going?"

"Out of this world, Bax," I said. "Out of this world. Remember Adriana Gray?"

Bax grunted affirmatively.

"Well, it turns out Ms. Gray lives in her own private little world, and there's trouble in paradise."

I caught Baxter up on the events of the day and my own suspicions about Gray's deeper motivations for hiring me, which amounted to very little more than basic paranoia at this point. Baxter listened quietly until I was done.

"Mist travel is rough," he observed.

"The choice, the charge and the challenge," I muttered. "Just another day at the races."

"What're you going to offer for the sacrifice?" Baxter asked.

"All my fond memories of high school calculus," I retorted snarkily. "How should I know what I'm going to offer? You think I think about that stuff all the time?"

"I think you think about everything all the time, Boss," Baxter replied with one of his deep reverberating chuckles. "But it's none of my business, I'm just morbidly curious."

"Nosy is what you mean," I quipped.

"You got it, Boss," Baxter agreed happily, again.

No matter how powerful the magic-maker you traveled with, everyone who made the crossing over from one world to another had to pay a price. Once the way was opened, my part of the operation would be simple enough: the choice, the charge, and the challenge. I had to consciously choose and willingly go, I had to pay a price that meant something to me, and I had to face some kind of physical, mental, or emotional challenge to prove my worthiness. All in all, it was a real pain in the ass.

"Do me a favor, Bax," I said. "Get a message to Tim. I think I'm going to need his help on this one before it's over."

"What about me, Boss?" Baxter asked. "You want me to get infiltrated someplace in this holdfast of Gray's? Nobody there is very likely to know me."

"Not this time," I answered thoughtfully. "It's just a gut feeling, but I don't think that's the right approach for this one."

"Or could it be," Bax rumbled good-naturedly. "That you just can't bring yourself to use the same trick two cases in a row?"

"It could be," I allowed. "But until we're sure, let's call it a gut feeling. That sounds more detective-like, don't you think?"

"Sure, Boss," Baxter reassured me.

"Tim's out running around Malachi-knows-where with Eel," Baxter said. "It might take a while for him to get the message."

I sighed. Tim the warlock was a good buddy of mine, but I totally fail to understand how he makes any money at all. He's a freelancer like me, a small business owner and a specialist, albeit in a very different field to mine. The thing that confuses me is this: There is absolutely no reliable way to get in contact with the man. How does a potential client even find him? I practically walk the streets wearing a sandwich board to drum up business.

I had to admit that I was pleased to hear that Tim was spending time with Eel. The three of us had helped the kid out of some serious trouble and his head still wasn't quite on straight. That wasn't entirely a surprise; Eel was half-angel on his father's side. That's right, Eel's father was an honest-to-gosh white-winged Angel of Salvation. Eel had grown up without any contact from or knowledge of his parentage. To say that his childhood had been messed up was an understatement of Biblical proportions.

Eel's biggest problem was a violent allergy to evil acts. They made him break out in flaming swords and homicide. He was working on it. We were all working on it. But there was no twelve-step program for righteous vengeance.

"Maybe I'll find some magical help on site," I said. "Whatever, I'll work something out."

"When are you leaving?" Bax asked.

"Apparently, whenever I feel like it," I replied. "The Almighty Ms. Gray doesn't need crutches like ley lines or rituals."

"Really?" Bax's voice actually went up half an octave he was so surprised.

"Apparently," I repeated.

"Huh," Baxter mused.

"That's what I said," I agreed.

We left off on that note of camaraderie and confusion and I dialed Carin's number. It rang once and she answered.

"Hello ... Carin Schein speaking,"

"Carin ... hi," I replied, pleased to hear her voice.

"Z," her voice sounded animated and happy. "What's up? I had a great time the other night..."

"Me too," I assured her truthfully. "Just touching base to let you know that I'll be out of town and off the grid for a while. Not sure when I'm leaving and I have absolutely no idea when I'll be back."

"Thanks for the udate," she laughed. "Think you might be able to vague that up for me a little bit? I think you accidentally gave me some actual information about your life there."

"Whoops!" I teased back. "I'll have to watch out for that. Seriously, though, it's a new case I'm starting up and I really don't know much about it. It pays well, but it could take a long time and I don't think I'll be able to keep in touch until it's over and done with."

"Fair enough, I guess," she said. "Take care, and get in touch when you're back so we can get together again."

I admit the prospect of getting together again with Carin sent a little thrill through me. I tried to get a handle on my racing hormones, but they were slippery little devils. I took a breath and cleared my throat before going on.

"We'll play calendar bingo and see if the stars align," I hedged.

"Sure thing," Carin replied with a hint of laughter in her voice. "Maybe you'll get lucky."

I chuckled at the thought.

"Listen," she said with a chuckle of her own. "I'd love to keep talking, but I have to go. Call me."

"Will do," I said, before hanging up the telephone.

I packed up my supplies, shut down the office, grabbed my hat and coat off the hat rack, and walked out the door. I took the elevator down twenty-two floors, wished Lem the security guard a pleasant afternoon and entered the city of New Jerusalem.

New Jerusalem was a big, loud, colorful explosion of life. The sights, sounds, smells, and feel of the city was unlike any other I had ever known. Some folks say they always feel the tingle of magic on their skin here. I'm not sure about that, but there surely is something special about my city.

I walked the three blocks to the Zohar coach station and soaked it all in. A small crowd of folk were looking up into the sky. I followed their gaze and saw a ghost barge serenely floating over the city center. The hairs on the back of my neck prickled up. Ghost barges are creepy, phantom dirigibles that appear seemingly from nowhere, criss-cross the New Jerusalem skyline and then vanish. What exactly they are, where they come from and go to (when they aren't spooking the locals) and what purpose they serve are all unanswered questions as far as I know. A lot of people have theories, guesses, and semi-educated ideas. Some say they appear right before or right after a murder to carry the soul of the victim away to eternity. I was pretty sure that wasn't the answer, or at least not the full answer. There are dozens of murders in New Jerusalem every week, just like there are in every city. Ghost barges only appeared once or twice a month at most. If they were here for the victims, how did they choose who was deserving of first class travel and who had to hoof it?

The rest of my walk to the station was nicely uneventful. Either the laws of chance or the powers that control commuting were with me, because the rest of the trip home went quickly and smoothly, relatively speaking, anyway. As a daily patron of public transportation, I had spent years honing my skills of patience and relaxation. To mixed success, I'm sad to say, but I'm better than I used to be and that's something, at least.

Eventually I came upon my destination: 2317 Enigma Avenue, the condominium complex that housed my home. I read somewhere once upon a time that homes should have names; I named mine the Hall of Justice. The appellation hadn't yet caught on with my friends and co-workers, but I was winning them over.

I checked my mail like I usually did and amongst the usual pile of junk and bills there was a card from the mail room indicating a package too large to fit into my box. That was exciting, but for dignity's sake, I maintained a sedate pace. Sure enough, there was a big box waiting for me in the mail room. The return label simply said 'Gray.' I scooped it up with a wide grin and childlike glee. Was there anything better than getting cool stuff in the mail?

The Hall of Justice was on the fifth floor; I took the stairs and was only wheezing a little bit by the time I got to my front hallway. I ran my finger along the rune carved into my lintel so the spell-lock would recognize me and was rewarded with the familiar click-clack of the door opening.

"Hi honey, I'm home!" I called out to absolutely no one.

"Hello, you," replied Audrey's voice from my bed room. "C'mon in and help me warm up your bed, would you?"

To my credit, I only started a little at the unexpected presence. I had set the spell-lock to recognize her, after all. I dropped everything, smiled wickedly, and swaggered into my bedroom. Audrey was posed artfully and totally naked in the center of my bed. Audrey was a natural redhead, a fact which was well-displayed at the moment. She also had generous curves and a very wicked mind. Her skin was very pale and lightly dusted with freckles. My blood began to flow away from my brain and towards more southerly locations.

"How was your day?" Audrey purred.

"Getting better all the time," I replied, loosening my tie.

"Take off your hat, why don't you?" Audrey invited.

I rolled my eyes and clapped a hand to my head. I was, in fact, still wearing my hat. I doffed it and tossed it frisbee-style towards the chair. It missed, of course, and Audrey giggled as it landed gently on the floor.

Audrey rose sinuously to her knees as she slowly tugged my tie loose and tossed it onto the chair. She then began unbuttoning my shirt slowly, spreading it open as she went, her fingers brushing against the bare skin of my chest. I shrugged out of the shirt as soon as I could. While I was doing that, Audrey busied herself with unbuckling my belt; she drew it slowly and carefully out of the loops, coiled it up and tossed it on the chair next to my tie. I wasn't nearly as tidy and dropped my shirt on the floor at my feet.

She kissed me softly on the chest and neck. I kissed the top of her head and smelled the clean scent of her hair and skin. Her hands fluttered across my back like butterfly wings. I kneaded her back and shoulders with my own hands and was rewarded with a moan. Since she was brushing her lips against my chest at the time, I felt her moan as much as heard it.

She went back to work on my trousers. She unfastened them and hooked her fingers into the waistband of my boxer shorts and drew them, and my trousers, down my legs; she pulled my shoes and socks off and I stepped gracefully out of my remaining clothing. We had gotten pretty good at the business of undressing each other.

She lay back onto the bed, drawing me down onto her; I didn't resist. Her skin felt marvelous, soft and cool and very, very inviting. I wanted to touch all of her with all of me. We embraced and the world fell away as I was drawn into the simple, sensual act of kissing a beautiful woman as she kissed me back. Our tongues leapt and slid along each other. Hers was smooth as velvet, soft and strong at the same time. My chest brushed against hers and we both shuddered with pleasure. My fingers stroked her arm and then her thigh, her hands tangled in my hair and we finally broke the kiss, both of us gasping a little for air and other things.

Our eyes locked and she smiled as she drew me slowly inside her. She made small sounds deep in her throat as we moved together. I would have gone slowly, but her needs were more urgent than that, and she quickened the pace in time with her breathing. She grinned wickedly and pushed me gently over, as she swung up to ride on top of me, her hands braced against my chest, her hips moving against my own.

"Don't hold back," she whispered. "I want it."

I never argue with a lady when she's right.

Chapter Four

The rest of the day and the night passed joyously but all too quickly and in the end we wrapped ourselves in each other's arms as we drifted off to sleep. I woke a little after dawn, which was unfortunate, but I've learned over the years that if my body is done sleeping, there's not much I can do to convince it otherwise. I slipped out of bed as quietly as I could. Audrey stirred in her sleep and mumbled something before rolling over and hogging the entire bed. I waited a moment as her breathing slowed and I was sure I hadn't woken her up, then scooted off to the bathroom to perform my morning ablutions.

The whole world seemed to be a much more pleasant place and I was momentarily confident about facing and surmounting all of the challenges that lay before me. I knew the feeling wouldn't last long, but I enjoyed it while it did. I pulled on trousers and a nice shirt, but in deference to the rigors of travel I wore a sturdy leather jacket in place of my usual worsted wool and forewent my usual necktie. I wrote a brief and somewhat sappy note to Audrey in my notebook, tore the page out, and left it on the kitchen table near the coffee golem where she was unlikely to miss it.

I hauled my travel bag out of the closet where it lived, threw it open, and loaded my toiletry kit and some spare clothing into it. There was still plenty of space remaining and I filled part of it with the contents of the package from Adriana Gray's magic shop. The bag was a genuine Pratchett, very expensive and magically-enhanced. One of my most expensive and most treasured possessions, it held more than it had any earthly right to and weighed less than it should have when full. I didn't much like to travel, but any excuse to pull this baby out was a good one.

I padded back into the bedroom in my stocking feet, planted a gentle kiss on a bit of Audrey that wasn't covered by sheets and blankets, retreated back out into the sitting room, laced sturdy boots onto my feet, shouldered the travel bag and glanced at the mirror by the door. I looked fine, albeit a trifle overloaded. I nodded approval and made my way out into the world.

It was a simply stunning autumn in New Jerusalem. The weather was just cool enough for long coats to be comfortable, but not so cold as to be unpleasant. The wind blew, turning the streets into a hundred miniature tableaux of drama. Did I mention that I love my city? Because I do.

I reversed my journey from the afternoon before, much as I did almost every day, stopped for a toasted bagel with cream cheese at a convenient shop – also much as I did almost every day – and found my offices where and how they usually were. I called the number that Adriana Gray had given me.

A crisp, professional-sounding young woman answered the phone, "Lady Gray's Tower, how may I direct your call?"

I was momentarily nonplussed but rallied rapidly to ask, "May I speak with Adriana Gray, please?"

"Of course," the crisp young woman replied. "Who may I tell her is calling?"

"Mr. Zachariah Monday," I explained. "She's retained my professional services."

The crisp young woman politely instructed me to hold, so I did. There was music. After about twelve seconds, Adriana Gray's voice came onto the line.

"Zachariah," Gray greeted me. "Are you ready for our trip?"

"Sure," I replied. "Shall we meet at my office?"

"Actually," Gray replied. "As lovely as the weather is, I thought we might do this outside. Perhaps in Echo Park?"

That sounded like a fine idea to me so I told her as much and we agreed to meet in forty minutes at the center of the hedge maze. Echo Park was thought by most to be the poor relation to New Jerusalem's more famous Ambrosius Park. But Echo Park more than made up for what it lacked in fame with style.

I swung by my favorite coffee place and picked up a couple of extra-larges. If Gray didn't want hers, I was confident that I could drink two of them given enough time. I whistled happily, if tunelessly and walked smartly uptown and towards the Weishaupt coach station.

Significantly less than forty minutes later, I hopped off at Echo Park Station. The vagaries of public transit had been in my favor for once and I had some time. Deciding that wandering the maze would be an excellent way to kill that time, I walked over to the park and headed directly for the hedge maze.

The park was mostly empty at this time of the morning, so I pretty much had the place to myself. I took a deep breath and relaxed. Something like a baseball bat slammed into me from behind. My hat and the coffees all went flying and I went down like a ton of bricks that weren't paying any attention to the world around them. I really had gotten too dependent on my pocket watch.

My back was on fire. Nothing felt broken. I was bruised, battered, and quite possibly sprained, but at least I wasn't broken. Yet. I rolled to the left as quickly as I could. A club smacked the ground right where my head had been. I was oddly fascinated by it. A club? Who uses a club these days?

A boot caught me in the gut and the air whooshed out of me like a flyaway balloon. There was more than one of them. Great, just great. I wondered what I had done to earn this particular beating. It wasn't my first such experience. I put people in jail for a living; I had enemies. I guess it really didn't matter much to me why I was getting curb-stomped just then. I'd worry about it later. Always assuming there was a later.

I tried to get my feet back under me, but I was still nauseous from the gut shot and it just wasn't happening. I saw another boot hurtling towards me out of my peripheral vision. I tucked my head, elbows, and knees in and curled up tight. Sometimes you just have to take a beating.

The good news was these guys weren't professionals. They wasted a lot of energy on flashy kicks. That was good for two reasons; first and most importantly, they didn't hurt as much as good strong kicks with a lot of power behind them, and second, they might get tired faster. Make no mistake, beating the tar out of a guy is hard work, even when he's not defending himself so well.

The one with the club was a little bit more of a problem. I tried to make myself a hard target. I squirmed around a lot; I offered no resistance and thus was hard to get leverage against. Basically I made them work for it. It hurt. It hurt a lot, but I was able to protect my vitals.

The bad news was that they weren't threatening me. They weren't warning me off or shouting at me to leave town or any of the usual stuff. (I get beat up a lot, okay?) That meant this wasn't a message, this was something else. Maybe revenge or maybe straight out murder. Either way, I really didn't want to hang around and see how it ended.

I had to convince them that it was over, and that meant playing dead. Fortunately for me, I'm real good at playing dead. I wrapped my arms around my belly; this served two purposes: one, it protected my belly and two, it allowed me to rub the charm inscribed on my belt buckle. It was a one-shot charm and an expensive one at that, but I didn't see a lot of options open at the moment.

Something went crunch in a sickeningly wet sort of way in my midsection, I spat up blood and I went loose and boneless. I stopped breathing. If anyone stopped to check my heart wasn't beating either. To all external observation, I was dead. My assailants didn't get the clue at first so they smacked me around a few more times. If I'd been truly dead that wouldn't have hurt nearly as much as it did. Eventually, they got the message and stopped hitting me. They checked for my apparently non-existent vitals and made tracks.

Mission accomplished; time for beer. I lay there for a while after my assailants were gone. I slowly picked myself up. That hurt, too, but not as much as actually getting beaten to death would have. I managed to pull myself up into a sitting position and gave myself a cursory examination. I was rough, and badly in need of an economy-sized bottle of pain killers, but not ready for the hospital.

I stood up, brushed myself off, found my hat and put it back on my head. I looked around for the coffee. Both cups were smashed beyond recovery. Now that really hurt.

Gray arrived just then. I noticed that she was carrying two extra-large coffees. Punctuality was an excellent quality, and one that wizards were well known for, relatively speaking, but this once I rather wished the wizard had arrived a little bit early. I gave her a jaunty wave.

"Stars of Salvation," she gasped. "What happened to you?"

"You should see the other guys," I said with a grin.

It hurt to grin, but the effect was important, so I sucked it up. She took a moment to examine me and rapidly came to the same conclusion I had, which is to say I that could mostly walk this one off.

"Here," she said. "I brought coffee."

Adriana Gray was wearing a black skirt that fell to mid-calf under a plain black blouse that looked like silk, and a short jacket that was also black. Rounding out the outfit was her hat. I can't quite say what sort of hat it was, but if a snap brim fedora and an old-fashioned witch's pointy-topped chapeau had a child, this could well be it. The peak of the hat rose only a few inches above her head, but it still made the point, so to speak. I guess this was business casual for a wizard, good clothes to travel in.

I accepted one of the coffees. I complimented her on her punctuality, which produced a thin smile as she took a sip from her own cup. Testing mine, I found it much too hot for my liking. I guess Ms. Gray could stand the heat because she didn't even blow on her brew before tossing it down contentedly. Hopefully the client wouldn't notice my hesitation and fault me for not being manly enough.

I told her about the attack and explained that it was likely a hangover from an earlier case. She seemed more concerned about the severity of my injuries than their source. I decided that a change of topic was in order.

"I'm ready to go whenever you are," I said, as much to distract her from my faults as a coffee-drinker as from my ignominious injuries.

"Not just yet," Gray said, smiling. "Let's talk for a while and finish our drinks. It's best not to travel on an empty stomach and coffee is an excellent choice of beverage."

"Coffee?" I asked. "Why is that?"

"Symbolically it stands for beginnings, awakenings, and preparations," Gray said. "Also many people feel strongly about it and so it accumulates spiritual energy."

"That makes sense, I guess," I said thoughtfully.

"And the caffeine doesn't hurt either," Gray added.

I snorted, which hurt a bit and not just because everything sort of hurt right then, but also because I had finally chanced a sip of my too-hot coffee. If Gray noticed my distress, she was good enough not to comment on it. Wizards could be polite that way, I supposed.

I waited a while and then had another sip; this time it was just about right. Mmm, I love coffee when everything is just right. The two of us sat in companionable silence for a time, enjoying the shared experience. It was one of the moments that mornings were made for. I was almost able to forget I had just been curb-stomped by persons unknown and at large.

After a while, Gray asked me where I had first learned about the mist realms.

"I had to do a bit of research once to solve a case," I lied.

Well, okay, it was only sort of a lie. It might as well have been a case. Sort of. I had learned about the mist realms during a whirlwind affair about 10 years back. I had just been dumped by my first serious girlfriend and it was a total rebound relationship … if you could even call it a relationship. It was exciting though, I'll give it that much.

Kelli had been wild and dangerous and very, very sexy. And when I was with her, I felt dangerous and wild too. And yes, sexy. (I was young and on the rebound, I make no apologies.) Kelli was a faerie commoner, who looked mostly human, but wasn't. She was a creature of magic and her flesh was made of lighter and fairer stuff than I was used to. And she moved like no one I had ever seen before or since. It was poetry just to watch her walk across a room.

She was also a renegade, on the run from both of the Courts of Faerie and hiding in New Jerusalem until the heat died down. But New Jeru isn't exactly the middle of nowhere as far as the Fae are concerned. Somebody saw something, somebody talked about it, and the next thing we knew, the two of us were on the run from the Wild Hunt. We had a few close scrapes, always managing to stay one step ahead of the hounds, but it couldn't last. Sooner or later, the Hunt would find us. Kelli had to run further away if either of us were going to survive.

That's when I found out about the mist realms, unclaimed lands that were beyond the reach of the Faerie powers. Neither of us knew much back then, but we learned fast. We gathered everything she'd need, and begged, borrowed, and stole enough power to bust open the ways between worlds, and together, we made it happen. But that had been a long time ago.

She had asked me to come with her. I refused. I hadn't even seriously considered it at the time. It seemed like an absurd thing to even contemplate; I had to finish school, get my degree, make something of myself, become an adult, all that important stuff. But after she left I had strange dreams for a while, crazy wild dreams of riding on some kind of elk or something through a sylvan paradise. It got to me, and I started to regret turning her down. It didn't matter by then because she was long gone. Some nights I still have that same dream, not very often anymore, but sometimes.

I realized quite suddenly that Gray had just said something and that I had no idea whatsoever what it had been.

"Um," I said in a totally unclever fashion. "What did you say just now?"

"I said keep your secrets if you must," Gray said with a laugh. "I was merely curious."

We finished our drinks, she before me by a little bit. We each crumpled up our mugs, releasing the one-shot magic charms that made them dissolve into a fresh lemony scent. She produced two chocolate chip cookies and offered me one. No dummy, I took it. There is no better cure for that which ails me than a chocolate chip cookie. Even my bruises felt better.

"Shall we begin?" asked Gray.

"Absolutely," I replied. "What do you need me to do?"

"Nothing," she said with a smile. "Just stand up, a foot or so away from me. Please don't touch anything until I tell you that we've arrived. Do you have your sacrifice ready?"

I nodded. The selection had been hard; by definition it had to be something I cared about but could still stand to part with. As a general rule, I like to keep the things I care about.

Gray's face took on an expression of concentration. An errant breeze stirred my hair, which was odd since a moment ago there hadn't been any wind at all. I smelled wildflowers and the featureless lawn began to feel like uneven ground under the soles of my boots. Ghostly trees formed around us, pencil sketches drawing themselves over the so-called real world. As I watched, doing as much nothing as I could, the trees became more real, colors filling in and shapes inflating. At the same time, the park began to fade, losing color and solidity rapidly.

"So, it's to be a Sylvan Crossing," Gray murmured. "Mr. Monday, we must pass through controlled territory, likely a personal hunting preserve."

"I'm not crazy for the sound of that," I replied, attempting to sound flip or possibly insouciant.

There were plenty of things that lived in the Mists. Most of them weren't strong enough to maintain a holdfast, but anything might be dangerous on its own ground. There were legends aplenty of people going missing one day only to pop back up again, weeks, months, years, or even decades later. There were things that could reach up between the worlds and just take you away, if you let them. And getting lost in a dream wasn't my idea of a retirement plan.

"The rules are simple," Gray said, more or less ignoring my words. "As long as we obey them, the hunter cannot take us. Soon a path will appear; on no account shall either of us step off that path. Not even for a moment, not even if I tell you to do so, should you leave the path while we are still in the dark wood. Do you understand me, Mr. Monday?"

"Yeah," I said. "I understand you. Feet on the path, check. What else?"

"Be nothing but polite to anyone you should meet, human, animal or otherwise in seeming," Gray said. "On no account trust any elderly women and keep your wits about you at all times."

"That all seems pretty basic," I said. "Anything else?"

"Yes," Gray said. "You must not use or even reveal your sidearm. The things that hunt the Mists are old and they view modern firearms as dishonorable."

"Really?" I asked. "Can a gun hurt anything around here?"

"Almost certainly not," Gray replied. "But they do not understand them and to be honest, I think they fear that which they do not understand."

Gray said something then, but I couldn't quite understand her. She spoke again, but I still couldn't make out her words. It was like she was in the next room and there was a wireless playing; I could tell she was speaking and the words all sounded like English, but I couldn't understand her meaning.

I could hear a roaring sound in the distance, so there was nothing wrong with my hearing, at least. I focused on the roar, but for the life of me I couldn't tell whether it was a waterfall or a bunch of lions. I found myself sort of hoping it was the lions. I mean you can get waterfalls pretty much anywhere but – hey, lions, right?

Chapter Five

"I said," Gray said at last. "Can you understand what I am saying?"

I could understand her. I shook my head as a wave of dizziness passed. I realized that my body felt well and whole. The aches, bumps, and bruises were gone as if they had never been. We weren't in the dark wood anymore, if we had ever really been there at all.

It was unaccountably cold though. I found myself huddling for warmth inside my coat. And my breath steamed when it hit the chilly air. So much for autumn.

I found myself in an office much like my own meeting room, only the chairs were nicer and the table was smaller. I was standing in the doorway while Gray was seated at the table across from another woman whose hair was snowy white and face was delicately traced with age. She wore a simple dress of white and blue with a rather nice fur coat on over it. The fur coat was also white and flattered the elderly woman's figure.

"Are you quite well Mr. Monday?" Gray asked. "I was introducing you to Mistress Dortchen Wild. Come over here and speak to her, please."

We were in the Mists. The crossing through worlds was over and we had arrived. Hadn't we? I couldn't remember the details. Perhaps that was a side effect of the magic? Apparently we had been here for some time. I shook my head again. What had just happened? I tried to reconstruct the last few minutes in my mind. Clearly, I had lost track of things somehow. And my mind wandered back to the crossing. Yes, that explained it.

I lifted my foot to enter the room and something stopped me. I lowered my foot again and paused for thought. Something had caught my attention and been flagged by my subconscious as noteworthy. What was it? What was my – occasionally paranoid – inner self trying to tell me? Experimentally, I lifted my foot again. There it was. Something bulky in my front trouser pocket had poked me in the leg.

I reached my hand into my pocket. Inside I felt the hard plastic case that enclosed one of my most treasured possessions. I remembered putting it in my pocket; it was a Black Lotus trading card, a rare collectible from my college days. I hadn't played the game in years, but the collection itself was still one of my pride and joys. Why had I taken out one my most valuable cards? For the sacrifice, of course. That made perfect sense. But if it was still in my pocket that meant that I hadn't actually sacrificed it. How had I made the crossing without making the sacrifice?

I took the card in its protective case out and looked at it. I looked at the familiar card art, the game text and the mana cost at the top. It was all exactly as I remembered it, even down to the tiny rips exposing white card stock along one edge that lessened its resale value.

"Please don't be rude, Mr. Monday," said Gray. "Come and join us at the table. We have much to discuss."

The other woman, whom Gray had named Mistress Wild, smiled at me. Her teeth were odd shades of brown and gray, and strangely fascinating. I still didn't move. Pinpricks of perspiration sprang out all over my body. I was mortally terrified of … something.

"No," I said. "I don't think I'll be doing that. Let's talk from here. Mistress Wild, please forgive my behavior."

After a momentary pause, I decided to say something nice; it was important to be polite. I smiled at Mistress Wild.

"You have a lovely office," I said unable to think of anything else nice to say. "Thank you for your hospitality."

The white-haired woman smiled wider and began to cackle quietly.

"Oh you're a cagey one," she said. "Manners as proper as you please, but not one step off the path have you taken."

I looked down. My feet were planted firmly on a dirt path running through a snowy field field. It occurred to me that it was odd to have a floor like that in an office building, but at least it explained why it was so cold.

When I looked back up again there was no office. I was standing in a dark and winter-frosted wood. One of my feet was on the ground and the other was poised to step off the path and into the snow. Across the field from me there was a small house on stilts. Mistress Dortchen Wild stood before the house, her hands clasped and a predatory look on her aged face. I put my foot down, both figuratively and literally.

"You are also cagey, Grandmother," I said as respectfully as I could. "But I do not wish to be your servant or your dinner, so I must politely decline your offer of hospitality."

"And why shouldn't you be my dinner?" Wild asked with a cackle. "These are my lands and you are trespassing. And old Mistress Wild has a large stew pot that wants meat in it."

Great, I was trapped inside a fairy tale. Things rarely went well for adults in these kinds of stories. Still, there were clearly rules. She was talking to me and not chasing me around with a knife. Or at least she wasn't doing it yet. I decided to try to play by the rules.

"I was told that as long as I kept to the path and minded my manners that I would be allowed to pass freely," I said.

"Freely?" she cackled. "Freely? None may pass freely!"

I took that as encouragement. If she was willing to set a price, maybe it was one I could meet. I had my sacrifice prepared for the passage. And if this didn't count as a challenge then I needed a new dictionary.

"Then will you agree to let me pass if I offer you a gift?" I asked.

"It depends upon the gift," she answered.

I held up the trading card and showed it to her. I thought I saw something flash in her eyes for just a moment. It might have been greed, or desire, or even lust. Then again, it might have been my imagination. She smiled widely, giving me an excellent – if disturbing – view of her dental work and she nodded her head.

"Your sacrifice is acceptable." she said, a hint of the cackle still in her voice. "I offer you passage through my lands without let or hindrance, provided you take nothing that is not yours and do not leave the path. Should you break my rules, then you must stay and serve me forever and a day."

"You are both generous and wise, Grandmother," I said, tossing the card up and towards her. Her eyes locked onto the card in its arc, seemingly hypnotized by its passing. I could have done something then, maybe, while her guard was down, but I didn't see any big ovens to shove her into, and she hadn't really offered me any harm. I decided that getting myself out of there as quickly as possible without losing the path would be well and good enough. So I did.

I walked for a few minutes until the stilt-legged house was out of view. I passed a hedgehog and an owl both sitting by the side of the road. I nodded politely to them and wished them both a good day. The hedgehog offered to tell my fortune in return for a silver penny. I regretfully told him that I didn't have a silver penny, so instead he blessed me. The owl said nothing. The Mists were a very weird place.

The path led up a hill and, at the top of the rise, I came upon Adriana Gray waiting placidly for me. She smiled and looked relieved to see me. I nodded to her. My travel bag sat on the ground at her feet.

"I think we got a little bit split up," I said. "How was your day?"

"Yes, my apologies," Gray said. "I underestimated the witch's power in her own lands. I shall not make that mistake again. Had you failed the test, I would have come for you. She would not have wanted to try my power, I trust."

Gray handed me my travel bag, which I gratefully accepted.

"Let's hope not," I agreed. "But frankly I'm just as glad not to find out."

"As am I," she said. "Ah, here is the end of the path. We're out of the woods."

"So to speak," I said, wryly.

"Indeed," Adriana said through one of her wan smiles. "Perhaps we are merely entering a new and different dark wood."

"I'll remember to be polite and keep my wits about me," I said. "Just in case."

We came over a rise as the last of the forest dropped away. It had been cold and a little bit foggy in the glade where Mistress Wild kept her house, but now it was warmer and the sun was burning the mist off the grass. The brim of my hat kept the sun out of my eyes, for which I was grateful.

All my battered bruises came slamming back home to take up residence where they had left off. I might have let out a strangled moan, but if I did Gray was polite enough to ignore it. The fog burned off completely, revealing a vista from our position atop the rise.

Gray gestured grandly and I saw the strangest land I had ever seen stretch out below me. It was a crazyquilt landscape of pasture jammed up next to bog, with a wide river abruptly beginning in the middle of dry land and ending the same way, neither flowing down from any highland nor towards any visible body of water. There was a set of picturesque hills planted incongruously next to an unnaturally-flat and perfectly-manicured lawn. Roughly in the center of it all was a city, or at least what I thought was a city. It looked more like parts of several different cities stitched together by some divine artist.

I took in a long slow breath. The air was fresh and clean. I could smell the hint of wood smoke in the distance and not one whiff of the not-so-pleasant odors that I was accustomed to from city life. There was birdsong instead of traffic noise. All in all it was a pretty big change from what I considered to be normal. I wasn't entirely sure I liked it, but I was willing to be open-minded. Hopefully, I wouldn't be attacked by some kind of rabid wildebeest. Did they have rabid wildebeests here? I resolved to ask somebody when I got the chance.

"Welcome," said Adriana Gray. "Welcome to Patchwork."

Chapter Six

Patchwork was the name of the holdfast, the name of the land, and the name of its largest – and possibly only – city. Apparently, if you were a native you just naturally knew which Patchwork was which in casual conversation. Gray led me towards the outskirts of that city. We walked for nearly an hour, covering distance faster than I believed possible.

When I looked at the road in front of my feet, everything seemed normal enough, but if I glanced to the left or right, the world blurred past like the landscape outside a moving coach. It was disorienting, so I resolved to face front. Magic can be subtle sometimes, but on those occasions when it wasn't I found it best to look in the other direction.

Mist realms are called soft for a reason; the rules are pretty much what you make them. The laws of physics are barely guidelines and reality is something you make up as you go along. Some mist realms are created, controlled, and essentially owned by a single guiding will. Most folks couldn't handle that kind of mental and emotional load so most of the soft lands are ruled by committee, or sometimes by no one at all. Those that are uncontrolled rarely last long, geographically speaking, holding shape for a few hundred years at best before they dissolve back into the Mists proper. Some of those abandoned realms become twisted, haunted places, traps for the unwary, or hunting grounds like the dark wood we had just escaped.

Gray assured me that Patchwork was a relatively normal place, ruled and maintained by a democratic community of researchers, specialists, and oddballs who just didn't fit into the real world. She also told me that these rulers were called 'pillars' which sounded nice and pretentious. Magic flowed strongly here, and some of the more romantic debunked sciences still held sway, but otherwise things like gravity, distance, light, and heat were pretty much like you would expect them to be. Until they weren't, of course, but I'd cross that Rubicon when I came to it.

For a city boy like me, Patchwork was a little bit off-putting. The air was filled with strange scents, strange sounds, and yes, even strange tastes. I was used to the tang of smog and the rumble of traffic as well as the other subliminal sensations of city life. I could hear buzzing insects, screeching birds, and the distant howls of who-knows-what kind of animals all around us. The smells were hard to describe, simultaneously sweet and musky. I sneezed explosively; this was going to take some getting used to.

Our destination was a private residence outside the city. I saw it coming quite a distance away. Peter Starbourne's home looked for all the world like the country estate of some fabulously wealthy European count or duke. The property sprawled over a dozen acres, including a number of buildings as well as some exquisitely sculpted lawn, a small patch of woods, and what looked like – but almost certainly wasn't – ancient ruins. The overall effect was absurd, like someone with absolutely no aesthetic sense trying desperately to buy his way into good taste.

"This place is owned by an artist?" I asked.

"An artist with a sense of humor, perhaps?" Gray replied. "Personally, I find Skywatch to be quite charming."

"Skywatch?" I asked.

"The estate's name," Gray explained. "Peter constructed it himself. It took him months."

"Months?" I sputtered. "To build all of this? How many hundreds of workmen did he hire?"

"Not built, constructed," Gray corrected me. "And Peter did it all himself. He was a most powerful will worker."

I nodded. There was clearly a lot I didn't understand about how things worked here in Patchwork. I had read that magic could be more powerful in some mist realms, and I was guessing that was the case here. Most buildings constructed out of magic didn't last long, or required such intense concentration from the maintainers that it wasn't worth doing. If

Starbourne had magicked this place up himself, it was doubly impressive that it had lasted beyond his own life.

"How long ago was Starbourne killed?" I asked.

"His body was found by a servant late Friday night," Gray answered.

"Today is Sunday," I mused. "Two days, that's not so bad. I'd like to see the body first and then look at the crime scene. I assume it's relatively undisturbed?"

Gray smiled thinly, "You can do both at once and the crime scene is completely undisturbed. You will find it exactly as it was."

"And the corpse is just lying there?" I asked dumbfounded. "Aren't there health codes against that?"

"Please," Gray said with a dismissive *tsk*. "We put the entire wing into an eternal moment recursively looping over itself. Nothing has moved or changed in any way since very early Saturday morning."

"Oh," I said. "That's, um, good."

I was simply not accustomed to the amount of magic being thrown around here. I was going to have to take that into account moving forward. I was off my usual turf and that made me uncomfortable. I'm good at what I do because of knowledge, experience, and instinct. I didn't have much knowledge or experience here, so I was going to be down two out of my three best tools. Having to pick everything up on the fly was going to be a royal pain in the posterior. Hopefully human nature would assert itself and I'd be able to rely on the good old-fashioned motives of love and money. If some kind of esoteric magical mumbo-jumbo was behind the murder I might be hard-pressed to earn my exorbitant fees.

We passed through the gate together. The path wound across a rolling lawn towards an enormous Victorian-influenced residence, the main building of the compound. A small man-like creature in footman's livery approached us with a rolling gait. He was a few hairs over three feet tall with proportionately over-sized head and hands. A bulbous nose and sparkling green eyes protruded from between bushy eyebrows and an equally-bushy beard. He trotted up and tugged the bill of his cap respectfully.

"Mister Zachariah Monday," Gray said formally. "May I present Algernon Tiberius McCumber Fizznorman, in service to the house of Starbourne, blessed be his memory."

"Blessed be his memory," repeated Fizznorman. "How may I be of service to you and your friend Mr. Monday, Lady Gray? I apologize, but we are not accepting callers at this time. Surely you understand. If you would both be so kind as to return another time, I can personally promise the legendary hospitality for which Mr. Starbourne was so deservedly famous will …"

"Algernon," interrupted Gray gently. "I have asked Mr. Monday to help us get to the bottom of who killed Peter."

"Ah, and that changes everything," exclaimed Fizznorman. "Surely you are welcome and well met. Even in this, our hour of mourning and sadness, let it not be said that the house and staff of Skywatch showed one frisson of disrespect to any legitimate visitor come calling upon …"

"Algernon," interrupted Gray again, indicating the house with an extended hand. "If you would be so kind?"

"Ah, and of course," said Fizznorman, trotting towards the house and waving us along with his stubby arms. "Follow me if you please, welcome and well met at Skywatch be you and yours. May no harm befall you under this roof and no crumb of bread nor drop of wine fall from your lips nor stain your shirt. The hospitality for which Mr. Starbourne was so deservedly famous is at your disposal, as am I. I have the honor of being Algernon Tiberius McCumber Fizznorman and at your service."

Fizznorman kept up a steady patter the entire walk to the front door. As far as I could tell he never paused for a breath. I stole a sidelong glance at Gray and she gave me a little nod and an eye roll as if to suggest that this behavior was nothing new and I was best off more or less ignoring it. The tiny fellow unlatched the large wooden double doors and swung them open before ushering us in, all the while chattering amiably about the origin of the wood the door was made out of (African Striped Ebony) and the significance of the door knocker (the Starbourne family crest rendered in three dimensions).

I listened with some fraction of my attention while the rest of my brain was trying to take in as many other details as I could. I couldn't be sure which tiny detail might become important. The odds were good that none of them ever would, but you never know. Besides, I had to do something with my brain.

The three of us walked to the soundtrack of Fizznorman's endless monologue. The inside of the house was surprisingly tasteful given the exterior. The walls were thick with paintings. The light was muted and diffuse, but sufficient to display the art. Every nook and corner had some kind of sculpture, either free-standing or on a pedestal. The floors were covered with soft carpeting.

"Did Starbourne make all of this art?" I asked, interrupting Fizznorman's current ramble.

"Oh my, indeed not," the little man replied. "Much of it, yes. And if you ask me, or indeed any of the household staff, we would say that the finest of the collection was all created by Mr. Starbourne, but he was also a collector and a patron of the arts. He supported many artists, both emotionally and financially. He sponsored many schools and offered grants and scholarships to the most promising young artists. He was also surpassingly fond of estate sales, auctions, and, sadly, yard sales."

I paused in front of a small statue of a female nude. It was about two feet tall and disproportionately slender. I had never seen it before, but something about it struck me as somehow familiar. I know just about jack zero about sculpture – or any art at all for that matter – but I looked at the way the stone had been carved and thought about how the artist would have been holding the chisel and the hammer, and at what angle would the chisel have been struck? I wondered if this was how artistic styles were created. Through muscle memory and quirk of nature? Were schools of art made up of people pretending to be left-handed because of one great artist they admired? I really had no idea. Perhaps I should do some research in that area. It rarely hurts to broaden one's knowledge base.

"Is anything missing from the collection?" I asked.

There was a moment of silence. Gray paused, her mouth pursing thoughtfully. I looked around and was shocked to notice that the two of us were alone. The small manservant was nowhere to be seen. Gray looked around as well before making a quiet *tsk* of dissatisfaction.

"Algernon," Gray said with an air of long suffering patience in her tone. "You're doing it again."

"Ah, and I'm terribly sorry, Ma'am," said Fizznorman who had apparently been present all along. "It happens, sure, and I'm terribly, terribly sorry. Never meaning any disrespect am I, surely you understand."

With that, Fizznorman began to ramble on again as he had been before I distracted him. I was still trying to figure out how I had missed his presence. Gray smiled apologetically at the confusion that must have been obvious on my face.

"A good manservant is unobtrusive and dear Algernon takes that adage a little bit too close to heart," Gray said. "When he isn't actively making his presence known, he tends to become, well, very unobtrusive. It isn't even anything he does on purpose anymore, it just happens. It can be rather disconcerting, but he doesn't mean any harm by it."

"Huh," I said, intelligently. "Let's, um, let's go take a look at things, shall we?"

We followed Fizznorman, who managed to avoid not talking again, until we came to a wide hallway. I looked down it and found my vision blurring and my eyes watering as I tried to focus. Magic: once again, I found it wiser to look away rather than directly at it.

"One moment please," said Gray and she began humming.

It sort of hurt my ears and my brain to listen, so I assumed it must be yet more magic. After a moment of conscientiously not listening, the hallway resolved itself and there was a sort of a pop inside my head, as if the air pressure had changed rapidly.

"It is safe to pass now," announced Gray.

"Well, and I'm sure that when it comes to disturbing poor Mr. Starbourne, the fewer the better," announced Fizznorman in the midst of an ongoing discourse about … something … before ducking a quick bow and withdrawing.

"He really is an excellent manservant," murmured Gray. "Peter was quite fond of him."

"I'm sure," I replied.

We moved on to the crime scene without further repartée, witty or otherwise. When Gray opened the door the smell of fresh blood hit my nose; this recursion magic was pretty impressive stuff. I stood in the doorway and looked around. It was a study or a library of some sort. The walls were covered with bookshelves crammed full of books with the odd knick-knack or decorative bookend to break up the flow. There were three comfortable looking-chairs pushed up against the walls, and a desk near the opposite wall. There was a small round table next to the desk filled with the kinds of odds and ends that accumulate on small round tables.

The body was between the desk and the door; it lay facedown on the floor in a pool of its own blood. I tried not to see a dead person; I tried not to dwell on who he had been and what he had dreamed of. This was a crime scene, a puzzle to be solved for now, not yet a loss to be mourned. The back of the head was smashed in and the obvious murder weapon – a bloodstained fireplace poker – lay on the carpet nearby. The obvious weapon wasn't always the actual weapon, but I'd assume it was in this case unless I found non-corroborating evidence.

"Can we get a post-mortem examination of the body?" I asked.

"Dr. Michelle Foucault is one of our citizens," said Gray. "She maintains a research laboratory. After you're done here, I'll see to it that the body is transferred there. I'm sure she'll be eager to help in any way that she can."

I nodded. I idly wondered what kind of research a doctor might engage in around here and what kind of practice, for that matter. Before I was done, there were an awful lot of things I was going to have to learn about this place. Some of it was going to be necessary to solve the crime, but more importantly, now that I was here, I wasn't going to pass up an opportunity to poke my nose into other people's business.

I plunked my down travel bag, opened it up and removed the case containing the first of the items I had ordered from Gray's shop in the Old City. It was a camera. It wasn't the kind of camera that fit in a pocket and it certainly wasn't one of those single-lens and single-button jobs that are popular with tourists the world over. This particular camera required more gear than the average golf foursome. I lifted the tripod out and busied myself assembling it and attaching the hood. The mount was designed to swivel so I could move the angle of the shot around without having to completely take down and reassemble the tripod, and for this I was grateful.

Next, I opened the leather box that contained the various lenses. Most of them looked familiar enough, short lenses for taking pictures up close and personal, longer ones for farther away and that sort of thing. But this camera also took different kinds of filters. The yellow one captured residual auras indicating magical devices, the red one took the auras of living creatures, and the black one would show any wraiths, specters, or other ghostly non-corporeal manifestations. Or so the marketing literature promised.

I had wanted one of these babies for years but hadn't yet been able to rationalize the expense. I'm as good at rationalization as the next guy, but this sucker would have cost me more than a month's work at standard retail. I hummed happily to myself as I selected a lens and attached it to the camera.

I took about a dozen shots, which used up the film I had pre-loaded. I considered putting in a second roll, but this film was very pricey, and I was pretty sure I had gotten at least one shot of everything I needed. I would regret it later if I had missed something, but I also didn't want to rely too heavily on the new toy.

"Okay," I said to no one in particular. "I'm going to flip over the body now."

I gently touched the body's shoulder. It was warm and a little doughy to the touch. There was a sharp metallic tang on my tongue and a wave of dizziness passed over me. I felt an odd rush of memory overtake me, sights, sounds, smells, and other sensations of my past paraded through my head. The smell of perfume, the thrill of sexual excitement, sadness, loss, loneliness, the feel of paper beneath my fingers, the sound of a man lecturing about … something.

I found myself experiencing a profound nostalgia for my youth, the time I spent at college, when I learned so many of the things that furnished the shelves of my brain to this day. I couldn't explain why it hit me now, of all times. I guess death affects us all; even the death of a stranger can make a man glad to be alive.

I turned the body over; the spell had kept it from stiffening with rigor. I looked into the dead eyes of Peter Starbourne. They were pale blue and whatever secrets they held were beyond me, at least for now.

"Who did this to you?" I asked the corpse. "And why? Help me find out."

Nothing unusual presented itself. He was wearing a colorful vest, a white linen shirt, dark trousers that fit him well and would have flattered his physique back when he was alive, and very expensive leather shoes. His skin was milk-pale; his thick hair was silver and lush and tied back from his face with a blue ribbon that matched his eyes. I examined the hands, the fingers, and the palms of his hands. The nails were painted to match the vest.

He appeared to be in excellent physical condition, apart from being dead. He had almost certainly got a lot of exercise. That was unusual for an artist, but not unheard of.

I looked up from my labors to see Gray staring at me with a peculiar intensity. Her dark eyes bored into my own. I looked a question at her.

"Nothing," she replied distractedly. "I thought I saw something odd, but don't let me keep you from your work."

"No, it's all right," I said. "We're not very likely to learn anything more of use here and now. The autopsy might tell us more, but then again it very well might not."

I thought about it while I began cleaning up after myself. The details of the murder looked pretty straight forward, but sometimes that's deceiving. If it was a crime of passion, the clues probably painted a straight trail, but if this was a premeditated crime the killer or killers might have gone to some lengths to obfuscate their trail. It had happened to me before. Given his position in society, I was inclined to suspect politics or some other even more complicated motive.

I took down the camera parts and loaded them back into the cases and the cases back into the bags and slung the bags back onto my shoulders. Why can't the really good stuff ever be small and light? I'm sure there was some kind of cosmic law at work here. The only thing I wasn't sure about was whether that law applied to everyone or just hard-working private detectives.

"There was a party here Friday night?" I asked.

"Yes," Gray replied. "A small gathering of friends, less than a hundred people, mostly citizens of Patchwork. Almost all of the pillars of our community were present. I wasn't here myself, although Peter invited me. I stayed home working."

Nearly one hundred people didn't sound like a small gathering of friends to me. There was no value to being snarky with the client at this point, so I declined to comment. Rich folks just did things differently, I guess.

"I'll check your alibi later," I said, mostly joking. "Can I get a guest list? Nearly one hundred suspects is a lot to go through, but I've had worse."

I took out my trusty notebook and a cheap ball-point pen. I always used the cheapest pen I could find. I inevitably left all my pens someplace and I felt worse about it if they were worth anything. I wrote down all my observations about the body, both what I found and also what I didn't find. Sometimes there were answers to be found in what wasn't there. Which reminded me of something.

"You never answered my question earlier," I said. "Was any thing missing, anything taken? Art, money, a book? Anything at all? Even something seemingly inconsequential might turn out to be important."

"I have no idea," Gray answered. "I'll ask Algernon to have someone look into that."

The wizard left to find the tiny manservant, leaving me alone with the body and my thoughts. Perversely, I found my thoughts turning towards Gray. What exactly was her status here? She claimed to be no more than one of many among equals, but the way Fizznorman deferred to her spoke volumes. It might just be the little man's nature, but my instincts told me there was more to Adriana Gray than met the eye, quite possibly a lot more. I jotted down her name followed by a question mark. Then I underlined her name twice and added two more question marks. Just for good measure I circled it. I can be very detail-oriented when I don't have any actual facts to work with.

Chapter Seven

There was an old-fashioned horse-drawn coach waiting for us outside Skywatch when were done. It was black as were the two horses hitched up in front. It seemed to be of excellent construction and in perfect order and repair. The only thing missing was a driver. That didn't seem to bother Gray who opened the door to the passenger compartment and waved for me to climb in ahead of her.

It seemed rude to point out the lack of driver, so I shrugged and climbed in. It was comfortable enough inside. Gray climbed in gracefully and took a seat across from me. She rapped sharply on the wall that separated us from where the driver would normally sit.

"Please take us to the tower," she said, annunciating clearly and speaking slowly.

The coach rolled forward and onto the road. The horses gradually picked up speed until we were moving at a smooth and steady canter. It wasn't exactly as fast as the kind of transportation I was used to, but it wasn't bad. I looked out the window and was a little bit shocked to see the world blurring by.

We rode like that for about fifteen minutes. I quickly learned that it was easier on my equilibrium if I didn't look outside. All things considered it was a nicer ride than many I had taken that featured actual drivers. Who was I to complain?

"I've arranged for a meeting with most of the movers and shakers of Patchwork," Gray said. "That will be tomorrow morning. For now, there's not much to do. I suggest you relax at my tower and heal up from your morning's adventure."

That didn't sound like a terrible idea to me. Normally I liked to get moving as quickly as possible on a new case. But things seemed to move at a more forcibly sedate pace around these parts. I guess it was a case of when in Patchwork do as the Patchworkies.

We arrived in short order at Gray's tower. It was more or less designed to specifications. It was impressively tall, but not impossibly so, it was constructed mostly out of some highly polished black stone, and seemed to feature absolutely nothing in the way of either doors or windows.

In some ways it reminded me of the place where my buddy Tim lived, but in others it was its own special snowflake, copiously decorated with brooding gargoyles, leering sheela na gigs, dancing kokopellis, and impassive green men. All of them seemed to be watching me suspiciously but I tried not to let it bother me.

"Welcome to my home, Zachariah," Gray said expansively. "Rooms have been set aside for you."

The lower floors of Gray's tower home were apparently open to the public. They featured an extensive library, several labs equipped with the latest scientific and/or magical equipment, and a top notch entertainment center that played a variety of educational programs. There were about a dozen young people wandering around, making use of the facilities.

Although there were also six or seven helpers cleaning, organizing, and generally minding Gray's tower, I didn't get the impression that any of them were quite staff. They seemed more like house guests that helped out with the chores. From the inside it didn't remind me of Tim's place at all.

Gray took me up the stairs and out of the public areas. The rooms that had been set aside for me turned out to be an opulent suite of three rooms. It was entirely too much, but it seemed rude to object too strenuously. Gray showed me around, careful to bring my attention to a tasseled bell cord that if pulled would alert the staff to any needs I might have. I assured her that I had no particular needs currently.

Gray wished me a pleasant evening and I installed myself in a comfortable chair. I sat there for a moment cataloging the things I had learned and stacking them against the injuries I had suffered. So far the injuries were outstripping the learning. Hopefully, that would dramatically reverse itself, and soon.

Rising, I puttered carefully about my suite. It was nearly as large as my condominium back in New Jerusalem and a good deal fancier. I found it a little bit hard to believe that Gray treated all the hired help this well. She had some kind of angle going on and buttering me up was part of it. Wizards always have some kind of angle going on but no one was paying me to figure out what her angle actually was. Gray had an agenda and that was fine with me. She had always done right by me, so I saw no reason to distrust her motives, secret or otherwise.

The suite included a small library and I did some light reading to pass the time. After a few hours, there was a knock on the door. It turned out to be a young lady bringing me lunch. I thanked her politely, but was unsure of the tipping protocol. Noticing my hesitation, the young lady assured me that no tip was required. Lunch turned out to be a savory meat pie, exotically spiced; I couldn't positively identify just what type of meat I was actually eating, but I tried not to let that bother me, because, whatever it was, it was really good. After lunch, I sat in the comfortable chair and read some more. Then I dozed. Maybe I could get used to this country lifestyle after all. The day's adventures must have gotten to me a little bit more than I thought, because my doze slowly slipped into a deep sleep. And then I dreamed.

In my dream I was walking the empty halls of Skywatch. I was looking for something, but I'm not sure what it was. I opened every door, but all the rooms were abandoned and empty. My footsteps echoed up and down the halls, sounding strange and hollow to my own ears.

I opened up a door that led to a closet. Gray was standing inside, gazing at me placidly. Algernon Fizznorman was suddenly standing next to me. He looked very unhappy with me for some reason. I apologized for disturbing Gray's privacy and closed the door.

I came upon a very long hallway that seemed to stretch on forever. The walls were covered with an endless series of portraits, the same man featured in every portrait. I didn't recognize his face, but I knew that he was important somehow. I kept walking but I didn't seem to be making any progress. The hall still seemed to go on forever. I kept walking because there didn't seem to be anything else to do.

I turned around to see how far I had come and found myself face to face with Peter Starbourne, the deceased master of Skywatch. He stared at me. His eyes accused me of slacking off when I should be looking for his murderer.

Starbourne didn't speak, but he raised a hand and pointed back down the hallway. There was a door there now where there hadn't been one before. I opened it and found myself in the room where I had examined Starbourne's body. It was still lying there, unmoving and unchanged.

I took off my hat and coat and dressed the body in my clothing. After I finished this, Starbourne's dead body sat up and looked at me. I knew that he wanted something from me; maybe he wanted me to tell him what to do. I didn't know what to do and I didn't know what to tell him. I looked at him and he looked back at me. After a while, he stood up and shuffled slowly away, still wearing my clothing. I turned back to the other Starbourne, the one who had pointed the way, but he was gone. I was alone again. Maybe I had always been alone.

I turned around and walked back the way I had come. The endless hallway wasn't there anymore. Instead I found myself in a courtroom. The jury box was full of my friends, Baxter, Tim, Jasper Mandrake, Audrey, and Carin were all there. My across-the-hall neighbors, the Gallaghers were there, Bruno and his adorable daughter the MOG, as well as the impenetrably dotty Miss Mulligatuck who lived one floor up. The judge was Peter Starbourne and he did not look happy.

I like dream symbolism as much as the next guy, but the guilt imagery here was getting a little bit over the top. I was acutely aware that I was dreaming, but that didn't seem to help much. I looked to Starbourne to see what my judgment would be. He banged the gavel and the sound of it echoed through the room.

"Hark! death is calling while I speak to ye," Starbourne intoned.
"The jaw is falling, the red cheek paling,
The strong limbs failing;
Ice with the warm blood mixing;
The eyeballs fixing.
Nine times goes the passing bell:
Ye merry souls, farewell."

"Well that's perfectly creepy, thank you very much," I said. "But not very helpful. Any chance you could give me some cryptic but still useful clue as to who actually killed you?"

Everyone in the room was standing now and they were all staring silently at me. Which was not very helpful. I stared back, but that didn't help much, either.

Judge Starbourne stood up and I noticed that he was still wearing my clothes. I realized then, in a moment of perfect dream-clarity, that he was also me. I was judging myself now? Good job, Monday. Judge Starbourne-who-was-also-me walked out from behind the bench and headed for his chambers. I followed and no one tried to stop me.

We went into the modest room and there was already someone sitting behind his desk. Or maybe that should have been my desk? Their desk? Dreams are weird. The judge addressed the person behind his desk.

"It went just as you predicted, Your Grace," Starbourne-Me said.

"Of course," replied the man behind the desk. "It always does, even when it doesn't."

I woke up then, still sitting in the comfortable chair. The final imagery of the dream haunted me. Did it mean anything or was it just the nocturnal wanderings of an over-active brain? Was my subconscious trying to tell me something? Or did the message – if it even existed – come from outside? I resolved to ask Tim the warlock about the dream the next time I saw him, whenever that might be.

I levered myself out of the chair and stumbled into the lavatory. I did what I needed to do in the mornings and then I washed my face and hands. By the time I came back out, I was beginning to feel human again. Coffee would be necessary for full functionality, but that would have to wait. At some point in the process, I forgot all the details from my dream and for the life of me, couldn't figure out what it was that I had wanted to talk to Tim about, just a moment ago. Oh well, it probably wasn't that important.

Chapter Eight

Adriana Gray had arranged a gathering of what she called 'Pillars of the Community' for me to meet. I could practically hear the capitalization when she said 'pillars' and 'community.' Usually when I heard a phrase like that it referred to the people who founded the local equivalent of the Rotary or Elks Club. Gray had already told me that there was a bit more to this group than the usual. Not-so-coincidentally, every one of them had been at Starbourne's gathering the night he died. Officially, they were all here to answer questions about Starbourne's untimely demise, but the important thing was giving me a chance to get a look at all of them. Or at least that was the important part as far as I was concerned.

I could have left my luggage at Gray's tower, but some of my gear might come in handy so I was still hauling my travel bag around. It didn't bother me much, in fact, it seemed even lighter than usual, despite being over full of my stuff. Perhaps the magics that held it together were more powerful here in Patchwork? Or maybe it was just that my gymnasium membership was finally paying off.

Skywatch wasn't exactly open to the public at the moment and Gray assured me that her tower was not an appropriate venue, so the meet was to be held at the Aristarchus Lodge, owned and maintained by one Oswald Quatermain, IV. Although the place was miles away from Skywatch, Gray once again suggested that we walk there, and once again the walk that should have taken hours seemed to be over in mere minutes with neither of us even slightly out of breath.

Seen from a distance, Aristarchus was a rather impressive classic hunting lodge; the exterior was unfinished, artfully rough-hewn, and in some places seemed to be assembled directly out of tree trunks. The whole thing squatted on top of a perfectly round hill surrounded by a startlingly picturesque forest. Nature in Patchwork seemed to specialize in looking kind of artificial in an aesthetically pleasing sort of way.

"Is this place for real?" I asked, mostly rhetorically.

"Yes," answered Gray. "And no. Like so many things, it is complicated. Perhaps we can explain a few things to you that may assist with your investigation?"

"Explain away," I replied.

"Let's wait until we are all gathered," said Gray. "It will be easier that way."

"Okay," I shrugged.

I was beginning to suspect that Gray had an agenda for this meeting beyond my own or anything she had shared with me. Wizards always seem to have an ulterior motive, a hidden goal, or a larger purpose to everything they do. They're a lot like private investigators that way, now that I think about it. Hoisted with my own petard once again. I resisted the urge to sigh theatrically, but it was an effort.

If I thought the sounds of wildlife were pervasive before, then the area immediately surrounding Aristarchus was a veritable zoo. I could see small animals scurrying around everywhere. Squirrels – or perhaps chipmunks, who can tell the difference? – stared at me with enormous liquid eyes from every tree. Howls, barks, and other animal noises periodically rolled over us. It didn't seem to faze Gray at all, so I tugged up my metaphorical big boy trousers and ignored it all. But I kept an eye on her, just in case; being eaten by wolves was not how I wanted to end my day.

As we approached within an acre or so of the lodge, the trees thinned out a bit and the undergrowth cleared away as if by magic. The lawn in front was the same postcard-perfect trim I had come to expect hereabouts. I knew a few groundskeepers back in the real world that would sell their mothers to be able to work the kind of magic that was so commonplace here. Quatermain must have had some kind of active watchwards because we weren't within a dozen yards of the place before someone – or perhaps something – came lurching out to greet us.

I had plenty of time to examine the greeter while we closed the distance. The greeter in question was about eight feet tall and nearly four feet across at the shoulders. He (or it) wore an old-fashioned tuxedo that couldn't possibly have come off of any earthly rack. The exposed skin was bark-brown and lumpy; the empty eye sockets revealed red pinpoints of light from somewhere deep within a hairless, earless, and noseless head. The toothless mouth yawned open to reveal more of the red glow.

It (or he) was a true golem: an animated statue with a strong work ethic and an indestructible, tireless body. True golems were as far from workaday coffee golems and dishwashing golems as an angel was from a dove. There weren't very many of them, seeing as the divine formula for their creation was long lost. Legend had it that an Angel of Salvation had personally delivered that formula to an ancient Rabbi in desperate need.

Whether the legend was true or not, no one was making any new ones. The old models didn't seem to be going anywhere, either. I had even heard tell of some of the really old ones achieving some level of autonomy and free will. But even the most emancipated of them still preferred to serve in some capacity or another. Apparently, it wasn't any easier for an animated hunk of rock to overcome its basic programming than it was for us mortal types.

"Greetings honored guests," the queerly polite voice emanated from somewhere in his chest and was unencumbered by emotion or inflection of any kind. "Please follow me. Most of the others have already gathered in the Great Room."

"Thank you, Roger," replied Gray sweetly. "Please lead the way."

The three of us entered the lodge. Roger took my hat and Gray's wrap and hung them both carefully on a stand near the door. I noticed a half dozen or so articles already decorating the stand. I kept my coat because I looked good in it. The others had indeed already gathered, or at least their outerwear had.

"Roger?" I asked in an incredulous *sotto vocce.*

"Hush," replied Gray in a matching whisper. "Be polite. Roger is perfectly harmless."

"Don't tell me," I hissed back. "He really is an excellent manservant and Oswald is quite fond of him?"

"Actually, no," Gray whispered back. "He's fairly dreadful, but be polite anyway."

I couldn't argue with that so we followed Roger inside what was essentially the largest and most impressive tree fort I had ever seen. The inside of the Aristarchus Lodge kept the promise of the outside. It smelled like a pine forest and looked like the sanctum sanctorum of the most pretentious of the Great White Hunters. There were stuffed animal heads on every mantel and the floors were constructed entirely out of rough-hewn (but highly polished) planks of hardwood. The walls were mostly covered with various animal skins while weapons of every make and historical period were fixed over doorways and paintings like deadly punctuation marks.

The walls were also liberally decorated with black and white photographs. Most of them were of safaris and featured triumphant hunters standing on top of dead animals. But sprinkled in and throughout were images of what I could only assume were Quatermain family gatherings. Generations of tall, slender, well-dressed children and adults smiled out at me with too-perfect teeth and glittering eyes.

The Great Room took up most of the center of the building. It was longer than it was wide, but that was still plenty wide. There were a number of trestle tables assembled cafeteria-style in the middle of the cavernous room, but the handful of people had restricted themselves to a far corner. Clever furniture arrangement and folding screens seemed to split the large room into several different spaces. The effect was enhanced by area rugs that dotted the floor. The room was lit by multiple chandeliers filled with burning candles.

"Lady Adriana Gray and Mr. Zachariah Monday," boomed Roger in an amplified version of his emotionless tones.

The cluster of people turned to look at us. They seemed to be mostly human, but even from a distance, I recognized the squat and inhumanly broad outline of a goblin and the diminutive form of a gnome or some other halfling. A man dressed all in white raised a hand and beckoned us close with a cheery wave.

"Come in! Come in," greeted the man. "Welcome to Aristarchus. Mr. Monday, I'm Oswald Quatermain. It's a pleasure to make your acquaintance."

Quatermain took a couple of steps forward and extended a hand to be shook. We were still a dozen paces away, so I had to hustle a bit not to leave him hanging. It made me feel a little bit awkward, as if I were a schoolchild trying to impress a stern headmaster. It was probably accidental, but it didn't immediately endear me to the man. You can tell a lot about a person by their handshake. His grip was firm, warm, and dry. He didn't try to crush my fingers to jelly and I returned the favor; maybe he was okay after all.

Quatermain appeared to be a fit and athletic 50, but you could never be sure about these things. There seemed to be something vaguely familiar about his face, but I couldn't place why or when. His hair was iron where it wasn't silver and his pencil-thin mustache was immaculately groomed. He wore a white suit, white shirt, white tie, and – yes, white shoes, which didn't look as absurd as you might imagine. He was carrying a walking stick with a pommel shaped like a cougar. He kissed Gray chastely on the cheek and murmured something that sounded reassuring. He turned slightly away from the two of us to include the group behind him and gestured towards them.

"Mr. Monday, allow me to make introductions," Quatermain said warmly.

I immediately recognized the diminutive form of Fizznorman standing next to a tall and broad-shouldered woman. He had changed out of his plain servant's suit and was wearing khaki pants and a gaudy Hawaiian shirt. Both articles of clothing were perfectly tailored to his form.

I leaned in close to Gray and whispered a question to her, "What's Fizznorman doing here? I thought he was Starbourne's butler?"

"Yes," Gray whispered back. "But he is also one of the Pillars. He is a servant by choice, a pillar by ability and destiny." She paused for a moment before adding, "Really, I think he just likes being a butler."

We joined the gathering. They were six in total. The tall woman was wearing a pale blue sundress, high strappy sandals and a hat that would have served perfectly well at any horse race or cotillion.

"Lady Gray tells me you've already met Algernon," Quatermain said. "And this is Dr. Michelle Foucault"

I shook Fizznorman's small hand before turning. Dr. Foucault was slightly taller than I was so I tilted my head to meet her eyes.

"Doctor," I said, taking her hand.

I was momentarily taken aback as I took the large hand in my own. I noted a certain thickness of the wrist and a strong jawline. Tiny and not-so-tiny details snapped into place and my world clicked slightly as a paradigm shifted. I tried not to let it show on my face, and I flatter myself that it didn't. One of the skills I've mastered over the years is the poker face. It's very useful in my line of work.

"Darling," Foucault exclaimed as she took my hand in hers, "So wonderful to meet you at last. Adriana has told me so much about you."

"Charmed," I said, a little helplessly.

"Did the, um, delivery I sent around from Skywatch arrive at your laboratory?" Gray asked, circuitously.

"Yes, yes, it did," Foucault said, her pitch lowering, perhaps subconsciously. "I haven't had a chance to look into it yet."

"Understood," said Gray. "We'll talk about it later."

The delivery that Gray was referring to had to be Starbourne's corpse. So the Dr. Foucault who was to perform the autopsy was also the Dr. Foucault who was one of my main suspects. That might well turn out to be inconvenient. Beggars couldn't be choosers, but I resolved to get some kind of third party confirmation of the hopefully good doctor's work. This was just another one of the many reasons I didn't like to work outside of New Jerusalem.

"And this fellow here is Gwynplaine," Quatermain continued the introductions, gesturing to a cadaverously-thin man with a profound widow's peak and an aquiline nose.

I shook Gwynplaine's hand, "Any relation?" I asked.

"An ancestor," he said diffidently. "Or possibly a descendent. It's complicated."

"I would imagine," I said, sympathetically.

The stocky form of the goblin shuffled forward and my eyes widened in sudden recognition. I hadn't seen the ancient goblin in years, but he literally hadn't changed at all. But then, why would he?

"And this is ...," Quatermain began.

"Visivald!" I exclaimed, happily. "How are you, your Grace?"

"Don't call me that," rumbled the ancient Duke, but there was no rancor in it. "How have you been keeping yourself, boy?"

"Fine, fine," I assured him. "I had no idea you were living here. How long have you been away from court?"

"A few years now," Visivald replied, his voice so deep, you felt him speak as much as you heard it. "There's no one left alive from my day, and

I was becoming something of an embarrassment," the Duke continued. "Couldn't have that, not when there's so much life left to live."

Visivald wasn't exaggerating; he was well over a thousand years old. As far as I was aware, he was completely comfortable with his immortality. Duke Sir Visivald had been a fixture around the Nome King's court for centuries. I didn't much care for the idea of him not being welcome anymore, and not just because I thought of the old warrior as family. Any change that excluded someone like Visivald was a change for the worse.

"And how are you treating that employee of yours?" Visivald rumbled. "Paying him well, I trust?"

"Your nephew is doing great, Your Grace," I said. "I pay him as much as he'll let me, but you know what he's like."

Visivald's laughter boomed out so loud and so suddenly that I actually took a half-step backward. If I had still been wearing my hat, I do believe it would have been blown off my head. I grinned a little weakly; it's always best to show courage in the face of people who are larger than life.

"That's Baxter," agreed Visivald. His voice thrummed somewhere in the vicinity of my solar plexus.

Technically, Baxter wasn't Visivald's nephew. All of Visivald's many, many descendants called him 'Uncle.' Great-great-great-great-great-great Grand Uncle was closer, but no one – to the best of my knowledge – knew exactly how old the Duke was or what precise relationships he held. Family is important to goblins, especially those of noble blood but details aren't and when you're family everything else is just details.

"Okay," I said, rubbing my hands together. "Now that we're all gathered, can we …"

"Excuse me, please," interjected Gray. "But we are not all yet gathered."

I blinked once or twice before I recalled that Roger had said that *most* of the others had gathered. Most, not all. That was exactly the sort of small detail that sometimes mattered. If I was missing stuff like that, I was more off my game than I had imagined. It was time to get my head back on straight. I wondered if I had missed something important already. I shook my head in frustration; that sort of thinking would get me spinning in circles and getting nothing done so I put the thought out of my mind.

"Sorry," I said. "I should have been paying more attention."

"Think nothing of it, old chap," enthused Quatermain. "Roger! Could you be so kind as to bring 'round the refreshments? What's everyone drinking?"

The next several minutes were taken up with the typical bustle and clatter of people preparing to settle down. Plates with several different kinds of cheese and crackers were produced, as were mushroom puffs, a variety of vegetables, two different kinds of onion dip (smooth and chunky), and as many different kinds of drinks as there were guests. I had an Arnold Palmer.

Everyone was very polite and friendly to me, but small groups of people aren't very good at waiting, I withdrew as much as I could so as to let them get past the pleasantries and maybe a little bit bored. People tell each other things when they're comfortable and bored, and I was listening.

Dr. Foucault asked how Gwynplaine – Lord Gwynplaine, she called him – was getting on in his new home. After a few polite exchanges, that question led to Gwynplaine wanting to know who was going to finish his castle now that Peter was gone. Quatermain had snorted derisively at that. Gray had hushed them both and both men quieted immediately. The ship of conversation then sailed for safer waters. After about fifteen minutes of nervous semi-party chatter, I had determined three things. One, Oswald Quatermain was an ass, two, she could deny it as much as she wanted, but Lady Adriana Gray was the de facto ruler of Patchwork, and three, Lord Gwynplaine was nervous about something – something that had him a lot more worried than floor plans and construction delays generally warranted.

There was a sonorous chime in the air. It emanated simultaneously from everywhere at once and nowhere in particular. Roger put down the tray of empty glasses he had been transporting to the kitchen and glided out the door. He was both quiet and fast, incongruously so for a creature that looked as ungainly as he did. I imagined those thick, blocky fingers could crush a man's skull as easily as they carried a tray full of champagne flutes. I started to ask myself some important questions. What did I know about golems? Did they have any weaknesses? And most importantly of all, was I being hopelessly paranoid?

"Ah," declared Quatermain, happily. "It would seem our final pillar has arrived. I do wonder what kept the girl?"

I rose from my chair, ostensibly to refresh my drink, but I was also sizing up the room. Roger would bring the final member of our little kaffeklatsch in through that door over there, people were mostly sitting on the couch. After a moment's calculation, I chose the best spot to stand, it commanded a fair view of the entire room so everyone would be able to see and hear me, and my gray suit would look better in front of the fire place than against a brown wall.

That may sound like a lot of effort, but this was my first contact with the principals of the case. At least one of the gathered was likely to either know something about the murder that I didn't, or have been actively involved; probably, it was more than one. Putting extra work in up front might well pay off big-time further down the line. Maybe if I was real lucky I could solve this case without anything becoming more deadly than it was boring. Hope springs eternal and all that.

Roger cruised back into the room, still quiet, but not as fast as he was on the way out. As expected, he was leading a woman into the Great Hall. The woman was hooded and cloaked for travel, but I could tell that she was tiny under the bulky clothing, less than five feet tall and willow-thin. She looked too regular of limb to be a goblin, but she was small for a human. Perhaps she was a faerie commoner of some sort. Something about her seemed familiar. Maybe it was the way she walked? I turned back to watch the assembly's reaction to her arrival.

Roger did that thing with his voice again as he belted out the name of the newcomer, "Lady Kellidwyn of Coldiron Keep, outcast of Faerie."

Everything slowed down. It took hours for my head to whip around and look at her. It took days for her to finish pulling her hood down. It took geological ages for me to regain the power of speech.

"Kelli?" I asked.

"Zack?!?" she gaped.

If anything, she sounded more shocked than I did, and somehow that helped bring me back to myself. It was Kelli. This was where she had gone when I sent her out of the world. This was the place she had run to. And here she was. It was simple really. I was just about to congratulate myself on how logical and in control I was being when I realized that I was standing stock still and gape-mouthed at Kelli, and she at me.

"Well, well, well," drawled Quatermain. "I can see you two already know each other? That will save time with introductions, I'm sure. Shall we begin?"

Gray hushed him with a sidelong gaze and a whispered word. Somewhere in the haze and confusion that my world had suddenly become, I remember thinking it was nice to see that I wasn't the only one Gray shushed so easily.

Chapter Nine

At the university I'd majored in Criminology, minored in Criminal Justice, and spent most of my time avoiding both in favor of booze and women. I'll leave it to posterity to determine how much each of these factors contributed to my success as a private detective. Suffice it to say that I learned a lot about the technical aspects of crime and crime fighting, not the least of which was how much the two fields have in common. But even more importantly, I learned a lot about motivation. Most crimes begin with a motive, and if you can figure out what that motive is, you're a long ways towards solving the crime. Trust me on this one, I'm a professional.

I met Kelli in junior year *Advanced Profiling 301*. She was eager, driven, smart, and did I mention sexy? We became friends and study buddies, but it rapidly became more than that. I had just been dumped and she was hyper focused on her grades; I wouldn't say our relationship was completely shallow, but it wasn't exactly a great love for the ages either.

None of which explained what was going on inside my brain in the here and now. I felt flushed and light-headed. My vision went a little swimmy, like I was going into shock. Shock? That didn't make any sense at all. Sure, I was surprised to see Kelli here, it was an incredible coincidence, but far from impossible. From what I had seen so far, Patchwork was exactly the sort of Soft Realm holdfast that Kelli and I had been looking for and hoping to find when we researched the ritual to get her out of the world and away from her pursuers. How many of those could there be? When I stopped and thought about it, it actually made perfect sense. But you could not explain that to my body – or my mind for that matter. I felt a moment of extreme disorientation as the world went wavery and I could have sworn I heard a swirl of harp music … and then I was someplace and somewhen else.

I was watching Kelli walk into the Great Room in Patchwork, but what I saw was something entirely different. I was back at college, sitting in the very back row of an under-filled auditorium. The professor was lecturing about the criminal mind, but I wasn't paying attention, I was waiting for Kelli and she was late. I checked my watch for the 100th time in less than a quarter hour. No one took attendance, so it's not like missing the lecture would hurt her, but it wasn't like Kelli to miss this class. Understanding the way criminals thought was her passion, it was all she talked about and the overwhelming focus of her studies. I was a little worried, but mostly I was just wanted to see her.

Something the professor said caught my attention, "… and money. If you stick to those basics, you won't often go far wrong. But if you're going to be truly excellent, you must also be prepared for the rarer criminal motivations. Things like frustrated ambitions, blackmail, curses, family pride, and yes – even the occasional geas or other mystical compulsion. Strange motivations can trick you into completely disregarding the guilty party because their actions make no logical sense."

The professor paused to let that notion sink in and for the slower note-takers to catch up. I wasn't close enough to see, but I felt sure that the professor was taking a moment to see how the class was reacting to his words. I had done a few teaching-assistant gigs already and I knew you could tell whether your words were sinking in or bouncing off just by the way a class looked. Some of the most on-the-ball professors could even change course in mid-lecture to bring the class back up to speed.

Someone sat down next to me and I started a little in my seat. I heard a familiar girlish giggle and turned to see Kelli smiling at me with mischief in her eyes. But time had fragmented for me once again, and it was hours later and Kelli and I were in my dorm room, and the mischief in her eyes had nothing to do with sneaking up on me in class while I was distracted.

She was curled up on my bed, artfully positioned to best display her physical charms. She was wearing a sleeveless blouse with a high lacy collar; there had been a sweater earlier but it was discarded now. A peasant skirt pooled around her folded up legs, I could see the shape of them moving beneath the light fabric, but there was some mystery there that intrigued me. Something about her position reminded me of something, but I couldn't place the memory. She crooked an inviting finger at me and beckoned me to join her on the bed; this I did eagerly. Kelli reached up and began slowly unbuttoning my shirt, her fingers lingering to tickle at my neck and upper chest as she did. The sensation was thrilling, I hadn't been touched quite like that in far too long, or had I? It was confusing inside my head. I decided to ignore my head and start listening to my body.

I touched her lightly on the shoulder; her skin was soft and cool to my touch. She made small murmurs of approval, so I ran the palms of my hand down her bare arm. She seemed to like that, and so did I, so I did it some more, drawing small circles on her flesh with the pads of my fingers and the heel of my hand.

"Your hands are so warm," Kelli said, approvingly.

"Are they?" I asked. "I thought your arms were cold."

"Can't it be both?" She giggled.

And then she kissed me, leaning forward and rising up a little off the bed to meet my lips. Hers were soft and they brushed against my own, teasing me with gentleness at first before pressing harder. Her lips parted and I felt her warm breath. I opened my mouth to match hers and her tongue slid into my mouth. Spasms of sensation exploded through my body, muscles in my legs twanged and my head went swimmy. It felt like my whole body was falling into Kelli.

Eventually we broke for air. We stared at each other for a moment and then Kelli pushed gently on my shoulders. I lay back on my bed, Kelli leaned over me, touching my chest; my shirt was open and mostly off. At some point when I wasn't paying attention Kelli's shirt had vanished revealing a rather fetching wine-red brassiere and an even more fetching expanse of luminous pale skin. I reached up to brush my fingertips lightly along her belly and she trembled a little at my touch.

She lay down, pressing her mostly-naked chest against my mostly naked chest as I ran my hands along her back, pressing her harder against me and murmuring into her hair. We kissed again, mingling our tongues and our desire. Kelli rolled off me a little without breaking the kiss and I felt her fumbling at my belt.

Time fragmented again (Damn it! Now? Really?) and I found myself in a small graduate-level seminar, *Criminal Geniuses: Know the Enemy.* Kelli had talked me into the class; she was obsessed with studying famous thieves, their methods, their styles, their successes and the mistakes they had made that led to their eventual downfalls.

"Lupin's ego drove him to commit more and more grandiose crimes, a spiral of consequence that led inevitably to his capture and eventual government recruitment. Another famous criminal whose career had a relatively happy ending is Alexander Mundy. Mundy's conscience and strict ethics restricted his targets and allowed an ironclad profile to be constructed. He was eventually captured and imprisoned; we don't have all the details, but his sentence was commuted to some kind of government service.

"And then there is Gwynplaine, who is surely, the most complicated and fascinating of real-life gothic villains. While we may never know what drove the renegade crown prince to the life he led, we can easily see what brought him low. The hunt for the master criminal was operatic in its sweep, continental in its scope, and tragic in its conclusion. Turn to page 269 in your textbooks …"

"Are you okay?" hissed Kelli in my ear. "You look all flushed and feverish."

I put a hand to my forehead; sure enough I was hot to the touch and a bit sweaty. I was also unaccountably aroused; college lectures usually didn't do it for me, but I felt like I was in the middle of some seriously sexy times. I put a hand to my mouth and coughed to stall for time.

"Excuse me," I said, a bit hoarsely.

If I could have stood without embarrassing myself I would have gone to the rest room and splashed some cold water on my face, but since that wasn't currently an option, I squirmed a little in my chair and waved an all-clear sign with my hand for the professor to continue. The professor smiled kindly and went on with her lecture. But I wasn't listening anymore. I was nearly certain that I had been someplace else just a moment ago. So either there was something wrong with my head or there was something else going on. No one else seemed disturbed so whatever was going on was only happening to me.

"I'll need to make some kind of sacrifice," Kelli said.

"What?" I asked.

"To make the passage," Kelli said, as if explaining something obvious. "I'll need a sacrifice, something I care about. Any ideas?"

I blinked rapidly and looked around the room, my dorm room. When had I gotten here? Kelli and I were sitting on my bed. I noticed belatedly that we were both naked. Had I just had sex with Kelli? How had I forgotten having sex with Kelli? Damn it! She laughed at the expression on my face and ran an affectionate hand through my hair.

"Don't worry, Zack," I'm not planning on sacrificing you. We just need to figure it out."

"Along with about five hundred other things," I agreed. "You could always sacrifice that bracelet I got you."

"No way!" Kelli cried. "I'm keeping that forever!"

In her defense, it was a really nice bracelet. I had spent a month's pay on it. It was an absurd extravagance and I can't remember what I had been thinking. Still, Kelli always smiled when she looked at it. And Kelli has a smile that was like the sun rising over the clouds. Somethings money really can buy.

I remembered when we were now. Kelli had found a book with some really solid information about passing into the Soft Realms. *Die Dornenhecke*, it was called. We had been excited; we had celebrated. We had celebrated quite a lot, actually. I leaned over and kissed her, she responded enthusiastically.

"We'll figure it out," I said after we broke the kiss. "It's all just details, and we're good at details."

"You're good at details," she corrected. "I'm more of a seat of my pants kind of girl."

I made an ostentatious show of checking out her behind.

"Not right now, you're not," I observed.

Kelli slapped me playfully on the shoulder and made a face that reminded me of Myrna Loy in *The Thin Man*. We both laughed, and we kissed again. Then we kissed some more. Her hand tangled in my shoulder-length hair and yanked my head back. She nipped at my throat and reached her other hand down. It looked like we weren't done celebrating yet.

• • •

It looked like we didn't have the answer yet. I threw the book down next to the pile of books just like it and sighed dramatically. Kelli looked up from her own pile of books and looked at me wearily. After a moment, she lifted her eyebrows questioningly and then winced slightly as if even that much effort had cost her dearly. I empathized with that wince; I was exhausted. Never had either of us worked this hard, not for any final or any project. It made sense I guess; this project was our best chance of saving at least one of our lives.

"The Erickson Operation won't work," I said at last. "I found more details. The ritual isn't compatible with the world passage. It can only be used to travel in this world. It's another dead end."

She sighed and threw down her book.

"Well, at least there's no point in me reading this old page turner then," she sighed and picked up yet another book. "And I was finally getting good at reading Old English, too."

For some reason that last bit struck me as hilariously funny and I started laughing. It wasn't even the hysterical laughter, which I half expected. It was just a small chuckle, a weary appreciation of Kelli's ability to crack wise in the face of exhaustion. After a moment, she joined me and we laughed together like we hadn't in weeks, not since we had first found *Die Dornenhecke*. It was good to laugh together.

The close calls were already beginning. Just the other night when we were out at a bar I had spotted some joker in a black hood and matching cloak trying to cast a spell. Lots of people cast spells – although it was certainly rude to do it in a public bar – and lots of people dress stupidly in public. Again, it's rude, but not against the law. If some guy or gal wanted to swagger around town doing a ringwraith impression, who was I to judge? I'm not paranoid by nature, but when there's a price on my girlfriend's head, I get a little twitchy. I got Kelli's attention, and with barely a glance she confirmed that it was faerie magic.

We had two choices, the most basic two choices there were, really. We could confront Mr. Ringwraith and try to figure out what he was doing and stop it if necessary, which would almost certainly involve violence. Or we could run: fight or flight. I was thinking at very high speed right now and I could tell Kelli was keeping up with me.

She looked at the cloaked and hooded caster and she looked at the door, then she looked at me and very pointed her jaw away from Mr.

Ringwraith and towards the door. In perfect unison, we both turned on our heels and bolted for the door. We were out and into the street in seconds. And sure enough we heard shouting behind us and the bar door banging open just as we tore around a corner and out of sight.

We didn't stop running until we had crossed three neighborhoods and two bridges. But as far as we could tell, nothing had chased us. We had gotten out before the real trouble could start, but our luck wasn't going to hold. We had to find a real answer and we had to find it now.

• • •

"We have to decide now, Zack!" Kelli shouted over the keening of the wind.

That same wind tore at my clothing as the cold bit through the four layers of heavy fabric and chilled me to the bone. I looked at Kelli. Tears were streaming down her face, cutting tracks through the soot and the blood caked on her cheeks. I noticed she was still holding the sword; her eyes followed my gaze and she looked at the weapon as if shocked to see it in her own grip. She let it drop to the stone with a clatter.

"The Hunt will be here soon," she shouted.

As if I didn't know that, but I bit back my snarled reply. We were on the edge of two worlds; the mists were thick and the stars in the sky weren't the ones I was used to. If I continued on this path, I would be leaving my world behind, perhaps forever. Kelli had to go, she absolutely had to go; there was no safety for her in my world, no life at all, really.

But could I go with her? Could I leave my life and my world behind? Somehow, I had managed to avoid making that decision, somehow I had put it off until this very moment. And now there was no time left and I still had no idea. No, that wasn't true. It wasn't true at all. I had every idea, I was just trying to convince myself that there was even a decision to make.

I loved my life, and I loved my world. I loved Kelli, too. But somehow, that didn't seem to be enough. I couldn't go with her. I guess I had known all along that this was the way it had to be, and my putting the decision off had just been me putting this moment off. The moment when I lost her.

"Go!" I shouted. "Go without me! I have to go back to New Jerusalem!"

For a moment she looked as if the wind had snatched away my words, but then I saw awareness dawn in her eyes. She had heard me, she just couldn't believe what she had heard. I saw a dozen emotions flash across her face in that one moment. Shades of anger first, then sadness, then grief, and finally something like acceptance. She didn't say another word, she just turned and ran. I watched her go and stood there in the mist for a long time after she was gone. The world shimmered and went wavy before my eyes, and I could swear that I heard a swirl of harp music.

• • •

All of that crashed through my mind as I stood there in the Great Room of the Aristarchus Lodge, seeing Kelli – pardon me, seeing Lady Kellidwyn of Coldiron Keep – outcast of Faerie, for the first time since we had parted in the mists on the edge of the worlds. I had a stunning sense of *déja vu*, not just because of the bizarre flashing mish-mash of memories, but because I realized this was the second time I had undergone this same torrent of memory. The first time had been just a few hours before when I had been looking at Peter Starbourne's corpse. I was absolutely certain that these were the exact same memories that had flooded through my head then. Why was I thinking about Kelli before I even knew she was here? Coincidences happen, sure, but not like this, not this powerfully and not this … well, coincidentally!

I figured I had been standing there gape-jawed and stupid for long enough. At least Kelli wasn't recovering any faster so there was some comfort in that. I cleared my throat and tugged on my lapels as if to straighten the coat on my shoulders. I wished momentarily for my hat so I could stall even further by straightening that as well.

"Yes," I said in a sort of brittle, chipper voice that surely fooled no one. "We've met before, in fact we're old friends. Lady Kellidwyn, I look forward to catching up with you and maybe talking about the old times later. It's wonderful to see you again, and in good health and comfort."

I held out my hand. Kelli smiled warmly and stepped forward to take my proffered hand. Her own hands were still cool, or maybe mine were still warm. Either way, it felt good to touch her again. It made her seem a little bit closer to real and a little bit less of the surreal fantasy that my brain was trying to make her.

"Zachariah Monday," she said, with all the composure and elegance of a queen. "It's been – what? Eight years since we've seen each other? You look fantastic. I'm so sorry that such a sad occasion has brought us together, but it is wonderful to see you again."

She smiled. I smiled. We both smiled for a little while. Everyone else in the room seemed to be holding a single breath. I released her hand and turned to Gray. With the instincts of a world-class hostess, the wizard sensed it was time for her to step in and she did so effortlessly and effectively, and for that I was grateful.

"Well," Gray said, archly. "No matter how many worlds I travel, they're always small ones. Oswald, would you be so kind as to have Roger refresh everyone's drink? We have a great deal to talk about. Perhaps even more than we suspected, hmm?"

Everyone had a little chuckle at that. Quatermain asked Roger to bring the drink cart around as well as the left over duck from last night's feast. This was a conversation that was clearly going to call for more substantial refreshments.

It occurred to me that if I didn't sit down soon, my knees would probably start to buckle, accordingly, I turned back towards my abandoned chair. Just as I spun around, I caught a flash of motion. Kelli and Lord Gwynplaine had been sharing a significant look, but when they saw me turn, they moved away from each other. The look itself wasn't suspicious at all. But the fact that they had tried to hide it from me? That was as suspicious as a Duke of Perdition in a gingham dress.

"Roger?" I asked, politely. "Could you bring me a whiskey sour, please? Arnold Palmer is not going to cut it today."

Chapter Ten

There is a law of inverse proportion when it comes to groups: once you get above a certain size, it is easier to organize large groups than small ones. The current gathering was the perfectly-wrong size, and roughly as organized as a litter of kittens. No sooner were we all about to be settled then someone had to run to the rest room for one biological reason or another. After each instance, we had to have another round of polite chit-chat.

"I see you've done the place over again, Oswald, bold choices," said Gwynplaine wearily, inclining his head towards Quatermain in a small bow, "It's very … rustic."

Gwynplaine had an old-fashioned aristocratic kind of accent, with long flat vowels and nasal overtones. His vowels had a languid drawl to them that somehow managed to feel contemptuous of other lesser vowels. He also tended to roll his tongue along any consonant that would stand still for it.

"Was this always the way you imagined it would look?" drawled Gwynplaine airily.

"Yes, well, of course," hedged Quatermain a little bit defensively. "It's authentic, don't you see? I'm as much of an artist as you are, in my own way."

"Of course you are," soothed Gray. "His Lordship didn't mean to suggest otherwise, did you Gwynplaine?"

Gwynplaine waved a languid hand and nodded, clearly agreeing with someone or something. What it was he actually agreed with was, however, perfectly unclear.

"So what kept you, Kellidwyn, darling?" asked Foucault, in a sort of a purr. "We were just about to start getting worried. You were running late even for your loose standards."

"Loose standards?" replied Kelli. "Look who's …"

"Canapé, Lady Kellidwyn?" interrupted Roger at a sharp gesture from Quatermain.

"Yes, Roger," replied Kellidwyn sweetly, "One of the mushroom ones, please."

Fizznorman sniffed loudly. Foucault started violently as the little man suddenly appeared right next to her. He had been there all along, of course, but we had all failed to notice him once again. Foucault leaned over as Fizznorman whispered something in her ear. Her eyes flicked towards Roger and she covered her face with her large hand as she tittered quietly.

"How fare your lands, Sir Visivald?" asked Gray.

"They are slippery," rumbled Visivald with a frown. "I am able to maintain the elements easily enough; the earth, the water, the fire, and the air are all well and good. But the higher orders are beyond me. Nothing flourishes."

"How dreadful," *tsked* Gray. "Perhaps Oswald will be able to help you with the fauna?"

"Well, of course!" Quatermain sputtered. "I've been meaning to, don't you know, but things have been so difficult lately."

Everyone nodded in an understanding fashion. Gwynplaine sulked and the Duke looked frustrated, but they still seemed to agree about how difficult things had been.

"What with Peter's death," added Quatermain hastily.

"Before that," countered Foucault. "Things have been falling apart for months. We all see it."

"Sure and losing Mr. Starbourne won't be helping," said Fizznorman, startling the assembly once again by his reappearance.

"Fear not, Algernon," said Gray. "We will hold until someone new rises to the occasion. I have faith in us, don't you?"

"Of course I do, ma'am," Fizznorman said, reassuringly. "All and all we do, it's just going to be hard times ahead, and that's the truth. What with His Grace barely to the wheel and things being what things surely are."

Once again there was general agreement; things were hard and everyone knew it. I started to know a few things too. There were some entrenched social dynamics going on. Quatermain and Gwynplaine didn't like each other, Foucault and Kelli – sorry *Kellidwyn* – didn't much care for each other, either. Gwynplaine and Kellidwyn definitely had something secretive going on; they were ignoring each other far too studiously. There was a rivalry of some sort between Fizznorman and Roger. Visivald and Gray seemed to be above it all, but most of the others were courting their favor, or at least their attention.

None of this was getting me much closer to learning whatever it was that Gray wanted me to learn, though. I probably could have moved things along, but I was learning plenty just sitting there, listening in and making the occasional neutral comment to keep things spun up. Eventually there was a pregnant pause long enough for Gray to seize control of the conversation and move things to where she wanted them. I wasn't under the illusion that she couldn't have done so sooner, but maybe she suspected that I was gathering important material. Or maybe she just liked polite chit chat with mysteriously Byzantine political undertones; you can never be sure with these wizard types.

"Yes," Gray said, rising to her feet and commanding attention. "Things are difficult; the realm is becoming – as Visivald said – slippery. We've all noticed it, and we've all started working harder to maintain our lands. Something is rotten in the state of Patchwork, and Zachariah is going to help us find out what it is."

"Or who," I interjected. "Sometimes it's a who not a what."

"Of course," Gray smiled her thin smile. "We all know by now that Peter was laid low by someone's hand."

There was a murmur of shock and grief that was as appropriate and proportionate as it was completely artificial; no one was surprised by this news, but most of the gathering felt the need to act as if they were. Gwynplaine appeared to be exhausted by his performance and looked for all the world as if he might faint at any moment. I noticed that Visivald just nodded grimly and folded his massive forearms over his barrel chest.

But then again, I don't think Visivald would look surprised if he suddenly noticed his underpants were on fire.

"What's this about maintaining lands?" I asked. "I'm guessing there's more going on here than agriculture and irrigation."

"Indeed," agreed Gray. "That is exactly what we have brought you here to learn, Zachariah. The land of Patchwork is, as you have surely guessed, unnatural. It exists solely through the exercise of our gathered wills. If we stop believing in the land, it will stop being. It is as simple as that."

"Simple isn't the same as easy," I quoted. "How exactly do you achieve this thing?"

"It's not something you can explain," said Quatermain with a hint of a sneer. "One must be born to the power to exercise it properly."

"Harrumph," said Visivald, quite plainly.

Quatermain rose to the bait, "Just because one hasn't done a thing before doesn't mean that one wasn't born to it. You are as noble as any among us, Your Grace."

"Don't call me that," said Visivald, his voice dropping even deeper until it almost hurt to hear. "I am many things, but graceful is hardly one of them."

"Each of us is responsible for a segment of the land," said Gray. "We each take on a portion of the load, diverse lands and aspects of reality all must be consciously maintained. Peter constructed most of the buildings, structures, and houses in Patchwork, and he maintained a significant percentage of the land. He was very important to us in many ways."

I stroked the stubble on my chin in a manner that I hoped looked thoughtful. This twist added a new possible motive for the killing. Did someone want to destroy Patchwork? What would anyone stand to gain from that? It could also be a gambit to replace Starbourne; if someone were in the running for a promotion that would be plenty of motivation.

"So who's in the running to take Starbourne's place?" I asked.

There was an uncomfortable silence in the room punctuated by some throat-clearing. Gray looked physically pained by the question. So much for that line of inquiry. Unless someone unexpected and lacking an alibi popped up in the next couple days, I could at least cross that motive off my list.

"Let's turn it around," I said out loud but mostly to myself. "What do people stand to gain from Patchwork? Why do people live here? If maintaining the land is such a strain on you all, why do you do it?"

"Freedom, power, and control," Gwynplaine declaimed, rolling each 'R' carefully.

"Because it is what my family has always done," replied Quatermain.

"It makes my research easier," added Foucault

"I'm safe here," admitted Kellidwyn.

"Because I can," rumbled Visivald. "These people need my help."

"It is my home and the source of my livelihood," said Gray.

"Your livelihood?" I asked. "How so?"

"Magic flows strongly here," Gray said. "Workings are fundamentally easier. Most of the items I sell in my shop are constructed here, in my workshop."

"Exactly so," agreed Foucault. "I can do so much more magic here than I ever could in the real world. My research has leapt forward since I came here."

I pulled my trusty notebook out and scribbled down a few details. I had a lot of questions and very few answers, but there was something here, definitely something that pertained to … something.

"So, let's get back to these difficulties you've been having," I said after returning my notebook to my back pocket. "How long have things been slippery?"

"Since Peter's death," replied Quatermain.

"Longer," countered Foucault. "Months, at least."

"Nearly a year," sighed Kellidwyn.

"Since I've been here," lamented Visivald. "But I credit that to my inexperience."

"I am still in control of my lands," Gwynplaine observed haughtily.

"As am I," agreed Gray. "But that doesn't mean I haven't noticed the problems."

"I am aware of everything that happens on my lands," Gwynplaine sniffed. "If there were something truly amiss, I would have found it and discovered a solution to it already."

Conversation descended into a general babble of agreements, disagreements, accusations, and counter-accusations. I tapped my pen against my lower lip and I tried to make sense of it all. There simply wasn't enough yet. I would need to talk to everyone separately, compare stories, find the holes and the places where things didn't quite match up. I could already see some inconsistencies, but they could be easily chalked up to rivalries and grudges.

"Miss Gray, you mentioned your livelihood earlier," I interrupted after letting things spin for a while. "I know you run a magic shop out of the Old City, but how do most of Patchwork's citizens make money?"

When in doubt I follow the money, and the money trail here looked complicated. Patchwork was either a bedroom community with the worst daily commute in several worlds or there was something else going on here that I needed to understand. Surely there couldn't be enough wizards here to make shuttling back and forth between worlds convenient.

"Some of us are self-sufficient," answered Gwynplaine with a hint of a sneer. "And we provide for our vassals in return for service."

"Vassals?" I asked. "Are we talking about a feudal society, here?"

"Nay," rumbled Visivald. "Gwynplaine betrays his ancestry. We have a responsibility to protect and provide for those who cannot create what they need out of the raw stuff of creation, but all they owe us in return is service, not servitude."

"Which is to say Gwynplaine's not exactly wrong, but he's still an enormous jerk about it," interjected Kellidwyn.

Gwynplaine shot Kelli a look that was pure acid; whatever they had going on between them it didn't seem to include friendship. Unless the exchange was for someone else's benefit, mine perhaps? I stole a glance at Gray, who was shaking her head with a weariness that suggested this wasn't an uncommon interaction for the two.

"So let me get this straight," I said. "The majority of the residents rely on you for – what? Shelter, food, leisure items?"

"In essence, that is so," said Gray. "We strive to teach them how to create and maintain their own demesnes but it is beyond most of them."

"Some of the citizens can maintain things that we create for them," added Kelli.

"But many more cannot and never will," Quatermain said. "Those people make up our working class."

"And in return we offer them a truly idyllic existence," said Gray. "They can live in any sort of home they wish, have any luxury items they desire, and make magic part of their everyday lives."

"I'm not judging anything or anyone," I lied. "I just need to know how the economy works here. A rich man has been murdered and money might be a factor. Or whatever it is you folks use instead of money."

"It's an elegant system without need to resort to such arcane abstractions as cash," said Quatermain. "If you think about it, it makes more sense. Why go through the extra step? Our citizens work and are compensated directly with whatever it is they want. As I say: elegant."

"So if Roger wants a new stereophonic wireless sound system and a complete Spike Jones discography, he asks you and you just magic it up for him?" I asked.

"More or less, and within reason," answered Quatermain. "Although in this specific case, I'd hand the job over to someone who knew what a stereophonic was or who Spike Jones is."

"Does that happen a lot?" I asked. "Passing the work around, I mean."

"Fairly often," replied Kelli. "We all have our specialties, and we owe it to our citizens to get them the very best we can manage."

I declined to ask whether Spike Jones' recording label would get their fair share of the transaction. While the global piracy implications were intriguing and perhaps troubling, I wasn't yet certain they were pertinent. This was exactly what I had been afraid of when Gray hired me. I didn't know what was pertinent and what was a waste of time. I have my specialties too, and I wasn't entirely sure I was offering my employer the very best service that could be managed.

"So aside from Fine Art and Architecture," I asked. "What else did Peter Starbourne specialize in?"

"He controlled the greater environment," answered Gwynplaine. "The weather and such like. Deucedly good at it, too. The man was a genius."

A thought occurred to me just then and I could see it mirrored on the face of everyone present at more or less the same moment. If Starbourne had controlled the weather and he had been dead for days, who or what was controlling the weather now? Would it just sort of cruise along until something or someone changed it?

"But does that mean ...?" I began.

As if in answer and with spectacular timing the sky turned dark and then blindingly bright with a flash of lightning. Less than a second later an ear-shattering boom rattled the glassware, and a heartbeat after that, the sky split open and we heard the sound of torrential rain and howling wind.

"Oh," I said. "I guess it does."

Chapter Eleven

After the first few dramatic moments, the storm settled down to respectable – but still impressive – levels. It showed no sign of abating anytime soon. Quatermain volunteered the Aristarchus as shelter for as long as anyone wished to stay, but no one seemed particularly interested in taking him up on the offer. Instead, he manifested umbrellas for everyone (mine was gray and Gray's was black) and we all began a soggy exodus.

"Miss Gray, Dr. Foucault," I asked as we arrived back in the lodge's vestibule. "Would it be possible for the three of us to go back to your lab to take a look at the body, er, I mean, the delivery? I'd like to learn as much as possible as quickly as possible."

Gray looked a question at Foucault who shrugged her broad shoulders amiably.

"I suppose," said Foucault. "Why not? We'll take my coach, it's dryer than walking."

As we stepped outside into the driving rain, a coach and two clopped up with perfect timing. The coach was a fairly typical Victorian-style brougham. It was painted a subdued shade of purple rather than the more traditional glossy black but that wasn't the strange part. The two weren't horses; they looked like horses, but instead of equine heads, they had the features of giant hawks, complete with wicked hooked beaks and unblinking yellow eyes. They also featured multicolored feathers in place of mane and hair; as I looked them up and down I saw great talons raking the ground where one might normally expect hooves to be stamping.

I snuck a quick glance at Gray. She didn't seem to be disturbed at all, so I tried to look cool. I would have convinced myself that I had succeeded too if not for Gray's half-suppressed snort of laughter. I reached up instinctively to straighten my tie before I remembered that I wasn't wearing one, so instead I adjusted my hat. Dignity was preserved after a fashion. I stowed my travel bag in the boot and we all got into the coach.

The inside was gorgeously appointed. Nearly half of the interior filled by a very well stocked wet bar. There was also plenty of room to stash our wet umbrellas away from our seats. I sank into the surprisingly comfortable bench with pleasure and listened to the sound of the rain pelting the roof.

"Is this memory foam?" I asked.

"Absolutely, darling," assured Foucault. "Imported. Magic isn't the right answer for everything. Would anyone care for champagne?"

She hoisted a chilled magnum out of the high-hat with one hand and an elegantly fluted glass with the other. She held them both up with a grin and wiggled them enticingly. Both Gray and I laughed before politely refusing. Foucault shrugged and filled the glass for herself. She restored the magnum to its sconce and saluted us with the bubbly golden liquid before taking a healthy swallow.

There was a communication rune carved into the inside wall of the coach. She brushed it with her free hand and announced, "Jonas, would you be so kind as to take us back to the manor?"

The coach tipped slightly upward and then smoothly began rolling forward. Either the hawk-horse-things had a remarkably smooth gait, or this buggy had a very impressive suspension. Or maybe it was both. The folks here in Patchwork seemed to live pretty well. A flash of lightning was followed almost immediately by a boom of thunder that rocked the coach before it became steady again. I amended my thought; the folks here in Patchwork seemed to live pretty well, apart from the newly-problematic weather.

"Dr. Foucault," I began politely. "You were talking about research earlier. Could you tell me a little bit more about that?

"Michelle, please," insisted Foucault with a grin I could only describe as wicked.

"Okay," I amended with a less-wicked grin. "Michelle, you were talking about research earlier, could you … ?"

Foucault favored us with her loud and totally unselfconscious laughter again. She finished her champagne, poured herself another and looked me up and down appraisingly. Her eyes twinkled a bit, so either she liked what she saw or her eyes were just generally twinkly.

"I would be glad to tell you about my work," Foucault said, licking the champagne off her lips. My field is biomimetics, the science of duplicating nature through machine or magic. My particular specialty is bolstering human recovery through biomimetic medicine."

"I have absolutely no idea what any of that means," I said with a smile. "But it sounds impressive. So it's easier to do your work here in Patchwork? Can you tell me why that is?"

"Two reasons predominantly," Foucault answered. "Firstly, I am magically very weak; in the real world I can barely do any magic at all. My instructors were always impressed by my powers of focus and will, but despite my academic proficiency, I was unable to master anything beyond the basics. Here, my grasp more closely approaches my reach."

"And the second reason?" I prompted.

"I met with considerable social resistance among my peers back home," Foucault said a little bitterly. "For my social and lifestyle choices."

"I can imagine," I said while Gray made sympathetic noises.

"Magic makes my research much easier," Foucault continued. "A simple montage spell lets me complete several days' worth of tests and processes in fifteen minutes or less, depending on the music, of course."

"Time doesn't always flow in a straight line here in Patchwork," Gray said, as if in explanation.

"I'm familiar with the concept," I replied, somewhat snippily.

We didn't talk for a while after that with only the rhythmic patter of the rain drumming on the roof of the coach disturbing the silence. I looked out the window past the gray sheets of rain and thought dark and moody thoughts. Experience told me that it was very likely that one of the people I had just shared drinks and conversation with was Peter Starbourne's murderer. There was always the chance of a one-armed man sweeping in out of nowhere, doing the dirty deed and vanishing back into the night, but usually people were murdered by their social peers. Despite what you read in cheap detective novels, murder isn't an everyday affair. Most people need to seriously psych themselves up for it, and most people are profoundly affected by the deed. The Mark of Cain isn't just metaphorical: murder changes people. I had only met three of the suspects before the murder, and even that much wasn't helping. I didn't know Adriana Gray all that well, but she seemed to be unchanged. I didn't seriously consider Visivald to be a suspect, but even if he did do it, nothing — not even murder — was very likely to change the ancient goblin's demeanor. And as for Kelli ... Well, time would tell how much eight years and living in a different world had changed the woman I knew. I realized quite suddenly that I very much didn't want Kelli to be the killer. I would have to guard against that desire as I began my investigation in earnest.

"What's the sentence for murder around here?" I asked.

"We've never had a murder before," Gray replied. "We've had theft, of course, assault, battery, destruction of property, all the crimes one might expect a community to face, but never before murder. Mr. Monday, I honestly don't know. There will be a trial, of course. Perhaps it will be exile."

I nodded as if that answered my question. Exile might well be a death sentence for Kelli. The people who wanted her dead were immortal; eight years was less than the blink of an eye. Of course the people who wanted her dead were also well known for having short attention spans and for being easily distracted, so who really knew? I knew that if I didn't stop worrying about what might happen to Kelli if she were guilty — which I did not think she was — then I wouldn't be able to do the job I was brought here for.

"How long will the local weather be out of whack?" I asked to divert my mind onto safer matters.

"That is a fascinating question," said Gray. "I have been trying, off and on, for quite some time now to take control of the situation. Thus far I have had no effect."

"What does that suggest?" I asked with more than academic interest.

"I have no idea," Gray replied. "It could indicate a systemic breakdown."

"That sounds bad," I said.

"Literally catastrophic," Gray said.

For once I was left without words; not a single response, witty or otherwise came to mind. We all just sort of stared at each other for a while. The coach rolled on, the rain poured down, and I began to feel profoundly depressed. After a time we arrived at our destination. Dr. Foucault's home was a Tudor-style mansion with many cross-gables. Exposed timbers and heavy chimneys dashed the stucco walls and dotted the slanted roofs respectively. It looked to house about 7 bedrooms on the upper floors, sat on what looked like two and a half acres of land, and – compared to everything else I'd seen so far in Patchwork – was conservative and tasteful.

The drive had a covered section that partially spared us from the weather in front of what looked like double doors. Gray glanced at our umbrellas relegated to the corner of the coach. She took on a look of concentration and waved her hand back and forth as if erasing a chalk board. The umbrellas wavered like a desert mirage and vanished.

"I must remember to return that to Oswald," Gray muttered.

I hauled my bag out of the boot and slung its strap over one shoulder. I normally would have taken the time to put bag across my shoulders so my neck could keep it from sliding around, but it was a short walk and I was feeling lazy. The strap lay very comfortably and didn't seem inclined to slide around.

The double doors swung open as we approached. Dr. Foucault led the way, I hesitated ever-so slightly to let Gray enter ahead of me and then I entered Foucault's home. The foyer had no mat for wet and muddy shoes, which I thought was odd until I realized that – until quite recently – inclement weather was vanishingly rare around here. There was a coat stand and a hat rack in the corner so I removed my hat and plunked it atop an empty peg. Depositing my jacket would have required unslinging the travel bag, and besides, I looked good in it. Foucault and Gray removed their wraps and hung them in appropriate spots.

Foucault noticed the small puddles our feet were making on her nice hardwood floors, *tsked* in disapproval and made an erasing motion similar to Gray's earlier one. This time, however nothing happened. Lines of concentration formed between Foucault's eyebrows and she made the motion again. Again, nothing happened. Foucault and Gray locked eyes; Gray shrugged. Foucault sighed heavily and went over to a nearby closet, opened it up and pulled out a mop. Truly, disaster had come to Patchwork.

In short order the mess was sorted and we got back on track. Foucault was no longer wearing the party dress I had first seen her in. She had changed into a conservative top, slacks, and sensible shoes, a change of clothes that had quite literally happened in the blink of an eye. I slid a quick glance in Gray's direction. She hadn't changed, which was good; I hate being the only one dressed inappropriately.

"The medical lab is back this way," said Foucault. "Please follow me."

The three of us trooped through Chez Foucault. I looked around out of habit, trying to note as many small details as possible. We went through a living space with two couches forming an 'L' around a low coffee table. The walls were mostly covered with shelves and the shelves were mostly filled with books. A predictable amount of clutter sat on one of the sofas and pretty much dominated the coffee table; the place was lived in. What I didn't see was any dust or dirt. Even the best kept homes usually had a little bit of grime in the corners. This one didn't.

Foucault led us down a long gallery, mostly featuring the work of Dutch Masters and Late Renaissance artists. The hallway opened up a bit and we passed a half dozen closed doors and a staircase before we arrived at our destination. All of the doors we had come upon so far were traditional 9-panel jobs, attractive and serviceable but not exactly secure. This door was a different model all together. It was a heavy security door with a latch and a security rune instead of a knob. It wouldn't have been out of place in a hospital trauma ward.

Foucault ran one finger across the security rune in a complicated pattern. The rune would not only recognize her unique aura, but also the specific motions she made. I approved of the double-fault security. I might have been able to get around it, but it wouldn't have been easy. There was a muffled *ka-chunk* and the door popped open an inch. Foucault pushed it open the rest of the way and gestured for us to enter.

The lab would have fit comfortably into any modern medical procedural. All exposed surfaces gleamed brightly and it was chock full of all sorts of advanced-looking doohickeys which I could not have identified to save my own life. I think I recognized the Machine That Goes Ping from an old British comedy sketch but everything else was a complete mystery. The far wall was covered with what looked like a giant refrigerator with a half dozen separate doors each with its own handle. One of the doors was open and a gurney was rolled out. The gurney was empty. The center of the room was dominated by an operating table, also empty.

I looked around ostentatiously. I looked at Foucault only to see that she was also looking around. That couldn't be good. She moved swiftly about the room, moving things and looking under them. No, definitely not good.

"Stop," I said. "Stop disturbing the scene."

"What?" Foucault and Gray asked nearly simultaneously.

"It's missing, right?" I said. "The damn corpse is missing?"

"But darlings! It was right here!" Foucault said excitedly. "No one could have gotten in. The door was locked. You both saw it!"

"Doctor, please calm down," I said. "Let me take a look around."

As I scanned the room for clues my mind started spinning wildly. Why would someone steal a corpse? Answer: Because examining the corpse would reveal something the corpse's thief didn't want revealed. Next question: how does someone steal a corpse out of a locked room with a sophisticated magical alarm system? The answer to that one didn't immediately pop into my head, so I filed it for later. I resisted the urge to rub my hands together in excitement. A locked room mystery? A missing corpse? Dramatic weather with rain sheeting down, flashes of lightning and crashes of thunder? It was like Chanukah in July for me. The whole scene was practically scripted for my entertainment.

I looked at the operating table.

"Is this where you left the body?" I asked.

Foucault nodded yes.

"Did you leave the cold chamber open?"

Foucault shook her head no. Her usual talkative nature seemed to have abandoned her. Apparently, she was a little bit freaked out. That wasn't entirely surprising, and it was actually useful to me. When people were alert and thinking too hard they often gave me too much information.

People generally want to help, so they leap to conclusions and try to do my job for me. I need raw data. When people who aren't trained in observation, deduction, and detection try to do these things, they make assumptions and they make mistakes. I'm fairly proficient at sorting those assumptions and well-intentioned errors back out, but it's still easier when they're not there in the first place.

There were smudges on the otherwise gleaming tile floor, too small to be drag marks. They might be caused by bare feet? Bare footprints? Who breaks into a lab in their bare feet? I looked at the open cold chamber.

"Was there anything stored in there?" I asked.

Foucault answered me slowly, "Um … just some raw biomimetic material. Nothing terribly valuable."

I drew out my trusty notebook and flipped to the last page. I wasn't sure what was happening here, but some disturbing possibilities were presenting themselves. I wrote down every detail I could think of; sometimes tiny factoids come back around later and bite me on the tucchus. I hate being bitten on the tucchus.

"What had you found out about the corpse?" I asked as my notes caught up with recent events.

"Nothing yet," Foucault sighed heavily. "I had to prepare for that little luncheon over at Aristarchus and he wasn't getting any deader."

I winced. Whoever took the corpse must have known about the meeting. Why else would they steal the corpse now? Answer: because the lady of the laboratory was out she hadn't had a chance to learn anything incriminating yet. That meant that the corpse thief was either working for, or was in contact with, one or more of the Pillars.

"Then whoever took the corpse got what they wanted," I said. "To keep us from finding answers."

"Not necessarily," said Gray. "Zachariah, you shot a roll of film with a Kirlian Camera earlier, mostly of the corpse, yes?"

"Yes," I said. "Will that help?"

"Darling! Of course it will help," exclaimed Foucault. "I need to see those photographs as soon as they're developed. It will be almost as good as having the actual body!"

"Magic to the rescue again," I said.

I was feeling less than spectacularly useful. So far the only progress on the case had come from my client or her associates. I doubted that I was going to see much referral business from this one. I had to get back into the game. A thought occurred to me then, and it was a welcome change.

"Dr. Foucault," I asked. "Have you done any significant magic here recently?"

"Nothing significant, no." she replied.

"Then there's something else I need to check," I said.

I unslung my travel bag and plunked it down, or I tried to anyway. It hit the ground and bounced back up into my hand. I caught it instinctively when it smacked into my palm. That was odd. I put it down more carefully and this time it stayed put. I shrugged and decided that it must have been just one of those things.

I reached into the bag and rummaged around for the Niven Disk. It was a copper plate about a foot across with a dimple in the center and lines engraved longitudinally across its surface. Actually, it was a variation on the classic Niven Disk, not a traditional one. Your typical Niven Disk was designed to use up all the magical energy in an area; this little devil was entirely different. Its enchantment was so delicate and so sensitive, that it would only spin in the residue left behind by a recently cast spell. It wasn't often useful, but when it was called for, there was nothing else quite like it. I set the disk down on the floor of the laboratory. I gave it a little spin to start it up and we all stepped back and watched.

"What's that?" asked Foucault.

"A little something I picked up from Miss Gray's shop," I answered. "It might tell us something."

Instead of slowing down, the disk picked up speed, spinning of its own accord. I nodded and started to bend over to recover it. Gray laid a gently restraining hand on my shoulder.

"Wait," she cautioned.

As we watched the disk began to spin faster and lifted itself a little bit off the floor. The disk spun faster still, picking up a bit of a wobble. Before our eyes, the disk began to glow like metal in a furnace. The disk blurred with the speed of its spin. I took a half-step back and saw that the two ladies had done much the same. Eventually, the disk began to cool and slow and finally settle down to the floor once again. The whole show had lasted about a minute, perhaps a little more.

"What did that mean?" asked Foucault

"Not just magic," said Gray. "Powerful magic. Very, very powerful magic."

"That's great," I muttered. "Just great."

Chapter Twelve

Gray assured me that she had a darkroom in her tower that was sufficient to the task of developing my film. In turn, I assured Foucault that I would look into the mystery of her locked room corpse theft. It was decided that Gray and I would go back to her home, leaving the good doctor to clean up her laboratory. I was also hoping that luncheon would be provided. I had gone light on the refreshments earlier and, although delicious, my breakfast at Gray's tower had been hours ago.

Foucault loaned us the use of her coach. Apparently it would 'find it's way home' if we just left it outside after we arrived at our destination. I must have been lower on blood sugar than I thought because that idea just about made sense to me. High-powered magic was woven into the structure of people's lives here, as common as door charms and wireless broadcasts. Or at least that was true of the people I'd seen. What was life like for the common working-class folk around these parts?

We clambered back into the coach and settled down onto the comfortable bench. A moment later the bird-horse-things pulled forward with their unexpectedly smooth gait. I eyed the wet bar for a moment before deciding against. Today was going to be a long and busy day and I had already had one whiskey sour before noon.

"Does it bother you that no one's driving this thing?" I asked Gray.

"The griffs are driving," said Gray.

"Does it bother you that the griffs are driving?" I asked.

"Not at all," Gray replied. "Do you have any idea who stole poor Peter's body?"

"Some," I allowed. "But I'd rather not speculate until I know more."

"What's your next step?"

"Besides lunch?" I asked. "Interviewing witnesses, suspects, and innocent bystanders, trying to sort out which is which, poking my nose into everyone's business and seeing who gets mad enough to try and kill me; pretty much the usual."

"Is that really how you work?" Gray asked in disbelief.

"Sometimes, yeah," I admitted. "People who have committed a crime are nervous; they're off their game and afraid of slipping up. When people are acting nervous and afraid, a nosy investigator can be a fairly unbalancing factor. If I turn over enough rocks, sooner or later, I'll either find something incriminating or scare a bad guy into doing something stupid and provocative, which usually leads to me finding something incriminating."

"Bad guy?" Gray asked archly.

"Would you prefer malefactor?" I asked. "Perpetrator is always nice, but I'm old school so I usually go with bad guy."

"What if it's a bad girl?" Gray asked.

"I choose to believe that guy is a gender neutral term."

"And I choose to believe that the world is full of good-natured people who only want to help others," Gray retorted. "That doesn't make it so."

"Okay, fine," I held my hands up in gracious defeat. "I'll try to scare the evil doer or doers into doing something stupid and incriminating. Better?"

"Much better," nodded Gray before favoring me with one of her thin smiles. "Thank you for your accommodation."

There didn't seem to be much more to add to this particular discussion, so I turned my attention to the rain-soaked window and gazed out into the gray landscape. No answers presented themselves, but I kept gazing just in case. Time passed and the rhythmic sway of the coach made me a little bit dozy. I must have started to dream because I would swear I heard the sizzle of cooking and smelled the heavenly aroma of beef roasting on a spit. I shook myself a little and sniffed. I was definitely smelling roast beef, and now that I was paying attention, I heard the clatter of silver on porcelain. I turned away from the window.

The empty space between the bench and the wet bar was now filled with what looked like a high-class hotel's room service cart, complete with white table-cloth. There were three covered dishes, two carafes, and two place settings, one in front of me and the other in front of Gray. She noticed me looking at the cart and nodded. She lifted one of the gleaming silver covers to reveal a round of roast beef, mostly carved into slices. There were small bowls with various condiments; at least two kinds of mustard, mayonnaise and chopped horseradish were represented.

"Where did all this come from?" I asked somewhat groggily.

"You mentioned lunch," Gray replied. "I saw no reason to wait until we arrived at my tower. We have roast beef, and some asparagus sautéed with garlic, and cold potato salad."

I blinked at her uncomprehendingly.

"Dig in," she said.

I shrugged and dug in. It was delicious. One of the carafes turned out to contain coffee and the other sparkling apple cider; I sampled both. The beef was tender and pink in the middle with that crispy brown stuff on the edges that is so delicious. The horseradish had a bitter bite that was perfectly softened and complemented by the mayonnaise, and the asparagus was quite simply out of this world. I didn't try either mustard.

"It's all delicious, thank you," I said. "But seriously, where does it actually come from?"

The food couldn't be magic; non-sustainability was one of the very few truly immutable laws of magic. It took energy to make things with magic; there was no way to get energy from magic. Magical food was completely non-nutritive, and this meal was definitely filling my belly and satisfying my hunger.

"It is will-worked," Gray said. "The stuff of mist is not just mutable on the surface; it can be fully made into a true thing. If one's will is strong enough and one has been properly trained, that is."

That explained a little more how people could actually live here. I wondered what the upper limits were to this will-working business. I wondered about a lot of things.

"So what happens to the leftovers?" I asked.

"When we're done, I will release my will and reabsorb the energy required to stabilize the mist. And the leftovers will be the stuff of mist again."

"Hmmm," I pondered that for a moment. "What would happen if you didn't release and absorb? What would happen then?"

"It would all remain and continue to exist and perform as I willed it to," Gray explained. "The dishes would be dirty; the food would spoil and rot."

"For how long?" I asked.

"As long as my will was maintained," she said. "Or, if another will worker chose to, they could lay their own will upon the leftovers, break them down, and claim my energy as their own. It's a matter of politeness to return the energy or make an item of equal complexity in recompense."

I remembered Gray mentioning something about returning 'that' to Quatermain when she had dissolved the umbrellas that we had taken from Aristarchus. It was a little bit awkward fishing my notebook out of my back pocket while sitting in the coach, but I managed it without knocking anything over or putting my foot into the horseradish dish. Hopefully Gray would excuse my rudeness, but I thought there was something here and I wanted to get this thought in writing while it was still fresh in my mind. I wrote down her words, '… [a created object] would … remain and continue to exist and perform as I willed it to ….' and 'another will worker … could lay their own will upon [them], break them down, and claim my energy as their own.'

I tapped my pen against my lips and read what I had just written. There was definitely something there. I'd let it simmer down in my mental kitchen for a while and see what it smelled like. I winced at my own metaphor; that was just awful.

"Something wrong?" Gray asked.

"Occupational hazard," I answered. "Listen, can you develop those photographs without me?"

"Of course," Gray replied. "Can I drop you off someplace?"

"I'd like to talk to Fizznorman," I said. "Would he be back at Skywatch?"

"Very likely, yes," said Gray. "I'll take you there and then go back to my tower and have your photographs developed and sent 'round to Michele's lab. Will that be acceptable?"

"Um," I said cleverly. "Yes, that would be great, thanks. Sorry for ordering you around like this."

"Think nothing of it," Gray said. "I want you to have everything you need."

Gray rose from her place on the bench and, leaning forward, rapped sharply on the front panel of the cabin. There was a moment's pause and the coach dipped slightly as the griffs came to a halt. Gray slid open a small panel and I could hear the rain and other outside noises more clearly.

"Please take us to Skywatch," she said in a clear and precise tone, speaking slowly as if to someone who's first language was something other than English.

The sensation of motion was restored as the coach described an elegant direction changing arc. Whatever else you could say about the griffs, they provided a remarkably smooth ride.

"Thank you," said Gray in the same slow and precise manner before sliding the panel shut with an audible *clack*.

"We're actually quite close to Skywatch," Gray said. "It will just be a few minutes travel time."

Gray waved the leftovers and catering cart out of existence while I went back to staring at the landscape blurring by outside the window. If everything here was consciously made by someone and all of it needed to be actively maintained by will and energy, then everything I saw was a choice, a decision. Unlike the real world, nothing here was random; here things didn't just happen. You could actually go bitch to the person responsible if you didn't like something. I looked at my notepad again and reread what I had just written. Something in the back of my mind was trying to tell me something.

The coach rounded a bend and I saw Skywatch looming in the distance. Once again the peculiar travel magic of Patchwork was present and my eyes were unable to focus on the individual buildings of the large compound as the coach hurtled forward faster than it possibly could in the real world. I looked away, blinking my eyes and shaking my head to clear it.

"It's easier if you don't look," said Gray sympathetically.

"Good to know," I replied.

A bare few moments later, the coach slowed and began making a number of course corrections, all of which indicated to me that we were approaching our destination. I imagined that I heard the scraping of talon on cobblestone as the coach came smoothly to a halt. I waited a moment to make sure that we weren't going anywhere and I rose to a semi-standing position, ducking my head slightly to avoid the roof of the cabin. I reached for the door just as it popped open without benefit of my assistance.

"Thanks for the lift," I said to Gray.

I ducked my head and popped out of the coach, my boots striking cobblestone. As I straightened up, I locked eyes with one enormous and unblinking yellow eye.

"Thanks to you two," I said somewhat awkwardly. "Very smooth ride, good job."

The closer griff sniffed, in what might have been appreciation but could just as well have been to determine whether I smelled edible. I gave both of the bird-horse-things a jaunty appreciative salute and made my way up the walk towards the front gate of the Skywatch compound. It never hurts to be polite.

The gates rolled open smoothly as I approached them. I guess they knew me now. That was nice. Passing through them, I walked across the rolling lawn that led to the main building. Fizznorman came rolling out the front door, ducking and bowing as he did. He was still wearing the Hawaiian shirt and khakis that I had seen him in earlier, but his manner was all servitude as he ducked his head and tugged on his forelock.

"Mr. Monday!" he cried apologetically, "Please be forgiving me for my appearance and my tardiness. Welcome be you in the house of Skywatch and may the hospitality that Master Starbourne was so justifiably known for be yours and your pleasure. How may I be of assistance to you on this fine and rainy afternoon?"

I started to answer him, but as soon as I opened my mouth, he was off again.

"Welcome, welcome, welcome," he cried. "Come in and out of the weather. Never let it be said that any guest was forced to tarry a moment in the elements while one brick stood atop another in the house that Starbourne built."

"Thank you, Algernon," I managed to jam into a slight pause. "The house of Starbourne is known far and wide for it's hospitality and I am both glad and fortunate to be beneath its roof."

I paused meaningfully and looked up at the rain falling down, then towards the aforementioned roof. Fizznorman's bushy eyebrows flew upward in what looked like genuine surprise as he apparently realized for the first time that I was still standing out in the rain. He stepped aside with a grand flourish and ushered me in. I walked inside the foyer, looked around for the little man and was immediately nonplussed to find he had somehow vanished.

"Algernon?" I asked the empty foyer.

"Oh and it's your pardon I'll be asking for, Mr. Monday," exclaimed the little man from right beside me.

I started violently but managed to clamp down on any unmanly noises. How did he do that? I put a hand to my chest and huffed out a breath to steady myself. Fizznorman had the good graces to look apologetic. I saw no trace of a smirk on his face, and believe me, I looked.

Fizznorman returned to his steady stream of nonsense chatter which in turn allowed me to keep noticing him. Which was good. Interviewing the fellow was going to be a challenge if he kept up his vanishing trick every time he stopped talking long enough for me to get a word or two in edgewise. Ah well, into the breach and Perdition take the hindmost, and so forth.

"Algernon," I began. "Would you mind if I asked you some questions? Some of them may seem odd or even intrusive, and some of them might not seem to pertain to the case."

"Sure and Lady Gray warned – er that is, told me – that you would be coming by and by, asking me all manner of interrogatives and such not. The good lady was most express and direct that it would be in the best interest of us all, and most especially in the line of finding justice for poor Mr. Starbourne if I were to be as complete and forthcoming as I could manage. So of course I'll be glad and glad to be of any and all help and service to you in your investigations as it is within my humble power to be and to be."

"Okay," I said in the first available moment. "I'll keep my questions brief and you give me as much detail as you can."

We walked together, Fizznorman rattling on about the weather or something equally interesting, into the mansion. The little man led the two of us into a small sitting room off the main gallery. He directed me into a chocolate brown leather arm-chair that was almost obscenely comfortable. I might never get up again. Fizznorman selected a foot-stool and perched upon its edge, pausing politely in his running lecture regarding the fascinating history of this particular room.

"First question," I began. "What can you tell me about your role as a pillar?"

Fizznorman's thick lower lip shot out in a classic expression of disapproval, or perhaps sulkiness. "Sure, and I'm not comfortable speaking of such things," he said. "I've always believed in my chest and in my gut that I'm presuming above my station and putting on airs and suchlike, which is very bad. But Mr. Starbourne and Lady Gray have assured me and assured me that the realm itself depends on me. That never did sit well with me and myself, don't you appreciate? I'm a humble-born man, a servant of servants born, generation after generation the Fizznormans have served gentlemen and proudly so.

"But this business of being … well, being a pillar," Fizznorman continued without seeming to pause for breath. "Well it just doesn't seem like anything a respectable serving man should be getting up to."

I looked at him expectantly in the hope that he might someday approach something resembling a point. Not that learning more about his nature and his motivations wasn't useful in and of itself, but there wasn't anything really noteworthy yet. I appreciated his discomfort and wasn't about to rush or pressure him. I settled in and practiced some active listening skills. I nodded appreciatively, made monosyllabic noises of affirmation and interest, and generally acted a little bit like an idiot.

"Mr. Starbourne and Lady Gray made it plain and simple for me, if you please. The land needed me and I had what you might call unique skills that I was never aware of having before it was put to me that I did and I did. So I did."

"And what," I asked at last. "Do you do?"

"Well now," said Fizznorman, an improbably huge smile stretching his face. "Why and why didn't you ask that in the first place? Once I was faced with the truth of the matter, I began to cast about for a place that was fit and true for the likes of me and I did see an opening, a lack as it were, that needed filling by one such as yours truly. The lords and the ladies, you know? The great and the good, they think great thoughts. But sometimes the low and the humble get lost in the tumble. I worry about things that the common folk need. When I first came to be here, I was always bothering Mr. Starbourne with my petty needs, a new mop, soap, detergent, a scrub brush that could reach higher-up spots and such and such like. If you take my meaning? And surely as soon as Mr. Starbourne stopped thinking about it, it was gone and vanished right out of the cupboard where I had been keeping it.

"And that's only right and proper and true as it should be," continued Fizznorman. "Why should the likes of them have to be filling their mind with such rubbish? Here and now was something that the likes of me and myself could be worrying about. I make certain that whenever anyone in the land opens up a closet or a cabinet or a cupboard it is filled with all the right and proper tools and accoutrements that anyone would be expecting to find in such a place.

"Looking out for the little guy, eh?" I asked, only a bit sarcastically.

Fizznorman gave me a look as if he were trying to figure out if I were making fun of him or not. I gave him my best Charming Zack smile and that seemed to put him back at ease. I made a polite 'please go on' gesture with my free hand.

"And there's plenty and plenty of little things like all of that," Fizznorman went on, sounding mollified-but-wary. "To make a world real there are tiny, small, little matters. I tend to those so my betters don't have to. And I have the honor of serving … had, had that is, the honor of serving one of the greatest men ever to live, Mr. Peter Starbourne. Oh, you'll have to pardon me, Mr. Monday, I'm getting a bit … a bit…."

Fizznorman's voice choked and cracked and he drew out a bright red handkerchief and blew his nose noisily into it. He sobbed quietly for a nearly a minute while I sat awkwardly in my extremely comfortable chair. After another minute passed and his sobs began to intensify, I decided to explore the house a little. I mumbled something about looking at the art. He waved me off with the hand that wasn't wiping his face.

I wandered out into the gallery and gazed absent-mindedly at the various *objets d' art*. I found myself looking at the same statuette that had briefly captivated me before. It definitely looked familiar, but I knew I'd never seen it before. What was it reminding me of? I pulled out my notebook and flipped back to before I had begun this case. The crooked cook, Nate Crane, Ginny Prescott, poor dead Malcolm Howard, and … I stared at a crude sketch I had made nearly a week ago. It was the Weeping Lady, or rather the counterfeit Weeping Lady.

My sketch lacked detail just as my notes did. Really the purpose was to trigger my memory. I had an excellent memory, but I found it useful to associate certain memories with notes, snippets of song, or sketches. Looking at this sketch helped me summon a vision of the Weeping Lady; my mind's eye roamed over its lines and shapes. I imagined how the sculptor must have held his tools, how he had struck the stone, how he had carved and shaped it. I was absolutely certain that the same artist that had created the counterfeit Weeping Lady had created this statuette.

What in two worlds did that even mean? Was there some kind of connection between Malcolm Howard's murder and Peter Starbourne's? Who was behind the counterfeit art? Was the scheme based out of Patchwork? It made a certain kind of sense. Where better to hide out? Magic flowed strongly here, it was off of every beaten path, and it was an easy spot to either hide or defend. But there had to be an easier path between Patchwork and the real world than any I'd yet seen. The logistics of it had to work or nothing made any sense. What was missing?

Chapter Thirteen

Fizznorman eventually came to collect me. He didn't mention any-thing about his emotional outburst and neither did I. If he wanted to talk about it, I'd listen, but I wasn't going to press the matter unless it became pertinent to the case. Somewhere in the middle of a lengthy dis-course on the absorbent qualities of various sorts of mops and rags, he asked me if I wanted him to contact Lady Gray for a pick up. I thought about it for a moment and asked if he could get in touch with Visivald instead. He assured me at some length that he could and I thanked him for doing so.

I headed out to the foyer to wait for transport. I collected my hat and smacked myself in the face as I suddenly realized that I had left my travel bag in the boot of Dr. Foucault's coach. I'd need that back, but there was nothing to be done about it at the moment. I sighed heavily. So much for how impressive my memory was; maybe I was getting old.

There were small planes of frosted glass set into the wall bracketing the front door and I watched as rain sluiced against them and listened to the quiet roar of the out of control weather. I wondered what the rank and file citizens were thinking right now. Had they heard that Peter Starbourne was dead? Did they understand why the weather was wonky? Did they know that catastrophic systemic breakdown was on the horizon? And even if they did, what could they possibly do about it?

According to Gray, about ten thousand souls called Patchwork their home and not two dozen of them could effect the trip through the Mists back to the real world. How many of them might die because of the intrigues and crimes that those two dozen had been getting up to? And how long did I have to figure out which one of those intrigues had gone fatally wrong for Mr. Starbourne before more people started dying?

The roar coming from outside suddenly changed pitch and became much louder. I threw open the door and saw a patch of ground about a dozen yards away erupting outward like a gushing fountain of dirt and rock. I had seen the effect before; it was goblin geomancy, earth magic … Or was that the wrong word, seeing as this wasn't an earthly place? As the showers of mud, dirt, and soil-blackened rocks settled to ground, I realized that my ride was here. His Grace, Sir Visivald always did like to make a dramatic entrance.

A metal coach lurched up through the newly created opening; it traveled on twin treads that wrapped around the coach from bumper to bumper and over the roof. As I watched gears turned, steam howled out through gaps in pistons, and the doors ratcheted open. Metal steps unfolded and plunged into the ground. There was a faint hissing as the entire contraption came to a rest. I turned the collar of my jacket up to shield the back of my neck from the rain and pulled my hat down hard on top of my head before dashing out the door. A half dozen running steps carried me from door to door; the mud splashed up in the rain, splattering my boots and lower pant legs but at least my socks stayed warm and dry inside my boots. And I didn't get any rain down the back of my neck. I celebrate the small victories when I can.

The interior walls were bare metal, the corrugated kind with lots of tiny screw holes for putting up shelves or hanging straps. Hanging off the walls currently were an enormous broadsword, a .50 caliber handgun of some kind whose make I didn't recognize, and a travel chess set, all secured and made ready for travel or a fast draw. I relaxed my jacket collar, removed my hat and shook a little water off each of them.

There were two sturdy benches on either side of the cabin. I plunked myself down on the closest bench. It was a metal grate, slightly rounded to accommodate the humanoid posterior.

The coach began to tremble and a deep growling came from somewhere deep within its mechanical guts. The front end tipped forward momentarily before some kind of gyroscope kicked in and the cabin stabilized. The sound of rain vanished, or perhaps was merely covered up by the sound of the works.

I turned to look at the occupant of the other bench. It was wide enough to handle three of me, but it was amply filled by Duke Sir Visivald, late of the Nome Court, and currently a Pillar of Patchwork. I grinned hugely and he returned the grin with about 300% more teeth. Unlike his distant descendant Baxter, Visivald had teeth that were quite pointy and wickedly curved, and they grew in rows, like a shark. It was quite a grin.

"Did you really have to dig up the front lawn like that?" I asked.

"I like to make an impression when I arrive," Visivald rumbled. "But don't worry your tiny pink head about it, I clean up my messes. No one will even notice a blade of grass out of place."

"You didn't used to be that good," I observed.

"This place is good for me," he rumbled.

"And you've been practicing," I added.

"A whole bunch," he admitted.

"It really is great to see you, sir," I said.

"I know," he rumbled jovially. "You're coming along nicely, Zack. You've got the stuff of heroes in you."

"Bullshit," I laughed.

"I didn't say you were there yet," the Duke rumbled back. "But enough small talk. What do you know so far?"

I considered for a moment.

"I'm still putting it all together," I said thoughtfully. "But my working theory is court intrigue; I'm betting that Starbourne was killed by one of the other Pillars, possibly over some obscure point of precedence, but counterfeiting might be involved."

I paused for a moment before adding, "And there might be a smuggling ring."

Visivald exploded into gales of booming laughter. I smiled ruefully and waited for the laugh storm to subside. Sometimes that took a while.

"Wonnaynge's Kneecap, boy!" he managed to get out between wheezes and chuckles. "You've only been here for 24 hours and you've uncovered an organized crime cartel?"

"It's not my fault!" I protested. "It's not like I bring the crime with me; I just find it!"

"How about that time I hired you to carry my ancestral shield to the bank deposit vault and you ended up stopping a robbery?" Visivald asked pointedly.

"Bad timing?" I asked, holding my hands up in a 'what can you do?' shrug.

"Whatever," the Duke rumbled. "For the record, I didn't kill him. I was at the party where he was killed, so we should put together a record of my movements all night."

"I'm way ahead of you, Your Grace," I said. "I'm the detective here, after all. I'm going to chart everyone's night, don't worry about that. Right now, I'm assuming you're not the killer and I want your opinion on a few things."

"I'll give you my opinion," Visivald rumbled dangerously. "If you stop calling me Your Grace."

I promised to try my best and then told Visivald pretty much everything I had observed so far. He didn't have any stunning observations right away, but I doubted he would. Duke Sir Visivald wasn't a fast thinker, but he had the mind of a thousand year-old military officer, and when he had something to say, you'd better believe I listened.

Although the details were not clear to me (or to anyone living as far as I knew) the Duke was suffering under some kind of ancient curse. The immortality was partial fallout of that curse. Immortality is a subtle sort of curse. I know an unusual number of immortal entities, and most of them seem to like it just fine, but it's bad news for us humans and goblins. It makes us crazy, detaches us from society, and usually ends badly for the cursed guy. I'm sure there was some 'on the day when three moons meet in the sky' escape clause that might yet get Visivald his happily-ever-after. But Baxter had convinced me to lay off this one, at least for now. I liked to think Baxter knew something I didn't, and in this case it was even more likely than usual to be true.

We rode together quietly for a time, me in my thoughts and, presumably, Visivald in his. I tried to read his face to get an idea of what was going on in his head, but I was never very good at reading goblins. Humans are usually an open book to me, but not so much with the green and scaly set. Different faces, different brains I guess. So I waited.

"What happened between you and Perdition last year?" he finally asked.

"First of all," I began, "it wasn't Perdition, it was just one devil, a friendly fellow that calls himself the Duke of Sorrows."

An animal sound rose from somewhere deep in Visivald's chest and his lips peeled back, revealing row upon row of pointy teeth in something that no one would mistake for a grin. My guts ran cold for just a second in purely instinctual fear, a sensation that came from nowhere near my conscious brain.

"He is no devil to trifle with," growled Visivald. "You were lucky to escape with your soul intact."

"To be honest, I'm not sure I did." I said. "It was a tough case, and I had to make some hard decisions. People got hurt. People died."

The Duke seemed to have no immediate response to this. He slowly composed his face while my heartbeat approached normal again. There was a certain tension in the metal cabin.

"Also I cheated." I confessed.

"That doesn't surprise me at all," Visivald said. "Just watch yourself. The Duke isn't the kind of entity that forgets that sort of thing. He'll be back, and I guarantee you will not see him coming."

"If that's the case," I said, "then there's absolutely no sense in worrying about it until it happens; is there?"

"That's not what I meant, you stubborn ..." Visivald began.

"Yoom?" I suggested, helpfully. "Pink skin? Crunchy?"

"Shut up," he said.

I shut up.

After a few minutes I felt our forward motion slow. Visivald rose and pulled a few levers, twisted a knob and paid careful attention to the juddering needles on a bank of dials. He removed a small box connected to the wall by a tightly curled wire from its hook and drew it towards his face.

"Captain to the bridge," he announced to the box, "bring us in steady and park in the trophy room, please."

"Captain?" I asked with a smirk. "Bridge? Really?"

"Just a harmless bit of fun," Visivald muttered.

We began to execute a series of small course corrections. Visivald kept a weather eye on the needles but didn't seem to see anything that troubled him overmuch. Eventually we came to a complete halt and the door once again ratcheted open and the steps unfolded with an audible *clunk*. Visivald invited me to disembark with a monosyllabic grunt and a wave of his hand. I accepted the invitation and stepped out into an unusually well-appointed cavern.

The cavern was cool and dry, with no puddles that I could see. There were numerous stalactites protruding downward and even more stalagmites rising up. Most of the latter had been sawn off at the top to provide flat surfaces. And every such surface was filled, mostly with weapons, armor, and chunks of masonry, but a few books, some jewelry and a crown were also on display. Each item was marked with a small plaque explaining its significance.

From the dates, names, and places, I gathered that each item was a memento of some kind from a battle that the ancient goblin warrior had been part of. There were many hundred such battles and the room was large and full. I walked around for a few minutes, reading plaques and dreaming dreams that weren't my own. Being in the presence of history often humbles me; being in the presence of living history always did.

"Visivald," I stammered. "Just … just wow."

The ancient goblin nodded his acceptance of the sentiment. We spent maybe fifteen minutes wandering through the underground gallery. I was honored that he had taken me here and I wished – certainly not for the first time, and probably not for the last time either – that Baxter was here with me. He would love this place more than anyone. Baxter practically worshipped his ancestor.

"I can't believe Banik kicked you out!" I blurted.

"His Royal Majesty Targamin Banik, 232nd Nome King of Goblin," Visivald corrected.

"Right," I agreed. "Him. It's absurd."

"Times change," the Duke rumbled. "Sometimes they change back. This isn't the first time I've left Court. It might not be the last."

That was news to me. I guess it made sense; Visivald had been kicking around for over a millennium. Stuff happened, but that didn't mean I had to like it.

"We should talk about the night of the murder," the Duke rumbled, interrupting my train of thought.

He was right. There would be time to talk about other things when I was off the clock. I took out my notebook and Visivald began talking. I asked some questions designed to jog his memory and between the two of us we reconstructed the entire evening from his perspective. I took copious notes.

As expected, no 'a-ha moments' leapt out at either one of us, but it was still a valuable conversation. Visivald was a good observer and his experience provided many touchstones. I asked him to recall where other party attendees had been at various points in the evening, who they spoke to, whether any heated words had been exchanged, and what the general emotional temperature had been.

In short, I asked for the kind of details that would give me a way to check other people's stories; small discrepancies were to be expected, but if someone went completely off the reservation, I would know that either they were lying or Visivald was. My money was on Visivald's version, but time would tell.

I noticed a shadowy object lying on the ground next to a stalagmite platform that featured a broken gear made out of some kind of stone. I nudged it with my foot; it was my travel bag.

"Did Dr. Foucault send you this?" I asked.

"Send me what?" the Duke rumbled.

I picked up my luggage and displayed it to the goblin.

"No," Visivald said. "I haven't seen that before. I wonder how it got in here?"

"Really?" I asked. "You're not pulling my leg?"

"Do I look like I'm pulling your leg?" the goblin asked darkly.

I opened up the bag and rummaged around inside. Everything was where and what it was supposed to be. Nothing was missing and nothing seemed to be altered in any way. I frowned and slung it back over my shoulder.

"This," I said slowly, "is damned peculiar."

Chapter Fourteen

I'm no expert when it comes to *objets d' magique*, but I did take a semester of basic theory back in college. And basic theory goes like this: performing a one-time spell, charm, illusion or what-have-you is easy enough … in theory, anyway. You conceive of what you want, you perform the ritual that has been established by warlocks past, you invest the operation with a significant portion of your will and that's all she wrote. Wham, bam, and so forth.

In practice, you had to have that certain special something which I – and 80% of the world's population – lacked. Without the inherent ability to perceive and manipulate magic, all the rituals in the world would never amount to a hill of magic beans. If you were one of the lucky 20% the only thing holding you back was training, experience, and will. Okay, maybe that was three things, but the general idea still holds true.

But none of that would cut it if you were looking to create a device that could be used by someone else. Even a trained operator couldn't activate a charm created by another, unless the charm was created using Vancian theories. Developed in the late 1960's, Vancian magic was a major technological breakthrough, giving magic to the masses. Devices created with Vancian magic could be operated by anyone with sufficient training and experience.

But those same laws of magic determined that once a device was completed, it could never get more powerful than it already was. The amount was fixed at the time of creation. That's why it was useful to create magical devices in a place like Patchwork, where the heavy lifting was a little bit easier.

None of which explained why my luggage had suddenly learned how to teleport. But that is exactly what seemed to have happened. Adriana Gray had shown up about a quarter hour after we contacted her and she had promptly commandeered Visivald's lab and locked both herself and my bag inside. An hour later she emerged and handed me my bag. Her conclusions were startling to say the least. Gray's Niven Disk confirmed what we all suspected: My luggage had seriously leveled up.

The three of us were sitting in a cozy little room somewhere in Visivald's home. Goblins traditionally build their homes underground, with only the front entryway and perhaps a small foyer exposed to the surface. Duke Sir Visivald was nothing if not traditional, so we had to be somewhere beneath the surface of Patchwork, but we were several levels above where the subterranean coach had docked.

Once we left the cavern of trophies, the walls and floor became much more like a modern building, smooth walls, carpeted floors, low humidity, good lighting, and all the other commodities you might expect to find in the real world. We passed enough rooms to make a mansion blush with insecurity, and I had the feeling I hadn't seen the half of it.

Baxter and I had been to the Nome King's palace once years ago and we had seen the rooms that Visivald had lived in. They were nice, don't get me wrong, but it was nothing compared to this place. It wasn't luxurious by any stretch, but it was large and impressive in a spartan sort of way.

The sitting room was definitely on the austere side; decorations were few and far between. But the chairs were comfortable and there was a coffee table, complete with coffee, although I was mostly ignoring mine while letting it slowly cool. The Duke and I had been sitting there together, mostly not speaking much while we waited for Gray to finish her analysis.

"So what can I expect?" I asked the wizard.

"It is difficult to speak accurately," Gray responded thoughtfully.

"Is there any danger?" Visivald rumbled.

"There is always some danger," Gray replied. "But I think in this case it is minimal. The original enchantment was designed to be a helpmeet, and Zachariah has never mistreated it."

"Unless you count forgetting it in Dr. Foucault's coach," I interjected.

"If the luggage objected to that treatment," Gray said, "it seems unlikely that it would have returned itself to you."

"Unless it wanted revenge," Visivald suggested.

"And people think I'm paranoid," I said. "Can we move away from what's possible in theory but highly unlikely and get back to what's likely to happen?"

"As I was saying," Gray said, smiling her thin-lipped smile, "it should still perform more or less the same tasks it did before. It is merely more puissant now."

'Merely' more puissant. To me that seemed kind of like saying the Titanic was merely wetter and riding a little bit lower in the water now. I decided to show restraint and not mention my thoughts to the room at large. I'm growing as a person. I made a mental note to tell Baxter about it; I was sure he'd be proud of me.

"As for specifics, I really cannot say," Gray continued. "Nor is there any reason to believe that it would perform for me in the same way it will for Zachariah. Magic isn't always consistent."

That last statement struck me as odd; Tim had always told me pretty much the opposite. It would seem there were more things in the earth and the Mists than dreamt of in Tim's philosophy. I was beginning to think that magic was a significantly more complex system than it seemed. That made a certain sort of sense and actually made me feel a bit better about my abject failure to create even the simplest of magical spells, rituals or charms.

"Does this sort of thing happen often?" I asked.

"Almost never," Gray replied.

"I've seen it three times before," the ancient Duke offered. "And once it was catastrophic."

That sobered me up a bit. Not the catastrophic part; getting up in the morning and walking to work could be catastrophic. That's just life. The fact that in all his hundreds of years of life Visivald had only ever encountered something like this three times, that was a compelling notion. Why had this happened here and now, and why to me, and why to a freaking piece of luggage? It all seemed to be simultaneously ominous and comedic. Still and all, there was only so much time I could spend sitting around thinking about it. I still had a job to do, a mystery to solve, and a fairly clear to-do list.

"I think we've covered all the ground we're likely to cover today," I said. "Let's table this discussion."

"All right," rumbled Visivald. "I say you should get rid of it."

"No," I said. "We're tabling the discussion."

"Right," said the Duke, agreeably. "Get rid of it."

"If I might interject here," Gray said. "Visivald, when Zachariah says 'table the discussion' he means that we should stop discussing it and move on."

"What?" rumbled Visivald angrily. "That's ridiculous. It means put it on the table for a vote."

"Um, no," I said. "What Miss Gray said is correct, I meant let's move on and discuss it later."

"Well," rumbled Visivald, "I'd still think twice before turning my back on it."

"Noted," I said. "Miss Gray, thank you for coming out here and helping. I think I should be paying you more than you're paying me."

Gray laughed her rich and melodious laugh, "Never fear, Zachariah. I am quite pleased with our professional relationship."

There was a funny thrumming in the air just then. I couldn't quite tell where it was coming from but I could tell that Gray noticed it too. Her eyes went unfocused for a moment, presumably to better see something that wasn't quite real.

"Excuse me,' Gray said. "I must attend to something briefly. Dr. Foucault has news."

Gray's eyes lost focus once more and I sat more or less patiently while she had the equivalent of a telephone call in her head. She didn't say anything and I didn't hear anyone else, but I could tell by her facial expressions and body language that she was getting important news. She was concerned, she had questions, and she was paying very careful attention to the answers. She held up a hand and her eyes refocused on the here and now. She gave me a significant look but said nothing. I raised my eyebrows and looked at her expectantly.

"Zachariah," she said. "Something very strange is going on."

"What else is new?" I asked. "What's the news?"

Gray hesitated as if unsure how to proceed. There was a pregnant pause as Visivald and I waited. I tried my very best to look patient. Patience is not my strongest quality, but faking patience is something I can do well.

"Michelle has reconstructed the body from the Kirlian Aura you produced," Gray began. "And ... well, she says it is not a real corpse."

"What do you mean?" I asked. "Her reconstruction didn't work?"

"No," Gray said. "The reconstruction worked exactly as expected. What was reproduced is not a deceased human body, but rather a reproduction of one. It is a counterfeit corpse."

"You're saying," I said slowly to give me time to work it out in my own head. "That Dr. Foucault has successfully created a copy of a fake corpse? And that fake corpse is the one that you found and I examined?"

"Yes," Gray said. "That is exactly what Michelle is telling me. What we found at Skywatch is not the corpse of Peter Starbourne."

My mind reeled. What was going on here? Nothing was what it seemed to be. Or at least the important things weren't what they seemed to be. Why would someone fake a murder, create a fake corpse, and then – presumably – steal that fake corpse? The first and most obvious answer? To convince us that a murder had occurred.

Was Peter Starbourne dead? Had his body been replaced? Or was he missing and presumed dead? And if that were the case, should we instead presume that he was alive and in need of rescue?

"What was it then?" I asked.

"That is uncertain at this time, but Michelle theorizes that it was crafted by Vancian magic out of biomimetic material and used a considerable amount of energy. It couldn't possibly have been meant to last long, considering the incredible amount of detail and realism that was achieved."

"How long would it have lasted?" I asked.

"Days at most, or so Michelle theorizes," Gray answered.

"That must be why the perpetrators stole it," the Duke rumbled. "To cover up the deception."

"That makes sense," I agreed. "They couldn't have known about the camera. That was a lucky break for us."

"But what does it mean?" Visivald asked.

"Salvation above and Perdition below," I swore quietly. "It's not a murder it's ... it's a kidnapping! A killnapping! Is that even a thing?"

Gray's eyes bored daggers at me.

"Zachariah," she said. "We are not going to refer to this as a 'killnapping.'"

"How about ... " I began.

"Or," she interrupted firmly. "A 'murdernapping' either."

I tried to hide my disappointment, but it wasn't easy. My excitement, on the other hand, I let show. We were on an entirely different timeline now; murder is a cold investigation, the victim usually isn't getting any deader, but kidnapping is hot. The victim could easily be in imminent peril or under duress, or both.

Usually I was in the avenging business; saving people was a luxury I rarely got to indulge in. I had come here to solve a murder, find the guilty party, and bring them to justice. That was what I did and it was usually enough. But this time might be different. Maybe, just maybe, I could still save Peter Starbourne. And that was very exciting.

I began constructing a plan in my head. This – quite literally – changed everything. The first thing we had to do was act like we still believed the corpse was real. The second thing we had to do ... well, that was a good question, actually.

"We must organize a search party immediately," Visivald rumbled.

"No," I snapped. "That is exactly what we should not do."

Both of them looked at me, eyes wide and mouths open. It wasn't too often that these people were caught off guard, let alone disagreed with. I rose, partly because I talk better when I'm on my feet and partly because I think better while I pace, but mostly because the position of authority would grant me the temporary illusion of command while I tried to convince two highly opinionated people of action to sit down, shut up, and listen to me.

"Right now we have a tremendous advantage," I said. "Whoever is behind all of this is confident right now; maybe even relaxed. He, she, or they spent a lot of time and energy setting this thing up, and they're probably feeling cautiously optimistic. We've been acting like we've swallowed their confidence game hook, line, and sinker. Mostly because, so far, we have. But if we start acting like we're onto them, they won't be confident and relaxed anymore. They'll start acting again. They might even decide to cut their losses and kill Starbourne – assuming he's still alive, which I think we have to."

I paused long enough for them to start thinking about everything I had just said. The trick to arguing with smart, knowledgeable people that were used to being in charge was to make them think your ideas were their ideas, or failing that, highly compatible with their ideas. I stopped pacing and turned to face them before they could actually form intelligent opinions and start to push me around.

"Here's what we do," I said willing as much confidence into my voice as I could possibly manage.

And then we made a plan together. All things considered, it was a pretty good plan. I called it Operation Hoodwink.

Chapter Fifteen

Operation Hoodwink was underway. I got to name it, partly in recompense for Gray having shot down 'killnapping,' but mostly because no one else had any ideas for a different name. It was small recompense, but I take what I can get. The key to the plan was to act like we were all still completely duped by the counterfeit corpse. That was easy enough for now, since we had, in fact, been completely duped. All we had to do was keep doing what we were already doing. The tricky part was running a second investigation in between the spaces and free time of the first. I had to assume that whoever had Starbourne wanted or needed him alive and secreted away somewhere, and as long as nothing disturbed that secrecy he was still relatively safe – if not particularly happy. For now, I'd take safe over happy.

The next step was interviewing each of the Pillars to learn as much as possible about as many things as possible as quickly as possible. It was back to school for me and today's subject was Oswald Quatermain, IV. My joy was underwhelming. What did I know about Quatermain? He was a Pillar of the community of Patchwork, which meant – as I currently understood it – that he maintained some portion of the holdfast's reality through the force of his will. He had told me that his motivation for doing so was family pride, or some variation thereof. And also, he was a jerk.

Visivald dropped me off at Aristarchus in his subterranean coach, with my little bag of miracles safely hanging off my shoulder. Okay, technically it was a medium-sized bag of miracles, but it seemed to roll better in my internal monologue as little, so sue me. I stood in the sheeting rain and watched with some fascination as the enormous mound of earth and rock formed in the wake of the subterranean coach's passage smoothed itself out and vanished. The entire process took less than ten minutes. It was more exciting than watching paint dry, but didn't exactly merit future viewings. Watching magic happen always made me a little bit twitchy, and this time was no different. I shuddered then shrugged, spun on my heel, and trotted the short distance to Aristarchus' front door. There was a small front porch with a roof that allowed me to take shelter from the weather.

Roger the golem greeted me and bade me enter in his disturbingly emotionless voice. I thanked him politely – you never knew when Adrianna Gray might be watching, after all – and I walked inside. I hung my hat and coat in the appropriate places, but held onto the bag. There was no sense taking chances with its favor at this juncture.

Instead of meeting in the Great Room, Roger led me down a different hall – albeit with the same charming décor – and up two flights of stairs. The rooms were much smaller on this level of the building and seemed more like the kind of places where people actually lived. A handsome and well-dressed young woman popped out of a door; she was quite pregnant, seven or possibly eight months along.

"The Lady Lillian Quatermain," Roger intoned placidly. "Mr. Zachariah Monday, here to see Oswald, Lord Aristarchus."

Lady Quatermain flashed me a dazzling smile, full of dimples and gleaming white teeth. She offered me her hand in a decorous manner. I gave her my most charming smile, took the proffered hand, and executed a cross between a slight bow and a head nod, with a little bit of a wink thrown in for good measure. If I scandalized her, she was polite enough to ignore it. I like to think she found me particularly adorable, but I was okay with easily ignorable.

Lady Quatermain continued on with her task, whatever it was, and Roger ushered me down the hall and into what appeared to be his employer's private office. Oswald Quatermain, IV, aka Oswald, Lord Aristarchus, sat at an old-fashioned roll top desk. The sight of that desk filled me with envy; it was gorgeous, and while it probably didn't have all of the aftermarket modifications my own desk sported, it was still much nicer looking. He rose and shook my hand once again.

Quatermain was once again dressed all in white, and his iron and silver hair and pencil mustache were immaculate, but he had clearly loosened up at least a little. He was now wearing a short sleeved shirt open jauntily at the collar and his trousers were what I would have called khakis if they hadn't been white. I brushed self-consciously at my own hair; mercifully, there was no mirror in the room to confirm my insecurity. Quatermain indicated a chair with his hand before sitting back at his desk. I sat and he spun his chair around to face me. I leaned forward to show him I was serious, briefly wished the chair had arms to brace my elbows against, and instead rested my left hand on my left knee and thrust my right hand forward to help emphasize my words. Trust me, this stuff really works when you get good at it.

"I'm sure Miss Gray has explained why I'm here and what I need from you," I said.

"Righto," Quatermain agreed in jolly upperclass fashion.

"I need to ask you a few questions," I continued. "Some of them may seem meaningless, or even impertinent, but please trust me that they all pertain in some way to the investigation. Or at least, they might pertain; they probably pertain, anyway. It's hard to know exactly what I'm looking for until I start to find it."

Quatermain cocked an eyebrow but said nothing. That was another reason to dislike him; I had never gotten the knack of eyebrow cocking and was often jealous of those who had it. He did it particularly well, probably just to get my goat.

"How long have you been a Pillar here in Patchwork?" I asked, moving past the eyebrow thing for now.

"Most of my adult life," Quatermain replied. "Ever since my grandfather retired nearly fifty years ago."

Fifty years? Okay, he was definitely older than he looked. That wasn't necessarily pertinent, but I did think it was interesting that he had a young and recently-impregnated wife. I wrote it down in my trusty notebook. It might not mean anything, but I figured why not. There were plenty of pages in my notebook and I had to fill them up with something.

"How long did it take you to get the hang of it?" I asked.

Quatermain stiffened a little bit at that. I had touched a sore spot of some kind. I was good at that. Some people can cock their eyebrows and others can honk strangers off just by talking to them.

"No longer than it takes anyone else," he said after a brief pause. "I was chosen from amongst all my brothers and sisters for this role. I was born for it."

"I'm sorry Mr. Quatermain," I said soothingly. "I'm new here. How long – approximately – is that?"

"A few months," Quatermain replied testily. "A twelvemonth perhaps. Why does this matter?"

"I already told you," I said patiently. "I'm not sure yet. I'm gathering information."

"Then why are you asking me?" Quatermain grumbled. "I'm not the expert on such matters. You should ask Lady Gray about this."

"I will," I said curtly. "I'm asking you because I'm asking everyone. It's called detecting; it's what I do."

Quatermain just stared at me. I held the stare, not for any good reason; I just hate to be the first one to blink. After a few moments of manly nonsense, I finally gave up, smiled to show him that there were no hard feelings, regardless of whether there were or not, and went on.

"What areas are you specifically responsible for?" I asked.

"The wildlife," he answered immediately. "Animals mostly, both the wild ones and the tame. Some plant life as well, but mostly the fauna."

"And you've been having problems maintaining the wildlife for how long now?" I asked.

"I couldn't really say for sure," Quatermain hedged. "It crept up on us all so slowly. Incremental difficulties are hard to notice."

I nodded in obvious appreciation of his difficulties. I was the soul of understanding. I made various sympathetic noises. I needed to get him talking and I needed him to forget that we didn't like each other very much. To do that, I needed to forget it myself. Easier said than done, but that's why Gray was paying me the big bucks. So once again, I had no choice but to pull up my metaphorical big-boy trousers. I smiled ingratiatingly.

"We talked about your grandfather earlier," I said after being agreeable for a while. "How long has your family been in Patchwork?"

"Generations and generations," Quatermain said proudly. "For as far back as the records go. Several centuries at least. There has been a Quatermain in service to Patchwork for several centuries, and there always shall be. Salvation willing."

"Do your family records have much to say about those earliest times?" I asked with genuine curiosity.

"Some," Quatermain answered uncertainly. "The oldest records were lost in a catastrophe of which we know rather little. The generations that came after did their best to reproduce the histories, of course. But much was lost."

"When did Adriana Gray first come to Patchwork?" I asked.

"What's that?" Quatermain asked. "She's always been here. As far back as the records go. Some say she discovered – or perhaps created – Patchwork herself."

This was exactly the sort of moment that called for a really good eyebrow cocking. I had to settle for raising them both, which was a decidedly inferior expression. How old was Gray? I knew that wizards were long-lived by nature, and spending time outside the real world allowed them to extend their lives even longer, but this was hard to believe in the extreme. She might be even older than Visivald, and I wasn't aware of any humans that could come close to that claim. Was Gray human? She seemed to be, but I knew well that appearances could deceive.

"Why was Patchwork created?" I asked. "Why was it carved out of the Mists in the first place? Do your family records have anything to say about that?"

"Not as such, no," Quatermain said, stroking his chin thoughtfully. "There are some obvious theories, of course. There is no better place for a man of power to live. Anything can be had if one's will is but strong enough. And there is the matter of magic. It flows more strongly here than anywhere else that I am aware of."

"But would Gray – or whoever created this place – have known that in advance? It seems like an extraordinary effort must have been taken. Most holdfasts are tiny. Patchwork is comparatively huge. If it were only a matter of making a workshop or some kind of supernatural bedroom community, why make the place so big?"

I was committing a cardinal interviewing sin here by trying to answer my own questions, but I found myself caught up in the wonder of it all. For a moment, Quatermain and I were united in our frustrated curiosity. Obviously this was something he had thought about before, and presumably, generations of Quatermains had pondered these same questions. If they had come to any substantive conclusions, they had either been left out of the family records, or the current Quatermain was better at keeping secrets than I thought he was.

"Perhaps Lady Gray – or whoever the founder truly was – had reason to know in advance what sort of place this was to be?" Quatermain suggested. "Perhaps it needs to be the way it is for some reason."

"Maybe," I said tentatively. "But couldn't Patchwork operate better with just Pillars and no citizens? Wouldn't it be less work that way?"

Quatermain looked as if he had genuinely never considered such a thought. He chewed on it for a little while, but it looked to me like he was trying to frame his answer in a manner that a man such as myself would understand rather than actually thinking about options. That was okay, it gave me a chance to watch how he worked things out, which was always useful information to have.

"Without vassals a lord is nothing," he said at last. "I wouldn't expect a man such as you to understand, but among the aristocracy, there is a … well … a need, really to make the world better for others."

I had heard variations of this line of bull crap before. It didn't impress me any more coming from Quatermain, but I dutifully listened and made all the muscles in my face work in such a way as to look like I was giving the matter all due consideration. At the same time, I paid attention to Quatermain. He was watching me, trying to read what I was thinking on my face, so I showed him what I wanted him to see. After I had done my best to broadcast how sympathetic I was to his white man's burden I brought myself back to the here and the now.

"I'm not sure I understand," I lied glibly. "But it's clear to me that this is important to you, and I guess that's enough for me."

I rose from my chair and tucked my trusty notebook back into my pocket. I offered him my hand; he took it and we traded grips once more. I adjusted the bag on my shoulder and gave Quatermain a small smile. It was a smile that said we might not be friends, but we could respect each other, he as the superior man, and me as a possible vassal. As far as smiles go, it wasn't my finest work, but I think it served its purpose well enough for now.

"I may have some more questions for you later," I said. "Thanks, you've been a great help to me."

"I just answered your questions," Quatermain said with just the smallest touch of carefully feigned self-deprecation. "Come back anytime you need to. Roger will see you out."

I turned and just about jumped out of my own shoes. Roger was standing right outside the door. How did a creature that big move that quietly? I had a momentary flash of panic. He could have staved in the back of my head with one of those massive stone hands and I never would have seen it coming. I threw a quick glance at Quatermain, he was doing a poor job of suppressing a smile at my discomfort. It seemed I wasn't the first one to be startled by Roger's stealthy presence. I gathered what remained of my dignity and nodded respectfully, first to Quatermain and then to Roger.

"Right," I said. "Let's go."

Roger led the way and I followed at a discreet distance that not-so-coincidentally put me just slightly out of his reach. I looked around as we walked out. Despite my hopes, nothing much had changed. Through a slightly open door, I thought I spied a flash of white marble oddly out of place with the great white hunter chic décor.

"What's in there?" I asked the golem.

"Master Quatermain's workroom," Roger replied.

"Mind if I take a quick look?" I asked.

"The master has offered you the hospitality of Aristarchus," the golem replied.

I pushed the door open and indeed saw a workroom with long tables covered by taxidermy in progress, partially cured furs, tusks in the process of being turned into scrimshaw, and all the tools and accoutrements I expected to see. There was a poster on one wall, bright, cute, and very much out of place. It was a watercolor of a ship with a poem about learning to chart one's own course. I used to have one just like it back in college. It had been a gift from Kelli.

But there in the corner, where I had seen a glimpse of it from the hallway, was the Weeping Lady, or a very reasonable facsimile thereof. Curiouser and curiouser as dear Alice once said. Was Quatermain involved in the art counterfeiting and smuggling ring? Was he another victim of it? Was it related to the Starbourne case at all, or just another coincidence to distract me?

Everywhere I looked I found more questions and fewer answers. The only solid fact I had started with was Peter Starbourne's death; now even that was gone and the ground kept getting less certain with every step I took. Sometimes my job really sucked eggs.

Chapter Sixteen

I was getting a little bit tired of being carted around everywhere like luggage – not that I had anything personal against luggage, mind you – so I asked Roger for walking directions from Aristarchus to Gray's. It might have been my imagination, but I could swear the golem looked at me kind of funny when I asked. I guess nobody walks around here. I swiped an umbrella from the front closet, mouthing a silent word of thanks to Fizznorman for its continued presence as I did, and started hoofing it back to Adriana Gray's tower.

In theory if I got really lost, I could send up a flare or something and get some help. Mostly, I just needed to walk. I did my best thinking while I was walking and I missed it. Plus, I was still a little bit stiff from my beating the other day and it would feel good to stretch. Worst-case scenario, I'd walk in a big damn circle back to Aristarchus and then get a ride.

The rain had settled down to a regular downpour and, although twilight was approaching, there was still plenty of light to see by, or at least there was enough light to avoid the really big puddles. The overwhelming animal noises that had greeted me when Gray and I had approached Aristarchus earlier were either gone or covered by the sound of the rain. Either way, it didn't comfort me much to think that all the wildlife out there was now silent.

A long and mournful howl rose up out of that silence from somewhere behind me. Deep in my primitive brainstem a word burned brightly: wolf! At the same time, the more reasonable parts of my brain told me that I was perfectly safe. This was a magical bedroom community, for crying out loud. That wolf was probably just wet and cold and miserable and felt like complaining to his maker, who in this case was most likely Oswald Quatermain, IV. I couldn't blame Mr. Wolf much; I felt like doing a little bit of howling myself. Sadly for the wolf, there didn't seem be much his maker could do about the weather. Some makers were better than others. That was bad luck for Mister Wolf; maybe it was bad luck for us all.

I like nature as much as the next born-and-bred big city boy, which is to say I don't like nature. Perfectly safe or not, I hiked at a brisk pace until I was well beyond the bubble of woods, wildlife, and wilderness that surrounded the hunting lodge and into the rolling fields and glades that made up Patchwork's default landscape. The road widened and flattened, but remained unpaved and slightly rutted. The non-stop rain was doing a pretty good job of turning the road into a flowing river of mud.

I slowed down to my normal walking pace. The ground had been a little bit surer in the woods around the hunting lodge, but in retrospect, I was still lucky I hadn't stepped on a rock and turned my ankle in my rush to get out of the woods. I saw no good reason to push that luck. Don't get me wrong, there are times when pushing luck is a good idea, and there are even times when it's absolutely necessary. But semi-rational mild discomfort wasn't a good enough reason to risk – well not 'life' – but certainly this qualified as 'and limb.'

Despite myself, my mood began to lift. Sure there were problems, lots of problems, and sure there were questions that I wasn't even close to answering, but for the first time since I had woken this morning, I felt like the problems were surmountable and the questions answerable. I just had to keep pushing until I found the answers and then I had to figure out how to use those answers to surmount the problems. Easy? Probably not, but it could be done. It all could be done. I just had to keep putting one foot in front of the other. I had talked to four people and I already knew a lot more than I had started with. Granted, not all of it was helpful and not all of it hung together yet, but solving mysteries was usually a matter of accumulating information. Sooner or later, you reached critical mass and it started coming together. That was the plan anyway.

I came around a bend in the road and saw a charming little copse of trees. It was so picturesque it could have come right out of a romantic fantasy novel. That was the thing about Patchwork: it was all so picturesque. Even if none of the pictures matched. I looked at the copse as I passed on by. If anyone had been watching, I would have given a little head shake and an oddly charming yet cynical smile; since I was alone, I decided to skip it.

I heard a noise from behind me: a sudden squelching sound, a foot hitting the mud perhaps. I spun around to see, lost my balance in the mud under my own foot, and stumbled to catch my balance. There was a man rushing up behind me with a club; my sudden stumble had caught him by surprise and his swing was off. He hit me in the right shoulder, hard enough to have bashed in my skull if he had been on target. The arm went numb and useless. The odd tingling sensations in my shoulder presaged massive pain in my future, but for now I was just down a limb. Fortunately, I'm left handed. Unfortunately, he had a club and two good arms. I had only the one arm and an umbrella to defend myself.

"Hey," I said. "That club feels familiar. Have you beaten me up before?"

"I thought we killed you," the club guy snarled.

"Nah," I replied with a grin. "Don't you know? I'm unkillable."

Okay, so that was a total bald-faced lie, but maybe it would shake my dance partner up and throw him off his game a little. It wasn't much as far as plans go, but I was improvising. I wasn't expecting to meet this guy again. In fact, I really had to wonder how he had gotten from New Jerusalem to Patchwork. Another man emerged from the picturesque woods; he also had a club. I had been wondering where the second guy was hiding. Last time we did this dance, only one of them had a club. Things were not improving.

Still, there was some good news. Normally I'm not exactly thrilled about being outnumbered in a fight, but these guys obviously didn't know how to work together, or the second guy wouldn't have waited so long to engage me. If he'd come up while I was getting bashed in the shoulder, it would have been a piece of cake for him to club me down from behind. This lack of coordination suggested a strategy to me, and I wasted no time putting it into effect.

I took a few quick steps until I was exactly between Club One and Club Two, then I whipped the umbrella around until I was holding it like a fencer's foil. I thrust my makeshift rapier into Club One's face. He snarled and backed up a little, getting ready to charge me. At the same time, I showed Club Two my undefended and delicate flank. If I knew my poorly-trained club-wielding thugs, he'd be getting ready to charge me too, or at the very least, take a mighty swing.

I waited two heartbeats before flinging myself to the ground; mud splattered everywhere and my attempts to make a controlled fall failed completely as I did an ungainly face plant into the road. My hat and my luggage tumbled off me and into the road. Above me, unable to stop their headlong flight on the uncertain footing that the road *cum* river provided, Club One and Club Two collided. Sometimes Lady Luck favors the unprepared.

I got up on my haunches, scrambled backwards and rose to my feet. I felt something pop in both of my knees as I rose; that was going to hurt later, too. The Clubs had gotten themselves untangled. Sadly, neither one of them looked hurt, but at least I had bought myself some time. And maybe I had even taught the Clubs a little bit of respect.

Respect or not, they were still taking turns. I guess I couldn't blame them after I had just showed them the disadvantages of attacking simultaneously. They looked at each other, trying to communicate without words. Eventually Club Two started moving towards me, cautiously, but still brandishing that club. I choked up on the umbrella and reversed it in my grip so that the hook-shaped handle was facing Club Two. I whipped it forward and hooked one of his wrists. I yanked back hard, messing up his club grip. At the same time, I launched a kick at his knee. I couldn't get enough *oomph* to deliver a really solid kick, but I was hoping it would be enough to put him on the ground.

Sure enough, the leg buckled and Club Two went down. I managed to keep hold of the umbrella, but he managed to keep hold of the club. You win some, you lose some. I gave him a boot to the gut to loosen his grip; it worked, his fingers went slack, and I was able to swing my foot back, reorient myself, and kick the club out of his hand. It didn't go far on the muddy road, but I'd take what I could get.

I got one more kick in before Club One got back into it; he screamed as he charged and took a vicious swing at the back of my head. In any fight, there are the kind of people who like to attack from the front and the kind of people who prefer to come at you from behind. Club One, it seemed, was one of nature's backstabbers. Or should that be backclubbers?

I let the umbrella slide forward in my grip until I was holding it near the tip, planted a foot hard in the mud, pivoted, and threw all my weight into a swinging roundhouse with the umbrella. The mud played in my favor as I spun a little bit faster than I could have on solid ground. The heavy metal of the hook handle smacked Club One on the elbow. I couldn't have planted the shot better if I'd actually been looking; the thug's arm was instantly paralyzed from the elbow down. This had the pleasant side effect of taking most of the power out of his own swing. It still struck me in the head and rang my chimes truly and properly, but it didn't feel like it cracked my skull too badly.

Club Two was back on his feet now and he was shambling around looking for his weapon. I ignored him for the moment and put some thought into finishing off his buddy. Thanks to the painful blow I had just delivered, Club One was moving a lot slower, it might not have been a vital blow, but never underestimate the effect of a whanged funny bone. I moved forward, choking up on the umbrella again to get more power, and jammed the handle as hard as I could straight into his throat. His eyes bugged out almost comically, he made a gurgling noise that I could hear clearly, even over the sound of the rain and my own heart slamming in my chest, and then he dropped to his knees before pitching forward. One down, one to go.

I was a little bit too slow; the rush of air and the grunt of the swing was the only warning I got of my impending danger. I tried to shuffle to the side, skidded in the mud and threw my arms out to counterbalance myself. Sadly, only my left arm responded to my urgent attempts and ended up spinning in a little circle. Embarrassing as hell, but the club barely brushed me as I dodged in completely unpredictable ways. Even I couldn't predict where I was going!

Club Two was getting bored with the game; he stretched his arms out and came at me, trying for a bear hug. I waited until he was right on top of me before going down on one knee; he came over me like a wave and bent over, reaching down for my head, his fingers thrusting towards my eyes. I thrust the umbrella up at his gut, sharp and hard; my own force combined with his, and gravity made three. The air rushed out of him, and he staggered back, losing his balance and going down in the mud. His breath came in ragged wheezing gasps. I walked over and gave him a kick for good measure. I can be a little petty sometimes, I admit it.

I thought about sticking around to ask some pointed questions, but thought better of it. By the time these guys could talk, they might be feeling feisty again, and it was only a matter of time before someone got seriously hurt. Even worse, that someone might be me. I recovered my muddy luggage and muddier hat, grabbed both clubs, tucked them and the mostly-ruined umbrella under my good arm and proceeded up the road at good speed. At least the rain was washing most of the mud off.

I was still panting hard from the fight and feeling a little light-headed from hyperventilation and the adrenaline crash, but I was pretty sure I could make it far enough down the road that the Clubs were unlikely to catch up to me without help. Right about then I was wishing that Patchwork's road magic would kick in and whisk me along my route. It was just a pipe fancy, of course. Without a wizard – or at least a warlock – to command it, no magic was going to happen for me on this road.

The world blurred, my feet skidded forward, but I did not fall. I shouted something that even I didn't understand. My left arm pinwheeled madly, spilling the clubs and umbrella to the road; still I plowed forward. The sensation was very much like falling, but I only 'fell' forward along the road. My momentum didn't slow. If anything, I was going even faster moment to moment. Somehow, miraculously, my travel bag stayed glued to my shoulder. I eventually came to some sort of an agreement with gravity. I no longer felt like I was pitching forward, it was more like water skiing along the muddy road. Only there was nothing towing me that I could perceive.

After several heart-pounding minutes of this bizarre travel, I started to slow down. Less than a minute later, my feet skidded to a halt, once again spraying up mud. I like to think that if both of my arms had been working, I wouldn't have fallen face first into the mud. Again. Sadly, I will never know for sure. I lay there for a few moments, catching my breath and marveling at how very comfortable I felt. The rain pooled at the back of my neck and trickled down my neck and under my shirt and jacket. Normally that would have been irritating, but in my current circumstances it didn't even make it onto my top ten list of irritating things.

I rose slowly and carefully to my feet. Sure enough, my knees were throbbing and felt swollen and very stiff. My right arm was more or less functional again, but my shoulder felt like it was being held against a hot stovetop.

"Ouch," I said to no one in particular.

I looked up and saw Adriana Gray's tower, a short distance away along the road. That much, at least, was going in my favor. I stumbled forward a few steps, getting the hang of walking again. I regretted the loss of the clubs and the umbrella; one of them might have been nice to lean on while I walked. I made do without the help, but I hoped that no one was watching me while I did it.

I got to the front door and raised my left hand to bang away unceremoniously until someone let me in, but the door swung open before my fist even got close. I staggered in and started looking around for a chair to flop down on. I didn't see one, and the floor was beginning to look awfully inviting, when the mistress of the house herself came upon me.

"Zachariah Monday!" she cried in horror. "What in Salvation's Name happened to you?"

I know I should have rushed to assure her that I was more or less fine, but I couldn't resist the moment. I grinned at her and tried to stand up straight. I cleared my throat theatrically and brought my hand up to the brim of my soaking wet, mud-caked hat.

"Ms. Gray," I said. "You should see the other guys!"

And with that, shock, exhaustion, and cranial trauma finally overtook me. I pitched forward and fell into the swirling black of my own pain, or possibly, the floor. Now that I think about it, it was probably the floor.

I awoke to muted, gray sunlight on my face and a soft pillow under my head. I cracked open an eyelid, even though it hurt to do so. I was in a large four-poster bed and my head was throbbing worse than the combined hangovers of an entire freshman dormitory. I started to look around until the pain in my head told me not to. So I just lay there for a moment, experiencing the pain of my own existence.

Eventually, I swiveled my eyes around to see as much of the room as I could manage. I was in a very nicely appointed bedroom. The comforter that lay atop me was pink and a little bit lacy. That was unfortunate, but I could deal with it later. The walls that I could see were adorned with pictures of puppies in various poses and situations. The door was across the room and closed. I wondered if it was also locked.

I gave my shoulder an experimental roll and was rewarded both with pain and the knowledge that someone had treated my shoulder.

The pain wasn't very useful, but the knowledge was. I risked a slight head movement to get a look at the dressing on my shoulder. I felt and heard gauze rustling against the pillow. Apparently, my head was also wrapped. The shoulder dressing looked good to me, but I was hardly in a position to be sure. I felt muzzy-headed; I was probably under some kind of painkiller enchantment. I was rapidly coming to suspect that it was a good thing, too. From the looks of me, I was pretty racked up.

There was a polite knock on the door and a moment later it opened. A stocky man dressed all in white entered the room and gave me a professional smile. He was balding, bespectacled, and bearded; his very-white teeth gleamed within the frame of his dark facial hair.

"And how are we feeling, Mr. Monday?" he asked in that friendly but detached tone that health care professionals often adopt.

"You look okay," I said. "But I feel like five miles of bad road. How does that average up?"

He laughed and shook his head, but didn't answer me. Why doesn't anyone ever answer me? He reached forward to the foot of my bed and pulled off a clipboard. He ran his eyes up and down whatever was written there, made a few interested noises, and scratched a note or two.

"Are you in much pain?" he asked.

"That's a relative question, Doc," I answered. "Compared to some days, I'm about normal, but all in all, I've been better."

He laughed again before replying, "I'm not a doctor. You can call me Lee. I'm a nurse."

"Glad to meet you, Lee," I said. "Can you tell me what kind of shape I'm in?"

"Pretty good, all things considered," Lee answered. "Nothing's broken and we've got the bleeding all taken care of. You've got a bit of a concussion, but you should be right as rain in a few days."

"That's great, Lee," I said. "I'm really glad to hear all of that. But I haven't got a few days. I need to be up and out of this bed as soon as possible. Can you cancel the anesthetic enchantments?"

Lee seemed to ignore me for a moment as he scratched another note onto the top page of my chart. He looked at me and sucked in a breath between his teeth thoughtfully.

"I can," Lee answered at last. "But I won't without the doctor's say-so. And I can tell you right now, she's not going to give it."

"Come on, Lee," I enthused. "I know my way around, one draught of healing and I'll be ready for swing dancing!"

"It's not that easy," Lee replied. "You've got head trauma, possible brain damage. There's a high risk in cases like yours that a healing draught will actually make things worse."

"Let's leave it up to the doctor then, okay?" I said. "When can she see me?"

I was hoping that the doctor in question was Dr. Foucault. I didn't want to tell Lee or another doctor that Peter Starbourne's life depended on my solving the case. The fewer people that even suspected Starbourne was still alive, the better. But I had to get out of this bed, and I wasn't going to be able to do that if I were magically doped up for my own good.

Lee shook his head as if to ask 'when will these patients ever learn?' and ducked back out of the room. About five minutes of pain exploration and boredom later, there was another knock followed immediately by the door opening again. This time it was indeed Dr. Foucault.

"Darling," she purred. "This is not the right way to get my attention."

"It was the first thing I could think of," I said with a smile followed by a wince as the smile caused my head to throb painfully.

She scooped up the clipboard and read what Lee had written. She made similarly interested noises, flicked her eyes up to my face and then back down to the charts she was reading. She made a *tsk* sound that was clearly disapproval. It sounded like she had picked it up from Gray, but Foucault was far from Gray's mastery of the form.

"You're really in no shape to be jaunting around," Foucault said as she replaced the clipboard.

"Be that as it may, Doc," I said brightly. "But we both know I don't have that luxury. Too much is resting on this case."

I tried to will enough urgency into my eyes to belie the lightness of my tone. I don't know whether my attempts at subtext worked or not, but Foucault was no dummy, and she wasn't slow on the uptake either. Her eyes widened a fraction as understanding came into them.

"You won't do Peter any good if you get yourself killed looking for him," she hissed quietly.

"Remember your Hoodwink Protocols," I cautioned her. "We don't know who the opposition is."

Her eyes flicked nervously to the door, "You don't mean? Surely not …"

"That's enough about that for now," I interrupted. "I'm not accusing anyone of anything. I'm just adhering to the protocols. Just like you should."

"Okay, okay," Foucault relented. "And I'll see what I can do about getting you up and around. But this is definitely against my better judgment."

"Mine too," I agreed. "But neither of us have much choice right now."

"But for now I insist that you rest," she said.

"I'll do my best," I said. "But I doubt I'll be getting any more sleep."

"We'll see about that," Foucault said ominously.

She reached towards the headboard behind me; I turned my head in time to see her finger tracing a glyph carved into the headboard. I had just enough time to wonder what kind of enchantment she was triggering before a tremendous exhaustion took me. It felt like a ton of soft feathers fell out of the sky and crushed me gently into the bed. My eyes slammed shut of their own accord and I fell into the most comfortable unconsciousness I had ever felt.

Isn't modern medicine great?

Chapter Seventeen

My eyes rolled open some time later. I could hear the rain still falling outside, but grayish light was coming in through the unshaded windows. I concluded that it was either still morning, or – far more likely – some subsequent day, hopefully the very next one. I had been hornswoggled, and as soon as I had enough energy to lift a limb or speak energetically, someone was going to get a piece of my mind. Hopefully, it wouldn't be the piece that had been scrambled by the vigorous application of a pair of clubs.

Adriana Gray was sitting in the room's only chair. She closed her book and turned to look at me, expectantly. I cleared my throat experimentally; everything seemed to go well so I figured coherent speech was probably within my current skill set.

"How long have I been out?" I asked.

"A day and a night," Gray replied. "It is Tuesday, about half past 10 in the morning. And Michelle says you are making excellent progress and should be totally recovered in a few days."

"Yeah," I said. "About that. I need to be out of this bed today. Now, if possible. Important things need to be done."

"I will see if I can convince Michelle to release you earlier than scheduled," Gray said matter-of-factly. "But it will scarcely do anyone any good if you are staggering around with mental and physical impairment."

"Miss Gray," I began, with a thin veneer of patience. "I spend approximately 40% of my professional career staggering around with both mental and physical impairments. It's part of the job."

"Be that as it may," Gray responded acerbically. "You are clearly not doing so currently. Perhaps we could spend your enforced convalescence productively. What have you learned so far?"

"That you and Dr. Foucault are in cahoots," I replied. "And if I don't get out of this bed soon, Operation Hoodwink will be in serious trouble."

"Hmmm," Gray said thoughtfully. "I seem to recall some key elements of that operation that would actually benefit from certain parties believing that you are out of commission."

"Believing it? Yes," I shot back. "Me actually being out of commission? No."

"Just think of it as undercover work," Gray said soothingly.

"You shouldn't do humor," I observed. "It's not working for you."

A single dark eyebrow arched elegantly over her left eye.

"I mean," I mumbled semi-apologetically. "There are other things that work better."

"*Hmph*," she muttered, obviously unimpressed with my diplomacy.

"As long as we're talking," I said. "Maybe you can tell me a little bit more about this place and exactly how it works."

"That would be a lengthy and complicated conversation," Gray said.

"I have specific questions," I said. "And we seem to have nothing but time."

"Touché," Gray allowed around one of her trademark thin smiles. "What are your specific questions? I don't promise I can answer all of them. At least not easily or to your satisfaction. But as you point out we have time."

I thought about it for a moment. The first and most obvious question to ask was why Patchwork wasn't falling apart worse than it was with Peter Starbourne out of the picture. But the both of us knew that Starbourne wasn't really dead. I had no pressing reason to believe the room was secure and I didn't want to go blabbing away our only advantage, but at the same time I didn't want to waste time discussing irrelevant details. Operation Hoodwink protocols had to be followed, but maybe we could still get something useful done.

"First off," I began. "Do you think the extreme weather could be the first indications of a complete systemic collapse?"

Gray pursed her lips and wrinkled her forehead. I gave her all the time she needed to catch up to where I was. She tapped a finger against her lips. I watched thought and emotion chase each other across her face as the implications worked their treacherous paths through her thoughts.

"It's certainly possible," she allowed. "And therefore it is in our best interests to find a solution as quickly as possible. But I don't think so. If we were facing imminent disaster, things would be degrading; the weather would be getting worse. What we're seeing seems to be stable. Dreary, depressing, and generally awful, but stable. Perhaps there is some meaning in the weather that we haven't considered?"

Now that was an interesting thought. Was Starbourne trying to tell us something? Was the weather a message? And if so, was it more than a simple distress signal? Maybe all he was trying to tell us was 'Hey! I'm alive and pretty freaking miserable! Come find me and rescue me!' It was also possible that he was being coerced into creating this weather for some unknown purpose.

"I can see where you might be going with this," I said, trying to will her to understand that I agreed with her even though we couldn't discuss the matter openly. "But I don't think we have the means to pursue it currently."

I watched Gray's face while she decoded my message. On some perverse level, I was actually enjoying the challenge. I was, however, beginning to have some sympathy for spies, criminals, and revolutionaries. If they had to communicate this way all the time, it was no wonder they were all so damn grumpy.

"I'll look into the matter privately," she said at last. "If I have time."

"I'd appreciate that," I said. "Has anyone learned anything about the thugs who tried to club me down?"

"Very little," Gray admitted. "We know that they are not citizens of Patchwork. We know that they entered the holdfast sometime within the last 48 hours. We do not know where they entered, or who brought them here."

"Brought them here," I mused. "How difficult is it to gain entry to Patchwork?"

"Extraordinarily," Gray replied without hesitation. "Only Pillars can bring someone over, and that authority devolves directly from my will. I have currently restricted access to humans, faerie folk, and goblins. Nothing else can enter this place without my direct and explicit action."

"No animals?" I asked.

"That is correct," Gray said. "Nor angels, nor devils, nor dragons, nor any other creatures of legend, myth, or other realm. Not even another Pillar can vouchsafe such an entity against my will."

I couldn't do Gray's one eyebrow trick, but I could throw them both up as well as the next guy. I did that now. Gray's will? Just how powerful was this woman? If she was personally maintaining the boundaries of Patchwork, how much else was she in direct control of? I decided it would be impolite to keep staring at her with my eyebrows up and my eyes all bugged out, so I decided to change the subject.

"That sounds good," I replied. "Next question: how long has each of the Pillars been in their position and how long before that did they come to Patchwork?"

"Hmm," said Gray thoughtfully. "Visivald has been here the shortest at five years. I recognized his potential very nearly straight away. He's held land here for more than four years."

Had it really been more than five years since the last time Baxter and I had been to see Visivald back on goblinside? I didn't want to believe that it had, but the evidence disagreed with my beliefs. Evidence can be a bitch that way.

"Your friend Kellidwyn has been for …"

"Eight years," I interrupted. "I know."

"Yes," drawled Gray. "So you do. She's held land for six, let's say six and a half years."

"Also a swift discovery?" I asked.

"The qualities that make one a good Pillar are easily recognized when one knows what to look for," Gray said by way of not really answering the question.

"Next would be dear Michelle," Gray continued. "The good doctor has been with us for nearly fifteen years, and has been a Pillar for over twelve."

"I like her," I said. "She's a fascinating character. You don't often meet someone with the courage to be as out there as she is."

Gray smiled, "She is far happier here than she was in the real world."

"I'm not surprised," I agreed. "The real world can be a difficult place for some of us."

"You might do well here yourself," Gray said.

"I believe you were about to tell me how long Gwynplaine had been here," I prompted.

"However did you know I was going to talk about Gwynplaine next?" Gray asked with what sounded like genuine curiosity.

Score one for the detective. Or score one rather for the con man. Human nature is fairly predictable, even when the human in question is a wizard. Gray would tell me about Starbourne as far into the list as possible. Some people would choose to organize the list out of respect for the victim; I'd do it that way because it was the most dramatic way to tell it. Either way, it didn't matter why, Gray would choose to talk about Starbourne last. Fizznorman was attached to Starbourne and Quatermain belonged to a family legacy. Therefore, Gray would choose to tell me about Gwynplaine next. Every now and then it's fun to play genius detective, even if it is a trick.

"Just a hunch," I said modestly. "It's a detective thing. Anyway, please go on."

"Gwynplaine is complicated," Gray said. "He's lived here more than once, but he doesn't seem to remember it. He's definitely the same man; he simply has no recollection of the years he lived here. We've given up on explaining it and we all write it off as one of the curiosities of a magical life."

"Or his personal time line is out of synch with yours and you're dealing with an earlier incarnation of the same man," I offered.

"Really now?" Gray laughed. "Isn't that a bit overly complicated for a first guess?"

"I know something you don't," I said airily. "He's got a date with a criminal history text book."

"Gwynplaine?" Gray practically hooted." A criminal? I find that hard to believe."

"Who knows for sure," I hedged. "Call it another hunch, then. Who's next?"

"Oswald of course," Gray said. "A member of his family has been a Pillar here in Patchwork since before I became Steward. And his child after him, I'm sure."

"Soon to be young Master Quatermain," I said knowingly.

"Yes quite," Gray said. "And Oswald a father for the first time at 90. It will be nice to hear the laughter of children in Aristarchus again after so long."

"Quatermain is 90?" I spluttered.

"Ah," Gray said mildly. "That's right, you didn't know. Although the citizens of Patchwork age normally – more or less – they do not weaken with age as people do in the real world."

"What do you mean by that?" I asked. "They age normally but don't weaken?"

"Just what I said," Gray said with a bit of a pedagogic flair. "A man's span of years is no longer here, but he will be healthful, vibrant, and vital for every day of it."

"That's bizarre," I observed. "But kind of cool!"

"Indeed," Gray smiled.

"And that leaves Starbourne and the motor-mouthed gnome," I said.

"Zachariah!" Gray snapped. "Please be more respectful. Algernon is a beautiful person. You shouldn't mock him for his disabilities."

"Disabilities?" I snorted. "Where I come from he's got a super power!"

"Be that as it may," Gray said, her voice losing its edge and heat as if by magic. "Please be more respectful. Algernon has only been a Pillar for twenty years. Regretfully, he served Peter as his chief domestic for fifteen years before we realized his ability."

I resisted the urge to say something about Fizznorman being overlooked, because I'm a better person than that. But from the look on her face I got the feeling that Gray knew what I was thinking. She had to give me at least some credit for not coming out and saying it, didn't she?

"And poor Peter," she said, keeping my unruly tongue at bay with a threatening eyebrow. "He has been at my side for well over 100 years. I hate to think how he must be …"

"Had been at your side," I corrected. "And how he must have suffered, I believe you mean."

"Oh," Gray said. "Yes, I do beg your pardon Zachariah. It is as you say. I hate to think how he must have suffered before his untimely death."

"What is Patchwork for?" I asked suddenly, derailing the conversation.

"I beg your pardon?" asked Gray, while once again displaying her excellent eyebrow skills.

Sometimes I do unworthy things. I admit it. I'm not proud, but I do at least try to make sure my actions serve a greater purpose. In this case, ambushing my friend Miss Gray was an unworthy act that I hoped would help me protect her friend's life. She had gone out of her way to mention that the Quatermains predated her, but I wasn't quite sure she wasn't fibbing a little. So I resolved to apologize to her later, but for now I pressed on with my impolite inquisition.

"This place can't have been easy to create or to maintain," I pressed. "There's no good reason for it to be as large or as complicated as it is. Why did you create it? Why do you maintain it?"

"I? Created Patchwork?" Gray sputtered. "Just how old do you think I am?!?"

"Um," I said cleverly.

"I will have you know," Gray said haughtily. "That I am 425 years of age. I am nowhere near as old as Patchwork, and in no way am I its creator."

"I would have sworn you weren't a day over 390," I said.

"*Hmph*," Gray muttered darkly.

"Okay, okay," I said. "It was the concussion talking, I swear. Can we move back to the topic?"

"Very well," Gray snipped. "What was the topic again?"

She crossed her arms beneath her breasts and her dark eyes bored into mine. Despite her words, I somehow suspected that she had not entirely forgiven my *faux pas*. If I were of a paranoid and suspicious nature, I would suspect that her snit was designed to distract me from the question. She was certainly giving me every opportunity to retract the question, change the topic, and generally not get the answers I was looking for. Unfortunately for her, I was more than willing to ignore the conventions of propriety when I was on the trail of knowledge.

"The topic was Patchwork and its purpose for existence," I said. "I can't figure it. The amount of energy required to keep this holdfast running ... it just doesn't add up. What am I missing?"

"Patience, forbearance, tact, and restraint," Gray commented tartly. "There are some questions that I cannot answer for you. At least not yet."

"Why not?" I asked.

Even to my own ears, it came out a little bit petulantly. It was obvious that Gray very much didn't want to be having this conversation, but I couldn't shake the notion that there was something important here. Maybe it was pertinent to the case, and maybe it wasn't, but I wouldn't know until I found it. Besides, I was in my sick bed. Surely I was allowed a little bit of petulance under the circumstances. Such rationalizations allowed me to stick to my guns where a lesser, or perhaps a more polite, man would have given in. I matched her stare with my own.

"Zachariah," Gray said at last. "There are forces in this world that no one can deny; not you, not me, not anyone. There is a time and a place for revelations. Let it suffice for now that Patchwork will serve a purpose – a significant purpose – in the struggle against Perdition. That purpose must not be revealed until the proper time or all might be lost. Can you please – for the time being, at least – accept that answer?"

Perdition? That was a curveball I didn't see coming. The two oldest forces in Creation were Salvation Above and Perdition Below. The two were locked in an eternal struggle for – amongst other things – the souls of all humanity. Salvation offered the promise of eternal bliss at some indeterminate point in the future if humanity would only hold to the compact. Perdition offered power, wealth, and certain less savory pleasures right away, in the here and the now, but the price was generally held to be rather higher than the value given. Still that didn't stop an endless horde of greedy idiots from begging the forces of Perdition for favors.

I had run afoul of the Duke of Sorrows, a ranking member of Perdition's aristocracy, more than once in my time, and he was – as Visivald recently reminded me – no devil to be trifled with. I had also tangled with the angel Carafael who seemed to be the Duke's opposite number in Salvation. Carafael had certainly had humanity's best interest in heart, but I was none too sure that he cared much one way or the other about me personally. And that was something of a sticking point for me. Still if I was forced to choose – and sooner or later, everyone was – there was no doubt in my mind which side I would have to come down on. I knew the Duke of Sorrows and his works too well to ever trust Perdition again.

"Okay," I said after thinking it through for a time. "I guess I can leave it at that. For now. But if it turns out that I need to know some of this stuff to solve the case, you and I will have words."

"That is well and fine," Gray agreed. "By my oath, I will share with you what knowledge I can as soon as I may."

That was an interesting choice of words on Gray's part. It implied that there was someone or something directly prohibiting her from telling me more. Was she prevented from telling this to anyone, or specifically to me? That was a fairly egotistical notion, but I'm a fairly egotistical man. I could certainly understand the notion of information containment and

I was already comfortable with the idea that we weren't secure here, but Gray seemed to be specifically concerned about the forces of Perdition getting wind of what we said. That didn't entirely jibe with her earlier confidence about the security of Patchwork's borders. Unless – and this was a sobering thought – there were humans, faeries, or goblins already in Patchwork that sympathized with Perdition.

"Okay," I said again. "Fine. Now can I please get out of this damn bed and back to work?"

"That much can certainly be arranged," Gray said.

"Good," I said. "I hate being useless."

"Waiting for the right time is not being useless," Gray scolded. "There will come a time and a place when you will find what you have been waiting for and that which has been waiting will find you. You and Patchwork both."

Chapter Eighteen

An interminably slow and frustrating two hours later, Adriana Gray's driverless coach dropped me off at the edge of Lord Gwynplaine's estate. There was an ornate gate and a high fence surrounding his lands. About a mile in the distance, I could clearly see the rambling Gothic monstrosity that Gwynplaine called home.

Gray's coach was much like Foucault's, but it was a perfectly respectable black color instead of the strange mauve-purple that the doctor preferred. Also, it was drawn by disturbingly intelligent and self-directed horses instead of disturbingly intelligent, self-directed griffs. I liked Gray's coach a little better; I wasn't entirely sure that Gray's horses wouldn't eat me if given half a chance, but I still felt a little bit safer than I did around the griffs and their razor-sharp beaks.

I rapped twice on the back of the coach. The horses snorted, stamped their hooves in the mud and clopped off down the road. Rain ran down the brim of my hat but didn't manage to get down the upturned collar of my coat, as I gazed up at the sheer enormity of Gwynplaine's home. It's crumbling walls and towers were liberally covered with ivy, while the central keep seemed to be mostly intact, but it was hard to tell for certain from this distance.

I sighed heavily for the benefit of no one other than myself. I slogged a short distance through the mud over to the front gate. Gray had told me that if I presented myself at the front gate I'd be noticed and, presumably, allowed entrance. I wasn't entirely sure what presenting myself meant, but

I was present and maybe that would be enough. I waited while nothing happened. I rapped on the gate. Nothing happened again.

"Hello?" I called out uncertainly. "It's Zack Monday. Adriana Gray might have mentioned that I'd be coming by?"

A fair amount of nothing continued to happen as I stood there getting steadily more soggy. At least the weather was warm. I pondered how long I should wait, what to do next, and how long it might be before Gray's coach came back to rescue me from extreme boredom and acute sogginess. I had the sense from meeting Gwynplaine earlier that this was just a little *comme il faut* style maneuvering on his part. He was home and he knew I was here. The lord of Gormenghul had done a lot of bragging earlier about how he knew everything that happened on his lands. And here I was literally on his doorstep.

I resigned myself to wait awhile. I'd dealt with ancestral aristocracy before, and I'd dealt with things that lived for centuries. Those experiences taught me two things about situations like this: Patience is very important and there are always rules. I learned how to fake patience and I pick up rules very quickly and on the fly if necessary. There are times to be a nuisance – and believe me, I could make a proper nuisance of myself at those times – but for now I was resigned. Mostly.

Eventually the gate rolled open, apparently of its own accord and to the sonorous tolling of bells. Lord Gwynplaine was definitely pulling out all the stops for me. I was honored, or at least I would have been, if it weren't raining. A dozen men in identical sack suits and moving in lock step came hustling up the cobblestone road that lay beyond the gate. Between them, they were carrying what looked for all the world like a portable gazebo. That is something I don't see very often, so I stood there watching as they marched up and deposited the gazebo on the ground in front of me.

"Master Monday," said one of the gazebo-delivering, identical suit-wearing men. "Please accept our lord's apologies. You are welcome in the hospitality of Gormenghul."

This all seemed just a little bit surreal to me, but I rolled with it. The men were obviously servants – or vassals – as Gwynplaine had so charmingly put it earlier. I guess the red carpet treatment around here included a team of ... what would I call these guys, gazebonauts, maybe?

Gazeboteers? I decided that I liked gazeboteers and resolved to think of them as such from now on.

"Should I step inside the gazebo, then?" I asked casually.

"The palanquin, yes. If you please," the gazeboteer agreed with a smile and a nod of encouragement.

I shrugged, 'When in Patchwork, step inside the gazebo,' as I always say. I stepped inside the gazebo. As I did so, a wave of warm, dry air washed over me. After being out in the elements for so long, it was like being wrapped in the warmest, softest, driest towel ever. Immediately, both my clothes and my person were perfectly dry and I was very comfortable. This was better than the best sunbeam ever. If I had been a cat, I would have curled up purring for hours. Fortunately, I am not a cat; I also resisted the urge to yawn, stretch or preen, but not without some effort.

The ground pitched slightly beneath me, but not badly enough to unbalance me. I felt a sense of organic motion, like a slow moving horse or a boat on calm waters. As I looked around I felt a vertigo that was growing unpleasantly familiar. The gazeboteers had picked up the gazebo, with me inside, and were marching back up the cobblestones at top speed. My ride remained smooth and pleasant and I found it easier to look at my feet until we came to a stop.

From outside my gazebo sanctuary, the immense, mostly ruined structure loomed hugely before me. I hopped out into what I expected to be wind and rain, but was pleased to notice that we were under a roof. It didn't even seem to be leaking, although from the looks of it, I couldn't figure out why not. The gazeboteer who had spoken earlier, indicated an open sally gate to the side of the huge wooden doors. The doors were covered with an intricate swirl of carvings that looked magical to me, but I couldn't figure out their purpose. I nodded to the lead gazeboteer before taking his directions and going in.

I found myself in a small and cozy library. Every surface was filled with books, including the tables, the desk, and parts of the floor. The room was lit by candles, all sealed inside glass lamps and hanging from the ceiling at regular intervals. There didn't seem to be any doors into or out of the room other than the one that I had just come through.

That was odd. I looked around. It was definitely a small and cozy library. I turned around and saw the door; overwhelmed with curiosity,

I ducked back through. I was standing outside the castle with the rain and the wind. I shook my head a little and walked back inside the library.

Gwynplaine was sitting behind the desk. Had he been there before and I had simply missed him amongst the stacks? He was wearing a burgundy smoking jacket and a matching smoking hat. He was smoking out of a silver cigarette holder and exhaling blue-gray smoke that rose to the low ceiling where it formed a small carcinogenic cloud that swirled in strange eddies and whorls above his head. He was as cadaverously thin as I remembered him to be, but the peculiar hat covered his Bela Lugosi hairline.

"It's smaller on the inside," I observed.

Gwynplaine's hand rose languidly to the cigarette holder; he removed it very carefully from between his teeth and he exhaled slowly. The smoke rose up to join the cloud.

"Clever," he said. "But no, what's actually happened is that I diverted your path from one doorway to another."

He waited a moment, perhaps for me to stare wildly around in shock or disbelief. I declined and instead took the time to read some book titles. Most of them seemed to be in French. I don't know any French, but I had some ideas. Words like *sorcellerie, puissance, thaumaturgie,* and *rituel* just sort of jumped out at me.

"That doorway right there," said Gwynplaine as he gestured with his cigarette holder towards the door behind me.

I smiled benignly at him. This was part of a tactic I often used to good effect, the slow count. I slowly counted in my head and didn't say anything until someone else spoke first. It was the only way to gain the respect of immortal powers, and it didn't work too badly on the mortal ones either. Gwynplaine had screwed around with me on his front doorstep, and now it was my turn.

"Do you need me to explain it to you any further or can we move along?" Gwynplaine asked.

"I'm fine," I assured him.

I gave him my blankly affable look and restarted my internal count. After a mere thirty counts, Gwynplaine was fidgeting and edgy. I had arranged the meeting, Gray had gotten him to agree to it, and now he wasn't quite sure what to do next. I was reasonably certain that Gray could get anyone one in Patchwork to do anything she wanted anytime she wanted. Gray had probably made him promise to answer my questions. His nobleman's pride had been wounded and so he had launched the stranded-at-the-front-door offensive. I was striking back with my not-doing-anything gambit. It was my hope that the conflict would end here, but I was prepared to escalate if I had to. I had 'pushy' and 'rather rude' in my arsenal and I wasn't afraid to use them.

"Very well," he said slowly and uncertainly. "How may I be of service to you, then?"

"Ah!" I exclaimed happily. "I'm so glad you asked. I was hoping that you could answer some questions for me."

"What kind of questions?" he asked, his eyes narrowing.

"A variety," I answered. "Mostly about Mr. Starbourne, as I'm sure you'd imagine, but I also need to learn more about Patchwork and your place in it."

"I must admit to some confusion," Gwynplaine said. "Haven't you spoken to your partner?"

"My partner?" I asked. "What about him?"

"He came by yesterday," Gwynplaine drawled slowly. "And questioned me quite thoroughly. Perhaps it would be best if the two of you compared notes more often?"

It's not terribly often that I find myself lost for words. Something wasn't right here. There was flat out no way that Baxter had arrived in Patchwork without contacting me. At the very least, I'd have heard about it from Gray. Gwynplaine had no reason to lie to me, and I'm a good judge of that sort of thing and he wasn't showing any of the usual tells. What was going on here?

"My partner isn't in Patchwork, Lord Gwynplaine," I said. "Can you describe the person you spoke to?"

Gwynplaine eyed me suspiciously. He was suddenly unsure of himself and clearly this was uncomfortable territory for him. Now he was trying to figure out what my angle was. Which was a good question from his perspective and also solid confirmation that he wasn't trying to work an angle on me.

"Average height and build," he began. "A lot like you actually. Your skin tone, dark hair like yours. Less gray around the temples, perhaps he's a few years younger than you are. In fact, I had assumed he was a younger relative of yours; the resemblance between the two of you is remarkable."

"He's not with me, whoever he is," I said. "He wasn't a local?"

"Certainly not," Gwynplaine replied with a sniff. "I know everyone who makes Patchwork their home. There have been a few unauthorized passages recently. Perhaps it was one of them?"

"I think I met up with those fellows," I said ruefully. "And they were a lot bigger than me."

"Well, at least now we know it wasn't one of us who killed Peter," Gwynplaine said.

"I think that's a bit of a stretch," I said. "It certainly opens up the field a bit, I admit. What kind of questions did this guy ask?"

"Mostly he asked me about my movements on the night Peter was killed," Gwynplaine answered. "He was really quite earnest and his questions bordered on the impolite from time to time. I had planned to mention his impertinence to you as his superior, but now that I realize he was an impostor, his behavior makes more sense. Clearly he is involved with the murder in some way and was looking to cast blame on the innocent. I'm no detective, Mr. Monday, but it seems to me that if you find this scoundrel you'll be a good way along in solving your case."

"Well I sure do want to have a few words with him," I admitted. "Listen, this is all fascinating, and certainly important, but I do still need to ask you some questions. I apologize for the inconvenience, but could we do the interview anyway?"

Gwynplaine's hollow face screwed up in an expression of distaste. I wondered idly whether he was in charge of all the creepy things in Patchwork. Somebody had to watch out for the creeps, after all. I resisted the urge to smirk at the image of Gwynplaine patiently and methodically creating all the creepy things, cobwebs in corners, spooky trees, and small creatures that scuttled and skittered. He looked like he'd be good at that job.

"Oh by all means," Gwynplaine said, languid sarcasm positively dripping from his words. "Let's do."

"Thanks," I said doing my best to ignore the sarcasm. "Since the other guy already tried your patience on one of the subjects I'm interested in, let's focus on the other. Can you explain – briefly – what it is you do as a Pillar of Patchwork?"

"I assume you are looking for an explanation in layman's terms?" Gwynplaine drawled.

"That is a safe assumption," I said, graciously.

"Very well," Gwynplaine sighed as if gathering the energy to pound knowledge into my thick head was almost more than he could manage. "In the simplest terms possible, I maintain reality."

"Can I get you to expand on that a little?" I asked after waiting a few moments.

"I'll try," Gwynplaine sighed. "But I doubt it will make much sense to you. Nothing that you think of as real happens naturally here. The sun does not rise at dawn, except that I will it so. Gravity does not weigh you down until I decide that it does. The air provides no sustenance to your lungs and no oxygen to your blood, but that I declare it so. Do you understand any of what I'm saying?"

"I believe I do," I replied. "That must be quite a burden. How long have you performed this service for Patchwork?"

"It has ever been the burden of the truly gifted to exercise those gifts, no matter the challenge," Gwynplaine replied loftily. "Lady Gray and the people of this land have honored me with this responsibility for twenty years and a half score of months. Although I should note that at some point I am destined to leave this place and to return to it earlier. I wouldn't expect you to understand that either."

I decided not to trouble Gwynplaine's evaluation of me, and my place in his world by disagreeing or arguing with his preconceptions. I didn't really need the ego boost and it sometimes helps to be underestimated. Don't get me wrong; I was impressed by Gwynplaine's job description, I just wasn't much impressed by his personality. He might have been overstating the case or inflating his own position a little, but I didn't think he was. I knew enough about how holdfasts worked at this point to make sense of what he was saying. The question wasn't 'Is someone making sure the laws of physics work the same way every day', it was 'Is Gwynplaine that guy.' I had no compelling reason to doubt that he was. I had to admit, the bit where he diverted the doorway was also pretty compelling.

I asked a few more questions, mostly to confirm things I had already learned from Gray, Visivald, and Fizznorman. Getting different perspectives was important, but to be honest, my heart really wasn't in it. I was preoccupied by the idea of the other guy running around asking the same questions that I was asking. Had Gray hired competition? That didn't seem likely, but it had to be ruled out. Something didn't add up and that meant I needed more information, information I wasn't likely to get from Lord Gwynplaine.

He was as eager to be rid of me as I was to be on my way, so it wasn't too hard to disengage myself. In relatively short order, I was shaking his skeletal hand and ducking back out the magical mystery door that currently led to the courtyard of Castle Gormenghul. The gazeboteers were there waiting for me. Had they been there all this time or had they hustled into position while I was making my excuses to their master?

I pondered such irrelevancies as I rode the gazebo express back to Gwynplaine's front gate. When we arrived, I was pleasantly surprised to see Gray's driverless coach waiting for me. I thanked the gazeboteers and wished them well. The fellow who had talked once or twice gave me a jaunty salute and a conspiratorial wink, then they picked up their gazebo and trucked off back to where ever they hung out when they weren't carrying me around.

I climbed into the coach and asked to be taken to Lady Gray's tower. The horses seemed eager enough to oblige me and so we trotted off. I hauled out my trusty notebook and wrote stuff down. I had no idea what any of the stuff I was recording actually meant, but I had hope that it would all come together sooner or later. Even if it didn't, I would at least have something to say for myself when Gray asked how I had been spending my time and her money. If I had competition for the job, that last part might become more important.

In shorter order than I had expected, the coach rolled up to Gray's tower. As I approached, the stone wavered like a heat mirage and a door appeared where only stone had been a moment ago. I walked in without preamble because I was getting tired of standing around in the rain. I took off my hat and coat but once again elected to hold onto my travel bag; I was trying to stay friends with it, after all. Gray strolled in to the foyer as I was about this task; she waited politely while I finished, her thin smile comfortably in place.

"So," I asked conversationally. "I don't suppose you hired somebody else to do my job while I was racked up in bed, did you?"

"Certainly not," Gray said, giving me the eyebrow. "Why ever would you think that?"

"Because somebody is going around asking people the same questions I am," I said. "I just got back from Gormenghul and Gwynplaine told me he got interviewed by some other guy Monday afternoon. You definitely didn't send anyone around?"

"I assure you Zachariah," Gray tutted. "I did not."

"Perdition," I swore quietly. "That's what I was afraid of. We've got another player on the field. I need backup. Can you get a message to Baxter Kline for me?"

"Certainly," Gray said. "Please speak clearly and slowly; I will relay your words and Baxter will hear them within the hour."

"Oh," I said momentarily nonplussed. "I thought you'd have to prepare."

Gray looked at me expectantly but said nothing.

"Right," I stalled. "Baxter, it's me – Zack – I need you to get yourself to Patchwork as soon as you can. Things have gotten interesting and I need backup. Send a message to Tim if you can – the usual method – and close up shop."

Gray remained impassive but attentive while I tried to think if I had missed anything.

"Oh," I added. "And have him grab one or two of my neckties if you don't mind. I'm tired of the informal look."

Gray rolled her eyes exasperatedly. Why does everyone do that?

Chapter Nineteen

Rationalizations are vitally important to my sanity, functionality, and stability. One of my favorite rationalizations is the firmly-held belief that everybody relies just as heavily on a good rationalization as I do. If this isn't actually true, I don't want to know the truth. There are some mysteries that even I don't want to solve.

Right now I was telling myself that putting off my interview with Kelli was a good and logical plan. Somewhere deep in my brain of brains, I knew this wasn't true. My prior experiences with Kelli made her an excellent candidate for interviewing. I would have a better chance of reading her body language and tells, a better idea of whether she was lying to me or not, and that would provide me with a valuable baseline I could use to test the other suspect's stories against.

But that ship had sailed and I was rapidly running out of non-Kelli suspects to interview. Sooner or later, I was going to have to face her. But that didn't mean I had to like it. In fact, I would have rather gone nine more rounds with the Club Brothers than be someplace alone and private with my ex-girlfriend. Some tough guy I turned out to be.

It was sort of funny, in one of those not-at-all-laughable kinds of funny; I was just about getting the hang of dating two women. Audrey and Carin were wonderful, smart, funny, driven, and powerful women; I was honored to be part of their lives. The fact that they wanted me in their beds was a source of constant wonder and joy to me. The fact that they gave each other space and respect and that we were all (mostly) willing to share nicely with each other was nothing short of miraculous.

The idea of potentially adding another relationship to my life was simply terrifying. Where would I even find the time, let alone the emotional resources and energy to date a third person? That was easy. Nowhere. It simply wasn't an option.

So why did I find myself thinking constantly about Kelli? Why was I remembering all the good parts of our time together and none of the bad? Why did I have a case of school boy nerves whenever I considered going to talk with her? The answer to that was easy, too. I was an idiot. There was still hope: If we were all very lucky, Kelli wasn't an idiot. She'd be helpful, polite, and totally innocent of all charges, but distant and professional. This behavior would make it abundantly clear to me that the past was the past and we would be able to look forward to a warm and utterly platonic friendship. That was the plan. It was a good plan.

I kept repeating these thoughts over and over again, mantra-like, as I rode Adriana Gray's driverless coach to Coldiron Keep. I had no idea where I was going, but I trusted the horses to find their way. With the front of my mind occupied, I let the accumulated facts of the case simmer on the metaphorical back burners of my brain's metaphorical stovetop. The soup was still a little thin. I needed more ingredients; I needed a recipe to put them all together in a way that made sense. Most of all I needed a better metaphor.

I wondered what Coldiron Keep would look like. So far I had visited crumbling gothic ruins, black marble towers, underground fortresses, Victorian hunting lodges, and two different sprawling country manors. What would Kelli's dream house look like? The name suggested something medieval and pretentious, but I had my money on post-modern.

Kelli had collected clippings and scraps from magazines and newspapers that intrigued her. She rarely did anything with what she collected. It all mostly lived in a shoebox, but every now and then, she'd take them all out and look at them. It wasn't all house stuff, but a lot of it was. She also collected pictures of clothing, jewelry, paintings, sculptures, architecture; there wasn't much she wouldn't take a scissors to and shove in that box. I'd get occasional tours of the box's contents. She'd spread it all out on my bed and explain to me why she'd grabbed each individual clip and what it meant to her. A lot of it had just sort of washed over me and been forgotten over the years, but I did recall her fondness for modern architecture.

I had learned not to look out the coach windows; the blurred terrain whipping past hadn't yet failed to cause me vertigo. So it was somewhat of a surprise to me when the coach rapidly slowed, executed a sharp turn and pulled up to a stop. I gathered myself up, opened up the door and hopped out into the rain. I was getting a bit tired of the rain, so I resolved to stop mentioning it, in the hopes that it would eventually get the idea and just go away. The horses snorted and stamped their hooves a little, rousing me from my contemplations. I looked around and locked eyes with the closer horse. He was looking at me quite pointedly. It was a little bit odd to say the least and I stared dumbfounded for a moment. Then I realized that the horses were politely waiting for me to tell them that they could go.

"Oh," I said, feeling a little bit embarrassed by my rudeness. "Thanks. You guys can go now. I'll be done here in a couple of hours."

The horse snorted again and began describing a small circle to turn around.

"Thanks," I said again.

The horses got the coach sorted out and they trotted off back the way we had come. I turned around and laid eyes on Coldiron Keep for the first time. I lost my bet with myself. It wasn't post-modern. It wasn't medieval and pretentious either. It was a perfectly normal three-storey Colonial, complete with gables, neatly manicured lawn, and white picket fence. Painted a pale blue color, it wouldn't have looked one whit out of place in the suburbs just outside New Jerusalem. I genuinely did not see that coming.

I squidged my way through the mud and over to the front door and, lacking any better idea, rang the doorbell. There was a thump and a scrape from within that sounded like someone getting up and out of a chair swiftly. I could hear a bit of a commotion and possibly more than one person moving around inside. A moment later, the light over the door went on, followed by the door opening. I could see Kelli's tiny form silhouetted against the glow from within. Which was odd, because it was daytime and even with the rain, it should have been a bit darker inside. Magic always pops up in the weirdest little ways.

"Hi Zack," Kelli said. "Welcome to Coldiron Keep. C'mon in."

She retreated back from the door to allow me entrance, a fact of which I took swift advantage. As I stepped inside, I had a brief sense of being inside a plain, unadorned box. I got a flash of pale yellow featureless walls. But it was only for the briefest of moments. It was a normal looking house. I was in the foyer and there was a perfectly respectable hat stand and coat rack. I racked my coat and stood my hat while Kelli waited politely. When I was done, I turned to her and we both smiled awkwardly and didn't say anything for an uncomfortable few seconds.

"Well," said Kelli. "This is awkward and uncomfortable."

"I was just thinking the exact same thing," I said agreeably.

"Right," she laughed. "You always could read my mind."

"I am not a mind reader," I objected. "I am a student of human nature."

"And I'm not human," she countered.

"A great ship captain," I began, adopting a stentorian tone. "Once said 'everybody's human.'"

"Nice one," Kelli said wryly. "For a crunchy."

I affected a huge wince of pain, held a hand to my forehead in dramatic fashion, and generally carried on. 'Crunchy' was a popular derogatory term for a human being. It was mostly used by goblins and faeries and I believe it derived from our fragility and short life span relative to members of those races. It didn't hold much sting for me. I had never been the subject of damaging racism. It was my experience, living in the world, that the goblins took most of the heat. After all, we humans were here first – even though the faeries claimed they were older than humanity – and it was our world. The faeries didn't suffer from racism much either. At least the ones who looked like humans, only prettier, didn't.

Kelli let me ham it up for a while. She was laughing at my antics and I was remembering how much I liked it when she laughed at my jokes. Eventually, our mirth subsided and we were smiling at each other again. But this time the discomfort was gone.

"Let's sit down and talk," Kelli said. "Can I get you anything?"

"I'd love a cup of coffee," I admitted. "It's been a long day."

"And you fresh out from Michelle's care," Kelli said. "And if you're anything like I remember, I'm guessing before she wanted to let you go."

"Guilty as charged," I admitted.

She led us down a short hallway and into an oval-shaped room with a couch, a love seat, and two armchairs. They all looked quite comfortable. I plopped myself down into one of the chairs and she took the couch directly across from it and perched on the edge of one cushion. She waved her arms dramatically and a coffee service rolled in apparently under its own power. It came to stop between us and I helped myself to a cup of the True. There were tiny bottles of single malt whiskey next to the cream and the sugar but I resisted the temptation.

"Would you like a cup?" I asked.

"Yes, please," Kelli replied brightly. "An afternoon without coffee is like a day without sunshine. Cream, sugar, and a wee drop of the Talisker."

I fixed our coffees, handed Kelli hers and set mine aside to cool. The delicious aroma of good coffee filled the room and I breathed it in happily. Soulful guitar music strummed from some hidden source. I recognized the song; it was one we used to listen to often back in the day. I wondered if she had chosen the music purposefully to remind me of those times. It was the sort of thing I'd do, but it wasn't the sort of thing the Kelli I remembered would think of. The burning question before me remained: was this the Kelli I remembered? Eight years is a long time; people change.

Kelli smiled at me as she sipped her coffee. She closed her eyes as a rapturous expression came over her face. When Kelli did something, she did it all the way. Right now she was enjoying her coffee and to all external evidence, that was all she was doing. No thought, no distraction, no niggling little worries about the thousands of other things that always came between me and whatever it was I was supposed to be doing. I envied her that ability. I always had.

"So," I said ungracefully. "I'm going around and asking everyone a bunch of pushy and intrusive questions that might or might have anything to do with Peter Starbourne's murder."

"And it's my turn in the barrel?" Kelli asked brightly.

"Pretty much," I agreed.

"Okay Mr. Big Shot Detective Man," she said. "Grill me."

"Let's start with the basics," I said. "You're a Pillar. Tell me what that means. What do you do around here?"

Kelli laughed. A lot of people talk about laughter being musical; her laughter was musical in the way that only faerie laughter can be. It made me think of waterfalls and rolling green hills. It also made me think of picnics and beds with rumpled sheets, but that was a distraction I really didn't need right now.

"Not much," she said after her laughter had subsided. "I maintain a couple hundred acres of land, and sometimes I support Gwynplaine when he has something simple that needs doing. I'm no heavy hitter, that's for sure. I don't have Adriana's knowledge, Gwynplaine's control, or even Visivald's raw power. Really, some days I don't think I do much around here at all."

I resisted the sudden and surprisingly powerful urge to comfort and defend Kelli against her own insecurities. That was so very much not my job here. I covered by jotting down some inconsequential notes. Good old notebook, it had gotten me out of more than a few scrapes over the years.

"What's it like working with Gwynplaine?" I asked. "After all those years of studying him and all the other master criminals?"

Kelli froze for just a second and her eyes darted around as if she were looking for a way out of the room, or at very least out of the conversation. But it was only for a moment. If I hadn't been expecting some kind of reaction, I'd surely have missed it. She tried to cover by taking another sip of coffee. I took the cue and sampled my own cup. It was still too hot, but I took one for the team and risked a tiny slurp.

"You mean a member of his family," she said.

"Sure," I allowed. "What's that like?"

"Well, incredible, right?" she didn't pause for me to answer. "He's told me so much about his home and what his family is like. The insights are …"

"Incredible?" I prompted.

"Exactly!" she effused.

"I mean sure, he's a bit of jerk sometimes," she said thoughtfully. "But that's mostly just the culture he grew up in. We come from different worlds, quite literally different worlds. There would have to be some friction just finding ways to communicate with each other."

"Sure," I said supportively.

"And the opportunity," she continued with barely a pause. "To work with a man … so much like the man we studied! It almost makes everything we went through worthwhile."

There had been a pause there. It definitely wasn't my imagination. She had been about to say something else. Had she wanted to say *the* man we studied? Did she believe that this Gwynplaine was destined to become the master thief of our history? I was pretty sure he was. But it almost didn't matter what the truth would end up being. Or at the very least it almost didn't matter right now.

"Tell me about what it was like for you when you first got here," I prompted, taking a generous gulp of my coffee.

"Oh," Kelli said, putting her hand to her mouth. "It was … it was like nothing I had ever experienced before. Going from all that stress and excitement and danger with you in New Jerusalem to this idyllic, magical existence. I think I had some kind of breakdown really. It was all so strange. I was always freaking out; looking for danger that simply wasn't there. I couldn't sleep. I lost weight.

"You what?" I asked. "How do you lose weight? You're barely there as it is!"

She laughed again, "I'm tougher than I look."

"You don't have to tell me that," I said. "I'd have you at my back in any fight, anywhere, any time."

Kelli actually blushed at that, which made me uncomfortable by proxy. I refreshed our coffees so no one had to say anything for a little while. But I could only be so worried about her feelings. Or so I kept telling myself.

"How did you discover your ability to … whatever it is you Pillars do," I asked.

"It was little things at first," she answered. "Things just went a little bit better than they had any right to do. I got places faster than I should have. Knives didn't get dull no matter how much I used them. Everything was just too easy all the time. It actually made me a little paranoid at first. I thought someone powerful was following me around, spying on me, and doing things for me."

"Someone like Gwynplaine?" I asked.

"Yeah," she said harshly. "Yeah, okay. You got me, Zack. I thought it was Gwynplaine. Happy now? I admit it."

"Um," I said cleverly. "No, honestly, no. That wasn't what I was trying to get at. Sorry. Really. Can you tell me more about discovering your powers?"

"Ha," Kelli laughed. "I really don't think of them as 'powers.' It's more like a responsibility … a burden or something. It's like having to do math problems in your head all the time, just to keep the world from blowing up. And it's getting harder."

"Since Starbourne died?" I asked.

"No," she said. "That's the funny thing. It hasn't gotten any harder at all since poor Peter was killed. Things got – what did Visivald call it? Slippery – about eight months ago and it's been that way ever since. You'd think losing Peter would have made it worse, but it didn't. I have no idea what's going on."

I felt a stab of guilt, keeping her in the dark about Starbourne still being alive, if missing, but information control was still the best way to keep him alive. I toughed it out. She was giving me good information here, and mentioning details that no one else had. I told myself that it would all be worthwhile when we got Starbourne home safe. I told myself a lot of things, but no matter how hard I tried, I never managed to believe my own lies. Being a jerk was still jerky, even if it was for a good cause.

"How do you know when it got slippery?" I pressed. "Did something specific happen around that time that made you aware of the problem?"

"No," Kelli said a little bit too quickly and forcefully. "There wasn't anything specific. It just all got harder. I remember it because I wrote it down in my journal. That's all."

"Okay," I said. "Thanks, Kell. You've given me a lot of good information here. You've helped a lot."

She smiled and I felt crappy. She'd lied to me. She'd just lied right to my face. The only question – and it was a big damn question – was why? Was she protecting somebody? Was she protecting herself? I was absolutely certain that she had nothing to do with Starbourne's disappearance. But she was hiding something that bothered her, something she felt guilty about. Well that made two of us I guess.

I wanted to be honest with Kelli. I wanted to sit down with her like regular folks. I wanted to talk over old times with her. I wanted to ask her questions that didn't have ulterior motives. Sometimes my job really sucked.

Chapter Twenty

Per Dr. Foucault's strict orders I was on a short work day, so Gray wouldn't hear of taking me anywhere but back to her tower after my 'obviously stressful' interview with Kellidwyn. I argued quite stridently for going back to talk with Quatermain again. My arguments were to no avail. Between the doctor and the wizard, I had no control over the situation at all. The most irksome part of it all was how right they both were. I really was exhausted, and the headache that had started when the club brothers had come a' pummeling was approaching epic proportions. And so it was that I half-walked, half-stumbled back to Gray's tower at the embarrassingly respectable hour of 4 o'clock in the afternoon.

Shortly after we got back, the lady of the house ceremoniously fobbed me off on a young gentleman named Tad. Tad was one of the people wandering around Gray's tower that I thought of as helpful houseguests. He looked to be maybe all of seventeen years old, and a particularly scrawny seventeen at that. But it didn't pay to assume anything around here. For all I knew he could be a thousand year-old vampire in treatment trying to kick the blood habit. I peered at him suspiciously.

"You're not a thousand year-old vampire, are you?" I asked.

"Nope," he replied. "I'm a seventeen year-old science major at Cal Tech. I'm interning for Lady Gray."

"And part of your job is ushering me around?" I asked somewhat taken aback.

Tad shrugged, "First off, it's the best paying internship, period. But secondly, I'm learning more about combined field theory helping Lady Gray out in her lab than I have in three semesters. I'm pretty happy with the job."

"You're seventeen," I said. "How many semesters have you been at Cal Tech?"

"I'll be graduating next year, sir," he said, very politely.

"Well," I said. "Can't argue with that. Lead on, Tad; lead on!"

Tad led us up a spiral staircase to the less public areas of the tower and into the rooms set aside for me. I sat in my chosen comfortable chair and started flipping through my notes. Tad waited for a moment to make sure I wouldn't – I don't know, explode or something – before making his excuses and assuring me that he was a mere pull of the cord away. I thanked him for his excellent service.

I sat there and tried to put what I knew into some kind of coherent system. I had gathered a lot of information, but I didn't know what it all meant. The counterfeit statues were at the heart of the matter, I was certain of that much. Someone here in Patchwork was making them and selling or otherwise distributing them to a variety of different homes in Patchwork. From what I had learned during the Malcolm Howard murder case, at least a dozen of them had been somehow smuggled into New Jerusalem. Were they being sold for profit, or being planted for some other reason?

Starbourne was wrapped up in it somehow. Either he stumbled onto the perpetrators or he was in it with them and they had a falling out. The second case was less likely but it couldn't be completely dismissed yet. Whoever was behind the statuettes was probably behind the killnapping as well. Knowing who that whoever was might give me a leg up on finding where the poor guy was stashed. So cracking the counterfeit/smuggling ring was the next step to finding Starbourne.

But I couldn't ignore the other guy, the one who had questioned Gwynplaine while I was *non compos corpus*. He might be working for the counterfeiters or he might represent a different faction entirely. I hoped that last option wasn't the case because it would make my life more complicated than I wanted it to be. Unfortunately, crime was rarely accommodating to my hopes.

A bell tolled from some non-specific location. I was just about to leap gracefully to my feet when the door opened and Gray walked into the room. She had changed outfits and was now wearing a conservative black blouse, a black A-line skirt, black granny boots, and a traditional pointy witch hat. It looked very much like what she had been wearing when I first saw her in back in the Old City.

"What's – ?" I started to ask.

"Nothing to concern yourself about," she interrupted gently. "Please stay seated and relaxed. We're about to receive guests."

The bell tolled more rapidly and louder and the room started to get brighter. I looked at the witchlamps, but the light wasn't coming from them; it was coming from a spot in the middle of the room. As Gray and I watched, the brightness became a glow, the glow became a glare, and two figures stepped out. One was average height and slender, the other was short and incredibly stocky. They were silhouetted and I couldn't make out their features but I knew those shapes. I'd know them anywhere. It was Baxter and Tim. My friends were here.

Tim was wearing a black and white bowling shirt with embroidered flames all over it and baggy black cargo shorts. His exposed arms and legs were liberally tattooed as was his neck. I had seen Tim without his shirt on a time or two, and I knew that the ink on his neck was part of an extended piece of work that covered most of his torso. His right eyebrow, left nostril, and lower lip were all pierced and I had long ago lost count of the piercings decorating his ears. His head was covered more or less uniformly with dark stubble except for a platinum-blond soul patch covering most of his chin. And lastly he carried around an ancient ruck sack, slung precariously over one shoulder. Over the years, I'd rarely seen the warlock without the ancient canvas construct, and I'd seen him pull the most amazing things out of it.

"Oi!" shouted Tim in his high and reedy voice, "Is everybody decent?"

That last was pretty much what Tim shouted whenever he entered a room. It was his version of, 'Hi, how are you?' and what his voice lacked in timbre and tone he more than made up for with gusto and volume.

Tim was just that kind of guy, and you forgave him for it, mostly. Master of the social niceties or not, Tim was a great friend in the clutch and had saved my life at least twice, probably more. Also, I had once been able to walk up to him and declare that I had come back from the future and I needed his help to save the past. Moments like that create a bond.

"Gentlemen," Gray said with frosty politeness. "Perhaps you'd like to explain why you've barged into my home without asking permission? To say nothing of disturbing my guest's much needed bed rest."

"Lady Gray," Baxter began in his deep goblin-rumble. "I'm sorry to barge in like this, but we got word that Zack was in trouble, so we came running. Tim here knew a spell that would rip through the Mists without having to muck around with the locals, but it required a direct connection."

"'At's roight," agreed Tim. "I used a bit of Zack that'd he left lying about in his boudoir. And as for bursting in? Well, I'm afraid that's just sort of a warlock thing."

"Yes," Gray said slowly, sarcasm dripping off each word. "I can see that it is. Well, no harm done, and three-fold return. Have your little chat with Zachariah, but please don't tire him out. He has a concussion."

"Aye?" Tim asked. "An' I've got a brace of healing draughts. What's the problem?"

Tim reached inside his rucksack and began rummaging around ostentatiously.

"The problem," Gray snapped. "Is that applying healing draughts to people with a concussion is a bad idea. We have studies that show serious trauma is likely to result."

"What?" Tim replied angrily.

I could see that Tim and Gray were ramping up to a serious argument. It wasn't entirely surprising. Tim was a warlock and Gray was a wizard. The two of them didn't agree on a single thing about magic. Not how it worked, where it came from, or what it was for. Both of them could manipulate reality to their wills, but neither of them agreed, fundamentally, on what reality actually was.

"Guys," I said.

I had meant to say it loudly and with force, but it came out quiet and with kind of a warble. It was the voice of a man to be reckoned without. I cleared my throat with a kind of desperation. All three of the others turned to look at me. If I couldn't be commanding, at least I could be manipulatively pathetic.

"Guys," I repeated a bit more loudly. "I really don't have a lot of energy right now. How about we table this discussion and get on with the larger issues at hand?"

"I'm game," said Tim agreeably. "I vote for giving Zack a healing draught!"

"Not this again," I groaned. "Tim! I mean we're not going to talk about it anymore."

"Oh," said Tim calmly. "Why didn't you say so?"

Grey turned slowly to look fully at Tim. To his credit, Tim maintained a perfect deadpan under the wizard's scrutiny. She gave Tim the eyebrow of death but Tim just stared back in a blandly agreeable fashion.

"Impossible man," Gray snorted at last. "You have fifteen minutes before you will be gone from my tower. Use that time as you will."

"Thanks Lady Gray," I said by way of making peace. "It really is important. And it's my fault not theirs."

Gray made a noise that sounded exactly like 'harrumph.' She did it without moving her mouth at all which was kind of impressive. The wizard turned to leave the room. The door swept open before her and she stepped forward.

"And Baxter Kline is it?" she asked over her shoulder. "Zachariah has told me many good things about you. Don't let your association with this man make your partner a liar."

And with that, she strode out the door. The door, of course, slammed shut dramatically right behind her. I had to give the wizard points for an impressive exit. I guess she was learning a thing or two from me after all.

"Everyone ready to get to work yet?" I asked.

"No need to get shirty," Tim said testily. "Just looking after me mate. Her Ladyship might be right about this concussion business, I'll look into it. But I ain't gonna take her word for it, am I?"

"Bax?" I said, trying to head off Tim's escalating anti-wizard rant. "Anything interesting happening back in New Jeru?"

"Meh," rumbled the goblinblood. "Some mooks with clubs tried to take me out."

"Huh," I mused. "That exact same thing happened to me. Must have been revenge for a job we worked on together. So what happened?"

"What do you think happened?" Baxter said, showing me his tombstone grin. "But they got away."

I briefly considered sulking but decided it was too unmanly, even for a guy on his sick bed. Then I remembered the reason I was on my sick bed was that I got beat up. Again.

"Tim," I said, changing the subject as best I could. "What did you do with Eel? Was he with you?"

"Too right," Tim agreed happily. "I was takin' 'im 'round, seein' the sights, an' meetin' some in'erestin' folk."

"And where is he now?" I asked.

"Stayin' with Audrey in New Jeru," Tim said.

"Good," I sighed.

It's not like Eel couldn't take care of himself; he really could. In most ways he was a fully-functional adult. He just reacted strongly to certain stimuli. Sin, mostly. And sometimes his reactions were violent. We were working through it, but some things were just sunk too deeply to be easily overcome. I was glad the half-angel was with friends.

"So there's an impostor posing as you, Boss?" Baxter asked, interrupting my thoughts.

"More or less," I replied, bringing myself back to the here and now. "There's someone described as bearing a strong resemblance to me, going around asking the same sort of questions I've been asking."

"And finding this other guy is the top priority?" Tim asked sharply.

"Exactly," I said in agreement.

At the same moment, I held out two fingers in front of my face and then pointedly lay my hand across my lap with the two fingers still splayed. This was a signal the three of us had long rehearsed. It was to indicate to them that we were being observed and that our communications had to be in secret. It was a game we were good at.

"So you figure the other guy's the one who whacked Starbourne?" Bax rumbled.

"I can't be sure," I said wiggling my fingers to indicate that I meant the opposite of what I was about to say. "But my instincts say yes. If we track down this other guy, whoever he is, we'll have the Starbourne case all wrapped up."

Tim walked slowly across the room. He flashed me a smile as he passed. Tim's smile was quite a sight to see. He had replaced all of his teeth with shiny black stones, each of them carved with an intricate rune. By running a finger or, more likely, his tongue – along the runes, he could quickly cast a variety of spells, charms, and rituals. It made Tim a warlock who could move magic around much, much faster than most of his fellows.

"That's that, then" said Tim. "Anyone watching or listening now will get a random memory of mine of the three of us talking about nothing noteworthy. They won't hear us; we can say what we like now."

"Good job, Tim," I said. "There's a lot going on here and I think there might be as many as three separate factions mixed up in this case. First thing you have to know: It's not a murder, it's a kidnapping. But Starbourne's life might be in danger if his kidnappers know we know he's not dead. Finding and releasing Starbourne is our top priority. I can't do it because if our kidnapping creep is watching anybody, he's watching me."

"How are we supposed to find him, Boss?" Baxter rumbled.

"You're a goblin warrior and a warlock," I said as if the answer were obvious. "If the two of you can't do this, it can't be done! I certainly couldn't do it if you guys can't."

Baxter turned to Tim. Tim shrugged and nodded. They looked a question and an answer back and forth, nodding their heads in agreement before turning back to look at me.

"You 'aven't a bloody clue, 'ave you, Zack?" asked Tim.

"Nope!" I agreed. "But I have complete faith in the two of you. Get on it, guys. All kidding aside, this one's important. Without Starbourne back in the saddle soon this whole place could fall apart."

Baxter snorted and Tim rolled his eyes at me, but I could tell they were both already thinking about it. They really could do anything they put their minds to. I was damned lucky to have partners as good as these guys and I knew it.

"Oh, one other thing," I said. "Bax, the Weeping Lady case leads right to Patchwork. The counterfeiters are operating out of here, and they're in this up to their necks, whoever they are. I'm sure of that much at least."

The goblinblood rubbed a blunt finger across his chin scales which he often did when he was deep in thought. Bax didn't make snap decisions like I did – not outside of a fight, anyway – but when he had time to roll an idea around in that great big, square noggin of his, he always came up with something good.

"It doesn't make sense Zack," he rumbled at last. "I poked around a bit while you were gone, and every one of the counterfeit statues is a magical construct. I don't have any idea what they're supposed to do; we haven't figured out how to activate them, or even if it would be safe to try. But here's the thing: I can't even imagine how much sorcerous energy went into creating these things, but there's no way it's a profitable operation. There has to be something else going on besides money."

"We've got one we can take a real good up-close-and-personal look at," I said, thinking of the statuette I had seen at Skywatch. "Maybe we can learn something from that. While you guys find Starbourne, I'll get one of the local eggheads to examine it."

"And then what'll you do?" asked Tim.

"What do you think I'm going to do?" I asked. "I'm going to go break up a smuggling ring."

Unless," I added a beat later. "The other guy has already cracked the case for me."

"If 'e does," said Tim gleefully. "I think her Ladyship should give 'alf your pay to 'im."

"That'll be the day," rumbled Baxter derisively.

"Hey," I muttered. "Sick guy here! Be nice to me. Or I'm telling Lady Gray."

That shut them up properly.

Chapter Twenty-One

Bax and Tim ducked out of my little suite of rooms comfortably ahead of Gray's deadline. They made loud conversation about going to see Uncle Visivald and about leaving me to my sick rest. In their case, it was cover for their real mission to go search for Starbourne. In my case, it was sadly true. My head was pounding and I didn't like my odds of standing up without passing out cold. Instead of taking my chances, I opted to doze quietly in my comfy chair; the carpet looked soft, but I had no interest in testing that softness by bouncing my poor, suffering noggin against it.

I woke to a ringing in my head. I felt good, aside from the ringing and wondered how long I'd been asleep. I desperately hoped it was still Wednesday. Surely someone would have woken me up if I'd slept the clock around again, wouldn't they?

The ringing refused to go away and it occurred to me that maybe, just maybe, it wasn't inside my head after all. I looked around and saw an antique telephone sitting on the nightstand next to my bed. That's where the ringing was coming from.

Exercising due caution, I levered myself to my feet and, with steadily increasing confidence, made my way across the room. I scooped up the telephone and held the bit you listened to up to my ear and the bit you talked into up to my mouth. I took this as clear and present evidence that I was completely recovered from my concussion.

"Monday," I said into the phone.

"Zack!" exclaimed Audrey's voice through the phone. "Are you okay?"

"Yeah," I assured her. "I'm doing fine. All better, in fact. Who ratted me out?"

"That's not important," Audrey's voice declared. "Why didn't I hear about it from you?"

"So it was Baxter, was it?" I accused.

"Stop changing the subject," she said.

"Fine," I said, surrendering to the inevitable. "What would you like to talk about?"

"Why didn't you tell me you got hurt?" Audrey said in an exasperated tone of voice.

"You found out about it without me, didn't you?" I asked in what I thought was a reasonable manner.

"Zack!" Audrey said, "Would you please stop being unreasonable!"

So much for what I thought. This was the way most conversations with Audrey went. I didn't think I was being unreasonable, so much as Audrey's definition of the term differed from my own. It wasn't generally a problem. Whenever anything controversial came up, we'd simply argue until I agreed that Audrey was right.

"I'm sorry, Audrey," I said after taking sufficient time to have thought it over and realized how wrong I was. "It was wrong of me not to call you. Things have just been kind of crazy here. At least Baxter told you."

"Nice try, Zack," Audrey said. "But you are not getting me to admit who told me."

"Can't blame a detective for trying." I said. "What have you been up to? Keeping busy?"

"Always," she said with a laugh. "Been flying all over for Samaritech; met twice with McGregor."

"Ouch," I said by way of consolation.

"You know it," she agreed. "I did get in a session with Dr. Bechdel. That was good."

"Nice," I said. "How's she doing? Did you talk about me?"

"Oh, Zack," Audrey said. "You know I never talk about you when I'm with Dr. Bechdel."

We both laughed at that. I was still a little bit groggy from sleep, but something was starting to tickle at the edges of my brain. I rolled the idea around in my head for a little while and then I found it.

"So," I drawled casually. "It's great to hear from you, but aren't we in different worlds?"

"Of course we are," Audrey chuckled. "I'm in New Jerusalem and you're in over your head."

"Nice one," I chuckled. "But seriously, now you're the one trying to change the subject. How in Salvation's Reach are you making a telephone call through the Mists?"

"Well, I'm not really am I?" Audrey said after a pause. "It's a spell I bought down in Merlintown. I hope you appreciate it; it cost a fortune."

Audrey had paid to have a spell crafted to contact me in the Mists? That was some serious magic. This was wake-Rip-Van-Winkle-and-Oisin-up-and-bring-them-home-in-time-for-dinner magic. I knew Audrey was rich, and I knew she rubbed elbows with the movers and the shakers. She told me about all the Senators and CEOs she stirred the tea with, and it had all sort of just rolled over me. I had to stop and think. Just how powerful was Audrey? And how much money had she just blown to give me the raspberry?

"Well, whatever," I said. "Listen, can you get a message to Eel for me?"

"Sure Zack," Audrey said. "We're having dinner tonight. I can get it to him then."

I gave her the message. Then I had her repeat it back to me to make sure she had gotten it exactly right. Of course she had it right the first time but she humored my obsessive nature and I appreciated it.

"Oh," I said. "One more question. This may sound kind of strange, but can you tell me what day it is?"

"It's Wednesday morning, Zack," Audrey replied. "How many times did they hit you in the head?"

"Too many," I said. "I gotta get moving. Give my love to McGregor next time you see him."

"Yeah," Audrey laughed. "I'll do that. Now take better care of yourself or I'll kill you."

"Yes, ma'am!" I agreed enthusiastically.

We said our farewells and we hung up. No, I am not going to say who hung up first. I stripped out of yesterday's clothes, made my way to the bathing area, took a nice, long, hot shower, and got dressed again. I slung the magical mystical travel bag over my shoulder and made my way down the tower stairs to the kitchen where I scored a muffin and a cup of coffee.

They had a very nice insulated travel mug in the cabinets, for which I mouthed yet another silent word of thanks to Fizznorman.

I strolled out of Gray's tower, feeling refreshed, rested, and ready to take on the world. Or at least ready to take on the holdfast. The rain was pretty light and the sun was actually kind of shining somewhere up behind the clouds. It was what passed for a nice morning these days in Patchwork and I decided to walk.

I grabbed an umbrella from the stand by the door. There were now fully stocked umbrella stands pretty much everywhere. The Pillars of Patchwork were nothing if not adaptable. I wondered whose job it was to handle that, or if maybe each landlord just covered their own territory.

I legged it on down the path and back to the copse of trees where I had danced with the club brothers a few days ago. It was further from Gray's tower than I remembered it being, but I was suffering from multiple concussions at the time so I forgave myself.

I found the copse of trees easily enough. I remembered that particular bend in the road vividly. The scene of the assault was completely unremarkable. There were no indications remaining of the fight at all, or at least none that were visible to the naked eye.

What I was looking for would require tools to find. I slipped my hand inside the travel bag and my fingers closed immediately on what I was looking for. I pulled the Niven Disk out and placed it on the ground. I patted the bag affectionately, muttering my thanks as I did.

I gave it a spin, and it slowly began to pick up speed. It wasn't the whirling dervish it had been back in Foucault's lab, but I was pretty sure it was picking up something.

I knelt on the ground in front of the spinning disk and placed my hands gently on its surface, letting it spin beneath my palms. I nudged it a little bit forward, towards the trees from which my assailants had burst forth. The disk spun a little faster, but when I shoved the disk forward a bit more it slowed down again. Two more pushes and I had a line of effect to work with. I picked up the disk, paced a few yards along the effect line and spun it again. It was definitely moving faster along the line.

I continued this somewhat laborious process for nearly half an hour. Sometimes I would wander off the line of effect and it would take me a few minutes to track it down again. Once or twice I misread the disk and had to back-track when I realized my mistake. It wasn't much fun, but it wasn't all that hard either and I seemed to be making progress, which was a nice change of pace for this case.

I eventually traced the magical emanations back to small depression behind the trees. At the bottom of the clearing there was a huge boulder wedged partly into the ground. The pattern of the disturbed grass and dirt suggested it had been placed here recently by someone of considerable size and strength. The boulder was surrounded by an irregular circle of flagstones.

Each flagstone was covered with intricate carvings. I licked my finger and held it above one of the carved flagstones. I felt a tingle as the moisture evaporated off my fingertip. This was an old charm, often used and brimming with power.

The more often a charm was used, the more residual energy it picked up. That's the origin of the old superstition of running your finger along a carved charm for luck. It might not bring you luck, but over generations, it would make the charm stronger and stronger. These stones were plenty strong already.

It was even theoretically possible that a portal this powerful would be able to circumvent the Mist travel. Skipping over the whole ordeal-and-sacrifice portion of the program would be pretty darn handy for smugglers.

I had no doubt that this was the spot where my dance partners had entered Patchwork. And that wasn't all I knew. I had seen carvings like these before and I had seen them recently. I knew who was behind the attack on me, and that meant I knew who was behind the smuggling ring, and was most likely also behind Peter Starbourne's killnapping. Everything was coming together nicely.

I heard a growl from behind me, smelling a sudden intense musk of wet animal as air rushed towards me. I threw myself forward but too slowly – far too slowly. Something slammed me hard to the ground and pinned me there. My shoulders blazed into pain as claws plunged into my flesh; hot breath from a throaty roar hit the back of my neck. Whatever was on top of me had come out of nowhere and taken me out faster than anything I had ever seen before.

I got my hands underneath my body and desperately tried to push up and roll over. I had to get it off me. I had to get up and into the fight. It was like trying to lift a building and burning agony flared in my shoulders. A scream tore involuntarily out of my throat. My legs kicked helplessly at the ground. I wasn't going anywhere.

"Hey!" someone shouted from above and behind me. "Hey!"

I heard and felt something heavy bounce off the creature that had me pinned. There was a roar of pure animal rage and suddenly the weight was off me. I would have loved to just lay there for a few minutes thinking about my shoulders, but that seemed like a really bad idea, so I flopped over, using my body instead of my arms.

A man was facing down a cougar, throwing rocks at it and shouting. The cat hunched its shoulders and bunched up its hindquarters; it was about to pounce and the man – whoever he was – didn't have a chance. He had probably saved my life and I was going to Perdition before I would let him die in my place.

I looked around for something – anything – to use as a weapon, and there, right next to my left hand, was my .38-caliber revolver. I had packed it along with the rest of my luggage, but unloaded. Yet here it was, all in one piece and I could see shells loaded into the chambers. I snatched it up, ignoring the howling of my shoulders as I did. My hands were slick with my own blood, so I steadied my grip. I'd only get one shot.

I saw the cougar leap, I saw the man throw his arms up in a nearly useless gesture of protection. I tracked the gun with the motion of the animal, as the cougar slammed into the other guy, knocking him to the ground. I exhaled, centered the sight, and gently squeezed the trigger. Then I squeezed it five more times, just to be sure. The recoil did horrible things to my shoulders.

With a hideous yowl, the cougar threw itself off its latest victim. It turned to look at me with its strange golden eyes. We stared at each other for a moment, then two, then three thunderous beats of my heart. And then it turned and loped away, vanishing rapidly over the rise. The empty revolver slipped out of my fingers and thumped on the ground beside me.

"Ow," I said. And then I called out, "You okay?"

Only a groan answered me. But at least that meant he wasn't dead; I had heard a dead guy groan before and that wasn't what it had sounded like. I scrabbled up to my feet and staggered over to my wounded savior.

He was pretty badly mauled. The cougar's claws had punctured his chest in several places. His wounds glistened wet and red. Blood leaked from the corners of his mouth as well; that was never a good sign. I looked at him. Gwynplaine was right, he looked an awful lot like me. The face was the same, but it was unlined, unscathed by time and the stresses of life. His skin was pale and from more than just loss of blood; it looked like it had never seen the sun. His hair was the color mine had been as a child, light brown with streaks of fair auburn. Over the years my hair had first darkened to a chocolate brown and then turned light again as it grayed. This hair had never seen any of those years; it was new.

"Huh," I said wonderingly. "That is not something you see every day."

I ripped what was left of both of our shirts into bandages and did my best to keep his bodily fluids on the inside. I checked his vitals. He was noticeably cold to the touch and probably in shock. No surprises there. I felt a little bit woozy myself. I stuffed rags into my shoulder wounds, wincing badly at how much it hurt. But I wouldn't be doing either one of us any favors if I passed out from blood loss, so I sucked the pain up.

We needed help and we needed it fast. I had precisely one idea and it was a long shot. But a long shot was better than a slow death, so I went for it. I leaned over and dipped my finger into the soft wet mud. I traced the curves of a sigil with my index finger, a sigil I had traced nearly a hundred times before, but never from memory. Tim's true name is a unique and very complicated series of strokes, lines, and curves. If I got one minuscule fragment even slightly wrong, it wouldn't be his name and it would have no chance of catching his attention. It took my shaking finger nearly a full minute to finish its work. And when I was done I started over and did it again. And after that I started a third time.

Tim had once yelled at me for transcribing his true name more than once in a week. He had mentioned something about me being an irresponsible, pushy, kit. He hadn't spoken to me for a week afterwards. I had just done it three times in less than five minutes, hopefully, correctly. If that didn't get the limey warlock's attention there was certainly nothing else I could do here that would. I was thinking about trying it another three times in a row when I felt a hand on my shoulder.

"Easy, mate," chirped Tim in his high, reedy voice. "I'm 'ere. We got ya."

"Oh good," I said.

I looked up and saw his freaky black teeth grinning at me. Behind him I could see Baxter surveying the carnage. The cavalry was here, we were saved. I felt the world start to spin and my vision blurred around the edges.

"Hey listen," I said to Tim. "You should really take a look at the other guy. He's a mess."

And then I passed out.

Chapter Twenty-Two

Iopened my eyes some time later. Baxter and Tim were staring down at me. Their faces both split into huge grins as soon as they realized I was awake. Their combined dental presence was enough to make me want to pass out again. But these were my people and I was glad to see them.

I suddenly realized that I felt great. My head wasn't throbbing, my shoulders didn't feel torn to shreds, my side wasn't aching, and I wasn't the slightest bit tired. I sat up. I was in the bed Gray had provided me in my rooms. Dr. Foucault was standing at the foot of my bed, checking my medical chart. I was really looking forward to waking up someday in a bed that didn't have a hook for a medical chart.

There was a general tumult of cheer at my being both awake and alive at the very same time. Lady Gray entered and suddenly it was a crowd. I was uncomfortably aware of the fact that I currently wore no trousers.

"Why do I feel so good?" I asked.

"Two words," Tim chirped. "'Ealing and draught. Specialty of the 'ouse and my very best-selling product."

Over the years I had bought and/or been given dozens of Tim's famous healing draughts. They were very good and very expensive, so on the whole I preferred the ones that were gifts. Right now I felt as if I had just slugged down two in a row.

"Concussion all better?" I asked.

"Near as," confirmed Foucault. "Perfectly safe to use healing draughts."

"Very fine healing draughts," Tim corrected.

"They most certainly are," agreed Foucault, before adding, "Darling."

"Yeah," I agreed as well. "They sure are. Now will someone please tell me what's going on around here?"

"Sure thing, Boss," rumbled Bax. "We found plenty of blood all over the place. And some of it wasn't even yours."

"Ho," I drawled. "Ho. You are a very funny employee."

"The critter that attacked you," continued Bax around a huge grin. "Wasn't real. It was a programmable homunculus built as a hunter killer. Somebody just put a whole lot of money into kicking your ass."

"Wow," I said, impressed in spite of myself. "Any idea why it looked like a big kitty cat?"

"Cougar," corrected Gray. "From the descriptions, it was disguised as a fairly common animal here in Patchwork. It's one of Oswald's favorite designs, apparently."

"How nice," I observed acerbically. "So we're presuming it came in through the portal I found?"

"Exactly so," confirmed Gray. "It would seem your investigations have finally had the result you were hoping for."

"Well," I admitted. "Maybe not exactly like this. But we're still in good shape to move forward."

I paused and looked around. There was one particular elephant that was missing from the room. And if everyone was in here with me, who was making sure my impostor didn't bleed to death in the other room. Or had they already been unable to save him? I looked again at everyone's face. No one looked especially sad or stressed out. I would bet even money that no nearby patients were in critical condition.

"Can we speak securely in here?" I asked.

"With an absolute certainty," Gray replied. "I have put an extraordinary amount of effort into a brief but impenetrable defense against espionage. Even your warlock friend Tim agrees. Don't you, Tim?"

Tim looked like he had swallowed a lemon, but he nodded and even managed a duck of his head in Gray's direction. I looked around at everyone's hands and no one was making even as much as a twitch of secret code. I was satisfied.

"So," I said brightly. "Where's the other guy? And do we have any idea what his story is yet?"

Everyone got real quiet, real suddenly. I looked around again. Now everyone looked kind of nervous, and a little bit ashamed. Now I had to know what was going on.

"The 'other guy,' as you call him," began Gray. "Is something of an enigma. We know that he is also a programmable homunculus, but a very extraordinary one. His structure is somehow infused with biomimetic material."

"Like the stuff that got stolen from your lab, Dr. Foucault?" I asked.

"Not like it, Darling!" Foucault chuckled. "It is the stuff that got stolen. But now it's all mixed up and distributed through the homunculus as though it was designed to work together."

"But what does it mean?" asked Tim.

"Among other things," Gray said. "It means he's alive."

"As for where he is," interjected Dr. Foucault. "He's in the next suite with Tad. I've just come from checking on him. He's stable, but complicated. I don't know how to heal him yet, but at least he's not getting any worse."

"Healing magic doesn't work on him?" I wondered.

"He's not made out of the same stuff as we are," Foucault said with a shrug of her broad shoulders. "I'm working on it."

"Why does he look like me?" I asked.

"We're not sure," Gray replied. "In fact, we're not sure of a great many things. But there is one thing we do know for certain. Whatever our patient in the other room has become, he used to be our counterfeit corpse."

"Say what now?" I squawked.

"What we're saying," replied Foucault. "Is that something has caused the programmable homunculus previously shaped to look like Peter's corpse to become – well – the other guy."

"Do we have any idea what that something was?" I asked.

"I have a theory," announced Gray.

There was a sort of a rolling gasp as everyone tried to talk at once and then thought better of it. Lady Gray was definitely getting better at her dramatic delivery. I grinned at her and she tossed me a wink before continuing.

"I believe," Gray said before giving a pause that was dramatic enough to impress even me. "That Zachariah created the other guy through the force of his own will."

I squawked again. Everyone looked at me. I cleared my throat and tried to gather what little dignity I had left before repeating myself.

"Say what, now?" I repeated in a pleasant and well-modulated voice.

Lady Gray favored me with an unusually warm version of her trademark thin smile.

"Since I first met Zachariah last year," Gray continued. "I have suspected that he would make a fine Pillar. He is in possession of all the qualities that indicate the kind of will power necessary to maintain the holdfast of Patchwork. That is why I agreed to help him with his efforts."

"I seem to remember you charging me rather a lot for your help at the time," I observed.

"That is true," Gray agreed. "But a girl does have to make a living, you know."

Baxter snorted quietly. Tim and Foucault didn't even try to hide their grins. I shrugged and gave Gray a jaunty salute. As a fellow small business owner I had to respect her style.

"I had been meaning to invite Zachariah to come visit for some time now in order to test my hypothesis," Gray continued. "But time got away from me until the dreadful business with Peter. I decided to further two purposes at once by hiring Zachariah's firm to investigate."

"You're trying to manipulate me," I accused.

"Wizard," she replied pointing to herself.

"Fair point," I allowed.

"Several events occurred that convinced me I had been correct," Gray continued. "The mystery of the luggage magic? Zachariah used his will to imbue it with more power and made it answerable to his desires. That is something that is only possible here and even then only by a very select few."

All eyes in the room turned to look at my travel bag. It sat innocently in the corner, acting more or less like an inanimate object. As we watched a tiny ripple went through its fabric. I got the impression of quiet contentment. Silently and unanimously, we all decided to ignore it and get back to the subject at hand.

"Then, after Zachariah was attacked by those ruffians with the clubs," Gray iterated. "He subconsciously used the travel magics to get him quickly and safely to my door. No easy feat for an untrained mind, I assure you.

"This latest revelation only cements my understanding of the situation," Gray concluded. "The details are simple enough to deduce. Our villain, whoever he or she may be, removed Peter from his own party, replacing him with a programmable homunculus of his corpse that fooled us all."

"Originally disguised as a statuette," I interrupted. "I don't know how it was smuggled in, but it's the one we were presuming was stolen."

"Just so," continued Gray. "Later when Zachariah examined the counterfeit corpse, he focused his will quite powerfully. Once again, just as he did with the luggage, Zachariah imbued the object with new and more powerful magic. It must have immediately imprinted upon you as its creator, but it took some time for everything to sort itself out.

"During that time, we transported it to Michelle's laboratory, where it was exposed to the biomimetic material. This is where my understanding is imperfect, but somehow all of these factors combined and the other guy was 'born.'"

"Are you saying the counterfeit corpse turned into a replica of me," I asked slowly. "Got up off the table and walked out of Dr. Foucault's laboratory?"

"That is exactly what I'm saying" declared Gray.

"And ran out into the night trying to solve Peter Starbourne's murder?" asked Tim. "Why in sodding Perdition would he do something like that?"

"Because Zachariah asked him to," said Gray.

I squawked a third time. This time even I wasn't sure what I had just said, so I decided to leave it be. I cleared my throat again and waved my hand for Gray to continue.

"I was standing right next to you when you created him," Gray said. "I could feel the magical power in the room, but I had no idea what was happening. But I do quite clearly recall the words you said next. You asked the corpse who did this and then asked him to help you find out."

"Did I?" I asked in an unsteady voice.

"That does sound like something you'd say to a corpse, Boss," Baxter agreed.

I had to admit, he had a point. It did sound like something I'd say to a corpse. We all sat in silence for a while. I can only assume that the implications of what Gray had just told us was affecting everyone. It was almost too much to think about. There was a new form of magical life lying in the other room.

The thing that I couldn't get past, the thing that my mind couldn't quite grip but was incapable of releasing was the thought that this new thing in the worlds came from me. It was my double, maybe even my nemesis. The stories that featured magical duplicates rarely ended well for the original. Was he here to replace me? Or was I just being pathologically paranoid?

Assuming Dr. Foucault could save his life and bring him back to consciousness, did the world really want or need another Zachariah Monday? What would it be like if he really were just like me? Did I want that? Did it matter what I wanted? This was a living creature with rights and needs. Did I have any responsibilities as his unwilling creator?

I had a lot of friends in the worlds and I took my duties towards them very seriously. Family was equally important to me, but I didn't have much of that. My father had died when I was very young. My mother meant the world to me and I visited her on most of the important holidays and even called sometimes when the rates were low. But I had never once thought about having children, so the idea of being responsible for another person had never really crossed my mind. Now the idea was crossing back and forth, jumping up and down, and generally waving its hands at me.

"Do you really think you can fix him up, Doc?" I asked Foucault.

"He's not getting any worse," Foucault said in a thoughtful tone. "I'm confident that I can come up with something. My work in biomimetics can only help. I can't promise you when, but I can confidently say I will have him up and around again, sooner or later."

"Well that's something anyway," I said. "Okay, we've got a lot of work to do. How far did you guys get on finding Starbourne before I got inconveniently mauled by an artificial cougar?"

"We have a plan," Baxter rumbled. "And we're ready to put it into operation. Tim worked out a ritual that will let me start tracking Starbourne. We're pretty sure it'll work, but it might take a while."

"Even with all the rain and time that's passed?" I wondered. "How's that even possible?"

"The trick is to start tracking before all that time and rain 'appened," said Tim casually.

"Now you're just messing with me," I grumped.

"Maybe," Tim chuckled. "But the point is we can do it. What 'ave you been up to? Besides getting stomped in a fight?"

"Again," Baxter rumbled cheerfully.

"All right," I said testily. "Let's move on."

"Sure thing, Boss," Baxter agreed.

"Ahem," I said, distinctly. "The three facets to any mystery are who, what, and why. We already know the what and I have some ideas on the who. The why probably has something to do with control over Patchwork."

I looked directly at Gray and held her eyes as I spoke. I had to convince her that whatever secrets she was keeping were less important that solving this mystery. I was convinced that something she knew and wasn't telling was the key to this whole mess. Hopefully I was right about both of those facts, but either way, I couldn't move forward without at least trying to get the answers. Getting the answers was what I did, after all.

"I see what you're trying to do, Zachariah," Gray said after a moment's silence. "You want to know why Patchwork exists."

"I think it's pertinent to the case," I said. "Very pertinent."

"I'm not sure how that can be," Gray said slowly. "But you're the detective so we'll assume you're correct. I must swear each and every one of you to absolute secrecy on this matter. It is quite literally more important than any of our lives."

"Darling, you've earned my trust a hundred times over," said Foucault. "I promise to keep your secrets, always."

"Why not?" said Tim. "I promise. One or two more dark secrets rattlin' around in this old noggin? What's the diff, eh?"

"On my honor and by my oath," Baxter rumbled without a trace of irony or sarcasm. "I swear to keep your secrets as my own."

"Unless it's absolutely necessary to save a life I'll keep your secrets," I promised. "And if there's any other way I'll keep them, even then."

"That's good enough for me," Gray said thoughtfully. "I trust each of you and always have. Even you, warlock, though Salvation alone knows why."

"Pshaw," snorted Tim.

"Not today, nor any time this decade – hopefully not even this century, but some day the final battle between the forces of Salvation and Perdition will happen. It is inevitable. Salvation works unceasingly to delay the horror and destruction that will result. But sooner or later – hopefully much later – the day will come and the world will end. Patchwork is a vital part of Salvation's plans to make the World To Come a better one. The war must come, and it can be won, but not without Patchwork."

"It's a back door from Salvation to the real world, isn't it?" I asked. "Patchwork is a way to move troops directly from Salvation to New Jerusalem."

Gray's jaw dropped open and for the first time since I'd met her she actually looked surprised. I took a moment to savor the experience. Foucault and Tim looked equally surprised, or maybe they were still stunned by Gray's reveal. But Baxter only chuckled.

"You already knew didn't you, Boss?" Baxter rumbled. "Is there anything that surprises you anymore?"

"Thanks for the compliment," I said. "But no, I hadn't figured it all out. I was working on it and I might've gotten it sooner or later but … yeah. It just makes sense this way."

Gray got control of herself and even managed a wan smile. She shook her head slowly. She folded her arms across her narrow chest and tried to look stern. I wasn't buying it; I could tell that she was impressed with me.

"I suppose I get what I deserve for bringing in a detective," she said tartly. "But now you all understand why this place is so important and why it cannot be allowed to fall. We must find Peter and restore the balance before it's too late."

"There might be a problem there," I said. "I'm nearly 100% certain that one or more of the other Pillars is behind this mess. That's a problem that'll need dealing with."

"I have a plan for that eventuality," Gray said confidently.

"That is exactly what I'm afraid of," I said. "Now let's get to work! Who wants to take down an inter-dimensional-mystical-counterfeit-artifact smuggling ring? I know I do!"

Chapter Twenty-Three

We talked for a few hours, discussing theories, plans, and methods of attack. By the time we were done, everyone was bushed except for me (a side benefit of the healing magic) and the other guy had woken up. Whatever Foucault was doing to treat him seemed to be working. Hooray. I know I shouldn't, but I had honestly kind of been hoping my *doppelgänger* wouldn't pull through. I felt pretty awful about it, but it was true. Fortunately for all of us, hope wasn't effective against modern magical medicine. Not even in Patchwork.

An hour had passed since the other guy woke up. Gray had spoken to him and apparently, he was 'quite lucid and rather well-spoken.' Then Foucault talked to him. She said he was 'just darling.' Tim went in to talk to him and declared him to be 'a right fine bloke.' A more precocious three-day-old was unlikely to be found. I was starting to get the impression that everyone was waiting for me to go talk to my double.

Baxter didn't go in, but I got the feeling he was just keeping solidarity with me. Bax knew me better than anyone else in any world, and he knew that I wasn't okay with the other guy yet. And until I went in and talked to him, Baxter had my back. No matter how stupid, bull-headed, or wrong-minded I cared to be, Baxter always had my back.

"I have a theory," I announced.

Everyone looked at me expectantly.

"I don't think I had anything to do with the other guy," I pronounced. "Sure it's pretty obvious that he's patterned on me. Like a baby duck imprints on the first animal it sees."

"Duckling," corrected Tim.

"What?" I asked.

"Baby ducks is called ducklings," Tim said helpfully.

"Right," I said. "Thanks. I guess I knew that."

"'Appy to 'elp," Tim said warmly.

"Anyway," I went on. "So there's some sort of magical flare that reactivates the homunculus' spell while I'm examining it and it just sort of imprints on me. I didn't have anything to do with it; I was just the closest guy."

"Perhaps," Gray said thoughtfully. "But even if that were the case, what does Spenser's Law tell us?"

"That's the Spenser Rule," I corrected. "It sounds more 'tough guy' that way."

"My apologies," amended Gray. "What does the Spenser Rule tell us?"

"That if we assume I had nothing to do with it, we have no where to go with the investigation. But if we assume I did have something to do with it, we have a way to proceed."

"Precisely," Gray agreed. "Why Zachariah, I do believe that you show some potential as a detective."

"Thanks a lot," I sulked, while trying to ignore the chuckles and muttered comments of 'burn!' from my so-called friends.

"Boss," Baxter rumbled quietly. "Are you gonna go talk to the guy, or what?"

"Fine," I sighed. "Fine. I give up. You're all right and I'm all wrong. I will go and talk to the guy."

And, as the man of action that I am, I stood up immediately to do what I had said I would do. Because that's the kind of thing that a man of action does. Yes, indeed.

"I have another theory," I said.

"Go!" shouted everyone at once.

"Okay, okay," I said. "You guys…"

I walked out of my little borrowed suite and to the hospital-like room that Gray and Foucault had established across the way. The other guy was lying in bed. He was awake and his eyes followed me, but he said nothing. The headboard featured half a dozen intricate runic carvings. I recognized the sedation one from my own experiences. I also noticed a clipboard with a medical chart tucked into the little slot for it at the bottom. I admit that I took a perverse pleasure in it not being my bed with the medical chart for a change.

"Hey," I said.

"Hello," he replied. "You're Zack."

"That's right," I said. "I'm Zack Monday. It's nice to meet you. You saved my life earlier. Thank you."

"You're welcome," he said. "I was glad to do it. I was coming to see you anyway. I need your help. I can't do it without you."

"Can't do what without me?" I asked.

His voice was similar to mine, but sounded a little more nasal and with less resonance. Was that what I sounded like to other people? I hoped not. I was going to have to take elocution lessons.

"I can't figure out who killed Peter Starbourne," he said sounding a little bit shrill. "I've tried and tried. And there's plenty of evidence, but it all points in different directions."

"Yeah," I said. "It really does, doesn't it? Between you and me, I'm beginning to think they're all guilty."

"Really?" he asked, eyes growing wider.

"Nah," I shrugged. "But they do all have secrets they're trying to hide. Come on, let's you and me talk it out and maybe between the two of us we can get it figured."

"I'd like that," the other guy said.

"Right," I said. "Where do we begin?"

"With the smugglers," my double stated. "It all has to come back that somehow."

"You're right," I said, impressed in spite of myself. "I keep coming back to that as the key."

"There are two of them," the other guy said.

"How do you figure that?" I asked.

"One them has to be Roger," he answered. "No one else would be strong enough to move the rock that blocks the portal. And they used that portal at least twice."

"Sound logic," I agreed. "But you have to be careful. Someone else could have used magic to move the boulder. But I have some corroborating evidence that strengthens the case for Roger. He was the only one who knew when and where I was going to be when the guys with clubs ambushed me."

"But Roger isn't capable of making the homunculi," he continued. "Golems are powerful, indestructible, and immortal, but they're not real smart. So he has a partner. Or more likely, he's working for someone else. Golems are always more comfortable working for someone else; they don't like to run things themselves."

"So that leaves out Visivald, Foucault, Kellidwyn, and Fizznorman," I said. "None of them have the magic mojo to do this sort of thing either."

"It must be Lord Quatermain," the other guy declared. "Roger is his servant and I think he has a magical workroom where he could have made the statuettes."

"Good theory," I said. "But there are problems with it. First off, never assume a relationship you see is the truth. Roger could easily be moonlighting for someone else. Secondly, I've been inside Quatermain's workroom, and I don't think it's sophisticated enough to create those statuettes."

My double looked crestfallen. I debated internally whether or not to tell him that I had been running with the exact same theory he just proffered until I saw the runes at the secret portal. They were the exact same style and hand as the ones I had seen on Gwynplaine's front door. The Quatermain solution was close, but it didn't fit as well as the Gwynplaine.

"I'll be honest here," I said. "For a while there, I wasn't actually sure who the bad guy was. Everyone here has a motive: power. Having a captive Pillar under your thumb? Who could resist that idea? And I'll tell you something else, everyone around here has a plan, a dream, or a scheme. Even Gray has secret motives that she doesn't want to share with the other children."

"Even Kelli?" asked the other guy.

"Yeah," I said. "Even Kelli. In fact, I'm almost completely convinced that Kelli is working with Gwynplaine The question I don't have an answer for is whether she knew what Gwynplaine was really up to when she did it."

"Why would she do that?" my double asked.

"Because she's obsessed with thieves," I explained. "Brilliant, unconventional master thieves in general, and Gwynplaine in specific."

"Lord Gwynplaine isn't a thief," he protested.

"Not right now he isn't," I agreed. "He will be, but that's not important right now. At least I think it isn't. That's one of the things I'm not sure about."

"I don't understand," said my double.

"That makes two of us," I said. "But let's table that discussion for now. And don't you dare make a vote. Tabling something means not talking about it anymore."

"I know," he said.

"Right," I agreed. "Sorry. I'm a little on edge."

"I freak you out, don't I?" he asked.

"Yeah," I admitted. "A little bit."

"I'm sorry," he said.

"Not your fault," I replied.

"Can I still be sorry?" he asked.

"Oh, yeah," I said with a sigh. "You can totally be sorry even when it's not your fault. Maybe especially then."

Neither of us talked for a little while then. I sat in my chair and he lay in his bed. I looked at him again. He didn't look that much like me, or so I told myself. It's not like anyone would confuse him for me. Maybe a younger brother at most. I could see a lot of myself in him, in the ways he thought and tried to figure stuff out. Also the guilt complex looked pretty familiar. I felt sorry for him; as far as personality templates went, he could have done a lot better than mine.

"So," I said at last. "You said you needed my help to figure out who did it?"

"That's right," he agreed.

"Did you have a plan?" I asked.

"Oh," he said, blushing a little. "Sure, but I know yours would be better."

"Maybe," I considered. "And maybe not. Let's hear your plan and then I'll tell you mine and we can maybe use the best parts of both. Okay?"

"Okay," he said enthusiastically.

And then he told me his plan. And you know what? It was a damn fine plan. Even if I do say so myself.

After we had thrashed through some of the details, he was looking pretty tired. I was still full of post-healing-draught energy, so I let him get some rest and I wandered back across the hall. Gray was already gone and Dr. Foucault excused herself to go check on her patient as soon as I returned. That left me, Bax, and Tim. If we had some beer and a wireless set, it would have been just like a typical Saturday night.

"Anybody know who won the game?" I asked.

"The Monday night game?" Bax rumbled back.

"Yeah," I confirmed.

"Circe," Tim said.

"Damn," I muttered. "I had Killgore."

"Yeah," Baxter said. "Me too."

Tim just chuckled and we both glared daggers at him until he stopped.

"You got a plan?" Baxter asked.

"Actually," I said. "The other guy has a plan."

Both Baxter and Tim looked at me, eyebrows raised.

"Yeah," I said. "I know. But what can I say? It's actually a pretty good plan."

Baxter stuck out his lower lip and made a sort of *hmph* noise. Tim just nodded his head and chuckled some more as if he'd known all along. Warlocks are annoying that way; they always act like they know more than everybody else does. It was all the more annoying because of how often they really did know more than everybody else.

"It ties in pretty well with a contingency I've been lining up," I said. "The last piece of it should show up soon. And then we've got work to do."

"Sounds good," Baxter said.

"Oi," said Tim thoughtfully. "Is there any chance 'er ladyship 'as some beer around 'ere?"

"That's a good question," I said. "Let's find out."

I reached over and gave the bell cord a tug.

Chapter Twenty-Four

The next morning dawned and the three of us rose with it. Bax and Tim had crashed out in my suite, on the couch and in the chair respectively. We had discussed the finer details of the plan all through the night and we all knew the whats, whens, wheres, and hows.

My double's plan really was pretty solid. But he had no way to pull it off. It required connections and resources that he simply didn't have. Fortunately for the plan, that's where I came in. Step one was to sow fear and confusion amongst the enemy, and confusion is a particular specialty of mine. We had to cause a rift between Gwynplaine and Roger and the best way to do that was to create the illusion of betrayal.

The thing about criminal partnerships is that, generally speaking, they're inherently unbalanced. There are always exceptions, but in most of my experience, it's true. Either the criminals have a strict hierarchy in place, or nobody trusts anybody else. Ever. When forced to operate from a position of equality, acute paranoia is the only safe option for a criminal. It's like I said earlier, real people in the real world don't just commit a brutal crime on Tuesday and then go back to their normal lives for the weekend. It changes you, fundamentally, and it changes your place in society. And these guys were so far beyond having a normal place in society, it wasn't even funny.

So, all we had to do was destabilize that hierarchy, or upset that balance of power, and the whole house of straw would come down. Simple in theory, but often tricky in execution. The biggest risk was of an innocent getting hurt in the crossfire. When violent criminals have a serious falling out, violence often ensues. After all, sometimes straw has an annoying habit of bursting into flame.

Like any good con, this one had a lot of different moving parts and needed a props budget. I had most of the talent I needed on hand so all I needed to do was convince Adriana Gray to donate the hardware. I respected Gray. She ran a small business much like my own; she was savvy, and had a healthy respect for her own profit margin. But none of that was going to stop me from trying. Fortunately for my own budget, I had an angle she couldn't possibly resist.

"I'm declaring martial law," I declared.

"I beg your pardon?" Gray asked, arching an elegant coal-black eyebrow.

"I mean it," I said. "For the greater good, and so forth and so on, the community needs to pull together."

"*Um-hm,*" she nodded in a thoroughly unconvinced manner.

"For the greater good," I repeated.

"What do you need?" Gray asked. "And when do you need it?"

"One of those homunculus gadgets," I said. "In the same style and fashion as the ones we've been finding. But more of a cheap knockoff. Like a half-talented amateur would come up with if she'd had a real good look at the original. And I need it for tomorrow."

"Indeed?" she said favoring me with the eyebrow again. "And are you suggesting that I am qualified to be that half-talented amateur? To build cheap knockoffs?"

"Think of it as a challenge to your artistry," I appealed. "You have to convince an expert that this thing was made by an amateur, but it's still got to work."

Her dark eyes pierced the air between us. This was clearly her Unimpressed Face. I gave her some patience. She kept glaring so I gave her one of my patented Very Charming Smiles.

"Harrumph," she grumbled, throwing her hands up. "I'll have it for you by dawn."

"One more thing," I said.

"Really?" Gray's tone couldn't have been icier if it had been found at the Arctic Circle.

"Yeah," I said. "I need you to make sure Oswald Quatermain is away from Aristarchus for a couple hours tomorrow morning."

Gray pinched her nose as if she were getting a migraine. Then she sighed and shook her head slowly.

"I hired you for your professional services Mr. Monday," she said with a smile that took all the sting out of her words. "You are the most demanding employee I have ever had."

"Don't think of me as an employee," I said. "Think of me as a potential member of the community."

Gray gave me her Unimpressed Face again. It featured both her thin smile and her cocked eyebrow. I had no defense against it and I felt my arguments withering.

"Well," I offered. "You did as much as invite me in, what with all of your tests of my potential."

"And if I thought your interest was sincere, Zachariah," she replied archly. "I should be delighted."

Damn. She had a point and we both knew it. It was very frustrating for me to have to work with someone who read me as well as I read them. Gray's ability to read my mind was almost magical. Actually, strike that last thought. I had been hit by some mind reading magic once, and Gray's methods were actually more effective.

"Nonetheless," Gray continued after letting me twist for a moment or two. "I agree that this is in the community's best interest. And therefore, I shall be glad to keep Oswald busy for the morning. I'm sure he'd be delighted to join me for tea and a poetry reading."

"The community thanks you," I said solemnly.

I shall not repeat her response, but suffice to say, it did not, strictly speaking, pertain to the case.

"Hey," I called after her. "Can you give me a lift over to Kelli's? No? Okay, I can get there on my own."

I got myself over to Coldiron Keep while everyone else was out and about and gathering what we'd need for the job, I had the unenviable task of confronting someone I'd once loved with uncomfortable truths. These conversations rarely go well. My hands reached up to straighten my tie and I was once again annoyed to notice that I wasn't wearing one. This informal country living was cramping my style. For lack of anything better to do with my hands, I rang the buzzer.

There was a very brief wait before the locks went *click* and *clack* and the door swung open to reveal Lady Kellidwyn of Coldiron Keep, outcast of Faerie. Her hair was pulled back in a loose ponytail, she was wearing a flannel pajama top and knee-high athletic socks and pretty obviously nothing else. She was holding a bowl in her hands and was eating cereal out of it.

"Morning Zack," she said around a yawn. "C'mon in."

She looked good. In fact, she looked very, very good. I tried my very best to ignore that as I followed her back inside.

"Want some chocolate frosted sugar bombs?" she asked, jerking her chin towards a garishly colored box sitting on her kitchen table.

"Sweet Salvation," I chuckled. "You're not still eating that stuff are you?"

"S'best stuff ever!" she grumbled, sticking out her lower lip. "Can't believe you're dissing my chocolate frosted sugar bombs."

"Make them yourself, do you?" I asked.

"You know it," she replied proudly. "Go on! Try some. They taste exactly like I remember!"

"They'd pretty much have to," I sighed.

I walked into her kitchen, guessed the cabinet that had the bowls in it on the first try, grabbed a spoon out of the dish drain and poured myself a quarter cup of sugar-saturated breakfast. There was a carafe of milk as well and I sploshed a generous amount over the top.

"Mmm," I said brightly with my mouth full.

She laughed and it made my heart skip a beat. She must have seen it on my face because she stopped almost at once. She cleared her throat quietly and we both ate a few more spoonfuls in silence.

"Why are you here, Zack?" she asked. "What do you want to know?"

"You're a thief," I said. "You've always been a thief. What did you steal that got you in dutch with both courts?"

"It doesn't matter," she said sadly. "It's long gone. Nothing left but the grudge."

"You studied the greats to improve your own game," I said.

"Is that a question?" she asked. "Or an accusation?"

"It doesn't matter," I answered. "Not anymore."

"Fine," she said. "I don't care what you think. I am who I am and I always have been."

"I need information," I said. "And I need you to stop lying to me. Lives are in danger, and I can't believe that's the way you want it to be. I know Gwynplaine was visiting you the other night when I first came to question you. He was warning you about what not to tell me, wasn't he?"

Her eyes got hard, but only for a moment. Then she turned away and I could see the tension going out of her shoulders. She sighed and then slowly turned back to look at me.

"What do you want to know?" she asked.

"A lot of things," I admitted. "But the most important thing right now is, what are the statuettes for?"

"I don't know," she said.

"I need better than that," I snapped. "You know something. You might not know it all and you might even be lying to yourself about what you do know, but you're not stupid and you're not blind. So tell me what you know."

The mood around the breakfast table had chilled. She sniffed a little bit and there might have even been a ghost of a tremble on her lower lip. I watched emotions chase themselves across her face. She was weighing her options and trying to construct a narrative inside her own head where she wasn't a bad guy. I had seen these emotions on a lot of different faces over the years, but it still hurt to see it on the face of a loved one.

"I'm not sure, okay?" she said at last. "I don't know what they're for, but I know Gwynplaine got some help designing them from someone outside of Patchwork. Probably very outside. And not from the Goblin-Faerie side, either."

"Perdition?" I asked as every short hair I had prickled up and seriously considered moving out.

She just nodded.

"Are you sure?" I asked.

"What am I, talking to myself here?" she said, rolling her eyes. "Of course I'm not sure! Do you think I would have gotten involved with him if I were sure he was dealing with Perdition?"

"How involved are you?" I asked, dreading the answer.

"I'm just the delivery girl," she said. "They give me a package, I put it on the right shelf. That's all."

"You break into people's houses and sneak fine art into their collections," I said. "So Santa Claus is real after all. I have to say you don't look like I pictured you."

"Ho ho," she said with nice timing. "When I first got made a Pillar, I couldn't handle it. Gwynplaine helped. He helped a lot."

"And it didn't hurt that he was one of your idols from college," I added.

"Sort of," she muttered. "But also sort of not."

"How many statuettes have gone to New Jerusalem?" I asked.

"A couple hundred," she replied. "At least. I have no idea how he makes them so fast without rupturing himself."

"A deal with Perdition can give you an awful lot of extra oomph," I said. "I've tangled with these guys before and they have got it going on."

"Gwynplaine has a greater understanding of the fundament principles of magic than anyone I've ever know," Kelli said. "And his power rivals Lady Gray's."

"That's good – if disturbing – to know," I said.

"I won't help you against him," she said. "He's got a destiny, even if he doesn't know about it yet. Somehow he gets to the world someday and becomes a legend."

"One more question," I asked very quietly, "How long have you and Quatermain been lovers?" I asked very quietly.

I didn't turn to look, but I heard her bowl clatter to the table. There was a moment of silence and I let it drag out. This I didn't need to know; this wasn't part of the case. But I couldn't help myself. There were some questions I just had to ask, even if I didn't want to hear the answers.

"Almost from the very beginning," she said, barely a whisper. "He and Lillian were fighting. They fought a lot back then. I wasn't sure what the heart of it was, but as a couple they simply weren't working."

"And there you were," I said. "No pressure, no complications, no commitment."

"It wasn't like that," she said. "Sure it was a just an affair, but we really had a connection."

"And things are better between them now?" I asked.

"Yeah," she said. "We haven't had a night together in months. I think it's the kid. They say it can do wonders for a marriage."

"This is their first child?" I asked.

"Yeah," she said again. "And with him pushing the century mark. Word on the street had him as sterile or her as barren. Everyone figured the Quatermain line was over."

There was something there, something that might matter. I didn't have time to worry at it right then and there. I resolved to get it down in the notebook before I forgot and then I moved on. Sometimes detective work is mostly fact-triage; you can't follow every lead every time or you'll never get to the bottom of anything.

"How can I break into Aristarchus?" I asked. "Without anyone seeing me?"

"Easy," she said. "You want to pick up or drop off?"

"Drop off," I said. "Basically the same thing you do."

"I can give you instructions," she said, confidently.

Frankly, I wasn't surprised. After all, there was nothing much of value at Aristarchus. Everything there was made out of Quatermain's imagination. How hard would it really be for him to just wish up some more? No, it made sense that security was low around here. Material possessions must mean next to nothing to a Pillar. But a place that held information? That would be locked up tighter than Koshey the Bone Man's hidden heart. Nonetheless, that was exactly where I had to go right after getting out of Aristarchus.

"That's good," I said. "How can I break into Gormenghul?"

"What?!?" she sputtered. "That's impossible!"

"For the greatest thief in any world?" I asked archly.

"Sure," she said. "But he's not here."

"I think between the two of us, we're more than a match for him," I said. "Besides, I have the funny feeling his reputation is overrated."

"You have an idea?" she asked, obviously intrigued in spite of herself.

"A couple," I agreed. "But I need some technical tips. Plus you've been there a lot more often than I have. I've got questions."

Kelli looked miserable and I felt like a class-one, grade-A heel. If this weren't so important, I'd honestly leave it be. Was it so important? All I had was Gray's story that someday, somehow Patchwork would be a big deal in a war none of us could possibly survive. Against that I had to balance the lives of everyone here, not to mention playing hardball with someone I loved. I should say someone I *used* to love.

"Are you sure, Zack?" she asked with something like desperation in her eyes.

"What am I, talking to myself here?" I echoed, gently. "Of course I'm not sure."

I paused for a moment, and I put my cereal bowl down and took her tiny hand in my own.

"But I'm right, and you know it," I said.

"Yeah," she agreed. "But you're also a real asshat."

I couldn't argue with that. So I just nodded. She got out a big roll of carpenter's paper and thick pencils for each of us. She spread the paper out on the kitchen table and started sketching details. We got to work.

Chapter Twenty-Five

Kelli was right about one thing. Getting into Aristarchus had been easy enough. She had given me a charm that made me invisible to most of the standard watchwards. That would stop the non-specific spells from finding me, but I could still put my foot into something and then the best charms in Patchwork wouldn't protect me.

Following her instructions, I popped the easy lock on the glass doors leading to the back sun-room. I spun the Niven Disk and was pleasantly surprised to find no magic of any kind in the sun-room. No magic meant no magic wards. I gave a cursory search for the old-fashioned non-magical tripwires, loose floorboards, and the like. A trap didn't have to be magical to be dangerous. I'd seen some completely mundane defenses that could reduce a full-grown adult to a sloppy liquid mess in seconds. Quatermain didn't strike me as the type, but better safe than slurry.

After ascertaining the lack of traps, alarms, and clutter, I crept quietly into the back sun room. It was exactly as Kelli had described it. Keeping as much out-of-sight and away from doors as I could, I followed the plan we had laid out together. From the sunroom, I found the back hallway that led to the servants' stairs. Those led upwards to the residential levels.

The place was nearly abandoned. Aristarchus was built to hold a large family, a full staff of servants, and still have room for plenty of guests. It was like a ghost town around here. I remembered all the family photographs in the front hall and wondered what had happened to them all. Quatermain had mentioned having lots of brothers and sisters. I could see not wanting to stick around after the family inheritance had been sorted out, but this place was just too big to be this empty. I shrugged quietly and crept on, leaving my questions to be answered for another day.

For what must have been the thousandth time, I patted the travel bag at my side. I could still feel the reassuring bulk of the statuette that Gray had provided me – as promised – first thing this morning. There were over a dozen of my toys, gadgets, and gewgaws stuffed into the bag slung over my shoulder, but the only one I could feel was the one I wanted to feel. This was a good bag. I patted it again, this time affectionately. I had no idea whether that meant anything to the bag or not, but I didn't want to take its gifts for granted. I made a mental note not to develop the habit of fondling my shoulder bag whenever things were going well. Because that would be weird.

I paused at the head of the hallway I was looking for, the one that lead to both Quatermain's office and to his workroom which was my target. This was also, by far, the area of the lodge where I was most likely to get caught. I scrunched down low and listened for all I was worth. I listened for the creak of a foot on a floorboard, or the squeak of a chair being sat in. I heard nothing. I listened for breathing, movement, anything, but the only sounds I could hear were my own. Hopefully no one else was listening for me.

I took a cautious step forward and then I took another, and then another. I was committed now, there was no place to hide between here and the workroom. I moved as quickly as quiet allowed and made it to the door. It was closed. I listened carefully but heard nothing on the other side. I breathed a silent wish that the workroom wasn't soundproofed and I tried the doorknob. It was locked. No surprise there.

I slipped a hand into my bag and my fingers closed immediately on my lock picks. Thank you, magic luggage. I brought them out, lowered myself to my knees and eye-level with the knob, I slid the first pick in until it was snug against the tumbler, and positioned the next one alongside it. Lastly, I put the fulcrum in. I moved the tools around carefully, trying to finesse the lock rather than force it.

Popping a lock in this manner takes longer, which can be agonizing when you don't know if the lady of the house might come around the corner and see you kneeling there like an idiot in front of her husband's workroom. The upside is that when you're done, it looks just like you used a key. There's no evidence of entry to be found. It doesn't keep you from leaving evidence on the other side of the door, but a lot of little things done right usually added up to a job well done.

I was at last rewarded with a *snick* as the bolt withdrew from the lock. I gently turned the knob, slid the door open just wide enough for me to slip through and then closed it quietly behind me. The room was exactly how I remembered it. I looked at the poster with the little sailboat poem. It was the exact same poster Kelli had once given me. There was no way it was a coincidence. Even if Kelli would have given the poster to a 'friend' there's simply no way the proud lord of Aristarchus would have displayed such a thing unless the giver was emotionally important to him. Sometimes detective work is mostly luck.

It only took me a few more moments to find what I was looking for, a small-ish box with a lot of other stuff stacked on top of it, mostly disused and preferably dusty. I hadn't specifically seen this box the last time I was here, but all workrooms have a few basic things in common.

I took me about fifteen minutes to set the scene just the way I wanted. Working with dusty scenes is hard, but it's worth learning how. Nobody believes a box has been tampered with if the dust hasn't moved. The thing was, most people didn't memorize their dust patterns, and it was easy enough to spray new dust after you were done. Easy that is, if you have a magic cobweb in your bag of tricks; and fortunately for me, I did.

I slipped back out with no incidents of note. Down the stairs, through the sun-room and out the glass door from whence I had come. A quarter of a mile up the road from Aristarchus a black driverless brougham cab awaited me. It was nice to have a getaway vehicle with style. I gave directions to the horses and clambered up inside, patting my luggage affectionately.

I arrived at the front gate of Gwynplaine's lands more or less on schedule. Hopefully Baxter and Tim were in place already, but if they weren't, I would be able to stall for time until they arrived. I checked the anti-ward charms Kelli had given me. They looked to be in place and functional. I took a moment to trace my finger along the charm; some superstitions were based on fact, and it only took a moment. Satisfied with my preparations, I slipped past the gate and took off through the rocky ground to the left of the road.

I couldn't move very quickly, not without risking an ankle, but I made decent time, all things considered. It took me ten minutes to get all the way up to Gormenghul. I was struck once again by the ramshackle glory of the place. A fallen tower had come to rest on a mostly collapsed outbuilding with a certain lunatic balance. The edifice was almost completely collapsed, but nothing short of a bomb was going to make it fall the rest of the way down.

There were no gazebos outside and the staff seemed to be elsewhere. That suited my purposes just fine. I moved up to the sally gate and looked again at the nest of swirling charms carved into the huge wooden gates. I was convinced that these charms were some kind of travel magic; a written version of the power that had carried me from the site of my beating to Gray's tower.

These markings were how Gwynplaine controlled where this door led. The charms let him bring me to the study where we had spoken. They could have just as easily taken me to his dining room, a bedroom, or a dungeon. As long as Gwynplaine knew how they worked and no one else did, they were his to control. They were also the same markings that created a gateway between worlds that skipped over the Mist travel, and that Lady Gray could neither detect nor prevent, so we were talking pretty high-level magic, here.

I could no more defeat this magic than I could lift a giant octopus over my head with one hand. It was too big, too heavy, and too flexible. But maybe I could pry it open and make it go off. It was usually easier to smash a lock open than to finesse it, and I had an idea for smashing open the magic of Gormenghul's front door. It would require the third of the toys I had finagled out of Gray's magic shop.

There is a device called a Babelbox. It's most often used as a practical joke kind of magic. It makes pretty much every sound that can be heard by a human ear and puts out a tremendous amount of light all over the visible spectrum, but all done so fast it's completely imperceptible; a neat trick, actually. It makes people unable to communicate and it messes with the way the brain processes information. I postulated that a device that produced magic in roughly the same way could be used to overload a spell. Tim helped me put it together; he did all the engineering and intellectual heavy lifting on the job, actually, and he won't let me forget it.

The device had saved my life and arguably the world, so I'd called it a success at the time. We never could get the darn thing to work again after that, which as you might imagine was frustrating. Once I explained the basic idea to Adriana Gray, she had taken to it like a phoenix to the fire. The result was a military grade version of the Babelbox that I never wanted to see pointed at anyone's brain, and especially not my own. Presently, I was pointing it at Gormenghul's front gate.

The Babelbox alone wouldn't be nearly enough. And there was no way I could pull a trick like this off anywhere but Patchwork. But nothing was quite real here; it was all the most advanced game of make-believe yet discovered, and I could use that to my advantage. I remembered what it had felt like when I had first touched the counterfeit corpse. I summoned back that sense of walking off the edge of the world and into a world of images and memories.

Those memories had poured into the counterfeit corpse, but I was also convinced that the emotions produced by my memories were the key. Those emotions were how the Pillars made their willpower into reality. I had always been stubborn, it was one of my defining qualities, and when I have a full head of steam going, I can deny reality better than anyone I've ever met. I was betting that this epic-level denial made the stuff of the Mists pliable, re-shapeable, and obedient. I had the equivalent of a kindergarten education in being a Pillar. But that was okay, because all I had to do right now was smash. And toddlers are pretty good at that. I focused my will upon the charms and told myself that they didn't exist. I told that to myself with all my might. And then I told it to the world.

I felt a profound vertigo. The world went swimmy all around me, the ground got softer than hot toffee and shook like there was a five point-toffee-quake going on. I activated the Babelbox and closed my eyes real tight.

There was no perceptible sound or light. A moment later, I heard a clunk and a creak and the sally gate swung open. I opened my eyes to confirm what my ears had heard. Sure enough, the gate was open. There was no saying where it went, but I figured I'd deal with one thing at a time. I stepped through.

Looking around, I found myself in a dining room. It wasn't big enough to bowl in, so I figured it was for intimate dining. I wondered who Gwynplaine did his intimate dining with. Or maybe he dined alone but felt that a crumbling ancient castle just wasn't a home unless it had every kind of dining hall in it.

This wasn't my target room so I shrugged my shoulders and did it again. Hopefully as long as no one was watching anything real closely, the pinpoint nature of my intrusion would go unnoticed. I scrunched up my brow and gathered my denial, and activated the Babelbox again. There were two ways out of the dining hall, a big set of sliding double doors and a modest little swinging door that most likely led to a kitchen. I focused on the kitchen door. It swung open and I stepped forward again.

And I landed in a hot tub. I was in a spa center of some kind. The floor, walls, and ceiling were all ivory-colored marble. And I was thighs-deep in hot, swirling water. It might have been nice without the trousers, shoes, and socks. I sighed mightily and tried for a third time.

And the third time was the charm; I stepped into an office of some kind. There were six filing cabinets in a row and a three-drawer desk. I retrieved my lock picks from the bag and began fiddling with the top drawer of the leftmost cabinet. This was exactly what I had been looking for.

I noticed that my legs were dripping and I was leaving wet footprints everywhere I stepped. I rolled my eyes. So much for the little things. The drawer opened up and I saw files, lots and lots of files. I was flicking through them, waiting for something to leap out at me, when a distant tolling of a bell sounded.

The door burst open and the doorway was filled with the form of the larger of the two club brothers. I could see it in his eyes that he recognized me, too. He was looking forward to a rematch. I took a step back to give myself some room and I felt iron bands wrap around me, pinning my arms to my sides and my legs together. I looked down but saw nothing. I was being held by magic. I had apparently attracted the attentions of the master of Gormenghul. Lucky me. I wobbled and would have fallen, but the same invisible bands that imprisoned me held me up.

The club brother smiled happily at me and thrust his fist into my gut. I saw it coming and did my best to clench my muscles, but not being able to turn or move my arms really cramped my getting-beat-up style. It hurt and my breath left me, along with most of my fight. I let it show on my face.

Club Two chuckled. It's nice when I can bring happiness to my fellow being. I smiled weakly at him to show I appreciated that there were no hard feelings. He punched me in the gut again. I considered throwing up. Maybe if I was lucky, some of it would get on him. That would show him who was boss.

"That will be quite enough, Tommo," Gwynplaine said as he glided into the room. He was wearing the same outfit as earlier, down to the hat. I guess it suited him.

"Y'know," I said thoughtfully. "Most guys really can't pull a pillbox hat off properly. Good for you."

"And that will be enough out of you as well," he said mildly.

I felt another band wrapping around my mouth. That was a shame, there was little in this world that I enjoyed quite as much as good banter with an unabashed villain. At least there was still hope for a monologue.

"Leave us," Gwynplaine said to Club Two, whose name must have been Tommo. "But remain outside the door. I shall have need of you shortly."

I was kind of annoyed to learn Club Two's name. Now it would be harder to think of him as Club Two instead of Tommo. I resolved to try anyway. I had been learning that I had untapped reservoirs of willpower, maybe it was time to start using those resources for something useful.

"And what might you be looking for," Gwynplaine asked, clearly hypothetically. "Some kind of proof that I killed Peter Starbourne? Or were you here to plant that proof, hmm?"

I looked him right in the eyes and shook my head profoundly in the negative.

"Well, of course you'd deny it," he said with a laugh. "Do you actually think your word means anything here? You have no rank, you have no standing, you have no history here."

His laugh was one of those that started out deep and rich, but had that twangy edge that suggested sooner or later it would crack and become a madman's cackle. I looked at him blandly, expressing neither fear nor anger. I was just waiting to have my say.

"Oh very well," he sighed and waved one hand languidly. "Come, tell me your lies so that we may get this over with."

The band around my mouth vanished. This was it. I had to sell this part and I had to sell it good. My hands twitched to tug at my shirt sleeve, or to straighten my hat. My feet ached to pace. This was all much harder without the gestures and the movement.

"Actually," I said. "I'm here because I convinced Roger that I could break in here and get the secrets of homunculus design. He wants to cut you out of the deal and take over the business himself."

"What?" Gwynplaine spluttered, inelegantly. "That's preposterous. Surely you can do better than that."

"Suit yourself," I said calmly. "I know when I'm rumbled. You've got me. It's no paint off my wand if my employer gets away. What do you know? If I live through this, maybe it'll even help with my reputation."

Gwynplaine sneered at me, but he didn't end the conversation. He stood there looking at me. I could see the gears working in that criminal brain of his. Roger had always been his subservient, faithful go-to guy. If the golem was even entertaining the idea of betrayal, the balance of power was off.

Gwynplaine's paranoia was waking up and stretching. Soon enough it would be telling him that the safest thing to do was get rid of Roger and get a new thug. Then his second thoughts told him that I was lying. It made sense that I was lying, but now he would have to be sure. If he asked me another question, I'd have him on the hook.

"How could Roger possibly run this without me?" Gwynplaine asked.

"He told me he'd been practicing for decades," I said in answer. "He's even managed to produce a crude knockoff of one of your statuettes."

"Aha," Gwynplaine pounced. "You've talked yourself into a corner. There is no such statuette. I'd know if there were."

"Maybe it's hidden someplace where it's hard for even you to find," I suggested reasonably.

"That's absurd," Gwynplaine scoffed.

"You're probably right," I agreed. "I mean you can read every inch of Gray's tower just as easily as you can see your own front door, right?"

"Harrumph," Gwynplaine muttered.

"Hey," I said brightly. "I bet Roger would have stashed it someplace inside Aristarchus, right? I mean that place is nearly as old as Patchwork itself, right? I bet it's bitching hard to get a read on that place."

"Hard," Gwynplaine agreed. "But not impossible!"

He took a pull of his silver cigarette holder as the tip of the cigarette magically bloomed into a cherry-red coal. He exhaled slowly and the smoke dipped and spun crazily through the still air, following air patterns that weren't there and never had been. His eyes lost focus and he hummed a little to himself. It didn't look like he was working up much of a sweat, but at least it had his attention.

Sadly, the strength of my bonds didn't waver any. I was still good and stuck. There was no way to force my way out of this situation. This gag had to work or I was one doomed detective. As surreptitiously as I possibly could, I began running my tongue along the inside of my teeth. I rapidly found the one tooth that had the backside carved up.

Tim himself had drawn this charm and it had felt damn peculiar when he did it. He told me that the charm included the rune that represented his own true name. I ran the tip of my tongue along it three times. That was the message to put his part of the operation into play. I hoped to Salvation Above that he hadn't been delayed by anything. It was now or never.

"There is such a statuette after all," Gwynplaine murmured. "But that in and of itself means nothing. There are many explanations for ..."

He paused. With his senses all out and open like that I figured there was no way he wouldn't smell what Tim was doing. After all, it was Gwynplaine's own spell that Tim was casting. Warlocks weren't so good at inventing magic, but as one of magic's natural tomb raiders, Tim was a real whiz at copying other people's work.

"Someone is opening one of my portals," Gwynplaine snarled. "Who could do such a thing?"

"I don't know," I said with faux-innocence in my voice. "Maybe somebody who's been studying your work for decades trying to learn how to rip you off?"

"That's enough!" Gwynplaine all but shouted.

He threw his hands up in the air and traced a rapid pattern, each hand going in entirely unrelated directions. I had to admit I was impressed. I couldn't even so much as rub my belly and pat my head at the same time. This took dedication. The will-worker vanished and his magic bonds vanished with him.

So much for the easy part of this operation. The next step required getting back out of Gormenghul and that meant dealing with Club Two outside the door. I looked around the office for something stout. I was pleased to find a heavy metal ruler with a T-square on one end. I smacked it experimentally against the palm of my hand and grinned. Sometimes I'm not a very nice guy.

Chapter Twenty-Six

One short but highly-satisfying fight later, I had free run of Gormenghul, at least for the very immediate future. I reversed my breaking and entering from earlier, only this time it involved more breaking and less sneaking and I found myself tumbling down a steep scrub-covered embankment just outside of the collapsed castle proper. I hit the bottom a little bit harder than I would have liked; my right ankle twisted beneath me, not badly enough to stop me but definitely enough to slow me down.

I half-ran, half-limped, half-staggered up to the muddy main road. And the fact that all added up to three halves can only help describe just how ungainly my locomotion was. I burst out onto the road and nearly knocked my partner over.

"Baxter!" I wheezed. "I almost knocked you over!"

"No you didn't, Boss," Bax assured me. "Run into me, maybe. Knocked me over? I don't think so."

"Ha, ha," I said cleverly. "Everything seems to be going according to plan. I got caught right on schedule, fed our mark the bait, and gave Tim the signal. And shortly after that Gwynplaine tore out of there like his little hat was on fire. I think it is safe to say that the seeds of doubt have been planted."

"Tim's done his part," Bax rumbled. "Now you have to do yours. Don't screw this up, Boss."

"What?" I sputtered. "Doesn't convincing him that Roger was trying to have him bumped off count as at least part of my part?"

"Sure, Boss," Bax agreed. "We can give you part of Tim's credit if you feel like you need it."

This was one of those times I so desperately wished that I knew the eyebrow trick. Nothing, and I mean nothing, would have put my mouthy employee in his place better than one single eye-brow arched sardonically in his direction. No words would be necessary, but we would both know who had gotten the better of the exchange. I had to settle for what I had. Which, frankly, wasn't much.

"Okay," I said in my best tough-guy voice. "Let's do this."

Baxter didn't look as impressed by my tough-guy voice as I felt he should have been, but he dutifully moved to the center of the road and handed me my bag. I had left it in his safekeeping, preferring to leave quirky and unstable magic out of my Babelbox equation.

The bag was heavy and awkward as Bax handed it to me, but as soon as I slung the strap over my shoulder its weight immediately vanished. Quirky and unstable it might be, but it was also quite nice. I patted the bag affectionately, (but only once). I pulled out the Niven Disk and sighed heavily. I had only owned it for a little while but I was going to miss this toy. I couldn't come up with any other options, though. Bax and I needed to get to the portal by the trees and we had to get there fast. We wanted to get there before Roger and Gwynplaine had a chance to talk to each other and compare notes, but we absolutely needed to get there before they discovered Tim and the fact that he had been the one to open the portal, not Roger.

And getting there fast meant using Patchwork's Travel Magic. The last time I had tried to use this magic, it had knocked me out for two days. Of course, some of that might have been the concussion, but I wasn't taking any chances. In Patchwork, a will-worker could suck the whammy out of anything, no matter who built it. I had seen Gray dissolve Quatermain's stuff easily enough, so, in theory, I could do the same. Gray had made the Niven Disk, and she had put an awful lot of whammy into it. I was going to pull it all out and use that energy to power up the Travel Magics.

It was an important element of the plan that Bax and I arrive not only fast, but also in style. We had to convince Gwynplaine that I was a powerful and competent Pillar, and that wasn't going to be easy. Even if I chose to become a Pillar, I was weeks of hard work away from being able to do anything solidly competent, much less impressive. But I had taught myself one trick already: and that was how to break stuff.

I centered myself and did my best to calm my busy mind. I focused my thoughts and tried to make my face look like Gray's had when she concentrated on magic stuff. It might not help, but it couldn't hurt. I reached out with my will and thought destructive thoughts.

I broke the Niven Disk. Bright silver light and sound blasted out of the space where the powerful charm had been. I closed my eyes, and imagined I could still see the silver light wadding it up into a big silver ball. I pictured it as a giant shiny piece of aluminum foil, I crumpled it up with my mind and then smoothed it back out again, all in my mind. I heard Baxter grunt meaningfully.

"You've got it, Boss," he called. "You're doing great!"

I had it. Now I had to make something with it. I pictured the foil sliding under our feet and lifting us up. Nothing happened. The foil just sat there in my mind's eye refusing to move. As if life weren't hard enough, now I had to deal with belligerent aluminum foil. I gave it an imaginary push, but my mind just sort of slipped off and couldn't get a grip.

"This isn't working, Bax," I growled through gritted teeth.

"Stop trying to get fancy," Bax rumbled back. "Just make it into a Coach Car, already."

I almost lost control of the foil completely. A Coach Car? I knew immediately that Baxter was right. There was practically nothing in this whole world that I knew better than the Coach Cars of New Jerusalem. As a long-time resident of a big city with a fantastic public transport system, I didn't drive. I walked as much as I could, but when I needed wheels, I used the Coach Cars.

I could picture a Coach Car perfectly in my mind. I knew how they looked, I knew how they sounded, smelled and felt. I had run my fingers along the pebbled metal doors thousands of times. The squeak of the tracks, the stink of the ozone, even the rocking motion that told me how fast we were going, were all captured in my memory with crystalline perfection. I thought real hard about a Coach Car.

"Good job, Boss," Baxter rumbled approvingly.

I cracked one eye open just wide enough to squint out of. Sure enough Baxter was standing next to a perfect replica of a New Jerusalem Coach

Car. The doors levered open with a hiss of released steam and a clunk of metal thunking against metal. There was no one on board.

"Bax," I said. "This is no good. There's no driver."

"Relax," Bax clucked. "Haven't you read your own reports?"

I had no idea what Baxter was talking about, but he strode forward and climbed up the short steps and into the Coach Car. I shrugged and followed suit. My partner clearly had a plan. Baxter was standing in the center of the car, his hand loosely wrapped around one of the floor-to-ceiling metal poles. I followed suit, but chose to grab one of the overhead handrails instead; handrails were cooler.

"Please take us to the portal," Bax rumbled politely to the empty air.

There was a shriek of brakes releasing and the driverless Coach Car shuddered twice and surged forward along the muddy road. In New Jerusalem, they ran on rails, but that didn't seem to be a problem here. The driverless Car molded tracks out of the mud and then ran along those. I looked out the window and saw them reshaping back into ordinary looking ruts behind us. I think Visivald would have been impressed.

The Coach Car picked up speed and I became glad of my handrail as we rocked back and forth and occasionally up and down as well. Outside the window, the scenery began to blur by in what was becoming a familiar fashion. I felt simultaneously smug at my success and profoundly concerned about the implications of that success. I was consciously and knowingly working the stuff of Patchwork. I was doing Pillar stuff. What did that mean? And what responsibilities was Adriana Gray trying to put on me?

These were not good thoughts to be having on my way to what was very likely a major confrontation and quite possibly, a big fight. I had to get my brain back into the game and I had to do it fast. Distractions could be deadly and if I were dead, I wouldn't be any use to anyone. Plus, I'd be dead, which would be a significant downside for me.

I shook my head to clear it. Bax looked at me inquiringly, but I gave him my 'don't worry about it, it's nothing' face and he seemed to accept that. It was a good face; it had gotten me out of a lot of uncomfortable conversations over the years. Now I just needed to convince myself not to worry. I didn't have a face for that yet.

I decided to distract my internal monologue by rehearsing the speech I planned to give whoever was left standing when the dust cleared at the portal. Then I started thinking about how dust clearing wasn't really the right metaphorical image, what with all the rain and mud.

I was busy pondering such weighty matters when the driverless Coach Car hit a bump, waking me from my reverie and obliging me to grip the handrail a little bit tighter. A new thought occurred to me. I rolled it around for a little while to get the shape of it fixed in my mind. I wasn't sure what it meant yet.

"Hey Bax," I said questioningly. "How'd you know the magic Coach Car would respond to verbal requests?"

Baxter snorted derisively, "I already told you, Boss. It was in your report. Everything around here responds to verbal requests. Dr. Foucault's purple buggy, Lady Gray's coach, and even Uncle Viz's subterranean job all did it. I figure it's just part of the way Travel Magic works around here."

"So the horses pulling Gray's coach and the griffs pulling Foucault's aren't real animals," I mused.

"I guess that follows," Baxter agreed. "All part of the magic. Hey, maybe there's one big sentient brain that controls all the Travel Magic in Patchwork? I bet Gray could tell us."

"Mm," I nodded. "But no real animals. Baxter, have you seen any animals since you got here?"

"Sure I have," Bax rumbled. "They're everywhere. Not to mention the cougar that mauled the crap out of you."

"Ah," I observed. "But that cougar wasn't real. It was a counterfeit cougar. And have you actually seen any critters? Or have you just heard them? Maybe seen them in the distance?"

Baxter stroked his chin scales thoughtfully.

"Now that you put it that way," he said slowly. "I'm not really sure."

"Me neither," I agreed. "I don't know what that means yet, but it means something."

With a hiss of steam, a screech of brakes, and a bone-jarring lurch, the Coach Car juddered to a halt. The doors hissed twice and clunked open. We had arrived at our destination.

Bax was first out with a bound that carried him off the road and half way to the copse of trees before I was even on the ground. Bax was annoying that way sometimes. I charged after him and was only a few paces behind by the time he got to the edge of the depression that hid the portal from casual view. The big rock was gone. Roger and Gwynplaine were yelling at each other. Club One was standing around looking profoundly uncomfortable.

That was good, actually. I was glad the argument hadn't broken out into a fight yet. Hopefully, I could gain control of the situation and put the next part of the plan into play. For the record, I was also hopeful that goblins would learn how to fly, the whole world would find a way to live in peace, and a leprechaun would personally deliver a tax-free pot of gold to my front door. I'm a hopeful guy.

"...nothing without me!" shouted Gwynplaine. "The design is mine, the work is mine, the portal is mine! No one but me could have accomplished this!"

"You couldn't have done it without my help," replied Roger in his emotionless, mellow baritone. "And I won't let you abandon me now, not when we're so close to the big payoff."

"I'm not abandoning you," Gwynplaine cried. "You're betraying me!"

"That is patently ridiculous," said Roger as calmly as he said everything.

"And yet I find you here, trying to escape through my portal!" Gwynplaine shouted.

"I have had enough of you and your baseless accusations," thrummed Roger's strange voice from deep within his chest. "And I shall stand for it no longer."

"Then why are you trying to escape?" Gwynplaine snarled. "The innocent have no reason to flee!"

Apparently Roger meant it when he said he wouldn't stand for it any longer, as he hauled back a massive rock slab of a fist and slammed it smartly into Gwynplaine's head. The fist stopped inches away, smashing into some kind of protective personal ward. A cascade of sparks flew up at the point of impact. Gwynplaine staggered back two steps but showed no other reaction. Apparently, the man was not without defenses of his own.

The fight was on. So much for world peace and the pot of gold. I looked at Baxter and he looked at me. I shrugged and ran towards the two combatants; the best plans always have a little bit of wiggle room built in.

"New plan," I shouted as I stumbled forward favoring my bad ankle. "Hit everybody really hard until they get agreeable!"

"I'm on it!" Baxter called back, as he bounded past me.

Chapter Twenty-Seven

For a short and stocky guy, Baxter can really move when he needs to. His leap carried him a good five yards past me, and he hit the ground running. Fast. He let out a bellowing roar that would have done credit to a bull elephant, put his head down and charged.

From my position, embarrassingly to the rear, I saw Club One and Gwynplaine freeze for a moment in shock. Roger, to his credit, ignored Bax's war challenge and instead slammed one huge rocky fist straight into the side of Gwynplaine's head. For the second time, Roger's fist stopped inches away from its target, throwing up another cascade of colorful sparks and making a scraping noise that hurt my teeth.

Bax slammed into Roger's back. The golem bent almost in double around the impact, but his feet didn't move an inch; I was impressed. Bax snarled and dug in. Roger tried to turn around and get a grip on the new target, but he couldn't get purchase against the massive goblinblood. Strong is good, but smart and strong is better.

Club One started maneuvering around to get behind Bax and I wasn't close enough to do anything about it yet. I scooped up a small rock, aimed for center mass, lead the target a little to make up for forward momentum and let loose. It clipped him hard on the shoulder. I had been aiming for the middle of his back, but I'll take what I can get.

"Hey!" I shouted. "Remember me?"

He snarled, looking around until he found me. I waved at him and grinned. Club One snarled again and charged towards me. This wasn't great, but it meant that he was no longer messing with my partner and that was also good enough for me. I gave him the 'come and get me' hand gesture that always seems to work in Kung Fu movies. I didn't know any Kung Fu, but I had been taught how to beat people up by some of the best fighters in professional sports. I liked my chances in a fair fight, even with a bum ankle.

My opponent drew his charge up short and studied me for a second. He slapped the heavy weight of his club against the palm of his hand. He liked his chances, too. I could hardly blame him; he and his partner had beaten me seven ways to Perdition twice already. But this time there was a difference. This time I wasn't outnumbered. Also, this time I had my luggage with me.

I slipped two fingers and a thumb inside the bag. My hand closed instantly and smoothly around the hilt of a wooden practice sword, the heavy kind used for serious sparring. I drew it out and tested its balance. It was exactly like the one I usually worked out with. For all I could tell it was the one I usually worked out with. There were some things about Patchwork that I was definitely starting to like.

Club One's eyes barely had time to widen. I took two rapid steps forward and then lunged. The blunt wooden tip of the blade caught him in the solar plexus. All the air and most of the fight went out of him at about the same time. He fell to his knees and stayed there. He wasn't quite unconscious, but he was definitely *hors de' combat.*

I flicked my eyes towards the center of the glen. Gwynplaine had staggered back a step or three and Roger was still struggling with Bax. Roger had managed to get turned around and the two of them were locked in a wrestling match. As I moved forward to meddle with that equilibrium, Gwynplaine's eyes snapped over to me, and our gazes met. His eyes narrowed. *Uh-oh.*

The next thing I knew, I was doing a face-plant on the ground. Ow. I couldn't move my arms or legs. It took me a second to remember that Gwynplaine controlled physics around these parts. I was pretty good in a fight, but physics are a bitch. I struggled to raise my head; it would have been nice, at least, to be able to see what was happening. I was straining with all my might, trying to get even my fingers into the ground, let alone get my face out of the mud. Nothing. I didn't move so much as a hair's width off the ground. I was helpless.

I hate being helpless. It gives me too much time alone in my head. I found my mind still racing at full combat-speed. Only now it was reminding me of every mistake I had made in getting to this point. There were a lot of them. Too many things just didn't make enough sense.

What was I missing? And what did it matter? If I couldn't get up, I was going to die right here. Lying facedown in the mud of a land so far away from my city that no maps had ever been drawn to show the way. I almost gave up. I almost stopped fighting. But I didn't, because I knew something that the other guys didn't know. I had brought backup.

I was still straining with all my strength to get up off the ground, when all of the implacable resistance suddenly vanished. Before I could adapt to the new situation, I threw myself up into the air and stumbled back, arms pinwheeling. Somehow I kept hold of my wooden sword. The guy who had trained me would have been proud. I'd have to remember to tell old Darius the next time I visited him in prison.

I saw immediately what had distracted Gwynplaine. A stream of knives, axes, spears, and throwing stars were careening off some kind of magical shield in mid-air a few inches away from his head. Colorful sparks were cascading in every direction. I followed the stream back to its source. Tim was standing at the edge of the glen. His scrawny arms were extended and flexing so hard the muscles and veins stood out, making his intricate tattoos writhe. His fingers were contorting bizarrely and his lips were moving around words of a language I didn't understand.

"About time we got some backup!" I shouted cheerfully.

Tim swiveled his left hand towards me, adroitly flipped me off, and went right back to throwing grief at Gwynplaine.

Thus freed from direct interference, I was able to survey the battlefield. Tim and Gwynplaine seemed to be all locked up as were Baxter and Roger. My dance partner was still sitting on the ground, sucking oxygen, and thinking peaceful thoughts. What could I do to swing the fight for the good guys?

I shuffled over and up behind Roger. I hefted my wooden practice sword and swung it towards the back of Roger's leg – right about where his knees should be – with all my might. It made a sort of a *clunk* as it impacted, and the vibrations shot back up my hands and arms, knocking all the feeling out of them for a second. If it weren't for my training, I would have dropped the sword.

Other than hurting myself, my actions seemed to have no effect. Roger ignored me completely, focusing all of his attention on my partner. Bax for his part, threw a hot glance in my direction. Roger noticed his distraction and redoubled his efforts. Bax's feet skidded back a few inches. Okay, not no effect; now I was making things worse.

"Get out of here, Zack!" Baxter growled. "You can't help!"

A lesser man might've been hurt by his partner's words. I took it as a challenge. I didn't have any weapons that could pierce Roger's rocky hide, and I had no way of getting through Gwynplaine's shields. Or did I?

I shoved the wooden practice sword back inside my bag. As soon as I opened my fingers, the hilt vanished out of my hand. I rummaged for about a nanosecond before my fingers found what I wanted. I pulled the Babelbox out, traced its rune three times until it glowed bright, and ran forward, past Bax and Roger. I darted across the road, only skidding slightly in the mud and fetched up short in front of Gwynplaine.

"Smile!" I sang as I thrust the business end of the 'box right into Gwynplaine's face and thumbed the activation rune.

Magical activity on every range of every spectrum blared out inches away from the Pillar's face. His magical defenses fizzled instantly. Tim's endless spray of magical weapons sailed through and smashed into the man's lanky frame explosively. A second later the weapons dissolved as well. I don't know whether Tim had dropped the spell or my Babelbox had interfered with Tim's magic.

I had a clear view of Gwynplaine's face as he turned to look directly at the Babelbox. He looked fascinated. Then his expression turned to horror, tears streamed from his eyes and his lips pealed back into a maniacal grin.

My fingers fumbled desperately for the shut off charm and at last I found it. The strange lights reflected in Gwynplaine's eyes flicked and went out. He stood there, swaying slightly and giggling quietly to himself. I swallowed hard and looked away.

Roger was finally getting the better of the fight. He was learning how to use his greater height and weight as leverage. I'll say one thing for golems, they're fast learners. I thought about turning the Babelbox on Roger, but the magics that animated him were covered by layers of impenetrable stone. There was no way they'd be affected, at least not fast enough to stop Roger from stomping me flat for trying.

I had to play my last trick. I hadn't planned on using it while Gwyplaine was still around, as there was no way it would have worked on a scholar of his level. I just had to hope that Gwynplaine would stay in la-la land long enough for it to work on Roger.

I reached into the bag and pulled out a single white feather and a pocket witchlighter. I held up the feather and thumbed the witchlighter into ignition. The feather caught fire immediately and blackened into char before my eyes.

"Enough of this," I shrieked. "Enough of this deception. See you all now the power that opposes you! I summon Carafael the Fallen to obey my bidding!"

The air was filled with the sharp tang of ozone and a light so bright it seared onto my retinas, followed less than a second later by the boom of thunder so loud it deafened me. I really should have prepared better for this entrance.

I blinked hard a few times and the sparkles and the blotches started to fade from my vision. Standing in the road, there was a gaunt blond man, naked but for a twist of dirty rag about his hips, ragged wings stretched out behind him. His skin was pale and almost translucent, blue and red veins tracing the underside of his flesh like miniature lightning bolts.

Roger and Baxter had staggered a few steps apart and were both staring at the new arrival. I could hardly blame them. There were very few things in this world that impressed me more than a really good dramatic entrance.

"Monday," hissed the winged man. "I swear by Samael's left tit that I will string you up by your own guts if you don't tell me why you summoned me."

The winged man's voice was soft, but it carried clear as the tolling of a bell to my ears. From the expression on Baxter's and Tim's faces, they could also hear it just fine. Roger was a rock and Gwynplaine was still giggling. I guess you just can't impress everyone no matter how hard you try.

"*Gulp*," I gulped.

"What's the matter, Monday?" the winged man sneered softly. "Can't you handle what you've dragged up?"

"I can handle the likes of you," I said trying to sound like I was trying to sound brave. "And I charge you to destroy this golem unless he flees this place now, never to return!"

"Wh- what?" stammered Roger, betraying for the first time in my hearing any verbal reaction at all.

"I said destroy the golem," I repeated helpfully. "Unless he flees this place now, never to return. Do you feel like being destroyed tonight Roger? Or would you rather flee?"

"You're bluffing," Roger said, recovering his calm. "Nothing in the worlds can destroy a true golem. We were made eternal."

"Ah, but who were you made by?" I asked. "Angels brought you into these worlds and a fallen angel can take you back out."

I was counting on there being some hint of an echo of divinity left in Roger's makeup. I needed him to be absolutely certain that he was dealing with a real honest-to-Salvation Angel. Because that's what he was, of course. Or half was at any rate. My message had gotten through to Eel, also sometimes known as Carafael, and he had gotten his half-angelic fanny to Patchwork. I wasn't sure how he'd done it, but with Audrey helping him out, I had been sure it would happen.

"This can't be," Roger said. "Angels and devils both are banned from this place. Gwynplaine said they were."

"And he was right as far as he knew," I replied. "But people who have cut deals with Perdition create a connection that works like a short cut. A Get Out of Perdition Free card. And it brought Carafael here."

"Nooooooo!" Roger screamed.

The sound of the golem's scream was horrible. It was long and drawn out and utterly inhuman. I had heard more than a few inhuman creatures scream in my time. But hearing it never got any easier. I shuddered inside, but tried not to let it show on my face.

"Get out of here," I said, putting as much menace into my voice as I could manage. "Before my friend here loses his patience."

"I don't want to die," Roger moaned. "Let me leave and I swear I'll never return."

Nobody fears death quite like an immortal does. Something about believing you can't die makes the possibility a lot scarier than it is for us poor mortals who know we're doomed to die. There have to be some advantages after all.

"Go," hissed the angel Carafael. "Now."

Roger moved as fast as his ungainly frame would carry him towards Gwynplaine's portal. He spoke a series of words as he did and the tiny runic lines carved all over the circle flared into vermilion light. As his foot crossed the circle, the light blazed up. Roger passed through the wall of light and both light and golem were gone.

We all just stood there for a moment, looking at each other. The glen was silent but for Gwynplaine's quiet giggling and the moans of the semi-conscious Club One. Tim moved to Gwynplaine and bound his hands behind his back. The Pillar stopped giggling, but otherwise did nothing to resist. Baxter walked over to the thug and produced a pair of handcuffs out of one trouser pocket. He snapped them shut on the equally unresisting thug's wrists.

"Is this guy evil enough to kill?" Eel asked earnestly.

"I'm honestly not sure, Eel," I replied. "But what say you practice a little restraint either way? It'll be good for you."

Eel didn't look too happy, but his flaming sword was nowhere in evidence so I figured we were all right as far as that went. The half-angel was getting much better at controlling his urges. Self-control was a good thing. When the loss of that self-control led to people getting dead, it was even better.

"So how was I?" Eel asked. "Was I scary 'nough?"

Left to his own devices, the half-angel tended to slur his words and was a bit of a sloucher. His wings drooped down and folded up against his back. He scratched idly at the side of his nose.

"Eel," I said. "You were fantastic. Thank you. I could not have asked for better. Bravo."

"Really?" Eel beamed with pride, and since he was half angel on his father's side, when he beamed it was literal.

"Too right," piped Tim. "That was fooking beautiful!"

"Good job, kid," Bax rumbled. "You were pretty freaky."

"Okay," I said. "We can hold the rest of the awards ceremony later. There's still work to do."

I walked over to Gwynplaine, laid one hand on either shoulder and leaned my face in very close to his. I looked into his eyes; they rolled around inside their sockets and focused on everything and nothing all at once. A tiny line of drool hung down from one corner of his mouth.

"Where is Peter Starbourne?" I asked. "Where are you hiding him?"

It took a while, but eventually both of Gwynplaine's eyes rolled towards me. He sniffed quietly and for just a moment seemed to be his old self. Then he started giggling again.

"Me?" he said around his giggles. "Me? I never had him. No, never. It was never me."

"Who then?" I demanded. "Who took Starbourne?"

"Oswald did, of course," Gwynplaine said. "Oswald Quatermain, IV. But you should know all about that, shouldn't you? After all he's working for the same people you're working for. Isn't he?"

Gwynplaine pointed to Eel and giggled so hard he fell into a coughing fit. When he recovered he looked at me with an unwholesome glint in his mad eyes. His smile grew wider and a little bit of his old contempt came over his face.

"Unless of course you were lying to poor, poor, Roger about that," he said. "You wouldn't lie about a thing like that, would you, Mr. Monday?"

I said nothing. My *doppelgänger* had been right and I had been wrong. Sure, Gwynplaine and Roger had been behind the smuggling ring. I had figured that much out correctly. But then I had leaped to the obvious conclusion that they were also behind the Starbourne kidnapping. That had been foolish in retrospect; I had made the oldest mistake in the book. It was the Unified Scheme Fallacy, the foil to the Spenser Rule. Everything wasn't always tied up neat in a bow. There was more than one set of bad guys operating here and I had missed it.

I had gambled and lost. There was no way Quatermain wouldn't have caught wind of this ruckus. If we had ever had a chance of rescuing Starbourne, it was gone now. For all I knew, the man was already dead and Quatermain had skipped town.

"It might not be too late, Boss," Baxter rumbled. "We can still put the plan Tim and I came up with into operation."

"The tracking ritual?" I asked. "Can that still work?"

"Maybe," Bax said. "Tim's end of it is fine. But I'm worried that I won't be able to keep my end up. There isn't much for me to go on."

"That's okay," I said. "We have another option now. We're tracking a violent crime of passion here."

Tim, Baxter and I all looked at Eel. Eel looked back at us. Eel scratched his nose again. I grinned. There was still a chance after all, but it depended on everyone pulling together on a very risky long shot. Also it would require me getting yet more free work out of Adriana Gray. I rubbed my hands together.

"Okay, guys," I said. "Here's the plan."

Chapter Twenty-Eight

The driverless Coach Car I had created screeched to a halt in front of Aristarchus. The ephemeral mud rails dissolved and the car promptly sunk about four inches into the mud. The doors *clunked* open and I stepped down and out into the ever-present rain of Patchwork. It was pretty obvious that Quatermain knew I was coming. All the tiki torches were out and the place was dark and silent. Even the animal noises were gone. The only sound was the squelching of my own shoes in the mud.

I limped towards the main lodge, rain streaming off my hat as fast as it seeped into my boots. I really missed the city. Sure it rained in New Jerusalem, but at least concrete didn't turn into mud when it got wet. I reached the door and lacking any better ideas, I knocked.

The door swung open. It was as dark inside as it was from the outside, and just as silent. I took a step forward and reached out one hand for the railing.

"That's far enough, Monday," Quatermain's disembodied voice echoed from everywhere and at once and nowhere in particular. "You can come in if you're alone, but no tricks."

"I need to see Peter Starbourne," I said in a firm tone, but at a conversational volume; there was no need to shout.

"He's close by," replied Quatermain's voice. "But give me your word that you're alone or I'll kill him right now."

"I'm alone," I said. "Show him to me."

"You don't get to make the demands here," Quatermain's voice replied, haughtily. "I hold all the charms. You've got nothing."

"Fair enough," I said agreeably. "So it's your show. What do you want to talk about?"

"Is it true that you once beat a Duke of Perdition at his own game?" Quatermain's voice asked.

So that's what this was about. Quatermain had cut a deal with a devil and now he wanted help backing out. That was both good and bad. It meant that he was desperate and desperate men were often willing to believe anything. That was the good part. On the flip side, desperate men were often also willing to do anything. And that was the bad part.

"We came to an arrangement," I said. "I was able to outmaneuver him, but it was a lucky break. And I never made a deal with him. Can you say the same?"

"You don't know me!" Quatermain snarled. "Don't judge me!"

The voice wasn't disembodied anymore, it came from right behind me. I whirled and there he was, still dressed in white from his toes to his neck. White shoes, white trousers, white coat, shirt, and a fluffy white cravat tied neatly around his neck. He held his cougar-pommeled walking stick in one hand and an egg in the other.

"Please stay very still, Mr. Monday," Quatermain said quietly. "If I crush this egg, Peter Starbourne dies. Messily."

I held my hands up in a placating gesture, but otherwise stood very still. Quatermain looked perfectly calm and was being reasonable and cautious. But I couldn't tell how far down his calm actually went. He had to know the forces arrayed against him were overwhelming. My guess was that he was putting on a good show out of some kind of aristocratic imperative. Underneath that casual, sophisticated super-villain stuff he was a frantic mess, one twitch away from screaming and frothing. I would have to play the next several minutes very carefully.

"What do you want me to do for you, Lord Aristarchus?" I asked.

"It was a mistake to treat with devils," Quatermain said, still oozing calm out of every pore. "I see that now. Agree to help me break my contract and I will release Starbourne. But you must swear an oath upon your honor."

I would have given anything to be able to raise one eyebrow at just that moment. Instead I had to settle for raising them both, but it just wasn't as cool.

"Assuming for the moment that I could help you," I said slowly. "I'd need more out of you than just Starbourne's release. Dealing with Perdition is dangerous; I'd be risking a lot."

"What else do you want?" Quatermain asked. "I'm a man of considerable means."

"Sure," I said. "Here. But what good is your imaginary wealth back in New Jerusalem?"

"Stay here, then," Quatermain purred. "Become a Pillar. Take my side in this matter, argue my case with Lady Gray. The rewards shall be greater than anything you can imagine."

"I don't know," I quoted. "I can imagine quite a bit."

"Good," Quatermain said, totally missing my reference. "Your imagination shall serve you well here."

"Maybe," I agreed. "But I want something up front. Something you can give me right now."

"And what, pray tell," Quatermain drawled. "Would that be?"

"Information," I said. "I need to know more about your deal before I know whether or not I can help you. What was your reward?"

Quatermain's manner changed. His jaw clenched and his chin lifted arrogantly. I saw the ghost of a doubt flicker across his face, but he mastered himself, and even managed to look down his nose at me as if it were something beyond my understanding.

"The continuation of my family line," Quatermain said at last.

"Your wife …" I began.

"Is barren," he interrupted. "My seed would not quicken in her womb. As the years went by and no heir was born to me, I grew concerned."

I kept my face calm and emotionless, but at the same time I had to forcibly stop myself from slapping someone's face; maybe Quatermain's or maybe my own. This guy had made a deal with a devil to get his wife knocked up? I was willing to bet my entire fee for this case that he hadn't even tried to get his wife to a fertility clinic, let alone been to one himself. I wanted to tell him what an idiot he was, how many options there might have been that he didn't pursue. For Salvation's Sake, he could have adopted somebody! Better anything than giving your soul to Perdition.

"But it went wrong," I said bitterly. "It wasn't the way you thought it would be."

"No," Quatermain agreed. "It wasn't. I thought he'd take my soul, but he didn't."

"He gets your soul no matter what," I said sadly. "That's the part of the deal they never tell you. The devils always take something else, something you never intended to give."

A single sob escaped Quatermain's otherwise perfect composure.

"What did he take, Oswald?" I asked as gently as I could manage. "What did the devil take from you?"

"My power," he said quietly. "My ability to control the Mists through my will. He took my Pillar from me."

Suddenly it all made sense. There were no real animals in Patchwork because he couldn't make them anymore. He was faking it with a fancy soundtrack and a few homunculi. Quatermain must have taken Starbourne to force him to do the job that he could no longer perform. If everyone believed that Starbourne was dead it might even have worked, for a while anyway. It could never have been a permanent solution.

"How long has it been?" I asked.

"Over eight months," Quatermain answered. "My powers faded as soon as Lillian was with child. It took me a while to realize what had happened, and by then it was too late."

That jibed with the timetable. The other Pillars had noticed the problems almost a year ago. Factoring in observer error and human nature, it jibed just about perfectly. I do love it when the answers come together and actually make sense.

"All right," I said. "All right. One more question: Do you know the name of the devil you cut the deal with? Different devils have different strengths and it always helps to know what we're dealing with."

"That's the only good news," Quatermain said. "It was the one you've already beaten once. I made a deal with the devil known as the Duke of Sorrows."

A cold stab of fear went straight through my guts and they turned to water. There were devils and then there were devils. And short of the Adversary himself, I had never known a deadlier one than the Duke. And he had a particular mad on for me and mine. Despite what you read in the detective novels, there are some coincidences sometimes. But the twisting sickness I felt was warning me that this – this – was not a coincidence. This was a plan. This was a trap. And I had walked right into it.

I felt tiny pinpricks of perspiration breaking out all over my body as my thoughts raced. Perdition had to know about Patchwork's tactical importance in the war to come. This wasn't about one soul. This was serious. This was about the whole ballgame and I was in over my head. As usual. The question was, how much time did I have to make this right? How long did I have until the jaws of the trap snapped shut?

"What were the terms of your deal?" I asked, trying to cover my desperation. "Did you get a guarantee of your own personal safety and autonomy?"

"What?" Quatermain asked.

"I'll take that as a no," I muttered.

This was bad. Without a personal safety and autonomy clause in the contract, the Duke owned Quatermain, mind, body, and soul. It was only a matter of time and devilish whim until the unholy bastard claimed custody of his property. Quatermain was doomed, no doubt about it. There was no way I could save him from the consequences of his monumental ego and folly. His wife and unborn child were probably beyond salvation as well. Not that I wouldn't try.

"Quatermain," I said as earnestly as I could manage. "You've got to listen to me. This was never just about you. This is a plot to destroy Patchwork. The Duke took your powers to destabilize the holdfast. I took Gwynplaine off the table. If you kill Starbourne there's no way the others will hold. This place will die. Your family's legacy will be destroyed. Don't kill Starbourne. Put the egg down!"

I locked eyes with Quatermain willing him to believe me. He stared back. The wheels in his head turned slowly, but they turned. I could see him thinking about it. Adding up what he knew, what he feared, and what he now realized. I felt a drop of sweat trickle down my forehead. It fell into my eye and stung, but I didn't dare move to wipe it away.

"I … I … I," Quatermain stammered. "I don't know."

"I do!" I shouted. "Don't be a fool, Quatermain. Your ego isn't more important than all of Patchwork. You were tricked! There's no shame in that; do your duty and protect the land and the people that you serve! Be a Pillar. It's not the power that makes you an aristocrat, it's your actions. Put down the egg!"

I saw it in his eyes. I had gotten through. I let my breath out and relaxed ever so slightly. Quatermains hand trembled, but it did not move. Then I saw surprise, confusion and fear flash across Quatermain's face. His hand wasn't moving.

"Monday!" Quatermain cried. "I can't move my bloody hand. What have you done to me?"

"What have I done to you?" I asked incredulously. "It's not me! Put the egg down!"

"I can't!" Quatermain all but screamed. "My hand won't move!"

"Try harder!" I growled, taking a step forward to help.

"No!" Quatermain shouted. "Stay back! I can feel my fingers tensing when you get closer. Something's controlling me!"

Something or someone. I'd bet dollars to doorknobs that someone was the Duke of Sorrows. I had learned to my great chagrin that the Duke gained powers over anyone he made a deal with. Adriana Gray's defenses might keep the Duke from physically manifesting in Patchwork, but his deal with Quatermain had given him a way in. The devil always takes more than his due.

"Take it easy," I said, taking one small step forward. "Try to relax."

The strain showed on Quatermain's face; he was trembling visibly. Veins stood out on his forehead and his lips peeled back from gritted teeth. He was losing, and if he lost we all lost. I lunged forward to join the struggle, but I even as I moved, I knew it was too late.

"Noooooo!" Quatermain wailed as his fingers inexorably tightened.

A flash of silver arced downward out of nowhere. There was a sound like wood being chopped, a gush of scarlet, and Quatermain's left hand hit the ground; its fingers still loosely clenched around the egg that was Peter Starbourne's life.

Quatermain stared in horror at the bloody stump where his left hand used to be. Algernon Tiberius McCumber Fizznorman hopped off the desk where he had been standing, and tossed a bloody axe into the corner where it clattered to the floor. He pried the fingers of Quatermain's severed hand open, scooped up the egg and cradled it against his chest, protectively.

"What took you so long?" I asked Fizznorman. "That was way too close!"

"It was a trick," the gnome shrugged. "I got an axe."

Quatermain collapsed to his knees, clutching the remains of his arm and trying to cut off the blood loss. He was having limited success. I moved forward to help when I heard a sound that stopped me cold in my tracks. Quatermain was laughing.

He looked up and his eyes were wild. The laughter turned into a shrill titter and I recognized it. It was a sound that I had very much hoped to never hear again. Coming out of Oswald Quatermain's mouth was the laughter of the Duke of Sorrows.

Chapter Twenty-Nine

Quatermain's face was a mask of blotchy gray and white flesh. His eyes rolled around crazily, focusing on nothing and no one. His mouth was slack, the tongue lolling out limply, and the sound that fluted out of that mouth wasn't Quatermain. It wasn't even human. It belonged to a creature that called itself the Duke of Sorrows.

The Duke was an immortal agent of Perdition, commonly referred to as a devil. I had gotten tangled up in the Duke's schemes before. Once I had even been instrumental in stopping him. And like Visivald said, Sorrows was no devil to be trifled with.

The devils were opposite numbers to the angels of Salvation, Eel's father, for example. Say what you want about angels; they may be high-handed, arrogant manipulative bastards, but at least they're out for mankind's overall good. (For whatever comfort that brought.) Devils, however, were a different story. Actually, devils were a lot like angels. They were also high-handed, arrogant and manipulative. In fact the only real difference was that the devils were most certainly not out for mankind's overall good.

"Mr. Monday," the Duke's queer, high-pitched voice issued horribly out of Quatermain's mouth. "It is so lovely to speak to you once more. How have you been? Was your reunion with the sweet Kellidwyn everything you dreamed it would be?"

Quatermain was still in there, and I could see the horror on his face as his body did things totally beyond his control. The Duke wasn't in

Patchwork, not really. He was just peeking through his pawn's eyes. It was a trick I hadn't realized he was even capable of. Live and learn, hopefully.

"Your game is up, Your Grace," I said. "We're onto you now and you can't hurt these people anymore. Give it up and get out of Quatermain. He's suffered enough."

"There is no such thing as enough suffering, Mr. Monday," came the Duke's answer. "And you are onto nothing. This time I hold all the cards."

From my experiences, the Duke never showed his hand until he was sure he had already won. Either he had another trick up his sleeve or he was bluffing. Either way I had to keep him talking. Like most egomaniacal arch-villains, the Duke of Sorrows loved nothing more than the sound of his own voice.

"Don't be absurd," I mocked. "You've got nothing. Quatermain is your only pawn here. He's helpless now, and so are you."

"Is he?" the Duke shrilled. "Am I?"

This wasn't helping. I needed him to brag more specifically. And I needed him to release his hold over Quatermain before the man bled to death. He started up that annoying titter of his again and I began to reconsider the pluses and minuses of Quatermain bleeding out.

"Look," I said. "If you're not going to brag about how you've outsmarted and defeated me, how will I ever learn?"

"You wish to learn?"

I clapped my hands to the sides of my head. Those words had just sort of slithered into my brain without passing through my ears first. I looked around for Fizznorman. I couldn't see him, but I didn't know whether he was actually gone or just hiding again. Either way I was on my own against Sorrows. Somehow that's the way it always seemed to go.

"You know I do," I gritted out through clenched teeth. "You know I want to know it all; I'm just not willing to pay your standard price. I prefer to go more *quid pro quo*."

"Very well," fluted the Duke's voice. "I offer you one piece of Truth, free of charge and without let or obligation."

"Why?" I asked.

"Because this particular Truth is one that you are ready to know," Sorrows replied with a titter. "And neither Adriana Gray nor that little bastard's father would ever tell it to you."

I thought about it for a second. My first thought was that Sorrows was stalling for time. I couldn't imagine what he was waiting for, but it was the sort of thing he might do. What did he have up his sleeve? I resolved to keep the conversation going. And I told myself that it was in the client's best interest that I did. Sometimes I'm so good at lying I even fool myself.

"I'm listening," I said.

"You've been told of the coming war between Perdition and its Enemy," the Duke intoned nasally. "But you haven't been told of the origin of the disagreement. When Creation was young the only beings in it were the angels of Salvation, and they existed only to fulfill the Ineffable Plan. When humanity was created, it caused strife among the angels for the first time in all of eternity. Some of the angels wanted to protect mankind and keep it safe from harm. But the bulk of the angelic host chose to follow the Ineffable Plan, which called for humanity to know lifetime after lifetime, generation after generation, of suffering and woe.

"The angels went to war over the fate of humanity," the Duke of Sorrows went on in almost a chant speaking words he had long ago memorized and was repeating by rote. "And the rebels lost. They were thrown out of the Silver City and cast down into the depths of the Mists. There they built an Iron City and there they still dwell. The Silver City is named Salvation and the Iron City is named Perdition."

Quatermain's body lurched to his feet without using his arms. It was kind of impressive, in a really creepy sort of way. Quatermain's face was white as a sheet and covered in sweat. I had no idea what was even keeping him conscious, let alone standing.

"We devils fell defending you from Salvation's cruel schemes," the Duke tutted, sounding like a disappointed parent. "And you humans still believe Salvation's lies. You believe the role they cast us in is true. We do not call ourselves devils, Monday. Among ourselves we have another name."

"And what name is that?" I asked.

"Free," hissed the Duke of Sorrows.

Was the Duke speaking Truth? If he promised me capital 'T' Truth and then lied to me, he would be breaking the Compact between Perdition and Salvation. That Compact was the only thing keeping the celestial war cold. I had to believe that Perdition wasn't ready to start the big one, not today. And if I was wrong, nothing much we did here today would matter anyway, so I figured I was better off believing it. For now at least. There's truth and then there's Truth; I wasn't egotistical enough to believe that the Duke couldn't tell me something that was true but so far beyond my comprehension as to confuse me into doing something wrong or foolish. Context is usually pretty important. Either way, I'd have to worry about it later. For right now, I had a case and this probably wasn't part of it.

"So why are you still here?" I asked. "You tried to destabilize Patchwork. I get it. But you're done now. It's over and you lost. Like I said, you're helpless."

"You're not a simpleton, Monday," hissed the Duke's voice. "My child is inside Quatermain's wife. Who's helpless then, hmmm?"

"Mmmmy wife?" Quatermain moaned in his own voice. "My child? Y... you k... keep aw ... aw ... keep away from them!"

"What?" the Duke shrilled. "You dare interfere with me, pawn?"

"G ... g ... get out!" Quatermain screamed.

There was a hideous stench and a sickening strobe of black light swirled through the room. My gorge rose in my throat and the room spun wildly. The floor smacked into my knees, or maybe I had fallen, it was hard to tell. When the light show faded and my vision returned Quatermain was on the ground bleeding and whimpering quietly.

He had thrown the Duke of Sorrows out of his body, as far as I could tell by sheer will power. For the first time I got an idea of what a Pillar of Patchwork really was. And I was impressed.

I rolled Quatermain over onto his back, pulled my jacket off and tied one sleeve around his stump to stanch the bleeding. His eyes fluttered open but it didn't look like he was up to answering questions, but I didn't care. I needed answers more than he needed his beauty rest.

"Quatermain!" I shouted into his face, shaking him by the shoulders. "Where's your wife?"

"Mmm. Guh... guarding Starbourne," he mumbled.

"Where?!?" I screamed.

"B ... basement," Quatermain mumbled.

"Fizznorman, where are the stairs?" I asked.

"I and I know the way," said the gnome, appearing next to me where he had apparently been standing. "Be following me and sure enough I'll be taking you there!"

He tore off with surprising speed, beginning a lengthy history of the Aristarchus lodge, so I could keep track of him as he ran. I kept up pretty well, despite my ankle; my legs were a lot longer. Fizznorman skidded around a corner and fetched up short in front of a black door. I grabbed the knob and yanked it open. It wasn't locked, thank Salvation for small gifts.

I blew past the gnome and half-ran, half-tumbled down the stairs. The basement of Aristarchus was all you might expect it to be. There were work benches every few feet, covered with dismembered – or possibly disassembled – animals of every size and description. It was mostly dark, dank, and dusty, except for a pool of pale witchlight in one corner.

Two people were in that pool of light, one lying down and the other crouching over the first. It was Peter Starbourne and Lillian Quatermain. Starbourne was wearing a colorful vest, a white linen shirt, dark, close-fitting trousers, and what looked to be very expensive leather shoes. His skin was milk-pale, his thick hair was silver and lush and tied back from his face with a blue ribbon that matched his eyes.

In short, Starbourne looked exactly as he had the night he died. The clothes and hair-do were identical. If it weren't for his eyes being open and the back of his head still being attached, I would have sworn it was the corpse I had examined just a few days ago.

The lady of the manor was crouched oddly, almost grotesquely for a woman as pregnant as she was. She rocked back and forth gently on her haunches and I could tell that she was holding something in her hands, but I couldn't see what it was. I stepped off the last stair and approached the tableau slowly. There was absolutely no sound other than my own footsteps.

As I moved closer I could see her hands. She was holding a pistol. And she was holding it up to Starbourne's head. What was this? Was it a hostage situation? Or was it something stranger? Her arm trembled and I leapt forward to grab her arm, but it was hopeless. I was just too far away.

The gunshot exploded, far too loud in the enclosed space of the basement. Peter Starbourne's head exploded in red. He had never said a word, nor made a single sound. I yanked the weapon out of her hand, thumbed the magazine release and let the clip clatter to the ground. I racked the slide to eject the chambered round, flipped the safety on, and tossed the pistol across the basement floor.

I put one hand on Lillian Quatermain's shoulder and attempted to spin her around. She offered no resistance and turned willingly. Her eyes were blank and staring, her jaw as slack as her husband's had been. As I watched, her eyes blinked and her face composed itself. She stared at me in confusion, but at least there was someone home again. She looked down at the lifeless body at her feet.

"He's dead!" shrieked Lillian. "Starbourne's dead! Someone killed Peter Starbourne!"

Her confusion turned to anger and she pointed an accusatory finger at me.

"It was you, wasn't it?" Lillian demanded. "Oswald warned me that you would try to destroy us!"

The pool of blood was rapidly spreading out from the lifeless body. We both stepped back and she twisted out of my grip. She spun to face me, face flushed and angry, breast heaving wildly.

"You've destroyed us," she insisted. "You drove Gwynplaine mad, stole my husband's power and now you've killed Starbourne. Nothing can save Patchwork now!"

I looked down at the lifeless body and then back up at her again. I looked around the room but saw no one else. I made my face hard and turned back to look at her, showing no pity.

"That's right," I said calmly. "Patchwork is doomed."

As if to underscore my words, an enormous crash of thunder peeled and echoed through Aristarchus. In the basement, it was even louder than the gunshot had been. Dust and dirt rained down from the ceiling. And then all was quiet.

Chapter Thirty

"Did you ever make a deal with the Duke of Sorrows?" I asked Lillian Quatermain.

"What?" was her only reply.

"Good enough," I nodded.

"Your Grace," I called out in my best public speaking voice. "I assume you can hear me through Oswald. Patchwork is doomed. It looks like you win this one. I beg a boon of you in your victory."

There was no response, but I hadn't really expected one. The old devil was listening; there was simply no way his immortal ego would pass up the opportunity to watch me lose. I was the one who had beaten him before, after all. To see me outwitted and trapped, about to die? There was simply no way he would miss it.

"Leave Quatermain now," I said. "Leave him, and do not return for the brief time he has left. Let the man and his wife have a moment together. They'll know you've tricked them, and Quatermain knows where he's going and how soon he's going there. Be gracious, your Grace. For humanity's sake."

If the Duke agreed to the boon, he would lose his connection to Patchwork. Without the permission of a willing host, devils and angels couldn't pass through the wards. But the Duke knew that Patchwork would destroy itself in a matter of hours, so what harm could there be in my little request? I kept my face down respectfully, my shoulders were slumped in defeat, but my eyes were cast up in hope. I was the perfect picture of a beaten man.

A strange shuffling and thumping noise heralded a body moving slowly and awkwardly down the basement stairs. Oswald Quatermain's body was clearly unconscious, but it still lurched drunkenly down the stairs, its head and shoulders bouncing off the walls as it went. Oswald's body staggered to the bottom step, and it turned to face me.

"Very well," the Duke's disturbing voice emanated once again from Quatermain's body. "I must say, Monday, I didn't think this was how it would end up. The plan was to trap you here, as a Pillar. With Gwynplaine and Quatermain off the table, that insufferable harridan Gray would surely have convinced you to stay and protect all these snivelingly pathetic sheep."

I stood impassively. I never interrupt a ranting bad guy when he's telling me what I want to know. The Duke had this figured for our last dance, so I really couldn't blame him for taking a few moments to gloat.

"I suppose I will regret the loss of my little operation here," the Duke mused wistfully. "The statuettes were flowing so smoothly too."

"Statuettes?" I said stupidly. "You were behind the statuettes?"

"Of course I was, dolt!" tittered Sorrows. "Alas now, they shall never be an army. But there are still enough of them to be spies, thieves, and assassins. And they are scattered throughout thousands of homes in New Jerusalem. Perdition's campaigns there will be greatly benefited by my work here. The Free will sing my name."

"And they will sing of your honor and nobility," I agreed. "When you grant my boon. They deserve a last moment together as husband and wife."

"So they will," the Duke crowed shrilly. "And also of my cruelty and my brilliance. Not only have I caused your downfall, but the plan I first put into motion eight years ago has finally come to fruition. And you, Monday, were instrumental to its success!"

"What are you even talking about now?" I sighed wearily.

"A deal I made with Lady Kellidwyn when first we met," Sorrows purred. "I gave her the ritual that let you send her to Patchwork. And after that, it was only a matter of time."

"What was only a matter of time?" I asked.

"You," the Duke tittered. "Today. All of this. Your pain."

I felt dizzy and nauseous. Could the Duke be telling the truth? Was it just a cruel lie to hurt me? If it was, I have to admit it worked. The idea that all of this was aimed at me somehow, just to hurt me, that it was all part of some weird revenge plot… It was just crazy. Simply insane.

"Wait," I stammered. "That can't be right. I screwed up your plans in New Jerusalem last year. You couldn't have arranged this eight years before. I had never even heard of you back then."

"You think so three dimensionally," Sorrows tittered. "Just because you hadn't heard of me didn't mean I hadn't heard of you. I knew you would wrong me someday, so I put my revenge into place long in advance. That is what it means to face an immortal."

My head was spinning. I genuinely wanted to throw up, but I fought it down, drawing in deep and ragged breaths as I did. I drew the back of my hand across my mouth slowly. My hand shook as I lowered it back to my side.

"Fine," I said quietly. "I don't have any idea what you're even talking about, but fine. I acknowledge your victory over me. Now get the hell out of here. Please."

"With pleasure," the Duke replied in a sing-song voice, drawing out every syllable in childish mockery. "I can't be here for the end anyway. I would be destroyed along with all of the rest of you pathetic specks. Oh, I suspect the bitch Gray will get out, and maybe even one or two of the others. But this place is done and Perdition has struck a major blow against the arrogance of Salvation."

The last time I had shown Sorrows the doorway out of my world, there had been a big black hole with crackly lightning and a wind-storm. It had all been very terrifying but a really great show. There was nothing like that at all this time. One moment he was there and the next he simply wasn't. Quatermain's body crumpled as though it had been fired at the floor out of a cannon.

"I hope the husband and wife enjoy their last … moment," echoed the Duke's voice hollowly, breaking into a titter before fading entirely.

The only sound was the dripping of water onto the floor and the quiet sobbing of Lillian Quatermain as she cradled her husband's body. Was he dead or merely comatose? I had no idea. I looked closer and saw his chest rising and falling, ever so slightly. He was still with us for all the good it would do him.

I stood there, my hands hanging at my side, the blood pounding in my head. My own breath sounded loud and ragged. I slumped slowly to the floor, leaning my back against a table leg. I was sitting in a puddle, and the dust and grime from the table was going to ruin what remained of my outfit. Long minutes passed.

Why was the basement even dirty? Did someone spend time and effort creating dust and cobwebs and mildew? Or was it simply this way because the Lords of Patchwork couldn't imagine it being any other way? I was too exhausted to care, but I couldn't stop myself from wondering. There was something seriously wrong with me.

"Okay," I said at last. "I think that's long enough. He's gone."

Nothing happened for a moment. Then another moment passed. The dripping sound stopped. The room grew brighter as the witchlamps flickered on. Four people were standing on the other side of the room.

Tim moved immediately over to where Oswald Quatermain lay sprawled. He uncorked a small tube full of milky-white liquid and poured a portion of it down Quatermain's throat. Immediately the blood stopped seeping from his wrist, the flesh rippling and flowing crazily, raw and red, but definitely healing before our eyes. As the color of his flesh grew less deathly, his breathing got visibly stronger.

"Pretty ballsy being here all along," I said wearily. "I seem to recall telling you to get yourselves out of here before I came down."

"Wasn't time," Tim replied cheerfully. "Besides, Yours Truly wanted to try 'is best concealment charm against the likes of the all-mighty pisspot."

"There really wasn't any time," Kelli said. "We barely made the switch before the Mrs. came down pulling her Lady Macbeth act."

"What?" Lillian Quatermain stammered. "What is happening? We have to get out of here! Won't someone help me with Oswald?"

"Relax, Mrs. Quatermain," I said gently. "It's okay. Nothing bad is going to happen anymore. It's over."

"Lemme try," mumbled Eel.

The scrawny blond man shuffled forward and put his hands gently on Lillian Quatermain's, touching the crown of her head and her brow, a soft and warm glow emanating from his hands. Her sobs slowed and then stopped, she sniffed once, hiccoughed in a genteel sort of fashion and was quiet.

"'At's a new trick," Tim said appreciatively.

"Shhh," murmured Eel. "She's had a bad day."

"But," Lillian said quietly. "What happened?"

"I think I can answer that," said Peter Starbourne, the fourth person. "Kelli and these other two folks snuck in here and replaced me with that."

Starbourne pointed at the lifeless body slumped on the ground. He looked at the awful head wound and shuddered visibly. But he turned back to Lillian and managed a gentle smile.

"That wasn't me who died," he said. "It was just a counterfeit."

"Programmable homunculus," explained Tim. "Courtesy of Adriana Gray."

"We stole the idea from your husband," I said modestly. "We made it from some pictures I took of your husband's version. I don't usually like to reuse a trick and I hardly ever steal other people's ideas, but this one was just too good not to. Not even the Duke of Sorrows saw this one coming."

"An' 'ose idea was this?" Tim asked archly.

"All right," I said. "All right. It was the other guy."

"The other guy?" Kelli asked.

"Long story," I said. "But remind me to introduce you two. I think you'll really like him."

"Mr. Starbourne!" Fizznorman shouted.

The gnome had appeared out of nowhere and shot across the room with surprising speed on his stubby little legs. The tiny man flung himself into Starbourne's arms and the two embraced each other. They stood like that, the large man and the small one, holding each other silently. I realized for the first time ever that I was looking at Fizznorman and actually seeing him while he wasn't saying a word. I felt myself getting a little bit misty-eyed. It must have been the exhaustion.

"How did you find him?" Fizznorman finally asked. "I thought the spells were hiding him too well to be found."

"It was a two man operation," Tim said, puffing on his fingernails before buffing them ostentatiously on his breast. "I cast the tracking charm and then we set i' t' 'one in on Eel's senses."

"We figured having somebody bound up and being tortured in the basement would set off Eel's righteous vengeance sniffer," I added. "And I guess it paid off."

"S'not like that," Eel mumbled. "I just knew something was wrong and I could help. I just followed the feeling."

"A' course none o' it would have worked if Kelli hadn'a snuck us int' this place," Tim piped in.

"Please," Kelli said. "I'm no hero. I'm just a naive thief who let herself be used to almost destroy the place that saved me. I deserve exile."

"Do not be foolish," said Adriana Gray.

We all jumped. Adriana Gray and Duke Sir Visivald were simply there, standing right next to us as if they had been there all along. The least they could have done was appear with a bang and a cloud of smoke. Some wizards have no respect for tradition.

"I am displeased," Visivald rumbled in a quiet but dangerous way. "You should have included me in your battle plans."

"Couldn't do it," I said weakly from my position on the floor. "Couldn't have the Pillars attacking each other. It had to be outsiders."

"Harrumph," Visivald said, very distinctly.

Gray lowered herself down to her haunches next to me, removed her pointy black hat, and kissed me gently on the cheek.

"Thank you, Zachariah," she said. "I am very pleased with your work and will write you a splendid letter of recommendation."

She rose and turned to face Kelli. She reached forward and took Kelli's hands in her own. She clasped them warmly and smiled her thin and frosty smile.

"And as for you, Kellidwyn," she said tartly. "I won't have any talk of exile. We need you. And we all have skeletons in our closets. None of us were born as we are. We all have dark pasts and disastrous mistakes we're running from. You don't have to run anymore. I knew very well who and what you were when I accepted you into our community. Please don't abandon us now."

There were tears running down Kelli's face, but she was smiling and nodding as she cried. I couldn't help but notice how beautiful she was. I remembered loving her and I thought that I could fall in love with her again if I let myself. But that wouldn't be fair to anyone. The past was in the past and sometimes it really was best to leave it there. It was never easy, but sometimes it truly was for the best.

"And what of myself and my lord husband?" Lillian asked.

"That shall be determined by the Pillars in due time," Visivald replied in a voice that was almost gentle.

Visivald looked to Starbourne and then to Gray. Something seemed to pass between them. Starbourne nodded and smiled, Gray nodded back, and Starbourne put his arm around Lillian's shoulders.

"But in the end no lasting harm was done, but to your husband himself," Starbourne said. "I'm sure we'll be lenient."

"He can't be a Pillar anymore," Visivald said. "But retirement to Aristarchus might suit you both. A quiet life together. That doesn't sound so awful now, does it?"

Lillian didn't reply, but the ghost of a smile touched her face and the tears that streamed down her cheeks seemed less of sorrow and more of relief. It was hard to say for sure, but I thought she would recover her strength eventually. She looked like a survivor to me.

I rose to my feet and moved to stand close to Gray. She was standing next to Visivald a little distance away from Lillian and Starbourne, giving them the illusion of privacy. I leaned close to her ear and murmured into it.

"You're going to keep a close eye on them, aren't you?" I asked very quietly.

"Oh, definitely, yes, Zachariah," she murmured back. "Very much so."

"I figured as much," I said.

That's wizards for you; even their acts of kindness, mercy, and charity had secret agendas.

Chapter Thirty-One

Sleep would have been nice. It would have been very nice. But both Baxter and Tim really wanted to get back to New Jerusalem and sleep in their own beds. And they were my ride back home.

I couldn't blame them. Frankly, I was itching to get back myself. I really needed to start looking into all of these statuettes the Duke of Sorrows was on about. If Perdition truly had thousands of remote-controlled homunculi infiltrated throughout New Jerusalem then we were in pretty big trouble.

And so it was that I had time to return to my borrowed suite of rooms at Gray's tower for a much-needed shower before my wrap-up meeting with the client, but not enough for sleep. I was feeling closer to human, but hardly at my best. Our luggage was all staged in the front room of Gray's tower. I asked my bag to stand guard and watch the other luggage. It practically snapped to attention. Magic is weird.

It would be a couple hours before the conditions were right for Tim's ritual of crossing, so we had some time to kill. Among other things, I was hoping to pick up a bonus from Lady Gray. If I was being totally fair and honest, I would also have to admit that I was avoiding Kelli.

Gray had asked to meet with me in her office. I had never been in her office here in the tower, but I had seen the one at her place of business in the Old City. The two were absolutely identical. The specific clutter had changed, but the bricks of the wall were the same, the carpet was the same, all the framed art was the same, it even smelled the same.

She was seated behind her modest desk. It was stacked high and wide with paper. In a small open space she'd hollowed out in the middle, she was scribbling away at some parchment or other. She looked up when I walked in and smiled her thin and frosty smile at me. It didn't fool me any more; I could tell she was pretty darn happy.

"You've done a great service to Patchwork," Gray said. "You have my sincerest gratitude."

"And you've paid my totally exorbitant bill," I said with a grin. "So in my book we're even."

Gray held her hands out and I – somewhat awkwardly – gave her my own. Her hands were surprisingly cool, but they were dry and her skin was soft. I've had worse handshakes. She smiled at me, for once wide enough to actually see the white of her teeth. I was impressed.

"Not even close," she said, shaking her head bemusedly. "But there is so much more you could do. If you stayed."

"Stayed and became a Pillar, you mean?"

"Yes," she replied. "That is what I mean."

"You don't need me," I said. "Starbourne is back on the job and now that he knows where the metaphorical ball was being dropped, he can compensate."

"Gwynplaine," Gray began.

"Gwynplaine will recover," I interrupted. "He may never be the man he was, but from where I'm standing that might be a good thing. He gets a chance to start over and maybe be less of an asshat this time. Either way, Dr. Foucault and Kelli are both working with him. Those two will have him nursed back to health and back in the saddle before you know it. Although I'm afraid Kelli might be a bad moral influence on him."

Gray laughed a little at that.

"The Pillars of Patchwork are not angels," she said. "They were never meant to be. This place works best – for now, at any rate – in the gray."

"So to speak," I added.

"So to speak," she agreed. "But we do need you. More people discover this land and request to immigrate every year. I have to turn almost all of them down. We haven't the resources to grow and thrive. We need you."

"You'll have me," I said. "More or less. The other guy is sticking around, at least for a while. He's already shown he's as capable as I am, maybe even more so. And how long will that biomimetic body of his last?"

"Hundreds of years in the real world," Gray replied. "Salvation knows how long here in the Mists."

"Exactly," I agreed. "He's your ideal Pillar. Smart, but without any real preconceptions, willful, but unfocused, and desperate to prove himself. And he's almost as good looking as I am."

"Almost," Gray said through her frosty smile. "Kelli is tutoring him as well as Gwynplaine."

"Yeah," I said. "I know. And that worries me almost as much as it pleases me. Kelli's one of the good ones. A little bit greedy with some pretty serious authority issues and bad impulse control, but still one of the good ones."

"She reminds me of a certain private detective I know," Gray observed.

"Yeah, well," I said. "Maybe I rubbed off on her back at school."

Gray arched an eyebrow.

"You know what I mean," I said. "Wizards have such dirty minds."

We both laughed then. Gray rose from behind her desk and walked over to her bar. She was wearing a black knee-length skirt below a black ribbed turtleneck sweater the outfit flattered her figure nicely. I resisted the urge to actively admire her figure. It never hurts to be extra respectful to wizards. She could most likely turn me into a toad, after all.

"May I fix you a drink, Zachariah?" Gray asked politely.

"One for the road?" I asked. "Is that a good idea right before heading into the Mists?"

"Probably not," Gray mused. "Have one anyway. Sometimes it's a good idea to act on a few bad ideas."

"I'll drink to that," I agreed.

She fixed our drinks and handed me mine. I took a sip; it was excellent, but I wasn't really surprised. Most wizards were also top-notch mixologists. It was just one of those things.

"Would you like a bonus, Zachariah?" Gray asked suddenly.

"For what?" I asked.

"For your exemplary service, of course," Gray answered.

"Okay," I said. "What kind of bonus?"

"I happen to know that you are a collector of rare truths," Gray said. "One might even say capital 'T' Truths."

"I dabble," I acknowledged modestly.

"I offer you one such Truth," Gray said. "In return for your giving serious consideration to returning here and becoming a Pillar some day."

"Well, that's not really a bonus then," I said with a smile. "But I'll take your deal. I give everything serious consideration sooner or later. Usually late at night when I'd much rather be sleeping."

I was willing to bet bed knobs to broomsticks that Gray's Truth would be exactly the sort of thing designed to convince me to come back and join her save the world club. I'd listen and I'd think about it. I had promised that much and I had no intention of breaking my word.

"There are only three real places in all of Creation," Gray began. "They are Salvation, Perdition, and the so-called Real World. Everyplace else, including Goblin and Faerie are just shadows of those true places. If any of the three are destroyed, Creation would be irrevocably altered, and while the creatures that call themselves variously the Free and the Angels could survive in that altered Creation, no mortal creature could."

"So if Salvation were to attack Perdition openly?" I asked.

"The world would be destroyed and the Ineffable Plan would be ruined," Gray replied. "They can't risk that."

"Wait," I said. "The Duke of Sorrows told me that the original war in Salvation was over the devils not wanting humanity destroyed."

"Ah he told you that, did he?" Gray mused. "I'm not surprised. It might bias you towards his words. His kind always have at least two reasons for everything they do."

"Angels, devils, and wizards, too," I said. "Pot, meet Kettle."

"Balderdash," she retorted jovially. "Wizards never do anything for merely two reasons. That's so terribly inefficient. But at any rate, what the Duke said was true in so far as it goes. The devils began with what could be described as noble intentions. But the war has been going on for a very long time and things change. There is now a ruling majority in Perdition that believe if humanity can't be released from what they call the yoke of Salvation, then we are better off being destroyed and 'put out of our misery.'"

"I'm not miserable," I protested.

"Indeed," Gray said. "I can see that much. But try explaining that to an immortal egoist who's already decided that he knows what's best for you and the rest of us poor mortals. Make no mistake, Perdition would gladly see humanity laid to ruin if it suited their plans. And some would even dance in our funeral flames."

"So what you're saying," I said. "Is that Salvation can't destroy Perdition because to do so would also destroy the world. But Perdition is willing to destroy either the World or Salvation to get what they want?"

"Essentially, yes," Gray said.

"So that's it then," I said. "Sooner or later, Perdition gets what it wants and there's not much Salvation can do about it."

"Not exactly," Gray said. "Salvation has a plan."

"That Ineffable Plan that Sorrows told me about?" I asked.

"The very one," Gray agreed.

"How could a plan made millennia before the devils rebelled take the results of their rebellion into account?" I asked.

"It's a very good plan," Gray replied.

"Any chance we poor mortals can get a peek at this plan?" I asked.

"That is not very likely," Gray admitted.

"I didn't think so," I grumbled. "But you know that Patchwork is part of the plan?"

"Yes," she said. "And I know that you are also a part of that plan, Zachariah Monday."

I just sort of stared at her for a while. She stared coolly back at me, sipping her drink from time to time. I realized I had forgotten my own drink. I reached for it and slugged a healthy portion of it down my throat. For purposes of my sanity and my ego, I chose to believe that Gray had meant that last bit in a sort of 'everyone is part of the plan' kind of way. That's what I was telling myself, anyway.

"Hey," I asked suddenly. "How come your office here looks exactly same as your office in the Old City?"

"I only have one office, Zachariah," Gray replied enigmatically.

Wizards are like that sometimes.

There wasn't all that much left to say, so I made my excuses, told her I'd say good-bye before I left, and wandered out and down to the public levels of the tower. There was the usual hustle and bustle of young people being earnest and insightful, but if you tried hard enough, you could ignore it. I eventually found Tim, Baxter, Eel, Kelli, and The Other Guy in a lounge area, eating popcorn, drinking coffee, and generally lounging.

"Hey Zack," Baxter rumbled amiably. "How'd the wrap up meeting with Her Nibs go?"

"Um," I said. "She's a wizard."

There was a general murmur of sympathy and understanding.

"Whyn't you 'ave a seat, Zack-man," Tim piped. "And look! What 'ave we 'ere?"

Tim's hands moved flamboyantly and when he drew the one across the other, a glass filled with amber liquid and garnished with candied fruit appeared in his hand. It was a whiskey sour. Now that's magic. I accepted the drink and the invitation to sit, both gratefully.

"So," I asked after getting comfortable and taking a sip of my drink. "What are we talking about?"

"You," said everyone more or less all at once.

"Ah," I said. "How … nice. Let's … um … let's change the subject?"

There was some good natured laughter at my expense then. I let it roll for a few moments and even joined in a little. I can laugh at myself when I have to. Sometimes I even enjoy it.

"You guys are all rat bastards," I said amiably. "And I love each and every one of you."

"Even me?" Other Guy asked.

"Even you," I reassured my *doppelgänger* amiably. "Hey. Have you decided on a name for yourself yet?"

"Well," he said a little bit hesitantly, "I was actually hoping you wouldn't mind if I kept Monday as a last name."

"I was voting for 'Tuesday,'" Kelli giggled.

"I don't mind at all," I lied. "Go ahead. What were you thinking about for a first name?"

"I was thinking about Jacob," he said.

That brought me up short. I guess he really did have all of my memories. Jacob was my father's name and my grandfather's name too. It was also the name given to my younger brother, who was born a few months after my father's death. Jacob, Jr. didn't live long. There were all sorts of complications and the doctors just couldn't save him. I wasn't quite ten years old when all of this happened, but it had affected me profoundly. The injustice of it bothered me then and it bothered me still. I missed my father terribly, and I was bitter that my little brother hadn't even gotten a chance.

"Zack?" Baxter rumbled gently. "You okay?"

"I'm fine," I said. "Sure. Jacob is a good name. You deserve it."

Jacob Monday and I looked into each other's eyes for a little while then. I saw understanding there, and I'm sure he saw much the same in my own eyes. He wasn't me, he didn't look that much like me, and he thought differently, but we shared a history that had never happened to him, but was still very real. It was at least as real to him as it was to me. That's what he was telling me when he picked the name Jacob. He knew what it meant.

"Can I call you Jake?" Kelli asked.

"Sure you can," Jake said with a smile. "It's what my friends call me, after all."

I saw something in that smile and in the way that Jake looked at Kelli. Kelli was looking at Jake in much the same way. There was something between them, or at least there was the chance of something between them. I wasn't entirely sure how I felt about that. Was I jealous? A little, yeah, but I was also happy and a little bit hopeful. Love made the world go 'round after all, every world no matter how magical.

I glanced at Bax and I could tell he saw it too. That's detectives for you. We were nosey that way. It's just how we're wired, I guess. Bax smiled and I smiled too. A happy ending was always the best kind of ending, and a happy beginning was even better.

The conversation rambled on like it does when a lot of smart, interesting, and opinionated people sit around in a circle. I contributed a little to the friendly back and forth, but I was off my usual game. Something was bothering me. There was some tiny detail that hadn't been resolved, some snag in the tapestry that hadn't been fixed.

I decided to ignore it. It had been a complicated case with lots of tiny details. Whatever was left unfinished would just have to stay that way. I finished my drink, and it occurred to me that I needed to find the facilities.

"Excuse me," I said to a nearby researcher. "Can you direct me to the nearest little human's room?"

He laughed a little and pointed down a hallway, adding, "Third door on the left."

I thanked him and ambled down the indicated hall. The restroom was gorgeous, featuring black, white and gold marble everywhere, gleaming tiles, porcelain, not one speck of grime anywhere. There was even a small couch in case I felt the need to actually rest.

I did what I needed to, washed my hands in the sink and waved them in front of the towel dispenser charm. I was rewarded with a fresh, clean towel that was slightly warm to the touch. I dried my hands, balled up the towel and tossed it into the air. The disposable magic was released and the towel vanished at the apex of its arc, a pleasant perfume filled the air. I do enjoy a classy restroom.

I stepped out and was mildly surprised to find Kelli leaning against the wall, waiting for me. She smiled a little hesitantly and waved greetings. I smiled back and leaned against the wall by her side. We both stayed like that what seemed like a long time, but in retrospect, it probably wasn't all that long.

"So," Kelli said at last. "You're leaving."

She left the again unsaid, but it was there nonetheless. I was leaving her. Again. Never mind that the last time she had technically been the one to leave. We both knew whose choice it had been. And we both knew whose choice it was this time, too.

"Yeah," I said. "I am. I have a whole life back there. Responsibilities, even."

"And love?" she asked. "Do you have that?"

"I do," I said gently. "There are people there who love me and I love them right back. My romantic situation is ... complicated right now. But it's good. Life is good for me."

"Life could be good here, too," she said.

"I know," I said. "And maybe someday it'll be the right good life for me. But not now, not soon, either. I still have my work."

"Yeah," she said. "That's what I figured."

"Yeah," I said. "I know you did."

We were quiet again for a while, but it was a comfortable kind of quiet. She put her hand to her wrist and slid a bracelet off. I recognized it as the one I had given her back at school.

"I want you to have this," she said. "It's been a favorite of mine for years."

"Why are you giving me this?" I asked.

"So you'll think of me whenever you look at it," she said.

She smiled then and it was like the sun rising over the clouds. I took the bracelet and dropped it into a pocket in my jacket. I kissed her very gently on the cheek. She smiled and teared up a little. I decline to disclose whether or not I teared up as well. That information isn't pertinent to the narrative, anyway. So there. We walked back together, chatting amiably about nothing in particular, like old friends do.

Chapter Thirty-Two

A couple hours later, we had all finally made our last good-byes. With groups like this, at times like this, saying good-bye wasn't an action, it was a process. A fun process, a warm and sometimes loving process, but also a lengthy and exhausting one.

And we still had to hit the Mists. I'll admit that I was nervous about this. My last trip had come seriously close to me getting eaten by Baba Yaga's little sister. I expressed my legitimate concerns.

"Trust me, Zack," Tim assured me. "I know what I'm doin' 'ere. The passage don't take physical strength, it takes strength a' soul. And what we're doin' 'ere is soul food. Also? Shut up and let me worry about things fer a change. I ain't no bleeding wizard, but I do know me way 'round the Mists, okay?"

"Okay," I grinned. "Sir, yes, sir."

"Zack can't help it, Tim," Bax rumbled. "He's a recovering asshat."

"Yeah," I agreed. "I – hey! Wait a minute!"

"I don' get it," mumbled Eel.

"Which part?" I asked. "The part where Gwynplaine was the smuggler but not the kidnapper? Or the part where Kelli is probably training Gwynplaine to become the version of himself that Kelli and I studied in school?"

"Or the bit where Zack tricked th' Duke of Sorrows into givin' up 'is connection to Oswald 'cause Patchwork was about to explode, killin' all of us and maybe even taking 'is Nibs with us?" Tim suggested.

"Naw," said Eel. "I get alla that. I just don't get why you guys are always so mean to each other. You make awful jokes at each other's expense, you insult each other, you act like you don't trust each other. An' you all know it's just acting. 'Cause everybody knows you guys would drop everything and do anything for each other. Even you guys have to realize it by now. So why the mean stuff?"

"Uh," I said cleverly. "It's just the way we are with each other."

"You know we're joking, kid, right?" Bax rumbled.

"I know," Eel muttered sullenly. "Doesn't make it not mean."

The kid wasn't wrong. Also the kid wasn't a kid. Eel was in his forties. His emotional maturity was more like a fifteen year-old and none of us were really sure why that was. We treated Eel like a kid, he acted like a kid, and it all seemed to work out okay. Maybe he was going to live a thousand years, and forty is the new sixteen for his people. The reasons didn't matter, we accepted Eel as he was and he seemed to like being around us.

But every now and then, Eel would come out with something like this. The things he said at those times usually stayed with us. He would spout something that sounded mushy and childlike all at the same time. But then when you thought about it, it started making a simple kind of sense. Eel had a lot of his father in him sometimes.

"A'ight," Tim piped. "Enough soul food for now, I'm bloody well stuffed. 'O's up fer a jaunt in the Mists?"

We all raised our hands and not one of us was noticeably misty-eyed. Because that's the way we are with each other, and it works. We'd explain it to Eel when he was older. Or something.

"Mind if I walk over with you?" Foucault asked. "I don't get to see many crossings."

"No worries," said Tim with a flash of black teeth. "I do me best work with an audience."

We hiked a short distance from Gray's Tower and stopped where Tim told us to. He had chosen a spot that was well off the road, but not really woodsy. The grass was ungroomed and weedy, but it wasn't hard to walk through. No cover though; hopefully no one was going to attack us. Then I briefly wondered when my life had gotten to the point where I regularly worried about sudden violent attacks.

Tim had us all stand inside a circle of braided leather. The braid work was intricate with many swirls and shapes woven into it. The leather hoop was also lavishly decorated with semi-precious gem stones, bits of carved bone, small coins from different countries, and what looked like shark's teeth. I stepped over it very carefully. In truth, it gave me the heebie-jeebies, but I tried not to let it show.

I glanced over at Dr. Foucault. Her eyes had lost focus and she didn't seem to be paying any attention to us at all. I recognized the look; she was communicating with someone in the way Patchwork's residents sometimes did.

"Problem, Doc?" I asked.

"Oh," Foucault murmured. "Please do forgive me, Darlings. I'm receiving a message from Peter. Apparently Lillian Quatermain is going into labor a bit prematurely. Nothing to worry about, I'm sure, but better safe than sorry."

It all hit me in a flash. Something the Duke of Sorrows had said about his child. Not Quatermain's child, but his child. That and the sly response he had given me when I told him he had lost his connection to Patchwork. What if it was never Oswald the Duke had connected himself to at all? What if the unborn child was the connection? The unborn are particularly vulnerable to a lot of things; they rely on the mother's protection to stay safe. But what if Oswald had abrogated that protection somehow as part of his deal?

What if this had been the Duke's plan all along? What if he had expected me to win? What would I do afterwards? I'd go home, of course, safe and secure in the knowledge that I had outsmarted the old bastard once again.

If I was right, this could be bad. If the Duke truly had his hooks into the Quatermain child, and that child was born into Patchwork, Perdition would have an irrevocable connection. Even if the child left the connection would remain. Birth was powerful magic. All of this rushed through my head in the time it took Foucault to step back a few feet and start concentrating. I could think fast when I had to.

"Peter is going to bring me through," Foucault announced. "Good travels my Darlings."

"Wait!" I shouted as Foucault started to fade.

"What?" Foucault asked. "What's wrong?"

"That child can't be born in Patchwork!" I cried. "It'll be disastrous!"

"Wot?" Tim squawked. "Why?"

"Connections!" I shouted. "Michelle, can you have Starbourne bring Lillian here? We have to get her out. And fast!"

"Is that safe for the child?" Foucault asked.

"As safe as it is fer us," Tim answered. "Zack, this'd better be bloody important."

"Biblical," I said.

"Bloody 'ell," Tim muttered darkly.

"Exactly," I said.

"Do it," Baxter rumbled. "Do it now, Michelle."

Foucault nodded and closed her eyes in profound concentration. After a moment she opened them again. She nodded again.

"Peter and Lillian are on their way," Foucault said.

"We're here," Starbourne announced. "What's the problem, Zack?"

Starbourne and Lillian Quatermain had simply appeared. The latter was reclining on a couch and looking romantically pale and wan, and very, very pregnant. Foucault strode purposefully over to her and began doing doctorly things.

"It doesn't look like true labor to me," Foucault declared after a moment. "That's still a little ways off."

"Sorrows has his hooks into the unborn child," I said. "We can't let him be born here."

"Are you sure?" Starbourne asked.

"Nearly," I said. "I know how the Duke operates and everything has just gone way too smoothly. There's a trap here, and we're about to stumble right into it if we're not very careful."

Starbourne considered all of this for a moment. His face was troubled, his eyes looked to the distance. His lips moved as if he were reading a particularly tricky section of a book. He was almost certainly talking to Gray.

"Take Lillian with you," he said. "Let the child be born in New Jerusalem. Michelle, please go with them and see to the birthing. If all goes well, the three of you can all return to Patchwork in a few days."

"And now is better than later," I said.

Starbourne bent over and lifted Lillian into his arms. He smiled gently at her and kissed her pale and sweaty brow. He then turned to us; Baxter held his arms out and Starbourne passed the lady of Aristarchus over to the goblinblood. Foucault looked at Tim who nodded, and she stepped into the circle of leather. With the six of us clustered together things were a little bit tight, but we arranged ourselves well enough.

"Time to go," said Tim.

Tim pulled a wicked-looking bowie knife out of his rucksack. He spit on the blade and nicked his hand with it, catching a drop of blood on the side of the blade. He opened his mouth wide, revealing shiny black, rune-carved teeth. He ran his tongue back and forth along his teeth, and he started humming an eerie little tune. At least I think he was humming, it might have just been the sound coming off his teeth. It was hard to tell which it was, and I'm not sure it really mattered either way.

A fog swept in, low and dense around our feet. I glanced down and I realized I couldn't even see the braided leather hoop through the fog. That was some fog. I looked around and saw ghostly shapes rising out of the fog. Low pedestals, or possibly shattered columns. Higher shapes, like walls or stalactites were less substantial, more misty.

Tim paced around the five of us, staying inside the bounds of where the leather hoop probably was. I imagined that Tim knew exactly where it was. Since I had no real idea anymore, I resolved not to move around much.

I heard a distant keening, like the sound of wind over the prairie, only distant and oddly hollow. At the same time, I noticed that the field was getting paler. The bright green vegetation was fading into shades of gray. It was like watching a color photograph turning black and white, only it was the whole world doing it, and it was kind of cool.

I looked back to where the columns and other wisps had been and saw them taking on color and a little more solidity. The keening was getting louder too, more like real wind and less like a scratchy recording of the wind. I looked up and saw what looked like a ceiling taking shape.

The phantom room slowly shifted into view. Becoming easier to see clearly. It looked like an ancient pagan temple that had long ago collapsed into ruin. What I had taken for stalactites were actually bits of column attached to the ceiling left behind when the rest collapsed. The floor was littered with piles of rubble and spots where the paving stones had buckled or erupted.

Now this, I thought to myself, this would be a great place to stage an ambush. You could hide a dozen guys behind that big collapsed column over there. And the broken ground would make it hard to sprint out of the way if gunfire came down.

"I would love to get a bunch of bad guys into a place like this," I said idly.

"What did you say, Boss?" Baxter rumbled.

"I said," I said. "That this would be a great place for an ambush!"

Baxter immediately produced a firearm. Or at least he produced that .50-caliber hand-cannon that he called a gun. I'm not sure I could have cocked it, let alone held steady against its recoil. But Baxter loved it. And only occasionally blew holes entirely through his targets.

"Nix, you guys," Tim called. "There's no ambush. This looks like a ruins crossing. We'll probably 'ave to answer some riddles; maybe perform a feat o' strength. Whatever you do, do not, I say, do not! disturb any tombs, read any inscriptions, touch any books, or drink any potions. If anybody sees anyf'ing that might be a bug scuttlin' around, do not ignore it, tell me. Same thing goes fer cats. Rats is no worry, you can ignore 'em."

"What about hounds?" Baxter rumbled anxiously.

"You won't see 'em 'ere," Tim declared.

"Then what about those hounds," Bax rumbled again, pointing towards a shadowy corner of the room.

"Blimey!" Tim shouted. "Those are hellhounds!"

"Can we run?" I asked.

"We bloody well better!" Tim shouted.

We ran then, the six of us. Baxter still had Lillian Quatermain in his arms, but it didn't seem to be much of a burden for him. We ran as fast as we could and we held nothing back. There was no negotiating with a hellhound, and death by hellhound wasn't pretty or fast. We might be able to fight a few of them, we were no pushovers, but hellhounds ran in packs and they knew how to fight dirty. We'd fight if we had to, but we'd run if we could. Eel and Baxter pulled rapidly ahead for a moment before realizing it and slowing down to keep pace with us more human types.

"Don't 'old back for us," Tim gasped. "If you make it to a bridge, I know how to stop 'em. Find the bloody bridge!"

"Where do we find it?" growled Bax.

"Just run!" Tim huffed. "The rules say you'll find what y' need, but they don't bloody promise ye'll find it in time!"

"Leave Lillian here," Foucault said. "She'll slow you down and it won't do her any good either!"

Bax nodded and lowered Lady Quatermain gently to her feet and then he and Eel were both gone like a shot. They really had been holding back. We all wasted a fraction of a second staring after them before we shook it off and got moving. Foucault and I supported Lillian and Tim led the way.

"It's the Duke," I said. "He's found us."

"Can't be," Tim puffed. "Immortals can't muck about in the Mists."

The hellhounds bayed. It was loud, much too loud for comfort. Loud meant close and close meant dead. I was cold suddenly, so cold I was shivering. Was I going into shock from fear or was something else happening?

The ruins were almost completely real now, and I could see that many of them were covered with heavy drifts of snow that had come in through the many holes in the roof. I realized that our gasping breaths were visibly steaming.

We needed to find someplace to hole up. There was no way we were ever going to outrun the 'hounds. We needed to find some place to hold out in, some place defensible. At least until Bax and Eel found whatever bridge Tim needed. I pointed to a snow-covered dais complete with a headless and armless statue.

I gave Tim a little shove in that direction. He took the hint and we used the last of our fear-based burst of energy to scramble over to the platform. We hoisted Lady Quatermain up. The snow made the going a little bit slippery, but we were highly motivated. We put our backs to the statue and waited.

I drew my .38 out of the travel bag. I checked, and found it was ready and loaded, again. I held it out, bracing my left hand with my right. Tim had an ornately carved drumstick clutched tightly in one hand. I hadn't seen that one before and I wondered what it did. Hopefully I wouldn't find out what it did now. All things considered, I could wait.

"Why can't immortals come here?" I asked.

"Too bloody big," Tim shot back. "They'd shatter whatever spot they tried to stand in."

"And what would that do to us?" I asked.

"We'd most likely find our way back 'home," Tim began.

"Oh good," I said.

"In two or three 'undred years," Tim finished.

"Not good," I said.

"Won't 'appen," Tim said.

"How can you be sure?" I asked.

"It'd kill 'is Grace deader than prohibition," Tim said. "And no immortal's ever gonna risk his life for reals and for actuals."

"So he has to be working with whatever's local," I concluded.

"Sounds reasonable," Tim agreed.

A dozen dark shapes melted out of the shadows. They were low and long and the way they moved reminded me of mercury flowing uphill. Snarling, they formed a circle around us.

"Go back," hissed a gravelly voice. "Go back to Patchwork."

"Back," keened a second voice. "Baaaack!"

A chorus of barking howls joined in, all urging us to go back. My blood ran cold. The voices were not even remotely human-sounding. The Hellhounds were speaking to us, but the message came straight from the Duke of Sorrows.

A gasp of pain came from behind us, followed by another. I spared a glance behind me, Foucault was mopping Lillian's brow as she groaned in obvious pain. Foucault met my eyes and I could see the desperation in her face.

"She's going into labor," Foucault confirmed.

"One more question," I asked. "How many different critters control large areas in the Mists?"

"Not more'n a dozen or two," Tim answered nervously. "An each of 'em are pretty distinct from each other. Easy to figure who you're dealin' with if you know a thing or two."

"That's what I was hoping," I said.

I pointed my gun up, away from us, and into the distance and squeezed off three quick rounds. The gun shots were oddly flat and quiet. The should have been explosively loud. I waited. The 'hounds didn't move. They sensed something was coming. Tim looked around curiously. He sensed it too.

"Mistress Wild," I shouted. "I beg your forgiveness for my rudeness with the gun. I know you object to such things in your land, but there is a situation that requires your certain attention."

An elderly woman had appeared just a few yards away from the circle of hounds and us in our marble tree. She had snowy white hair and wore a green and white dress under a white fur coat. She wasn't smiling. Which, for the moment, I still considered a good thing.

"An intruder from Perdition has invaded your lands, seized control of your hounds and is using them to kill your guests."

Mistress Wild looked at me quizzically.

"Us," I explained.

"My guests, are you?" Wild asked.

"Did you not invite me to sit with you?" I asked. "These are my friends. May we share your hospitality briefly?"

Dortchen Wild cackled. Her laughter was harsh and frightening and very, very cold. The hellhounds shivered and their fur shimmered from coal black to snow white like a desert oasis vanishing. The hounds whined a little and then slowly sat down on their haunches. Tongues lolled out in the hellhound equivalent of a doggie smile.

"I smell you, Old Bones," Wild said then. "You don't dare poke more than a finger into my business do you, Old Bones?"

There was only silence in reply.

"Fine then," Wild sniffed. "Hide from me for as long as you can. But if I were you, I'd be gone before I find you here."

There was more silence.

Tim and I began to crawl down from the platform. The hounds didn't seem to mind and they weren't really surrounding us anymore so I viewed the situation as a general improvement. We started to walk away, but the little old woman was between us and where we needed to go.

"And what shall we do with you, then, my guests?" Wild asked, with the barest hint of a cackle in her voice.

"We thank you for your hospitality," I said politely. "My friend Lillian is, as you can see, in need of medical assistance. And we wish only to pass through your lands without let or hindrance. We promise to take nothing with us that is not ours."

"Very good," she croaked. "Very good. But what gifts do you offer me?"

"I offer you a drop of my blood," Tim replied smoothly. "Warlock's blood."

Dortchen Wild's eyes gleamed with obvious greed. She even went so far as to lick her lips in obvious anticipation. I wondered what was so great about warlock blood.

"I offer you my secret," Foucault said. "As long as you promise to share it with no other."

Wild's eyes narrowed for a moment as if in consideration. Then she smiled broadly, showing her disturbing teeth to the world. She nodded.

"I," Lillian managed to grit out between moans. "Promise to name my child after you."

"And oh, how I do love children," Wild cackled. "Your boy child shall not be born here. Name him Dorian Wild Quatermain and go in peace."

Lillian gasped then and her tremors and moans faded slightly. Had Dortchen Wild just un-induced labor? I resolved not to think about it too much, at least not until we all got back safely to New Jerusalem. All eyes turned towards me and I knew it was my turn to offer a sacrifice. My mind raced. I licked my lips and tried not to look as nervous as I felt. I'm pretty sure I failed.

"And what do you offer me, cagey man?" Wild asked. "Do you have another precious bauble like the one you gave me before?"

"Nothing like that," I said. "I could offer you magic wonders or weapons from my bag of tricks. I could offer you gold earned from the sweat of my brow."

"And for mere passage," Wild said. "I would have accepted that. But you drew me into your war with the Duke of Sorrows. You made me your protector and the protector of the child unborn. And that I did willingly, but now you must pay the price. What do you have that is most valuable to you?"

I thought about it. She was right. I had manipulated her into helping me. I hadn't asked for help, I'd insulted her to get her attention and then played to her ego. It hadn't been polite or mannerly. I wasn't sure I had anything of sufficient value to make up for that.

"Mistress," began Tim. "If you release me friend, I offer you me ..."

"Wait," I interrupted. "I have the price."

I had no idea what Tim had been about to offer. Whatever it was, I was pretty sure I didn't want my friend giving it up on my account.

I reached into my jacket pocket and pulled out the bracelet that Kelli had given me. The same bracelet I had once given her. I felt a tear trickle down my cheek as I looked at it.

"I offer you this," I said, brandishing the bracelet. "A twice-given gift. A gift of love, freely given and freely accepted by two lovers. A sacrifice from one to the other and back again. A perfect circle. And I offer it to you, in apology for the wrongs I have done you. I am sorry, Mistress."

The bracelet vanished out of my hand and sparkled on Dortchen Wild's wrist. She smiled her disturbing smile and nodded to me. She swept her arm up and pointed in the direction that Baxter and Eel had made off in.

"If it were not for the child I would have you all in my cook pot," Wild said. "But I dislike it when the great powers manipulate children. The innocent should be free to make their own mistakes. They taste so much sweeter that way."

"Thank you, Mistress," I said, repressing a small shudder.

"Go," she said. "Go and join your friends at the bridge. You have the freedom of the passage. Use it swiftly and be gone from my holdfast. Take your wars with you, Zachariah Monday, I want no part of them."

We didn't exactly run, but you couldn't call what we did walking either. We moved swiftly. It didn't take long to find Baxter and Eel. They were standing at the head of a bridge. The bridge extended out into the fog and vanished from sight. They waved to us as we approached.

"We shouted your names when we found the bridge," Bax rumbled. "Did you hear us?"

"Nah," Tim admitted. "Turns out me plan wasn't so good. Zack got us out of it, but I wouldn'a 'ave believed it if I 'adn't seen it with me own eyes."

"What happened to you guys?" I asked. "Have any troubles?"

"Nah," said Eel. "We had to answer a couple riddles. They was pretty easy."

"What did you sacrifice?" Tim asked. "I gave 'er a drop o' blood."

"A tie that belonged to my father," Bax rumbled. "I have dozens of them."

"A feather from my wing," Eel said. "They grow back."

"That just doesn't seem fair," I grumped.

"Life isn't fair," Bax said. "Get used to it."

"Thanks a lot, buddy," I said sarcastically.

"My pleasure," Bax replied.

The six of us stepped onto the bridge and began walking along it. The fog grew thick around us and our footsteps sounded oddly hollow. I felt pretty good, all things considered. It was going to be nice to be able to relax for a change. And I was looking forward to sleeping in my own bed.

"You know we've got a lot of work waiting for us back there," Bax said. "Those statuettes of the Duke's. They're going to be trouble. We gotta tell the police about it."

"The police?" I said incredulously. "And what do you think they'll do about it? Nobody's going to pay them to protect the people of New Jerusalem from a boogey man they don't believe can hurt them."

"Then I guess it's gonna have to be us," Eel mumbled.

"What?" I protested. "Nobody's paying us either."

"It's not always about the money," Tim piped. "Sometimes a bloke's gotta do the right thing."

"You're a lot of help," I accused. "You don't need the money like I do."

"You don't need it as bad as you think," Baxter rumbled.

"Maybe," I said. "But either way, the statuettes are tomorrow's problem."

"You might be right," Baxter agreed. "Oh, that reminds me … I picked up your pocket watch."

Bax fished around in his trouser pocket and proudly presented my pocket watch. I took it from him. It buzzed once in my hand and then began pulsing warmly. I grinned. I had missed this little toy in Patchwork. It would have come in handy in a lot of different ways. I flipped open the lid and looked at the hands and checked the time. It was one minute past midnight.

"Aw," I said. "It can't be."

"What is it," Tim asked. "What's wrong?"

"It's tomorrow," I said.

"Then I guess it's time to start working on some problems," Bax said.

The End

Monday and the Counterfeit Corpse

About the Author

Andrew Kirschbaum was born in Nebraska in 1967. Education, employment, and an overseas war kept the Kirschbaum family on the move for the next ten years, living in Nebraska, Iowa, Nevada, and Florida before settling in Massachusetts. A basic ineptitude at anything not related to reading and writing his native language led to a B.A. in English Literature from Brandeis University and a short-lived career as a technical writer. In 1991, he started 3 Trolls Games & Puzzles – a traditional board game and puzzle store in Chelmsford, MA – with his family and has been running it ever since. In 2011 he collaborated with a group of friends and family to produce *Verdigris,* an interactive novel for the iPhone and iPad; his first traditional novel, *Monday and the Murdered Man,* followed shortly thereafter. *Monday and the Counterfeit Corpse* is his second and he is currently working on the next Monday adventure, another interactive novel, and various live action role playing games.

Follow the Author

on Twitter: @Baron_Saturday
Facebook: Andrew Kirschbaum
Google+: Andrew Kirschbaum
www.andrewkirschbaum.com
for current scheduled appearances, blog, and other allegedly
interesting stuff
Zack Monday will return

Made in the USA
Charleston, SC
13 February 2013